SINOPHAGIA

A CELEBRATION OF CHINESE HORROR

First published 2024 by Solaris
an imprint of Rebellion Publishing Ltd,
Riverside House, Osney Mead,
Oxford, OX2 0ES, UK

www.solarisbooks.com

ISBN: 978-1-83786-117-0

Designed & typeset by Rebellion Publishing

Printed in Denmark

SINOPHAGIA

A CELEBRATION OF CHINESE HORROR

TRANSLATED AND EDITED BY
XUETING C. NI

SOLARIS

For all my readers

For Chris A. Jones (R.I.P.)

CONTENTS

CONTENT WARNINGS

THE IDEA OF content warnings is relatively new and, especially in a horror book, could be considered a spoiler. I wanted to make this collection as accessible to as many people as possible, so have decided to include what are probably the most important ones, on a story-by-story basis.

If you do not need the warnings, or just want to experience the stories cold, stop reading here.

Or fold the page over.

Or, if you are a true monster, rip it out.

In no way can I promise that this list is exhaustive, and I have tried to be as broad with these terms as I can, to avoid ruining these exquisitely crafted stories. There are many triggers you would expect, such as death, blood and the supernatural. I am well aware of the microfractures of the human soul, where a seemingly innocuous detail may have a deep impact on a single reader. This book will be disturbing in places, but hopefully, for all the right reasons.

The Girl in the Rain 雨女, Hong Niangzi
Childhood trauma/neglect, coercion/gaslighting, corpse/body parts, suicide.

The Waking Dream 清醒, Fan Zhou
Coercion/gaslighting, corpse/body parts, drugs and alcohol, imprisonment, insects, mental illness depiction, needles, torture.

Immortal Beauty 红颜未, Chu Xidao
Coercion/gaslighting, corpse/body parts, domestic violence and abuse, graphic violence, imprisonment, sexual abuse/violence, torture, weapon use/firearms.

Those Who Walk at Night, Walk With Ghosts 但行夜路, 必见鬼, She Cong Ge
Corpse/body parts, disabled distress, drugs and alcohol, familial trauma/neglect, insects, needles, torture, weapon use/firearms.

The Yin Yang Pot 鸳鸯锅, Chuan Ge
Coercion/gaslighting, imprisonment, torture.

Shanxiao 山魈, Goodnight, Xiaoqing
Animal abuse/death, coercion/gaslighting, domestic violence and abuse, imprisonment, torture, weapon use/firearms.

Have You Heard of Ancient Glory? 你听说过古辉楼吗, Zhou Dedong
Coercion/gaslighting, corpse/body parts, drugs and alcohol, imprisonment, mental illness depiction, PTSD-related trauma, suicide.

Records of Xiangxi 老九门之湘西往事, Nanpai Sanshu
Animal abuse/death, child abuse/death, corpse/body parts, drugs and alcohol, graphic violence, insects, racial/religious slurs, torture, weapon use/firearms.

The Ghost Wedding 喜结鬼缘, Yimei Tangguo
Animal abuse/death, child abuse/death, childhood trauma/neglect, coercion/gaslighting, corpse/body parts, disabled

distress, domestic violence and abuse, drugs and alcohol, graphic violence, imprisonment, insects, mental illness depiction, PTSD-related trauma, self-harm, sexual abuse/ violence, strangulation, torture.

Night Climb 夜攀, Chi Hui
None.

Forbidden Rooms 禁屋, Zhou Haohui
Child abuse/death, childhood trauma/neglect, coercion/ gaslighting, corpse/body parts,
graphic violence, imprisonment, PTSD-related trauma, strangulation, suicide, torture, weapon use/firearms.

Ti'Naang 替囊, Su Min
Child abuse/death, childhood trauma/neglect, coercion/ gaslighting, corpse/body parts,
racial/religious slurs.

Huangcun 荒村, Cai Jun
Childhood trauma/neglect, coercion/gaslighting, domestic violence and abuse, drugs and alcohol, graphic violence, racial/religious slurs, self-harm, suicide.

The Death of Nala 娜娜之死, Gu Shi
Animal abuse/death, child abuse/death, childhood trauma/ neglect, coercion/gaslighting, corpse/body parts, graphic violence, imprisonment, mental illness depiction, PTSD-related trauma, strangulation.

INTRODUCTION
Xueting C. Ni

I HAVE ALWAYS had an active imagination. I was the sort of child who would see all kinds of things in the indistinct shapes of the dark, and of course, I loved ghost stories.

One of my earliest memories of horror was watching the 1986 TV adaptation of Pu Songling's famous Strange Tales from a Chinese Studio. Its opening titles, a single, dimly lit lantern, hovering unsteadily over a desolate nocturnal field, to the sound of ghostly, whispering wind, gave me unspeakable chills. During my childhood in Guangzhou, I would often visit Yuexiu Park, which, for a period of time, housed a replica of the underworld scenes from the fantasy epic Journey to the West, meaning I could visit the grim scenes repeatedly. I remember really wanting to live in a cave like the White Bone Demon.

Just where does this penchant for the dark and mysterious come from? I am sure I could lay on a psychiatrist's couch, and attribute it to some rather frightening traumas during my childhood. At the same time, this fascination with fear is natural to us all. This emotion is one of the primal human urges, and whilst it is not one that everyone finds easy to face or admit, or even one that certain societies and cultures are comfortable presenting to the world, we need the ability to be afraid in order to truly know what it is to be brave, calm and safe. One of the things I appreciate in both the writers and readers of horror, is their willingness to face fear.

Over a rather complicated and fragmented life, I have been no stranger to different kinds of fear. I have found myself part of many social groups and enclaves, who have shared their fears with me. Fears that range from facing life in an unknown place, and being different, to fears of those who are different coming into their safe spaces. I have seen, and felt, fear of not achieving, not being good enough; fear of social ostracization, fear of being misunderstood, not being seen, heard, and fear for personal safety in a space which should be the most comforting. Whilst what one is frightened of is entirely subjective, there is no shame in fear itself.

After moving to the UK, I fell in love with gothic fiction. I spent an adolescence reading authors such as Charlotte Brontë, Wilkie Collins, Alexandre Dumas, before following them with the likes of Horace Walpole, Charlotte Gilman Perkins and R.L. Stevenson at university. As an adult, I also found myself sitting down to Hammer horror films, eighties American cult classics and Hong Kong zombie films, and later finding out about mainland Chinese Qingming and Zhongyuan releases. I found myself drawn to the likes of Susan Hill's The Woman in Black, and films like Guillermo Del Toro's The Orphanage. Whilst gore has its place, it does not affect me nearly as much as that suggestive sense of eeriness.

The Chinese view of Horror has always struck me as being unique. Where nearly every horror myth I have come across in the West is a cautionary tale, China has a long tradition of journal and documentational style writing, referred to as the zhiguai, or tales of the strange, that mixes history with legends and hearsay. Traditional culture assigned these stories of the supernatural and paranormal to the classical literary cannon, which is why back then, five-year-olds like myself were able to watch series like Liaozhai on prime time national broadcasts. Moreover, the mishmash of Chinese beliefs did not label spirits and ghosts as something evil and unnatural, but rather, just part of the normal order of things, with their own place in the world, and traditionally, the 'frights' have only arisen when the spirits are angered, restless, or the boundaries trespassed.

As I began to put this collection together, I came upon a new horror. The more I spoke with agents and editors in China, the more I discovered that there had been a certain 'poisoning' of the genre through a slew of gratuitously violent, gory, and sexualised content, and a string of real-life deaths, all of which were blamed on copying films, books and series with a horror theme. Nobody over there wants to publish Horror.

My own research had shown me that China's horror fiction was at the same stage science fiction had been around a decade ago, and would also be ready to find an international readership, but whilst there was an amazing love for horror literature here in the West, it seemed that people did not want to be known as horror writers within China. I had paved my way into China's publishing industry with my first collection, but even with these contacts and avenues, how could I find those excellent writers I had read and written about, if they did not want to be found? There had been several online short story platforms specialising in horror, which would have been perfect selection pools, all of which seemed to have shut up shop at the start of the pandemic, and never reopened.

One of the few horror storytellers I managed to get in touch with, was unwilling to collaborate unless the entire collection was just his work, whilst another showed great willingness, until I mentioned the 'H' word, at which point he politely, but rapidly, fled from the conversation. Another dead end.

I had bid farewell to a day job of fifteen years in print production, in order to concentrate on creating and curating this ground-breaking first anthology of contemporary Chinese horror, and I was already experiencing the abject terror of not being able to deliver this book.

I was not going to give up. I was going to find these voices, by any means. I emailed, sent voice messages, held international phone conversations, stalked and pestered people (in an amicable and courteous manner) on social media, and did my best to explain that Horror fiction is much more established and recognised in the Anglophone market. I could see there was a lot of excellent writing in this genre from the last thirty years, especially around the period of domestic boom, which readers around the world would find fascinating and love to read. I thought how tragic it would be to see these works and creative voices buried. I hoped to gain new recognition for these writers with my anthology, and for this positive interest outside of China to feed back to the domestic market, in the same way it had done with kehuan (sci-fi), and we may just be able to alter attitudes and perspectives within the country. Obviously, a lot of this fell on deaf ears. After all, I had come to them about a sensitive topic, seemingly out of the blue, and pranks and scams are rife throughout Chinese net space. I held my breath, but my already low expectations were lowering still, until one day, my heart leapt at the notifications on my phone. Whether it was the earnestness of my words, the desperation in my tone, my sheer bloody-mindedness, or the scent of opportunity, they started to respond.

The next few months were punctured by immense ups and downs. Word of mouth about the project opened more and more doors, until I had a submission pile threatening to crash my little inbox. I read and read until my eyes felt ready to pop out of their sockets, but this was still only half the battle. I now had access to works and writers in the genre, but assembling the collection I wanted was going to take very careful curation. I have often said that Chinese literature is either very short, or very long, and in horror, it seemed like the best writers worked predominately in the long form. It took a lot of cajoling and discussion to convince writers to share shorter pieces with me, or let me take stories out of the context of larger collections, to try and merge those with some shorter pieces, "Tetrising" them into a collection I feel shows the gamut of contemporary China's Horror scene. I have to say that some of what I was sent just felt like a gratuitous collection of foul language, violence and gore, as well as a level of misogyny that no rural setting or uneducated characters could excuse. These had to be filtered, before quieter voices of solid skill could be allowed to stand out. Like other genres I have been working in, such as science fiction and Wuxia, horror literature is still dominated by male voices at the most visible levels. What was initially put in front of me was almost entirely from male writers, some of whom, unfortunately, were the ones who made the most demands, from content coverage to contractual terms. I had to specifically request those female writers whose works I had had my eye on, either by reaching out to them myself, or insisting to agents that they also submitted some women's writing. There is still the assumption that I would only want 'famous' voices, rather than those who are just starting to have their skills recognised.

I was given collection after collection of stories that were suspenseful or dark in tone. Authors who considered their work "Thriller" or "Mystery" stories. I had to spell it out bluntly. Whilst I would happily look at different themes, styles, and tones, I wanted stories that induced nothing less than intense fear in the reader.

One of the organisations who really understood the project, though, and who were instrumental in helping me seek out new voices, women's writing and a wider range, was the Future Affairs Administration (FAA), whom I had met at LonCon 2014, back when they were still a group of sci-fi fans. It has been heartening to see them grow into a company and leading brand in the industry with a multi-channel network under their belt. Their core business is to develop new sci-fi products ranging from books and films to TV shows and video games, but also to nurture writing talent and grow the community. One of the many projects they run is an annual SF Gala, for which writers from around the world are invited to create work around a different theme each year. In fact, one of the stories in this collection (Ti-naang) comes from that project. The fact the FAA pivoted so quickly to helping me find the new generation of Horror writers is a testament to the cooperation, perceptiveness, resourcefulness and proactivity of this young team, and their involvement in the editorial process of this story was one of the most rewarding and fruitful collaborations I have had in these projects.

Whilst this collection is meant to introduce you to the

wonders, and terrors, of Chinese Horror, it is still climbing out of a pernicious, exploitative era, and in doing so, many current attitudes and the representation of genre in China are problematic, and that extends all the way down to what you actually call it. For example, whilst there are specific terms for certain sub-genres, such as lingyi (paranormal), the most common term for Horror as a whole, is kongbu wenxue, the same "kongbu" (恐怖) that is the term used for Terrorism. Understandably, the word is filled with negative connotations. An alternate name for Horror is jingsong wenxue, but jingsong (惊悚) meaning "shock and fright", has come to be the Chinese equivalent of the term "Grindhouse", or "Goreporn".

Neither of these terms really describe Horror beyond the most superficial and stereotypical elements of storytelling, and certainly fail to illuminate exactly what this kind of literature is really about. Just as science fiction explores the hopes and dreams of a culture or people, their Horror stories examine their fears and anxieties, an equally important undertaking for anyone hoping to understand a society. At its beating heart, Horror as a genre is about human nature, and even when it extends beyond humanity, utilising the full toolbox of fantasy and the impossible, it is still about the impact on the frail human mind and body. Yes, what it shows can be our failings, weaknesses, cruelty and selfishness we would love to pretend did not exist, but without doing this, we cannot improve, progress, or regulate.

Most horror writers I spoke to in collecting these stories preferred to use the term 悬疑 *xuanyi* (suspense), or thrillers, which puts them on the same shelves as spy stories, or detective novels. In not naming a genre, or employing euphemisms, we risk it disappearing from literary history.

I have, in my correspondence, used the term kongxuan(恐悬), in an attempt to invite a more nuanced approach to the genre, and express its diverse nature. A constant reminder that Horror is a lot more than jumps, shock, and gore, though each of those has its place. It tells of the fearful things we encounter around us, and within ourselves.

As print publishing began to shy away from Horror literature, the rise of internet platforms in China became a haven for writers. In fact, many of the stories featured here, whilst being written by well-established authors, only saw the light of day due to social media and horror blogs, which kept the dwindling flames burning at a time when it risked being extinguished by public outcry.

In Sinophagia, I have tried to take a broad approach to the subject of Horror, where much of the selection engages on a psychological level. Chinese society is such a broad and diverse group, with regional concerns and habits usually hidden away in front of a Western audience, to show a unified "Chineseness". But here you will see the urban fear of the rural, the rural fear of the urban, the traditional fear of modern living, and Modern China's fear of its past.

So much of China is still wild land, from mountainous regions and forests to wide barren deserts, and so much of the supernatural thoughts of China surround the ghosts, spirits and monsters that seem to inhabit these places. In fact, there is certainly an idea that Chinese Horror is overwhelmingly rural, but with Chinese society becoming more urbanised, I knew there were some excellent horror stories inspired by urban legends, and based on social sources, and I made a consolidated effort to include those.

My first collection of Stories, Sinopticon, was very much about the visions of China, but Horror is a far more visceral thing, and whilst this may be considered a companion piece, I also wanted it to stand out as its own thing. We wanted a title that sounded unsettling, but without fuelling any sense of Sinophobia. '-Phagia' was chosen because of its association with 'devouring'. If any student studying this is seeking to increase their wordcount, you could consider it an ironic statement regarding the rising Sinophobia around the world, rooted in unfounded fears surrounding Chinese and Asian eating habits.

As always, the primary aim of this collection is to entertain you, the reader, with well-written, enjoyable works, even if that enjoyment is a little macabre, or sadistic.

The writers in this collection are varied. Not just in style, but age, gender, background and importantly, location. Whereas science fiction by nature transcends geographical boundaries, Horror traditions are intensely regional, with strong emotional energies, such as fear, very much embedded in our natural and manmade surroundings. Sinophagia reflects a society still dealing with recent histories of war, invasions, and revolutions, who still have a deep-rooted connection to a land that has not always been hospitable, and a cultural memory of the dangers brought by floods, famine, and the inhospitable terrain which surrounds the flatter cradle of early civilisation. What emerges is a very regional horror landscape, with the ethnically diverse mountains of the South and West, such as the imposing Zhangjiajie range of Xiangxi, providing the perfect sublime, but terrifying backdrop for the Chinese Gothic, whilst the equally impressive glass and steel 'mountains' springing up through urbanisation, fulfil the 21st century literary imagination to engage with the real-life horrors around them. In Sinophagia, we see a contemporary society that is concerned about class, the rural and urban divide, unaffordable housing, the aftermath of biopolitical policies, the alienating impact of urban living and how the growing consumerist economy and overwhelming pressures of the jobs market affect businesses and families. Whilst these issues are present in many non-genre books in China, they are often downplayed, or given imaginary happy endings, or in typical Chinese fashion, endured for a greater good. Horror allows the suffering in these situations to be explored unchecked, and often unresolved. In this collection, you will also see much violence against women, and the obliteration of their agency. China's improved awareness is reflected in its fiction, especially in the works of female writers who boldly tackle this alongside wider humanist concerns.

One thing that I have really enjoyed about putting this collection together, has been the way Horror plays with perspective and voice, and there is certainly a vast array in this book, from conventional omniscient narrators and intimate first-person storytelling, to an unusual second person viewpoint, and the marginalised voices of the non-human and non-mortal. There are neuro-divergent characters, and those who are being deliberately misled or manipulated, and sometimes, a combination of these, suddenly, rapidly switching, which make the stories all the more interesting. Whilst the styles and tones vary from story to story, from literary to journal-like reportage, from grave voices of gravitas, to the darkly comical, each of them has a sense of the uncanny, with themes of entrapment, secrecy and concealment, running through them. I truly believe that many of these stories can be read as archetypes for "The Chinese Gothic".

The last few years seem to have thrown even more darkness into our everyday lives. I sat, a few years ago, feeling surreal whilst translating zombie sci-fi during a tide of infections and lockdowns, and working through this anthology whilst myself becoming infected with COVID added a horrific dimension to the project. Not only are we dealing with a general collapse of society amidst a worldwide health crisis, and wars and conflict on every front, but also a seeming return to old lines of hatred along race, sexuality and gender. To some extent, horror literature helps us work through bad experiences and trauma. Experiencing frightening stories in fiction and emerging from them (relatively) unscathed gives us hope, and helps us think about our own suffering in a wider context. Whilst they are not meant to be a panacea, they do help to move us towards new courage, and towards healing. I am writing this introduction during Halloween, a time when we set up an elaborate space of themed horror fantasy to give the local children the most memorable trick, or treat, depending on how they see it. I have only recently started to appreciate their faces lighting up with not only fear, but also excitement, and then joy, and I can think of no better way to consider how horror can bring a renewed sense of life, as well as fear and reflection.

You may notice that I wrote (relatively) unscathed. You may think that you are going to read this book, and when you finish the last page, you will calmly put it down and get on with your lives, but I hope that as the curator of this collection, it will change you a little along the way. Whether it's a moment's hesitation before you step out on the balcony, or the speed with which you slam the book down after the last twist, I hope that some of it will stay with you for a very, very, long time.

THE GIRL IN THE RAIN

丂姆

Hong Niangzi

PRELUDE

A STARLESS SKY. From behind an obfuscation of clouds, the silver moon scattered a few dismal rays into the silent night. From a distance, tall, grim and cadaverous white, the hideous exterior of the women's halls of residence resembled a coffin.

The early spring night was a little too cold, and a little too quiet. Beating its wings, a little bird flew past the halls, offering a semblance of life to the otherwise still nocturnal landscape.

"You all made me do it!" A shrill, hoarse scream stabbed through the silence, permeating the entire university grounds. A muffled thud, and the night plunged back into a brief silence.

And then, the girl's dorm broke into a frenzy, the sounds of lights being switched on, yelling, slippers slapping the floor, all intertwined. A ghastly ray of pale lightning slashed the sky, closely followed by rumbles of thunder. A few slanted, withered trees around the building's edge cast elongated shadows on the wall, stretching longer and longer... the jumble of shadows shifting over the gloomy stairwell seemed so eerie.

On the flower bed by the front entrance, she lay, her

body twitching haphazardly. Dark red liquid oozed out of the five orifices of her face, like a beautiful flower blossoming in stealth. Her eyes were round and wide, glaring malevolently at the balcony of room 402. Her mouth was wide open, as if she wanted to speak, but she could only hear a choking gasp as the sound escaped her throat, until the twitching stopped...

ONE

H******* University was an ancient institution.

Like all older campuses, it had many, varied legends, such as the human head mop in the water room, and the headless doll that walked the women's dorms barefoot, but the most famous, or infamous, were the legends of "Yunü, the Girl in the Rain" and "The Red Umbrella". Because of these two stories, whenever it rained, the whole of H University would grow heavy with a ghostly atmosphere, and even the groves of cherry trees seemed to be hiding countless phantasmal shadows in their foliage.

No one was quite sure when the legend of Yunü, the Girl in the Rain, had planted itself, quietly, like a piece of wet moss, in the grounds of the university. The legend told that in rainy weather, if a single boy saw a lonely girl smiling at him in the rain, then he would be caught in the grip of Yunü, and even if the rain stopped, he would still find himself drenched from head to toe. The most frightening part, though, was where that water came from. Whoever had been caught by the Girl in the Rain would stay dripping wet on the outside, while all the insides of his body would start to dry up, eventually losing every drop of moisture, and through Yunü's curse, become a desiccated husk.

The Legend of the Red Umbrella would make you shudder even more. This story also began on a rainy day. There was a girl who took a stroll in the rain with a red umbrella. Suddenly she noticed that the water running off the edge of it had turned crimson. Disgusted, she tried to throw the umbrella away, but found her hand tightly stuck to the handle, as if it had dug into her hand, and was sucking her blood out of her, eating away at her flesh, until in the end, all that was left of her was a white skeleton, which had sunk deep into the sodden ground. The red umbrella was nowhere to be seen.

Since then, word had spread that no one should carry a red umbrella, ever, and the phrase had become taboo among the students. Even if you were just to touch one, without using it, it could very well be the thing that consumed your flesh and blood.

These two terrifying legends had enshrouded the otherwise beautiful university grounds in a grim and ghastly haze, ruining the mood of everyone whenever it rained.

It was another night of torrential rain, and outside H University's main teaching building, Jiang Ruohan, who had been studying late that night, raised her eyes. Gazing at the narrow path leading to the women's halls in the distance, she shook her head helplessly. Running back in such heavy rain would turn her into a soup-soaked chicken for sure. A cold would be inevitable, and if she slipped and fell, she'd be in big trouble.

"Ruohan, why are you standing there like an idiot?"

"Oh." Jiang Ruohan turned back, and found Luo Xi, her best friend, and Shen Jie, her boyfriend. Looking at them nestling together sweetly, Jiang Ruohan felt a sour ache in her heart.

Luo Xi's gaze fell on Jiang Ruohan's empty hands, as if she had worked something out, and tentatively asked: "Ruohan, haven't you got an umbrella?"

"Uh, no." Jiang Ruohan shook her head.

"Doesn't matter, I've brought one." Shen Jie whipped one out from behind him, as if with a magician's flourish, and waved it in front of Jiang Ruohan.

It was a red umbrella, the kind of glossy, fresh red that looked like a fresh wound. Its sudden appearance shook Jiang Ruohan, and she screwed up her eyes.

"Red... red..." Jiang Ruohan felt a chill in her heart. Rainy day, red umbrella... She was remembering the college legend.

"Ruohan, what are you mumbling about? Take it and go first." Shen Jie held the umbrella out in front of Jiang Ruohan, who stared at it with dead eyes, too frightened to take it.

"Ruohan, are you feeling unwell?" Luo Xi stepped forward and took Jiang Ruohan's hand. It was ice cold.

Jiang Ruohan forced out a weak smile and shook her head. "No, just a bit cold. If we take the umbrella, then what about Shen Jie? Why don't the two of you go first?"

"A gentleman would never sit back and allow ladies to get soaked. Don't worry, I am fit as a fiddle, and a quick sprint will get me back to the dorms." Shen Jie struck his chest, a wide, charming smile bloomed over his face, but to Jiang Ruohan, it gave out an impression of ill intent.

"But..."

"No buts, let's go." Luo Xi held up the umbrella and opened it; a skyful of red clouds seemed to enshroud them both. Jiang Ruohan's eyes widened. Luo Xi flashed Shen Jie a charming smile. "Jie, we're off, then."

"See you tomorrow." Shen Jie leant in, and suddenly

kissed Luo Xi on the forehead.

"Don't be a letch, we're in public!" Luo Xi blushed, and taking hold of Jiang Ruohan's hand, pulled her into the rain. Jiang Ruohan happened to look back and saw Shen Jie's face, which revealed an expression of mocking sweetness.

"Ruohan, are you really that cold? You're shivering like a leaf." Luo Xi looked at her best friend with concern. From the moment they'd left the building, Ruohan had been shaking and looking around her nervously.

"Red... red..." Jiang Ruohan spat out vague sounds from her trembling lips.

"Red what?"

"Red... red umbrella! Luo Xi, It's a RED UMBRELLA!" Jiang Ruohan took a deep breath and was at last able to get the whole sentence out in relative clarity.

"Red umbrella?" As she repeated Jiang Ruohan's words, Luo Xi subconsciously lifted her hand to look at the umbrella, and that one look was enough to send her whole body into violent tremors.

Deep red liquid was flowing along the skeleton of the umbrella, dripping with the slow insistence of an opened vein. One drop, a second... a third... the little splashes fell on the back of her hand, blooming into tiny red flowers, before spreading out over her hand. The air became filled with the nauseating metallic scent of fresh blood, while the giant umbrella felt like a great hand, looming over their necks, each shiny spoke of the frame resembling the fangs of a python, poised at any moment to snap shut at their throats.

The Red Umbrella... at last, Luo Xi understood the words choking up in Jiang Ruohan's mouth.

"It's got us, it's got us!" Clearly, Jiang Ruohan had also

noticed the dripping ichor and the smell; shouting like a lunatic, she ran out in the rain in the direction of the halls.

There was no time to think. Luo Xi dropped the umbrella and ran after Jiang Ruohan.

The normally well-kept narrow path had become muddy and slippery under these storms, and after running just a few steps, Luo Xin slipped and fell to the side of the path. The rain had soaked her through, her hair scattering down from its neat clips, and now it clung to her like encroaching seaweed. Struck by the icy rain, her already pallid complexion looked even more bloodless. She struggled to get up, but felt as though all her strength had been sucked out of her. Utterly drained, she could only sit where she had fallen.

She looked up in the direction Jiang Ruohan had run, but her figure had already disappeared. The halls were so close, yet they felt so far away. Luo Xi could see the lights of the building, and held out her hand, but could not grasp one ray of that light.

"Pah, pah, pah..." A strange noise echoed behind her, like someone slowly approaching. The icy feeling behind her grew colder still, as if an invisible hand was stroking her, from the middle of her back all the way to her forehead. Luo Xi shuddered, and mechanically turned her head. A flash of red filled her vision, like a warning signal. When she saw it clearly, it was a vast, thick band of red liquid, snaking along the ground through the rain and swimming towards her like a serpent, the head of which was the red umbrella.

The gory viper, spitting out its vile-smelling tongue, slowly slithered towards her. The night was so dark, and her vision so obscured by the heavy curtain of rain, but the only thing it could not hide was this crimson snake. Luo Xi could not believe how an umbrella from her love could have been the legendary Red Umbrella. Was it unintended, or had Shen Jie really meant to...? When she got to this point, she dared not think further, because countless wild thoughts had already flooded her brain.

Why would Jie want to harm me? Does he no longer love me?

Maybe it didn't matter anymore, because she knew that before long, she would become another victim of the legend, adorning it with another halo of horror.

The crimson snake had already slithered to her pure white ankle, its tongue "kissing" Luo Xi's feet. When a cat catches a mouse, it would usually toy with it like this before eating it, Luo Xi thought, as she closed her eyes, waiting for that moment to arrive, with a calmness in her heart. So, this was what it felt like to wait for death.

"Luo Xi, get up!" A voice, like a saviour, sounded by Luo Xi's ear, and an enormous force pulled her up by the arm, out from the jaws of the red snake. She looked up and saw Jiang Ruohan!

"Ruohan, Ruohan..." Gratefully, Luo Xin gazed at her friend's rain-splattered face.

"Don't just stand there, you idiot! Run!" Jiang Ruohan put her arm around Luo Xi's waist, half-pulling and half-dragging her, as they dashed towards the halls.

The rain still fell. On the small muddy path, the bright red liquid was no longer writhing around, but lay there limp, as if paralyzed, letting the rolling rain pummel and wash it away with abandon, the thick dark red gradually diluting into nothingness...

"Breathe! At last, we're safe!" Jiang Ruohan shook the rain from her hair. The light of the dorm made her feel extraordinarily warm, encouraging a sense of security. Her tense nerves relaxed, and a feeling of infinite exhaustion inevitably followed.

"Luo Xi, come and dry off." She pulled out a towel and passed it back to Luo Xi. But Luo Xi did not respond, and Jiang Ruohan realised that she was the only one in the room.

A gust of icy cold rose from behind her again, numbness creeping over her scalp. She dared not turn around, because she did not want to know who, or what, would be looking at her.

"Luo Xi, Luo Xi..." Jiang Ruohan plucked up the courage to call out a few times, but there was still no reply. The usually bustling room 402 was, at this moment, unusually quiet, so quiet that she could hear her own heartbeat.

Jiang Ruohan put down the towel, and mechanically shifted her body towards her bunk, climbed in, put the duvet over her head, and curled up into a ball. The whole time, she dared not look back.

Outside, the rain continued to beat down. This was destined to be a sleepless night.

TWO

Luo Xi HAD disappeared.

After three or so days, her classmates were slowly beginning to accept this reality, and rumours flew around the university. Some said that on that night, they had seen Luo Xi vanish, holding a red umbrella in the rain, others said they had heard the faint sounds of a girl crying out for help. All sorts of rumours mixed and fed each other, like a beast portending Luo Xi's ill fate.

Yet Jiang Ruohan could not bring herself to accept this truth. That night, she had first abandoned Luo Xi and run off by herself. She was not only scared, but secretly pleased. She had hoped that Luo Xi would disappear into the mud, because she envied her. Envied her looks and talent, envied that in every exam Luo Xi would always take the top spot. No matter how hard Jiang Ruohan tried, she could only be the green leaf to Luo Xi's flower.

Luo Xi was a distinguished beauty, whereas Jiang Ruohan was merely pretty, and pretty average. After showering, Luo Xi would stand in front of the communal bathroom's huge mirrors, naked, twirling her hair and striking alluring poses. Standing behind her, Jiang Ruohan would feel like an ugly duckling. The most hateful thing, though, was that she was the one who had met Shen Jie first. It was they who should have been the sweet couple. At the time, Jiang Ruohan had only wanted to share with her friend the happiness she was feeling. How could she not have known that Luo Xi would bare her blade and snatch away her love?

She hated Luo Xi to the bone. Even though, to other people, they were the best of friends, diehard comrades. Was this the friendship between all women?

But that night, Jiang Ruohan had still gone back to rescue Luo Xi, because even as she was running away, all the happy memories with Luo Xi kept flashing up in the febrile sea of her mind. She could not lose Luo Xi, who was, no matter what else she did, her only friend.

So, she went back, and stepped in to rescue Luo Xi.

But just as Jiang Ruohan had thought they had escaped from hell, Luo Xi disappeared, as if she had just...

evaporated into thin air. For the last three days, Jiang Ruohan's mind constantly returned to the scene that night. "Were these all figments of my imagination?" Jiang Ruohan kept asking herself. She did not know. She only knew that when she woke up on the second day, her bedsheets were soaked through.

"Was it him?" Jiang Ruohan suddenly thought of one person – Shen Jie, the one who had given them the red umbrella. At the time, she had clearly seen his expression, and had known that his intentions were suspect. It was him, it must be!

When Jiang Ruohan found Shen Jie, his face was ashen, as if he had been very ill. His long, usually shining hair was clammy, sticking to his neck, while his creased shirt clung to his flesh.

Seeing her former love like this, Jiang Ruohan felt a pang in her heart. The countless conjectures of before were now quickly tossed to the back of her head, as she took hold of Shen Jie's hand. "Jie, why are you sweating so much, are you ill?"

Shen Jie swallowed painfully a few times, and with effort he squeezed out the words, "All good, just a bit hot."

"Look after yourself."

"Mm," Shen Jie replied perfunctorily and nodded, his gaze locked on the middle of Jiang Ruohan's forehead, as his mind retraced what had happened two days earlier...

IT HAD BEEN an exceptionally beautiful morning after the rainstorm of the previous night, as if heaven and earth had been scrubbed and rinsed, looking all bright and new. Petals bearing the last raindrops floated down, gently settling on Shen Jie's shoulders. Gazing across the sports field, aflame with cherry blossoms, Shen Jie was stunned. The layers of flowers jostled each other for space, as if wishing to squander all their life force during this spring rain.

Perhaps the beauty of life was its transience, to be a summer flower was the ideal, and these flowers were drawn to it like moths to a flame, burning to attain the ideal. If Shen Jie had received the news of Luo Xi's disappearance, then perhaps he would not have felt so at ease, and maybe what happened next would not have happened.

Picking a scenic spot, Shen Jie unslung his camera from his shoulders, set up the tripod, and began a day of photography.

All he needed to do right now was to capture the beauty of these cherry blossoms in their prime. If we could not keep beauty for eternity, then let photographs retain it.

Shen Jie's hobby was photography. He loved to photograph beautiful things: flora, fauna, pretty girls – Luo Xi was not the only one on his computer. Even though there was no one quite as beautiful as her, everybody had a flavour of beauty in them. Shen Jie's heart could never be truly filled with just one. Was this not the way of all men?

Shen Jie adjusted the angle and fine-tuned the focus, wanting to produce something exceptional. He had taken a lot of photos before, which when viewed on the computer were beautiful, but somehow, they lacked a little soul.

He was quite vexed by this, but self-criticism was not going to solve anything. At that moment, another shower drizzled down from the sky, into the puddles on the playgrounds, which expanded just a little.

Early spring days were always full of this cotton wool rain.

"Zhanyi yü shi xinghua yu, chuimian buhan yangliu feng" – "The rain patters in the almond blossom season, as if wishing to moisten my robes; the soft wind strokes my face, it does not feel cold, but makes the young willow branches dance."[1]

A rainy mist had indeed wrapped around the cherry tree groves; the flower petals, as if rouged in the rain, appeared hazy and unreal. Perhaps a long exposure shot could be interesting, but then, this camera was the only expensive item he owned, so reluctantly, he packed it back into the dry safety of its case.

Shen Jing decided to simply take a stroll among the cherry trees and appreciate this beautiful scene properly. Falling petals brushed past his eyelashes, carrying with them the damp mist. The whole world became purer.

He meandered around the grove in lazy circuits, when a girl's figure passed in front of him and disappeared into the clusters of falling petals, but not before Shen Jie caught the sway of her graceful curves. It was a magical moment, and he was compelled to see more of her.

He took out his camera and followed her, wanting to capture this figure in a moment of delicious frisson.

Now the girl appeared among the flowers, now she vanished, but slowly, then came more steadily into view. She was heading towards the sports field beyond the groves, holding a transparent umbrella, the handle of which looked old and very worn.

The girl was wearing a green dress, paired with snow-white trainers. Her long hair flowed as she walked through the grove, framed by the deep green trees around her. Her tread was very light, as if she were afraid to wake something. Shen Jie followed her carefully.

She walked across the sports field, stopping in the middle

1沾衣欲湿杏花雨，吹面不寒杨柳风。From a jueju quatrain by Song Dynasty poet Zhi Nan.

of it, and then, slowly, half turned and looked towards Shen Jie, who pressed the shutters in an instant, before lowering his camera and smiling apologetically at the girl to demonstrate that he meant no harm. The girl was about to turn back and walk away; her expression had been so indifferent, even wooden, but seeing his smile, she appeared to contemplate for a moment before revealing the hint of a smile. It was so bewitching that all the flowers around them paled against it. Even a girl with Luo Xi's beauty was not worth one percent of her.

Shen Jie rubbed the back of his head shyly and lowered his eyes in order to pack up his camera. When he looked up again, the whole field was deserted. He felt as if his heart had been stolen away. Was it by this flowering season, moist with promise? Or by that single look from the girl with the long hair, in the green dress?

Shen Jie returned to his halls, dumping all the photos from his Canon onto his hard drive and launching the editing software. He was looking forward to seeing the day's achievements, and most importantly, that photograph of the girl in green.

He sat down and flicked through the day's output impatiently. The Canon had worked well. Everything had come out so clearly, and all the angles were perfect. But as he progressed through the files, Shen Jie began to feel a chill across his body, as if he had been wrapped in a wet towel, especially around his neck, as if something was breathing cold air onto it.

In that last photo, every element was perfect. The composition, the clarity, beautiful in every aspect except where the subject should have been brilliantly framed in the centre of the image. The half-turning girl in green with the flowing hair was not there. Shen Jie could not believe his eyes, rubbing them with enforced calm. There was no doubt that this was the sports field, but there was no sign nor shadow of any person. He was so sure he had captured the girl in green, but she had not stayed captured.

Steadying his heartbeat, Shen Jie zoomed in and carefully examined the photo, before shooting back so suddenly he fell out of his chair.

In the space that looked empty was a transparent person-shaped shadow. If you did not zoom in carefully, you would miss it entirely. His heart beat faster still as he remembered one of the scare stories that was going round the university – the Girl in the Rain. He raced to delete the photograph and unplugged his computer.

THREE

SUPPRESSING THE FEELING of being soaked, Shen Jie made it through the day. To him, that legend had merely been a thing pulled out of thin air by someone bored, as a trick to dupe the sillier girls. On the second night, he was woken by the sound of dripping water, the clear and crisp sound of droplets hitting the floorboards. He sat up.

Where the hell would the water be leaking from? He was in a ground floor room!

He looked everywhere for the leak, and his bunkmates thought he was overreacting, but the water was still making a noise. Eventually he realised why he could not track the noise. It was coming from him. He lifted his hand and saw, under the pale light, that his palm was soaking wet, and tiny trickles were creeping down his fingers, slowly gathering into crystal clear drops at his fingertips, on the verge of falling, but hanging on. They seemed to be reflecting a figure in green, whose face was lit up with smiles.

Shen Jie tried to recall the legend of Yúnü again. Fear numbed his scalp. His hand flew to wipe itself on his bed cover, but when he touched it, it was already cold and soaking wet, like touching a pool of water, and when he lifted the cover, it felt like fishing something out of a pool.

As he forced himself to at least seem calm, he heard footsteps from outside his room, growing closer and closer, each one feeling like a step directly on his heart. The footsteps stopped, and the air was rich with the damp, light fragrance of cherry blossoms mingled with darkness. Shen Jie felt as if he had fallen into the sea. The darkness, the pressure, the asphyxiation... He was not sure if it was terror he felt, but he could not move. The light went out, and a pair of hands came towards him through the darkness. They were gentle and cool, but cut through his thoughts like a knife of ice.

SHEN JIE OPENED his eyes, woken by Jiang Ruohan's phone call. He forced himself to sit up in a bed that felt like an ocean; his body felt light, and his throat was on fire. He had to down two bottles of chilled water just to take the edge off that scorching feeling. He slowly dressed and headed out.

When he walked through the main hall of the building, one of the cleaning aunties was sweeping the floor. As he squeezed past her sideways, she mumbled, without lifting her head, "Touch your finger to someone's méjiānlún, and Yúnü will move on to them, and leave you alone."

Shocked, Shen Jie turned back immediately to look at the old lady, who appeared as calm as if she had not spoken.

He knew he would not be able to get any more out of her. Would touching someone at the point between the eyebrows really work? That auntie looked like she had been at the university for a long time, so she must have known all these legends, and might just know the ways to break them.

"JUST ONE TOUCH between the eyebrows, and my hands will dry, and everything will go back to normal, and I will never have to sleep in a soaking bed or touch a soaking anything ever again! My body will recover, and I won't turn into a dry corpse!" Shen Jie's eyes were locked dead onto the spot on Jiang Ruohan's forehead, an odd excitement welling up in him.

He held out his hand, feeling his fingers trembling. The woman before him had loved him with an affection no less than Luo Xi had expressed, he clearly knew this in his heart. Now that Luo Xi had disappeared, there was only one woman he could turn to: Jiang Ruohan. You might ask how a man could push such a venomous curse onto a woman, not to mention a woman who loved him this much.

Shen Jie's hand, now just a finger's length away from Jiang Ruohan's forehead, stopped rigid. A sense of frustration rose, followed by the burning sensation flaring again, and like a volcano erupting, he could feel the evaporation of the remaining moisture in his body.

Women, there were loads of them. Love could be induced, but he had only one life! A trace of malice flashed in Shen Jie's eyes, and he no longer trembled. The paused finger continued to move towards Jiang Ruohan. Watching the innocent expression on her face, a kind of disdain arose in

Shen Jie. Farewell, stupid woman!

Closer, even closer, just as Shen Jie thought the curse was about to depart from him, a shadow dashed across his vision. It was Jiang Ruohan's hand, which had flown ahead to cover his forehead first.

"Shen Jie, your head feels very cool – shall I take you to hospital?"

Through the cracks between Jiang Ruohan's fingers, Shen Jie clearly saw that her lips had curled up to form a mocking grin of concern. The whole world went quiet, as his ear drums dried out to tatters. Slowly, Shen Jie got up, and shakingly, he walked back to the dorm building...

WHEN THEY FOUND Shen Jie, he was already dead, lying in the dormitory bathtub, curled up like a sleeping baby.

FOUR

IN ONE SHORT week, two students had come to harm, one missing, most likely dead, and the other having died in onsite accommodation. The leaders of H University could no longer stay silent, with the daily pressure of public opinion and parents requesting transfers, forcing them to pay attention. The police had also investigated, but had concluded that Shen Jie had committed suicide.

Rumours flew around the university, some saying that Shen Jie was distraught by his girlfriend's murder, and had chosen to follow her in the end; others said that it was Shen Jie who had killed Luo Xi, and then her ghost had come back to seek revenge, but the most popular one was that Shen Jie had succumbed to the curse of Yúnü, and his roommates had even testified that Shen Jie had been soaked through for the two days leading up to his death.

The panic continued unabated for a time, but university campuses were a breeding ground for fresh gossip. One day, as rumours of the human head mop in the water room came back into circulation, and there was talk of piano playing coming from the music rooms at midnight, nobody noticed that the stories of the Red Umbrella, the Girl in the Rain, Luo Xi and Shen Jie had faded from everyone's memories.

Everyone except the one whose heart and soul were forever marked by these incidents, and this person was Jiang Ruohan.

"Dead, all dead..." Jiang Ruohan sat in front of the mirror, looking at the girl who stared back. The corner of her mouth rose into a victor's smirk. "All dead, how lovely! University is such a good place, where even murders can be buried in legends. Hahaha, only fools face the law! So, what should the next legend be? The headless doll... or the ghost in the mirror?"

"I think it should be the ghost in the mirror!" said a cold voice behind her, in a dark tone. A gust of cold penetrated Jiang Ruohan's body as she stared straight into the glass, and in the reflection, she saw someone who should no longer be in this world – Luo Xi.

Time passed, second by second, Jiang Ruohan and Luo Xi's reflections glaring at each other. The dormitory became silent as an oppressive atmosphere enveloped the room.

At last, Jiang Ruohan cracked, and asked, trembling, "Luo... Luo Xi, are you alive? Or are you a ghost?"

The Luo Xi in the mirror smiled contemptuously and raised the red umbrella in her hand. "What do you think?

Oh, my friend, it's so cold under the cherry tree!"

"Ahhhhh..." Jiang Ruohan sucked in a mouthful of frosty air, her whole body shaking uncontrollably, the self-confident vigour she had cultivated in her gaze replaced by dread.

"It can't be. I made up the Red Umbrella and Yunü, there's no such legend! There is no such thing as ghosts!"

"Really? Because Shen Jie is here, too. He says he doesn't want to see you, though, because you were such a disappointment. Listen, he's just outside the door."

Half doubting, half believing, Jiang Ruohan turned her ear to the door. From outside came the sound of leather soles pacing the floor. That rhythm... she could tell it was Shen Jie's gait. He had come back, too? Had they come to seek revenge? Jiang Ruohan bit her lip so hard, a patch of gory red blossomed on her bluish lips. She widened her eyes, watching helplessly as the shadow in the mirror slowly approached her.

In the mirror, Luo Xi's face twisted with rage. "Did you know, on that rainy night, how much it hurt when you stabbed that damned umbrella spike into my chest? You killed me and buried me under the cherry tree. And then you killed Shen Jie. You killed the man I loved so dearly! Didn't you love Shen Jie, too? Is this what friendship is to you? Is this love? Are we all just fancy dolls for you to play with and break? Jiang Ruohan, you cannot be forgiven!"

"Nonsense! Friend? What friend? Did you ever treat me like a friend? I was a clown you kept by your side. I was greenery to complement you! You took everything away that belonged to me. My Shen Jie! Luo Xi, you deserved to die! And Shen Jie, too, the man I loved so dearly? Haha, he was a liar as well! He was seeing me behind your back. Every Friday night we would get a room just outside the university, and can you guess what I thought of when I was screwing him? I thought about you daydreaming over him! But he toyed with me. I gave him so much, but got nothing back. So he deserved to die, too! Luo Xi, you had no idea any of this was going on, you stupid little girl!"

"Oh? Well, now I know."

"What's the use of knowing? You're all idiots! Idiots who deserved to die!" Jiang Ruohan shook her head indifferently – she knew that there was to be no escape tonight.

"Haha, of course it's worth knowing." In the mirror, Luo Xi's smile brightened, as she brandished the umbrella in her hand at Jiang Ruohan, pulling a microphone from its rolled canopy.

With a crashing thud, the door of room 402 was kicked open, and two police officers rushed in. Guns drawn and pointing at Jiang Ruohan, they barked, "Jiang Ruohan, you are under arrest for the murder of Shen Jie and the attempted murder of Luo Xi. Raise your hands and come with us."

"So..." Jiang Ruohan looked into the endless pitch black of the gun barrels, a moment of understanding beginning to break. Viciously, she roared at Luo Xi, "You liar, you aren't dead!"

Luo Xi threw Jiang Ruohan a disdainful glance, and then unbuttoned the top buttons of her shirt. Jiang Ruohan saw the ugly scar across her chest. "The doctor said you missed by seven millimetres. I was in a coma for a fortnight. When I came round, and learned that Shen Jie had committed suicide, I knew it must have been you. When I reported it to the police, they said they had no evidence to arrest you on, so I created this trap to bait you. Our conversation is all on the recording. Jiang Ruohan, there is no way you can escape the law now. I want to see your execution with my own eyes!"

"Hah." Jiang Ruohan laughed bitterly, holding her forehead. "Luo Xi, you are smarter than me. Looks like I can't escape, but let me tell you, I'll never let you get what you want again!" With that, Jiang Ruohan lifted the stool she had been sitting on, and hurled it with force at the three intruders before rushing towards the balcony.

"Stop!" the two police officers both shouted out at once, blocking the flying chair in one swoop. They sped towards the balcony, but they were one step too late.

"You all made me do it!" A shrill, hoarse scream stabbed through the silence, permeating the entire university grounds. Jiang Ruohan's body cut a graceful arc against the night sky, ending in a muffled thud, and the night plunged back into a brief silence.

On the flower bed by the front entrance, she lay, her body twitching haphazardly, dark red liquid oozing out of the five orifices of her face, like a beautiful flower blossoming in stealth. Her eyes were round and wide, glaring malevolently at the balcony of room 402. She could see a grim smile spread across the face of a strange girl in white, who was leaning over the railings. Her mouth was wide open, as if she wanted to speak, but she could only hear a gasp as the sound escaped her throat, until the twitching stopped...

BECAUSE OF THAT recording, the murder cases that had shaken the university were speedily resolved in a few days, putting a stop to the pervasive wave of horror and panic. As the students sighed over the machinations of

Jiang Ruohan, a new cycle of legends and scare stories began to ferment in their heads.

EPILOGUE

TONIGHT IS JIANG Ruohan's touqi[2], her first offering day, and cotton wool showers of rain float down from the sky again. On the balcony of room 402 of the women's accommodation block, a basin of fire and two candles burn. Next to the candles are two photographs, one of Jiang Ruohan, the other of Shen Jie. Luo Xi is sitting in a black dress, constantly feeding mingzhi, paper funeral money, into the basin, while the licking flames roast her face red.

"All dead, all dead... how excellent!" A cunning smile rises from the corner of Luo Xi's mouth. "Shen Jie, how does it feel to die at the hands of the woman you love? Is it comforting? Do you know why Jiang Ruohan would kill you? It was me. Me who pushed her, this neurotic cow, with just a little medication and some psychological suggestion to bring her fully under my control. Sometimes I've got to admire that wretched woman for fabricating the stories of the Red Umbrella, and the Girl in the Rain, all to use as cover for her perfect murders. I only discovered it because I was flicking through her diary, and do you know? When I saw that idea, I was so excited, because I knew that my day of vengeance had finally arrived!

"Jiang Ruohan, you stupid woman, so stupid you died in your own murder plot. Such a shame that throughout the

---

2 Touqi 头七, part of traditional mourning rituals. The Chinese believe that the souls of the deceased remain in this world for forty-nine days, before they move on to the netherworld. Offerings are made to them every seven days by different members of their family, in the form of food and drink so they would not go hungry, and underworld money to send them on their way. Should the rituals not be performed or carried out properly, then the soul is likely to remain in this world, and cause trouble.

whole affair, you were too doped up and twisted round to get it, right up to the moment you died. What a shame." Luo Xi strokes the scar on her chest. "This was a huge risk. If I'd died doing this, it would have been ridiculous. But it worked. I bit down the pain and crawled to the hospital. I think I carried myself on vengeance and spite alone. Ah, I'll have this scar for the rest of my life, but if it wasn't this bad, how could I make the police believe me? Jiang Ruohan, this time, I gambled, and won!

"Shen Jie, Jiang Ruohan, you little shits, did you really think I had no idea? Yes, I didn't know straightaway, but perhaps heaven wanted me to see your ugly little affair. I went out to treat myself for breakfast and was shocked to see the two of you coming out of that hotel. I wanted to kill you both right then, and heaven help me, I've done it. Haha, this feeling of getting away with murder, it's so good! Farewell, my dearest friends, may the pair of you rot in hell!"

The flickering flames illuminate Luo Xi's face, her beautiful features mangled in the leaping light. The rain falls ceaselessly, and a flash of lightning streaks over the horizon, turning the pitch-black night white for a split second, before returning to the dark. Luo Xi does not notice that as the lightning flares, the glass window behind her reflects three figures...

NOTES

UNIVERSITY IN CHINA is a time for great emotional upheaval. The pressures to get in, the pressure once there to succeed, and those first few steps at independent living mean that it is a time of heightened experience. It is no surprise then, that this sense of great inner turmoil and emotions can so easily coagulate into the terror of urban myths and ghost stories. I remember, during my time at Minzu University in Beijing, being told that the dormitory was haunted by a lank-haired ghost who would hang from the ceiling when you showered and trick you into washing her hair whilst you were blinded with shampoo. The Xiaoyuan Jingsong (college horror) tradition may have grown out of the age-old oral storytelling forms, but since the 1990s, these fearful schoolyard legends began to spread via university BBS and internet horror fiction forums, until, coinciding with the maturing of China's film industry in the 2010s, and the revival of traditional festivals like Zhongyuan (Ghost Month), it resulted in a plethora of college-based horror films. Since Hong Niangzi is considered by many in China to be a 'must read' for the genre, I cannot think of a better author to start this collection with.

Hong Niangzi, whose penname translates as "The Red Lady", cemented her fame with the "Seven Colour" horror series. Dynamic in style, they range from dark psychological urban horror to traditional ghost stories, steeped in strange antiquities, often drawing from the rich folklore and culture of her Miao heritage.

The author wrote this story during the monsoon season in Shenzhen, when the summer heat makes the whole world feel like it is wrapped in a blanket of hot, humid air. She happened to be living by a university at the time and took daily strolls in the vicinity with her umbrella. One day, she saw two girls walking side by side with a tall boy in the grounds, and wondered what was going on between them. To most people, they would probably assume the general 'courting couple and chaperone', but to the mind of Hong Niangzi, she imagined emotional entanglement, subterfuge, and happenings possibly even leading to fatality. During her own time at university, she had heard some similarly ghastly tales, so the rain, her umbrella and a love triangle formed the ingredients for her story.

Hong Niangzi grew up in Miao communities in the mountains of Hunan, which existed alongside many other ethnic groups in neighbouring villages, many of which held an abundance of oral storytelling traditions. As an adult, she moved to Shenzhen for work, and was surprised to find that people in the big cities had never heard the tales from her hometown. So, she set about retelling those stories for an urban audience. At first, it was just for her own enjoyment, as a way of celebrating and maintaining the wonderful memories of her rural upbringing, but this creative flow coincided with the rise of the internet in China, and she found her words reaching a much larger audience than she had anticipated, so her writing became very much about exchange and connecting with the world at large.

THE WAKING DREAM

清醒梦

Fan Zhou

THE SPACIOUS, CIRCULAR meeting room is bathed in sunlight. Shen Yue sits with the two other architects at the long, snow-white, solid wood table, listening to the eloquent speech of their chief. The blue sky beyond the curved glass wall is so perfect it looks fake. From time to time, birds swoop past, spreading their wings. Shen Yue pretends to lower her head casually, focusing her gaze on the grain on the table surface, and avoiding what is pacing behind the chief: the giant spawn monster with countless eyes.

Like a spider, the monster has eight long, thin and crooked legs that step across the thickly carpeted floor noiselessly, its rubber-textured body constantly secreting a transparent sticky fluid, leaving a suspicious trail on the grey carpet. Drops of this viscous liquid are falling onto the back of the chief's chair, but he seems scarcely to notice. No matter where it goes, the monster's gaze is permanently fixed on the chief – who is excitedly introducing Phase Two of the Mars Base Construction project, like a hunter drooling over prey that is just out of its reach.

The plans are so familiar to Shen Yue that she does not need to look at them, so she just listens, respectfully. The chief is now actively seeking her input. "Shen Yue, which plan do you think is better, the multi-layered column solution? Or the hexagonal one?"

The monster seems to hear the chief's words, and without any telegraphing, stops behind him. Shen Yue lifts her head up to face the chief and the monster, and replies in a controlled tone, "Each solution has its benefits. The multi-layer form has top notch anti-radiation provisions, and allows for fairly large laboratories and common areas, which would make the lives of the staff living there very comfortable. Yet the hexagon has the budgetary advantage, allowing for economically spaced living quarters with greater privacy. Precisely which one should be chosen still depends on the client's requirements and budget."

"What you're saying makes sense, though personally, I think…" The chief continues his lengthy commentary. Shen Yue lowers her head, and surreptitiously breathes a sigh of relief. The withered, branch-like claws of the monster are now gripping the back of the chief's chair, its dull, lightless many-eyes boring into the back of the chief's head.

It feels like a century before the meeting finally finishes. The chief walks out of the meeting room, glowing with an air of vitality, followed closely by Shen Yue and her colleague Zhao Zhijian, with whom she shares an office. Zhao Zhijian leans in close to Shen Yue and says in lowered tones, "Thank goodness we're not in a real office right now, or I'd have developed haemorrhoids." Shen Yue humours him with a chuckle, and surreptitiously sidesteps around the monster's sticky secretions smeared across the carpet.

To get from the meeting room to her office, Shen Yue has to pass through the open-plan lobby, in which the display is simply dizzying. A cephalopod monster stands behind a female colleague, its tentacles tightly wrapped around her like a lover. Another creature, resembling a completely skinned human, crouches on the desk of a male colleague, its bright red gore flowing down, pooling onto the carpet and staining a large patch of it crimson. A moth-like monster is perched on the back of another member of staff, like a woodpecker perched on a tree, constantly piercing his chest with its furry claws. Nobody else in the hall seems to be aware of this nightmarish scene, just busying themselves with their own affairs. Shen Yue also pretends not to see this, and makes her way back to her office, bantering along the way with Zhao Zhijian.

Before the start of virtual working, Shen Yue had thought, like others, that working in the online world would be more relaxing than the real world. The principle behind virtual working is to transfer people's consciousness to the Yuanjie metaverse, so their cerebra work at full capacity, while their bodies lie in the Consciousness Converter (CC), in a deep sleep induced by a gas. To quote the media, virtual working is like a twelve-hour long, diverting dream, in which all the activities of the dream can be controlled. When VW really began, Shen Yue realised that she had been naïve. In real-world working, although her body would feel tired, her brain could make use of all those little moments of downtime; even when she was working, her mind could occasionally wander and relax. But in the Yuanjie, even though her body is in deep sleep in a CC, her brain is in a state of constant wakefulness, a kind of enforced focus that makes every second spent in the metaverse interminable, and inescapable, turning her twelve hours of work into a daily nightmare from which she cannot wake.

Almost another century passes, and it is lunch break. Shen Yue heads to the "canteen" with a group of colleagues.

When eating in the Yuanjie, the CC stimulates the taste cortex in the parietal lobe of the cerebrum, to simulate the sensations of ingesting food, but this kind of illusory pleasure cannot replace the *se'xiangwei*, appearance, aroma and taste, of real food. So Shen Yue places a lunch box full of food, like an accessory, by her hand, and instead focuses on listening to the chattering of her colleagues.

Someone mentions the name of the client they are working with. "Apparently, Hongda is now allowing employees to turn up at work using an avatar that looks different from their reals, so yesterday, a whole bunch of fire-breathing dragons turned up to the meeting. I laughed so much I nearly died."

Someone else immediately answers with a sigh, "I wish I could come to work with a different avatar. There are a few virtual skins I really like the look of, but we're not allowed to, so I couldn't buy them, even if I wanted to spend all that money."

"This is the consumerist trap," says Zhao Zhijian, who is sitting next to Shen Yue and wolfing down some *daoxiao* beef noodles. "In order to sell more skins, the operating companies offer clients that allow their staff to wear different avatars a month's credit on their maintenance fees. You don't think the boss at Hongda is doing this out of charity, do you?"

"Money is for spending. I just want to come to work with a different skin every day."

Another male colleague expresses his agreement, and pats Zhao Zhijian's shoulder. "I agree. If our company lets us change avatars, I will buy Old Zhao a female avatar with great tits and a perky bum right away, just to put us in a better mood looking at it every day."

He makes everybody laugh, including Zhao Zhijian.

Having finished her laughing, Shen Yue lowers her head back down.

Someone brings up another topic: "I heard on the news that some experts have suggested extending VW from twelve hours a day to fourteen – their reason being that sleeping more hours a day is better for your health."

Their neighbour complains, "Extend it? Sleeping for twelve hours a day is making me feel light-headed as it is. Another two hours, I'd be worried my body would waste away."

His comment generates a wave of agreement. "If you sleep for too long, you might not wake up."

"There's been cases abroad where people have been in the CC for a prolonged time and turned into vegetables."

"That's all rumours, and already officially denied. That person just had a particularly realistic nightmare."

This topic piques Shen Yue's interest. "What's the most terrifying nightmare you've ever had?"

"Caterpillars," blurts out a female colleague. "When I was little, I went on a school trip to the botanical gardens, and a caterpillar fell into my clothes. It crawled around on my back all day. After getting back, I had a month of nightmares about caterpillars." Shen Yue believes her, because a monstrous green caterpillar covered in downy black fur is currently sitting on her back.

"I dreamt of skeletons," says another female colleague. "I went to an escape room with my boyfriend and got a shock from a skeleton prop. That night I dreamt of the same thing happening, and it frightened me again." A skeleton with its hand full of needles is standing by this colleague right now, poised to jam them into her eyes.

Zhao Zhijian pushes aside his empty bowl and looks at Shen Yue somewhat curiously. "What are you afraid of?"

He is the only one around Shen Yue who does not have a monster behind them, only a faint pink glow of light issuing from the sleeves of his pale blue shirt.

Shen Yue does not answer immediately. Her middle school classroom floats into her mind's eye, in all its minute detail. The nightmares she has experienced, from which she cannot wake, took place in this all too familiar classroom.

DURING THE SUMMER of her second year at university, Shen Yue flew home after exam week. As soon as she got in the door, she flung herself onto the bed, and had the most terrifying dream of her life. In it, Shen Yue is only about thirteen or fourteen. Carrying her heavy school bag on her shoulders, she is frantically running to school to get ready for the big tests. When she gets there, she finds the school completely empty, only the blood red setting sun filling the classroom with its remnant rays. Young Shen Yue stands next to her seat, listening to heavy footsteps approaching from a distance. As they draw closer and closer, her heart is about to leap out of her chest. The door of the classroom opens, and she sees a tall, headless monster carrying a mirror on its neck. Shen Yue opens her eyes.

When she wakes up, she finds herself back in her bedroom. Having heard movement, her mother pushes open the door. Seeing the doubt and concern on her mother's face, Shen Yue feels so moved she nearly bursts into tears.

"What's the matter?" her mother asks, but Yue shakes her head without saying a word. Her mother does not press the issue, but instead hands her a peeled tangerine.

"Here, eat some fruit."

Obediently, Shen Yue puts a piece of tangerine into her mouth, but cannot taste the cool sweetness she is expecting. Having noticed that something is wrong, Shen Yue looks up at her mother, but all she sees is the tall, headless monster, with a mirror on its neck. She races out into the living room, picks up a fruit knife from the table and stabs her arm with it. Blood oozes out, but she feels no pain.

Shen Yue turns around to face the creature and sees her father's face in the monster's mirror. At that instant, her desire to wake up exceeds her terror. Shen Yue runs into the wall with all her might, but still feels no pain. Without further hesitation, she steels her resolve, and jumps off the balcony.

From then on, Shen Yue had begun to understand that in real nightmares, waking up was not the end of terror, but the beginning. Death, however, could be the shortcut to liberation; perhaps sometimes, it was the only way.

SHEN YUE OPENS her eyes and stares at the perfectly blank ceiling. She lets her breath out slowly, with a sense of relief, and sits up from the Consciousness Convertor. Her bedroom is barely three square metres and reverberates with monotonous mechanical noises. Sensing that their owner has woken up, the smart curtains slowly part, letting sunlight flood into the room. Shen Yue switches off the CC and stands up to stretch her stiffened limbs. Even though she has slept for twelve hours, she is still aching all over.

After a simple breakfast of fried eggs, noodles and a glass of milk, Shen Yue sweats out an hour on her running machine. After her workout, she does not want to go anywhere, so collapses, as if paralysed, on the sofa in front of the TV. Lunchtime soon arrives, and Shen Yue pours the lazi spicy chicken and meicai pickle steamed pork into a bowl, putting it into the microwave with some cold rice to heat up together. While waiting for lunch, she flicks over to the news. The anchorman is reporting that the creator of virtual working has been awarded a spot in the Top Ten Greatest Entrepreneurs of the Year. "This era-marking invention not only saves office space and energy, but has liberated billions of workers from the servitude of 996 and 007 living, enabling them to create value whilst staying free from the exploitations of the flesh. This is not only an illustrious technological advancement, but an advancement towards humanitarianism..." Hearing this, Shen Yue snaps off the TV instantly. No matter how you dress up the package in rhetoric, the essence of virtual working has never changed – it is nothing short of forced sleep and forced dreaming. Unfortunately, she is prone to nightmares.

After finishing lunch, Shen Yue leans on the windowsill with her chin on her hands, alone, and continues her contemplation. As far as the eye can see, skyscrapers cover every inch of sky. Every building in turn is covered in deep black holes, making them look like ant nests. Over every hole are solid metal anti-theft grilles, like dense and stuffy cages. Countless people live totally unrelated lives within these cages. Shen Yue has never found the view appealing, but when all those different kinds of monsters began appearing in her dream, she almost fell in love with this monotonous and dull world of reality. In the realm of dreams, those who were frightened of caterpillars were pursued by furry bugs, those who were scared of skeletons had skeletons keeping them company; there was nowhere to hide or shelter from fear, and no way of concealing it. At least here, she is safe.

Shen Yue gently swirls a glass of water in her hand, listening to the soft and delicate sounds coming from the ice cubes as they collide. The afternoon sun is warm and wholesome; she feels like a pile of snow about to melt away in the strong sunlight. She turns her head sideways, feeling drowsy and muddy-minded, and looks into the dressing mirror, seeing a tall, headless monster carrying a mirror on its neck, quietly gazing back at her.

The glass in Shen Yue's hand falls to the floor and shatters into a thousand shards.

THE NEXT DAY, Shen Yue sits in the chief's office, eyes lowered and fixed on her own interlaced fingers. The chief sits at his black solid wood desk, looking at her, evidently displeased. The ceiling above his head, the walls behind him and to either side, are all embedded with scores of malicious eyes. Like stage lights, they are universally trained on his person. From time to time, they make vague, whispering noises.

"Don't you think you owe me a reason for this transfer request? I think this role suits you very well. You've done your job excellently. So why change?" The chief's face is full of incomprehension.

Shen Yue replies tactfully, "I have no complaints about the workload or the nature of the tasks. I just haven't been very well lately, so the doctor suggests that I take a break from VW."

"What do you mean by 'not very well'?"

"It's mainly the headaches, occasionally losing my balance, also blurred vision sometimes. The doctor has given me a full check-up and says that this has been caused by cerebral hypertension over a prolonged period. They have suggested I reduce the amount of time spent in the CC."

"What if you don't get better after the transfer, what do you plan to do then?"

This is not a question Shen Yue has had time to consider. Lowering her head to look at the smooth surface of the table, from the corner of her eye, she notices that her monster is now on all fours, sitting by her feet, looking up at her in a confrontational manner. Its mirror shows a reflection of her own, totally distorted face.

Seeing that she is unable to answer, the chief says sincerely, "Considering you haven't thought it through, I suggest that you stay in the same position for now and try to adjust your state of mind. All the symptoms you mention are common features of stress-related health problems, experienced by practically everyone these days. Just try to relax regularly, keep up with the exercises, and you'll be fine. I've been living virtually ever since my car accident during my last year of university. I was receiving a virtual education, and when I started working, it's always been in the Yuanjie. So that's been over ten years now, and I'm doing fine, aren't I? There's no need to treat the CC like it's some kind of world-eating flood monster."

Shen Yue keeps her silence, knowing that the more the chief speaks, the more excited he gets, and that it's time for another great long monologue. "Virtual working is a great invention. In the past, everybody was restricted by the limitations of their physical condition, so there would be unfair situations such as men having the advantage over females, or the healthy having the advantage over the disableds. VW, however, has levelled all these differences in physical health, so that everyone with the talent and skills could stand on a level playing field and compete fairly…"

The chief grows more and more loquacious, occasionally gesturing with his hands. Shen Yue stares at the silver lotus patterns on the grey wallpaper behind the chief, his voice seeming to grow softer and softer. By the time she walks out of his office, the outside world is totally silent. Shen Yue watches her colleagues' mouths as they constantly open and shut; returning to her desk, she continues to work as normal. Struggling, she makes it through to the end of work hours, and the moment she's out of the office, all the sounds that had disappeared rush back in. Shen Yue opens her eyes, and feeling completely lost, she looks at the chief, who is still waxing lyrical, and at the grey wallpaper with the silver lotus patterns.

"Are you even listening to me?" The chief now looks hurt as well as angry.

Shen Yue casts a glance at the malicious eyes on the ceiling, and realises that she's still in the Yuanjie, and says softly, "Sorry, my headache just started again."

TWO DAYS LATER, during lunchtime, Shen Yue made light of her experiences in the chief's office to Zhao Zhijian. Today, Zhao Zhijian is wearing a short-sleeved polo shirt, and his lower arms are covered in shining pink lines, like some kind of strange vine, or the wiring in a gaming PC.

Zhao Zhijian looks at her, full of concern. "You're in a pretty bad state, aren't you? Having optical illusions in the real world, and a fake-wake inside the Yuanjie is evidence that your cerebrum has reached a state of extreme exhaustion, to the point where the boundaries between illusion and reality are blurring. I suggest you take some time off straight away and rest. Work can't be more important than your health."

Shen Yue does not reply. She has been focusing on Zhao Zhijian's arm. When he talks, these thin lines flicker along with the rise and fall of his speech. She has only ever seen these lines on Zhao Zhijian.

Unexpectedly, she says, "It's my 'monthly holiday' this weekend – do you want to come mountain climbing with me?"

Zhao Zhijian is clearly startled by this, but then replies immediately, "Sure. Just the two of us?"

"Just the two of us." Shen Yue sees it very clearly now – after her comment, the colour of the tiny lines on Zhao Zhijian's arms darken a little. At once she understands what these lines represent. This is the first time she has seen the manifestation of any emotion other than fear inside the Yuanjie.

Seeing that she has no intention of taking any proper time off, Zhao Zhijian decides to tell her a story. "Actually, I've always had my doubts about the security of virtual working. I have a friend who works at the operating company. He was the one who told me about this mechanical engineer abroad. While he was working in VW, he discovered a toxic gas leak at a factory near his home. Theoretically, when the toxicity in the air reaches a level that's harmful to the human body, the CC automatically wakes the user up, and that's what happened. All the other workers in VW were woken up and successfully moved out of danger. But that one engineer was not. In the end, he died in the CC, and the company paid a lot of money to keep the incident out of the media."

"Why didn't he wake up?"

Zhao Zhijian shakes his head. "Nobody knows. According to the engineer's colleagues, for some time before he died, he had been in a state of mental distraction.

Sometimes he couldn't tell the difference between illusion and reality, just like you, now. Before he dropped offline for the last time, his last words were 'snakes everywhere', but his colleagues had seen nothing."

"Snakes?" Shen Yue feels a chill run down her spine.

"The engineer said that snakes had been the thing he was most frightened of. The police deduced that this was the warning his body tried to give his brain. His body had sensed danger, but his brain was still dreaming, so his body was attempting to send messages to his brain to wake it up. Shame that he never got the message." He sighs. "I don't want the same thing to happen to you. Shen Yue, take some time off."

Again, Shen Yue makes no reply. Leaning on the railings, she gazes out at the forever sunny skies of the Yuanjie, but is thinking about all the food in her fridge at home, about the luxurious changrong cotton four-set linen on her bed, and the countless clothes and dresses in her wardrobe. All these have, of course, been purchased with money. She cannot lose this job. Poverty is more frightening than nightmares.

After the conversation with Zhao Zhijian, Shen Yue continues to work as usual. In the following week, more and more monsters appear in the company, and they grow stranger every day. After the weekend's rest, Shen Yue arrives at the office nice and early, as she does every Monday. Gazing at the lift doors that are slowly sliding open, she finds herself too petrified to step into the lobby.

The floor, which is usually carpeted with mute grey, has now become a surface of black water, and all the monsters she has seen in the company are either swimming in the water, or wading through it. Their long hairy legs and tentacles, dripping with viscous secretions, form ripple after ripple as they make contact with the watery surface, their fangs and sharp claws gleaming slightly in the reflection. Even below the dark waters, where the light cannot penetrate, a low grunting noise emanates. Shen Yue has no idea what kind of monster this guttural noise could be coming from.

"Why don't you come in?" The colleague that had stepped out of the lift ahead of her looks puzzled. Shen Yue sets her mouth, and begins to take feeble, floating steps towards her office. The way has never felt so long. With every step she takes, the breathing and moaning of the monsters seems to become more distinct; she can smell the putrescence of rotten flesh and blood from their bodies. These were other people's fears, and also her nightmare.

Her only sanctuary is her office. Zhao Zhijian's chair rests calmly on the water's surface, which is clear and gleaming with ripples. He is working, as calm as Mount Tai. Seeing her come in, he smiles and greets her: "Morning." As usual, there is nothing around him.

"Morning." Shen Yue sits down opposite Zhao Zhijian, feigning nonchalance, but bursting with jealousy. In the same suffocating work environment, when everyone else is battling with their own fears, Zhao Zhijian is somehow unaffected by it all, and able to live without worry or fear. Shen Yue finds it hard to describe with words the degree of envy she feels toward Zhao.

While typing, Zhao Zhijian says to her, "I've already sent you the proposal that the chief asked for last time. Take a look – if there are no issues, send it off."

Mechanically, Shen Yue nods her assent, and instinctively switches on her computer to begin work. The tall headless monster carrying a mirror on its neck, now draped in a black cloak, has been at her side this entire time, stalking back and forth, patrolling, as if holding its breath and observing her every move. Every time she taps on the keyboard, Shen Yue tells herself it is all an illusion, nothing to be scared of.

Word by word, she reads the proposal that Zhao Zhijian had written, correcting the places where there is an omission or a mistake. Having amended the proposal, she starts filling in an evaluation form to HR that serves as the seasonal report. The black-cloaked monster is now leaning over the desk by her hand; this time there's a head on its neck instead of a mirror, and two gory, gaping mouths where its eyes should be. All three of its maws are stretched wide open, as if about to gobble Shen Yue up and swallow her. Even though she knows it's an illusion, she can do nothing about it.

During lunch, Shen Yue does not go to the canteen with her other colleagues, but instead collapses over her paperwork, trying to take some rest. The monster squats on her desk, still watching her. The head on its neck has now turned back to a mirror, which reflects the features of a father Shen Yue is determined to forget, along with those memories from childhood.

These are all just illusions, she reminds herself yet again, but it feels like her cerebrum is now almost incapable of telling the difference.

At last, determined, Shen Yue gets up and marches out of the door in huge strides, and then she starts running, heading straight for the chief's office. This time, no matter what the cost, she is going to put an end to this nightmare. Or else, one way or another, she will go crazy in the Yuanjie.

Shen Yue knows that the chief never goes to the canteen

at lunchtime, but takes a break in his office. Today, though, his office is empty. The sound of faint footsteps comes from the lobby. Shen Yue pushes the door open and follows the sound.

The hall is also empty, and all those monsters that had been strutting around have, for the moment, disappeared. On the ceiling and the glass walls, dozens of malevolent eyes are fixed on the chief, who is standing in front of the wall. As Shen Yue approaches him, she hears him murmur to himself in dismay, "Why are there so many eyes?"

As if struck by lightning, Shen Yue freezes in her footsteps, her head running through the conversation with Zhao Zhijian on the balcony at lightning speed. When she comes back to herself, she grabs hold of the chief by the lapels and demands, "You can see these eyes?"

With a ghastly pale face, the chief reverses the question. "You can see them, too?"

Immediately, Shen Yue puts her hands around his neck and wrings it. "You have to wake up now, your body is in grave danger!" She does not waste time explaining, but grabbing hold of the chief, she rams as hard as she can into the wall of glass, repeatedly, again, and again. The chief, scared into a stupor by her violent behaviour, is unable to say a word. Seeing that it's no use crashing into the wall, Shen Yue lifts up a chair and brings it down on the chief's head over a dozen times, but instead of passing out, he sits paralysed on the floor, staring at her, completely bewildered.

Shen Yue looks around, trying to find some way to wake the chief out of his dream. Spying the balcony, she smiles. Ignoring the chief's attempts to struggle free, she drags him to the open portal, and with all the energy she can muster, pushes him over. The chief's body instantly turns into a nondescript grey dot, disappearing into the artificially straight lines of traffic on the road below.

THE MAN OPENED his eyes, sat up from the CC, and was immediately choked into a cough by the thick clouds of smoke rolling into his bedroom. Covering his mouth and nose, he strained to look through the house. Fire was raging in his living room, while his robot assistant and PA had disappeared. He pressed the release button and attempted to prop himself against the CC in order to crawl out of it, but his broken body felt like it was filled with lead and would not listen to his mind. The man managed to free himself from the machine, but he had used up all his strength. In the end, he lay collapsed by the bedroom door, unable to do anything but tremble. At last, he grabbed hold of a comm that had fallen on the floor.

"HELP!" He gave out a heart-tearing and lung-rending scream.

THE SIGHT OF the man's struggling and his calls for help during the last moment of his life are freeze-framed on the screen, motion trapped in blurred static ghosts. After pausing, the viewer exits the viewing interface, selects "delete document", and then, extracting the back-up hard drive, throws it onto the floor, crushes it to shards, and throws the broken fragments into the bin. Just like this, a man is disappeared into the obscure blue light of the screen, as if he never existed.

*　*　*

WHEN THE SOUND of knocking comes, Shen Yue is sitting quietly on the side of the bed, gazing at the mountaintops embedded in the square window. The scenery is a world away from the steel forest she is used to. Milky white mist floats like thin gauze between the mountains, a constantly undulating forest sea of crisp green. Facing this flock of mountains and sea of clouds every day, her previous life seems like a dream that is fading daily in Shen Yue's memory.

When the knock comes, Shen Yue does not answer it. The robot assistant pushes open the door, and says to her attentively, "Miss Shen, you have a visitor."

Shen Yue follows the robot nurse, shuffling behind them at a pace that would have frustrated anyone else towards the visiting room. This is her first visitor since she moved here. She is neither pleased nor curious.

There is only a square table and two chairs in the visiting room. Zhao Zhijian is waiting for her. Shen Yue sits down at the table. The robot assistant turns to leave the room.

The door is closed. Zhao Zhijian looks all around him, confirming that the indicator light on the CCTV is off, before saying to Shen Yue in a suppressed and lowered voice, "I gave the supervisor some money. This meeting will not be recorded. I have something important to tell you."

Silently, Shen Yue waits for him to tell her why he has come here.

"I have confirmed with my friend who works at the operators, the hard drive containing the last recording of the chief before he died wasn't destroyed in the fire – someone had smashed it. Someone had seen that video. After you'd pushed the chief off the balcony, he did indeed wake up. What's more, the company had given money to many of the chief's neighbours. If my guess is correct, somebody must have heard the chief's call for help, so the company wants to shut their mouth."

"But in the end, I couldn't save him. Does it matter if he did or didn't wake up?"

Zhao stares at her, astonished. "Of course it matters. If he woke up, then the company is trying to put the blame on you, when CC was at fault! According to them, the chief didn't wake up because you pushed him off the balcony, and the big shock gave him a stroke. But the reality is that he did wake up, but could not get out because of his disability. If the CC had woken him up earlier, he would probably have survived. The responsibility lies with them, not you."

Indifferent, Shen Yue looks down at her interlaced fingers. "What's the use of knowing all this? The evidence has already been destroyed."

"Even though the video no longer exists, the witness still does. I will find a way to drain the water out and reveal the sunken stone of truth." Zhao Zhijian gazes sincerely into her eyes. "Shen Yue, whatever happens, don't lose heart. I'm going to get you out of this."

Confronted with Zhao Zhijian's passionate declaration, Shen Yue remains silent, and continues to investigate the patterns on her palm. Zhao Zhijian seems a little disappointed, but after a moment of silence, opens his mouth again to test the waters. "Shen Yue, I've been curious about one thing. How exactly did you find out that the chief was in danger in the real world? In court, you said he actively asked for your help, but I can't help but think that you two weren't on such good terms. If he were really feeling unwell, he could have just requested to go offline from the administrator. Why would he ask you?"

Shen Yue freezes. "What have you heard?"

Zhao Zhijian hesitates for a while before replying,

"Recently I found a private forum on the net, and there are some discussions on there about virtual working. Several users said they've seen strange things on the Yuanjie."

"What things?" Shen Yue pursues.

Zhao Zhijian scratches his head. "It's hard to say. Everyone sees different things. It's all grotesque and strange illusions anyway. None of them seemed to understand what was going on. One user wrote a very long post commenting on this thing, saying that what these people are seeing are their subconsciouses."

"Subconsciouses?" Shen Yue frowns.

"The principle behind VW was to transfer people's consciousnesses into the metaverse, so that their brains can work in the Yuanjie. But what is being uploaded isn't just our conscious minds, but also the subconscious. The two parts make up one's whole personality, but the subconscious data on the metaverse far exceeds conscious data, like the part of an iceberg hidden under the water being far larger than the exposed tip. The computer cannot process the subconscious stuff, so most of it just isn't visible, but without it, the Yuanjie can't function. The operators call this invalid data. This guy suggested that some people are seeing illusions in the metaverse because of their unique cerebra, which allow them to somehow parse these things from the ID. In other words, they can read other people's subconsciouses. Because of this, the user has named these people Dúxīnzhe, the Heart Readers."

"All this is merely his conjecture; so far, nothing can prove it," Shen Yue says lightly.

Zhao Zhijian agrees. "You are right. That user must have some insider information. My friend who works at the operator has confirmed that his theory about the ID is correct. As for the Dúxīnzhe? If they exist, there's no way the operators will let them live. Being able to read other people's inner thoughts and feelings is a terrifying thing in itself, but these people could identify the thoughts present in other people that even they *themselves* are not aware of. At the moment, there are over seven million businesses around the world that have adopted VW. With the existence of Heart Readers, all the big enterprises would have to re-evaluate the risk of VW on confidential information and privacy. The operator would never allow that to happen." Zhao Zhijian leans in closer to Shen Yue, his face full of anxiety. "Shen Yue, the day that the chief died, what exactly did you see?"

Slowly, Shen Yue shakes her head. "I know you are worried about me. But I really didn't see anything."

Having got the answer, Zhao Zhijian breathes a sigh of relief. "Oh, good. Considering you're not a Heart Reader, the operator won't see you as a threat. I'm going to get you out of this as soon as I can."

After seeing Zhao Zhijian off, Shen Yue returns to her room, and continues to stare at the continuous green mountain range, like a grinning fool. She doesn't regret lying to Zhao Zhijian. The way things are now, Zhao Zhijian is her only worry outside this institute. She will do anything to keep him out of danger.

Shen Yue walks to the window, letting the moist and nourishing mountain wind stroke her face. If Zhao Zhijian is telling the truth, then the secret of the Heart Readers will come out sooner or later. Her next visitor will either be someone from the operator, or someone who wants to fight against them. Either way, it will provide her with some opportunity for revenge. But until then, Shen Yue is content to wait patiently.

Time ebbs away silently, and tenderly, the night descends.

At ten o'clock, the lights go off throughout the institute. Shen Yue is in bed. The tall headless monster with a mirror on its neck crawls out from under the bed, trailing its hands, which are now little more than bone, along the side of the bed, quietly watching her. Shen Yue closes her eyes, and in the clear and bright moonlight, serenely waits for sleep.

NOTES

THE INCREASING PRESSURES of the workplace are a universal experience. The climate of fear, and the pressure to overperform have been ramping up in both China and the West, until they have really begun to take their toll on the mental health of a generation.

Over the last few years, the inhumane working hours at many large corporations in China have become an unspoken norm, especially in technology, e-commerce and services. The expectation of 996 (nine to nine, six days a week) and 007 (midnight to midnight, seven days a week), has become so ingrained that workers are often bullied into meeting them by bosses and colleagues, with subtle suggestions that they are wasting a chair if they are not keeping up with the team. Articles were published by major newspapers, and campaigns begun over social media, deploring these tactics, and encouraging people not to tacitly accept them, quoting the maximum of 44 hours of work set by China's labour laws. Activists boycotted their hours, forcing major companies to put reforms in place, though it has not stopped entrepreneurs and business owners accusing their workers of tangping ("lying down"), or as we call it, quiet quitting.

The Waking Dream is a story of this environment taken to the extreme, and, as Fan Zhou has said, a voicing of her innermost fears, not just those of workplace exhaustion. The creatures in the story are drawn from her own nightmares, including those which had stayed in her thoughts since childhood. Again, the very nature of the Yuanjie is wrought with anxiety. Even though Fan Zhou loves science fiction, she holds reservations about uploading one's consciousness online, believing that whilst it would multiply all the possibilities that online living and working has produced, it would also exacerbate all the problems already rife in modern social media. "There, people could easily conceal their anxiety, worry and pain. These negative emotions won't just disappear, but flow on in the dark, like a silent current under the ice." The ability to tap into this stream, like Shen Yue and the Heart Readers, is not a superpower the author would ever wish for.

Fan Zhou is not unfamiliar with the idea of a virtual presence. She writes under a chosen pseudonym, and keeps her identity a secret behind avatars, which in a way, has its charm. She has more than hinted that the secrecy is necessary due to the nature of her day job and the sensitivity of the subject matter she delves into. I am grateful for Fan Zhou's brave contributions in the discourses of these contemporary issues and am delighted to include this very new voice in horror. The story was only published in Chinese in 2022.

IMMORTAL BEAUTY

红颜未老

Chu Xidao

WHAT DOES BLOOD taste like? When you have tasted it yourself, you will understand. Drops of strange, discarded gore trickling by the lips, so much like tears, with the same taste of the irreconcilable.

Blood is bitter, printed on robes, tables, walls, floors, the inexorable pain of parting mingled with fierce new jealousy, combining into dark, gory curses. Lord Liu, it was not until *I had drunk your blood dry that I truly understood the depth of my love for you. From now on, you will be with me always, never apart, never abandoning me. Do you want to flee? You cannot. There is no longer escape.*

Twenty-six years ago, when your mother pointed at my mother's swollen belly, she laughingly declared, "If it's a girl, then she will be my daughter-in-law." From that moment on, our lives were entangled.

Ten years ago, during that winter of goose feather snow, eight palanquins laden with the joy and wishes of two families and their forebears welcomed me through the gates of your home. Through the curtains of the bright red bridal litter, I watched the snow. Boundless, it seemed to cover heaven and earth. Its thickness blanketed my heart. Its brightness made me dizzy, and unexpectedly in this cold, sweat oozed from the palms of my hands. A crow sat upon a withered branch of a weeping willow by the river, glaring coldly at me. It was then I felt the foreboding, that there would be no return from this journey. But at the age of twenty-eight, my eyes could see only spring. Besides, this was an auspicious day, and what was there to be afraid of? The unease passed, like a gust of wind sweeping over the face, and I forgot it.

Exquisite moments are worth a thousand pieces of gold. Once you have seen the sea, no other waters compare.[3] Qimei jü'n. Xiangjing rubin[4]. We treated each other with decorous care and respect, like a model husband and wife. You have a great deal of talent, and I, of beauty. Why would we not be in love, even if it was just for a while? I still remember you dressing me with your very own hands, combing my hair into a spiralling, serpentine lingshe bun. *The flower that blushes to be plucked brims thick with nectar.*

Desires swelled as your brush ran over my brows, like passing mist, like sweeping clouds. Lips stained with the crimson of a million rich autumn reds. Then one day, you suddenly grew tired of my face, and during some moment of small talk, you looked out the window and were drawn by another's fresh spring sunshine.

So, another palanquin swayed joyfully through the mighty Liu threshold. Bolting the door of my chambers, and casting aside the revelry without, I slowly pulled out my bridal robes, which had been lining the bottom of the trunk. Stroking them, they still felt new, even though they

---

3 The first half of this sentence references the poem Spring Night (今宵一刻直千金), by Song Dynasty scholar and statesman Su Shi. The second half of the sentence (曾经沧海难为水) refers to one of the Five Poems of Yearning For the Departed by Tang Dynasty official and scholar Yuan Zhen, on missing his late wife.

4 Two idioms, both of which describe the deep Confucian respect a married couple should have for each other. The first, 齐眉举案 "serving dishes raised up to the brow", when serving each other food, raising the dish to the level of one's eyebrows as a sign of respect. The second 相敬如宾, "courteous as treating a guest".

were only ever required to last for that one day of dazzling, splendid beauty.

Staring into the mirror, unloved, I painted my own eyebrows.

Like the new moon, like a string of pearls, like the crest of mountains. The brush lightly swept towards the temples, gliding over fine black hairs like satin. *Pity that there is no audience for such a display.*

You look gaunt, I sighed, stroking my own face. Out of grace before old age, how could you regard the ravage of time with disdain?

What a shame, the young madam is barren.

By the window, the servants sighed, too, every word of their gossip piercing my ears, justifying his fickleness with reason.

Lady Qian, don't blame him. He is the eldest son.

Mother offered her earnest advice. Even though her temples were greying, wealth had taken good care of her, and she looked at peace; the skin on the hand holding her teacup was smooth and fine, nourished daily in goat's milk.

These are the best rouge and powders. Lady Qian, dress yourself finely, don't let him sow his wild oats.

It was too late, the prized beauty of youth no longer belonged to me.

Peerless beauty, that which could overturn cities and nations, was still no match for the murderous years that would kill youth in an instant.

I dragged my form around, worn thin by the multitude of sorrows and ailments, against the endless days and nights, in desolation.

Sometimes I saw an old crone with wild, white hair, her body crouched into a tiny lump, scuttling about like a rodent, salivating and latching onto passers-by to pester them for food. They say she was the last survivor of the many wives and concubines of Lord Liu's grandfather. I heard he was once a high-ranking official, and held great fame for a while, but no matter how hard I tried, I could not find a wisp of the charm, or a morsel of the beauty that the old crone must have held in her heyday.

Ten years passed like a moment.

You took seven wives, but not one produced an heir. It was not your fault, or so the priest had said, pasting fu charms wherever the eye could fall. There was an evil energy in the house. Mother had taken to chanting sutras, thinking this would release whatever was causing the blight, and help it to the next world.

When the lamps were lit, you would walk past my room, and always see me sitting alone, withering away in front of the mirror. Another fine line, like an enemy from the looking glass, mocking me from the corner of my downturned mouth. Silently, I followed your shadow as it moved further and further away. Night blurred my vision, but the shape of your back looked long and lonely, slightly hunching. Your head bent low, your brow must have been furrowed, traversing the long huíláng walkways, eventually swallowed up in the tangled vines and sinister mountain rockery.

The Young Master has been visiting Peony House every day. According to those who live to gossip.

The Young Master likes to hear Hongyan sing. According to those who love to embellish.

Her ladyship made the Young Master kneel at the eastern gate. According to those who laugh at suffering.

The Young Master is going to clear Hongyan's name. According to those who whisper directly into my ear.

I listened silently, tears washing my cheeks.

Qian, the Liu family must not permit an actress to enter its house. Absolutely not. Mother struck her hand on the table and rose furiously. A few days later, she fell gravely ill. She was old enough that reaching this stage of invalidity was natural. I took care of her, bringing tea and water, while the other mistresses hovered around and asked after her. The room was packed with fragrant beauties. You stood by, arms by your sides, the picture of filial attention, and yet Mother pressed on, demanding that you live by the vows you had sworn. So you fell silent.

Qian, be my eyes. You must not let her slip over the threshold of Liu. Or I will never spare you, even after my death.

Mother's hands finally loosened their grip. Your eyes, red from tears, glowered at me coldly, and then you were gone without a trace.

One night, after drinking, you burst into my room, embraced me, and wept in pain. I thought you had finally come back to me, but then you said that Hongyan was the love of your life, that you must marry her. For an instant, in your arms, I forgot myself, and, like a mother who could not help but indulge every whim of a beloved child, I said that in that case, you may as well.

Tired of the old and enamoured of the new, is this not the nature of all men? Head bent and brows drooping, I watched the candles weep wax as they crawled, exhausted, through the long dark night.

You shouldn't be a pining wife. Brother-in-Law's face flickered with an ambiguity in the candlelight.

Brother, you are drunk.

Suddenly his arms came together, locking me in a tight squeeze. I burned with a red-hot flush in the heat of his body. Long forgotten desires began to flow, and a shiver

79

of intoxication ran along my entire back, turning me limp and intricately smoothing out every little crease of ill-content. I was falling into a cloud, inch by inch, sinking further and further.

Brother, you must not.

But oh, the pleasure, as if all my bones were sliding away. A snake wandered wantonly through my body, and who could I blame for my wild and riotous sensations? My soul rushed for an outlet, and in an instant, it must have forgotten there was no way back.

He has his Hongyan; you, you can be mine.

Brother's smile, youthful and full of vitality, made me think of my Lord Liu when he was young. Greedily gazing, and in that moment, I fell into him.

Once fallen, I forgot the day. I watched you live out your amorous dreams with indifference. Every day, in front of the mirror, I still painted intricate huahuang flower patterns on my forehead. *But who do I do it for? Who will they please?*

Qianqian! What... what are you doing?

My Lord! I cried out in fright, pushing Brother's body violently away. Suddenly freezing, I gripped the corners of the embroidered bed covers, struggling to cover my embarrassed heart.

You dashed towards me, crimson threads criss-crossing your eyes, full of fiery rage. A slap stung over my cheek, forcing two streams of tears from me. I locked my gaze onto the headboard, its sculpted relief depicting the story of Consort Yang's tragic death on Mawei Hill, or was it Pan Jinlian's bloodbath before the altar[5]?

---

5 Women of notorious repute in Chinese history. The Tang emperor Xuanzong was so captured by Consort Yang's curvaceous beauty that he forced his son to give her up so he could take her for his own. He was also said to have neglected his duties for her. An Lushan, a young general under Yang's patronage, rebelled and forced Xuanzong's court to flee. Yang and her cousin, the prime minister, were executed on Mawei Hill. Pan Jinlian is the heroine of The Plum in the Golden Vase (jingping mei), a Ming Dynasty novel about

Silence. Waiting for the oncoming storm. Yet was there fury in your eyes? Was it jealousy? The thought induced a faint spark of joy.

Shhllloook.

Blood. Why is there blood?

I touched my lips, outraged to find them covered in crimson gore. I looked beyond you, and saw Brother like a ghost, light shimmering across the dagger in his hand. I was so shocked, I forgot to scream.

Your eyes were frozen, as if lost in contemplation. Turning your head, barely a sound could escape your throat, but muffled and vague, I heard, "Fifth Brother…"

The Young Brother chuckled coldly, replying with a kick, and the mountain crumbled to the ground in a heap.

I threw myself forwards and caressed your face, my heart aching at this shock and tragedy. But forever ruthless, you used the last ounce of strength to force my hand away.

And then you were gone. Eyes so wide open that they could not be closed.

Gazing at those enigmatic eyes and brow, I wondered who had been in your thoughts during your last moments. If it had been me, then your heart must have been filled with hatred, as was mine. But if it were not me?

I would rather you hated me than thought of another.

Numbly, I tidied your robes, knelt down, and lifted your head onto my lap. Regarding you, you were as handsome as when I first stepped through the doors of this house. With you here, in my arms, I found I had stopped hating you. This was ill fate; I must have owed you from my past life, or perhaps you owed me? *In our next lives, who will*

a serial adulteress that was famous for its contributions to the realist tradition and its explicit sexual content. Our story refers to Pan's ultimate fate of being sliced open in front of the memorial tablet of the husband she murdered, and having all her organs pulled out and placed on the altar as an offering.

pay for this love, and who will pay for these tears?

Lowering my head, I gently kissed your lips, and in that moment, smelled the scent of death. Tenderly, I bit open your neck. The blood was warm, like wine, burning my throat, burning my heart. My tears, mingling with the bitter blood, added an astringent note.

If I had only known...

Brimming with tears, I lifted my head. Brother was nowhere to be seen. Let him go. *He was merely a piece of flotsam, but you are my one and only. Even though I am not the one and only for you.*

I had only ever cared about your life. Was I destined to cause this, too?

When the *bukuài* burst into the room, I was still submerged in this scene of blood, lost in my own mind...

I had often thought that dying like this would be preferable.

DEATH IS BUT a moment of pain, better than a long life of endless suffering. But, as I stand on the execution ground, my long hair falling loosely about me, my heart begins to tremble, looking at the bound bodies around me, their faces ashen in death. Will I, too, share this fate?

The bare-chested executioner holds up his treasured blade, displaying it with great theatrics. The glare of the blade overwhelms my eyes, its blazing glint reflecting the last warmth in this world.

Who am I? Why am I here? For my whole life, I have been entrapped by love, and now, I am unwilling to resign myself to losing it.

The spectators, whispering their gossip and small talk, are indifferent to my fate. A faceless woman, fated to become an example to all. Looking through my mat of tangled hair, I see a swarming crowd, and cannot know what is in store for any of those fine round heads. We shall leave that to the hands of fate. Once, I was part of that audience, watching the show, but in the end, I have become a player.

What do you want to be after you die?

A butterfly. You?

Dew.

That's such a short life, why take the trouble?

The dew comes every night, I do not think that is a short life.

But once the splendid sun comes out, it melts away.

That is the most beautiful moment of its life.

Liu, my love, the thing that I remember just before my death is making wishes with you at the temple. I was only seven years old. Have you turned into a butterfly and already flown away?

If I had only known!

Suddenly, glimpsing a familiar face – no, two familiar faces – I cannot help but feel my blood boil and roil around my whole body.

Hongyan. Brother.

Her pretty face is suitably cold and frosty, but he is all smiles around his eyes and brow. Even as his gaze lands on me, it is all gratitude.

Arms lift, the blade falls!

My scream of terror is drowned in the cheering of the crowd.

Heart-rending pain cuts its unhealable wound through my neck; hot, stinging blood rushes out with urgency. Flowing, flowing, merging into streams and pooling around my head as my body lay twisted, trembling and twitching on the ground.

Liu, would your spirit come and drink my blood, too?

The ire—

With a dark flutter, a streak of dense *hunpo* rises, and flutters melancholically above my corpse, in time taking form, and becoming ligui, a vengeful ghost. I linger along the empty streets.

Passing through the many pavilions, I enter Brother's room. Under gold drapery hooks, and jade-sewn bed curtains, his broad arms are wrapped tightly around another kind of demon. Under her long hair, I see Hongyan's soul-enslaving smile. No wonder two men had both been stolen from me by this Yao.

Is this what you wanted? Brother twirled her smooth, soft, black locks around his long slender fingers.

I'm just worried you are still pining for Qianqian.

Hongyan arranges her crimson lips into a subtle pout, embodying the very word "charm".

How could she compare to you?

Brother's laughing mockery echoed against the walls, leaving strange, ringing sounds that grated in ghostly ears.

Roused, the ghost tried to rush, crash and lash out in frenzy, but the shadow just floated clumsily across the room without connection.

How can I let this go?

Your Dao is too weak!

From nowhere, another ghost appeared, smiling and drifting in

the air in front of me.

With cultivation like yours, trying to kill a human is a waste of time.

I shall have my vengeance! The thought feels as raw and incandescent as freshly shed blood, so dazzling it is blinding.

Your heart isn't nearly callous enough. Go, gather up all the grudges and envy of the world, all the selfishness and cruelty. When your malcontent distils into true malice, only then shall your *sanhun qipo*[6] have the power to harm the living.

I float away, my hatred rising.

I thought seeking vengeance would be arduous and my road of cultivation long, but after just a month, my claws are already beginning to sharpen, my tongue could snatch away souls, and my hair bind and choke. The world actually full of sharp tools I could use to kill.

Choosing an auspicious day, I revisit these familiar rooms.

Peals of laughter emanate from Brother's room.

Stroke, stroke, stroke. Every pass of the comb, brimming with conjugal bliss, eventually coiling the hair into a lotus style *furongji*. Darkly, I stand beside Brother, observing the love flowing through his fingers.

"Doesn't it look fine? Isn't it better than my big brother's?" Brother asked like a petulant child.

Hongyan seems to have not expected this question, and freezes. He never combed my hair.

I am about to attack, but pause in mid-air, until the malice and malevolence engulf me, and drive my invisible claws down, slicing through the chest of my enemy. Brother's smile becomes rigid with petrification, as he stares down at the gaping hole that seems to appear out of nowhere. Hongyan has no time to even scream, before her jade-white neck is constricted by my long hair.

---

6 Sanhun Qipo三魂七魄 – in Daoist philosophy, there are ten parts to the human soul, which are split into Yin, Yang, heavenly and earthly. Sanhun, the three hun that govern the spiritual and higher mental faculties, tianhun (heavenly hun), dihun (earthly hun), and minghun (life hun); and qipo, the seven po that govern the physical faculties, and correspond to the seven mailun (chakras) around the body. The tianhun and dihun are believed to often exist outside the body, which is inhabited by the minghun that governs the qipo.

Those that deserve death, have received death. For a moment, emptiness fills my eyes. With indifference, I watch two little souls slowly rising in front of me, too pathetic and weak to withstand even the casual strike with which I send them again out of this world, still bearing their grudges.

I am just about to cast away these stinking mortal remains, but such a beautiful countenance would be a shame to waste.

I peel Hongyan's skin from her body smoothly, without rips or snags. Luminous and translucent under the candlelight, it lures me in with the desire to slide into it. I cannot resist. I wipe the blood away, paint the eyebrows with umber, and smudge the cheeks with rouge. A remarkable resemblance to a beautiful living face.

Holding the skin up and turning it, I admire it again. Fights were fought, heads cracked open and blood shed, all because of you. I left the world in obscurity, all because of you.

Yet, even with city-enslaving looks, you were not allowed to live long, and nor did I let those who loved you grow old.

Dimples blossom like flowers... but ultimately, *huoshui hongyan:* "beauty brings calamity."

Holding this painted human skin in my hands, I begin to weep...

HIS BREATH IS like gossamer as the Yang energy leaves this man. Fleeting like so many transient memories. If the men of this world are so keen to pursue affection, you cannot blame me for being so merciless.

I don't even remember his name. Zhang? Wang? Li? Too many deceptions.

The soul emerges from its shell, and it is time to paint

the skin again. The human body is fated to wear out. Even one imbued with a thousand sweet charms will fall to the blustering blade and frosty sword of time.

One stroke, another stroke, it is so easy to ensnare them. If fate can all be written out by this one brush, I will see it through to the end.

Time has passed, and I have fallen in love with beauty, even though I had once regarded it with enmity. I understand that, one day, I will have to move to the next world, or reincarnate, or perhaps my hunpo will just dissipate. Should I forget my malice, and no longer remain a vengeful ghost?

May beauty never grow old;
May it be as bright as the peony blooms.
I wait, day in day out;
Yet alone, I paint my brow.
Beauty, don't you dare grow old;
Stay bright as the peony that blooms.
Though one day heaven and earth may fold,
My future will still hold,
For my heart shall never grow old.

Later generations sing this song. Those tens of thousands of women painting their skin in the mirror, waiting for love. Do I not possess them all?

NOTES

IN THE TRADITIONAL ghost stories I grew up with, there is a veritable army of female ghosts and yao, usually taking the form of ethereal femmes fatales that lure unsuspecting scholars in ruined temples to their demise, usually told from a viewpoint that marks out these supernatural beings as malevolent forces, supposedly transcribed by the (inevitably male) author. The most famous of these stories is Painted Skin, the tale of a fox demon who devours mortals, peels off their skin, wears it to live among humans, refreshing it with paint every night.

Immortal Beauty subverts this whole tradition, telling of a woman's tragic life in ancient China. To contemporary eyes, Lady Qian might seem weak, pining and unenlightened in her pursuits and desires, but as an ordinary lady living in a wealthy household during the dynastic times, with values moulded by social disciplining, the story reveals how so many women's lives would have been buried under the harsh societal and familial restrictions imposed on them by the patriarchy. If they were even considered to stray from the rigid morals they were supposed to guard, no matter if it was by choice, deceit or force, they would eventually, in one way or another, end up as the wronged ghosts of those tales.

This story came about because of a Cantopop song, Sandy Lam's "Beauty Never Grows Old", which I remember hearing from a lot of radio stations in China during the early 1990s. The author, Chu Xidao, made a connection in her head between this song and the legend of Painted Skin, in Pu Songling's Strange Tales from a Chinese Studio (Liaozhai Zhiyi). This was a story that frightened her most as a child, so she decided to turn this inner fear into a beautiful piece of fiction.

Chu Xidao has been an unrepentant spinner of fiction since primary school, writing for her own enjoyment and friend groups until she found the opportunity to publish her Wuxia and Qihuan fantasy works online during university, and now writes successful fantasy universes, screenplays and multimedia tie-ins. Writing women that kill seems to have become a speciality for Chu Xidao, ever since her early short pieces on female assassins. After seeing the list of contributors, she told me she was delighted to be curated into the same book as a few of her old friends and fellow web novelists, with some of whom it is the first time she has shared the printed page. It goes to show how nourishing and positive a community can be, even when its main preoccupation is blood, death, and the supernatural.

THOSE WHO WALK AT NIGHT, WALK WITH GHOSTS

但走夜话，见见鬼

She Cong Ge

PROLOGUE 1

HAVE YOU EVER taken a walk at night...

In the depths of the night, out on the mountain ridges covered with dense forest. You are alone, and all around you, the night sky is painted black. The surrounding farmlands, waterways and trees, all shrouded in boundless darkness. All you can do is feel your way forward, relying solely on the feeble light of the torch in your hand.

You cannot see what lies in wait, even a few feet ahead of you, you can only imagine, and feel, with every single nerve in your body... for no reason, your pulse quickens, the hairs begin to stiffen. You cannot help but look back, but there is nothing there, except the dark...

Just when you have barely calmed your nerves, you hear an eerie cry, not too far from you. You jump, and your heart leaps further, trying to escape your chest. You desperately try to soothe your frightened spirits.

But you frantically understand that it is Them...

Exactly what They are.

And that They are here.

PROLOGUE 2

PEOPLE HAVE HUNPO[7], which is invisible to them during the day. If walking at night, the hunpo would walk ahead of the flesh by three steps, so that it may detect any Yin, or evil energy lurking. So, when roaming at night, it is advisable not to outpace it. If you overtake your own hunpo, there is a danger that you may run into some strange phenomenon. Do not panic, or else your hunpo will scatter, and then nothing can save you.

When walking during choushi, the Hour of the Rooster, you must be alert. Be aware of any jumping of your eyebrows, any twitching of your eyelids, or a ringing in your ears. These are all signs of evil spirits circling you. You can bite your finger open and ward them off with the fresh blood. If you can stomach it, light a cigarette. Or carry an iron implement, like keys, or old coins.

Do not recite incantations, or chant sutras whilst walking at night out in the wild. Do not do this! Unless you happen to be a monk or priest of the most accomplished Dao and highest cultivation.

Do not ask after the name of any unknown person or thing, and do not share your own true name. Unless you are a *shushi*[8] of extraordinary skill.

Do not run.

Do not step on the gas. It is always better to clearly see the path ahead than rush blindly.

Even then, if you adhere to all these rules, what is meant to find you will come to you, and will never let go...

* * *

---

7 For Daoist ideas of the soul, see the footnotes in Immortal Beauty.

8 术士, folk practitioners of fortune-telling, astrology and exorcism who were particularly popular in the early dynasties.

XINGSHAN COUNTY, HUBEI Province. A remote county in the lofty Zhongshan mountains to the west of the province, located in the same administrative region as Shennong's Ladder. The epic Han poem of Hei'An Zhuan, The Legend of Darkness, came from this region, and was chanced upon, by some cultural worker, during a local funeral.

I had a university friend from Xingshan, named Li Yi. After graduation, he worked at a certain village hospital in Xingshan as a clinician, whilst I, on the other hand, had been unemployed for some time, and hung around at home with too much time on my hands.

Li Yi came into town on some business and, knowing that I was having no luck finding work, he invited me back to Xingshan with him, for a change of scenery in the mountains. I eagerly accepted his kind offer. That same afternoon, we took the bus to Xingshan, towards the endless, unbroken chain of mountains. I fell asleep on the way and was woken up by the rocking of the bus as it swerved around the poor road wildly. Looking out of the window, it was already dark, and checking the time, I saw it was past midnight. The bus was still rapidly descending from the peaks down the winding mountain road.

On the silent and empty road between the mountains, the headlights flashed over a single figure walking slowly along the thin verge.

I shot a question out at Li Yi, who was sitting next to me, "Why is that man out walking this late, on such a deserted road?"

Li Yi seemed to find my question odd. "Living in the mountains, walking at night is pretty common."

"Don't you get frightened?" I asked.

Li Yi seemed surprised – clearly, it had never occurred to him.

It was the early hours of the morning when we finally arrived at the remote village where Li Yi worked. As soon as we got off the bus, we slouched into his hostel, and fell asleep. It was night again before we woke up. Sitting up in bed, looking out of the wooden window frames into the dark, I could vaguely make out those chains of endless mountains. At first, it felt quite poetic, but the more I looked, the more I began to feel an inexplicable sense of dread.

Li Yi had a few friends in that hospital accommodation and invited them over. Together, we sat drinking and eating larou ham hotpot. Outside the window, the mountain wind blew strongly with a rattling 'gegege', and on it was carried a strange scream. Hearing it terrified me, but I was too embarrassed to let it show.

Towards the end of the drinking session, one of the friends said he had some matters to take care of at home and needed to leave early. As he walked out and off into the night, I could not help but worry on his behalf, so I asked, was he not scared of bumping into something dangerous at this time of the night?

Li Yi's other friend turned to me. "Since you're so interested, let me tell you one of our local legends. I can't say for sure that it's true or not true. It's just a story."

I nodded enthusiastically, showing my interest.

There was a guy, who went to visit his relatives dozens of li away from home. After dinner, he remembered that his sow was expected to have her babies that night and insisted on going back. According to the rules of the mountains, any visiting guests would be offered overnight accommodation, so he did not have to leave until the next day. His relatives tried to convince him not to go, there was no need to walk back so late at night. The mountain paths were rough, and it was easy to have an accident. Besides, he didn't know for sure the pig would give birth that night, but the guy was worried about his sow being in labour and stuck to his decision. No matter how much his relatives tried to keep him back, he steeled himself to go. Unable to deter him, they gave him a burning torch, to light his way home.

The guy had a drink before he left, to get up enough courage to step out of the door. It wasn't until midnight, when the wine was wearing off, that he began to feel afraid. It was the wild mountains after all, with an untended burial pit and no living households for miles. Apart from mountains, there were only other mountains.

As he walked on, he got more and more scared. If he had known, he would have listened to the persuasions of his relatives, and at least agreed for someone to walk home with him. A companion would prevent him from winding himself up, like he was doing now, walking alone in the lonely wild mountains.

The mountain paths undulated, up, down, and up again. The distance wasn't actually that great, but a lot of the route was stretched out by the rise and fall of the mountains. It was during this moment that he saw, on a peak across the valley, another burning torch. He felt very glad that, like him, someone else was journeying at night. He yelled towards the flames, "Hey, friend! Are you walking alone?"

"Yes, someone died at home, and I need to go back to take care of the burial," the person across the valley shouted back.

What the guy wanted more than anything right then, was company on his walk, so he yelled back immediately, "Can you wait there? I'll come over and we can walk together."

"Great!" came the voice from the opposite mountaintop:

"I'll wait for you here."

Even though the two people could hear each other, it would take at least an hour to walk over. The guy saw that the flame had stopped moving, and was waiting for him, so he flew down the mountain, all the way to the foot, before rushing up again with flying steps, eager to find the stranger who was waiting for him.

When he got near the flame, he froze.

You see, once he saw the flame up close, he could see it wasn't from a torch like his. It was the light of a changming lamp, specifically placed next to unburied coffins at night, before they are lowered into the ground.

There was an open grave next to the coffin. It must have been a long funeral, and the family had decided to leave the coffin by the pit to continue the burial rites the next day.

The guy was paralysed with fear. The voice that had spoken to him just then, must have come from inside this coffin...

What happened next, he couldn't remember. He was carried home the next day by his family who had come out to look for him. He had just enough sense left to tell his story – and the moment he finished, he died.

The story seeped into my bones. I pretended to look out the window, but was, in fact, a little too troubled to really do so, and was secretly thankful I did not have to walk out at night in these monstrous mountains, which seemed to be flexing their jaws with impunity. I simply did not think I would have the guts to do it.

But I was wrong. A few days later, I really did have to take a nocturnal walk deep in those mysterious mountains, and compared to what I experienced, this tale of Li Yi's friend would seem like a gentle midday stroll.

* * *

I SPENT A few happy days in this mountain village, set back from the provincial thoroughfares, drinking, sightseeing, and generally having a good time.

One day at noon, I was out with Li Yi, when a middle-aged woman saw him, and greeted us warmly. "Li Yi, will you come to Meiyou Plain soon? In the last few days, they... they came again. Not even Xianghua can control them."

"Auntie Zhu, it's not evil spirits, it's hysteria, it's a condition. Don't listen to Xianghua and his superstitions, I've told you before. Didn't someone bring you some medication?"

"We took it, we all took it." Auntie Zhu touched her hair and blinked. "But no one's got any better. They have been at it again, all the time."

"Oh, how's Uncle Tian? Any improvement?" Li Yi changed the subject – he seemed to know everyone in the village.

"Same old." Auntie Zhu's voice grew a little softer. "I don't know if he can get better." She turned and went on her way, her back bending under the weight of her beilou basket.

DURING DRINKS THAT night, Li Yi told me, "Fengfeng, tomorrow we're going into the mountains."

I asked, "To the Meiyou Plain where that auntie asked you to visit this afternoon?"

"Yes."

When Li Yi said "the mountains", he meant the really big, old mountains, and the primaeval forest which surrounded Meiyou Ping, "The Plain of Enchanted Plums". He told me that the hospital he worked at regularly sent doctors to cover the villages in the forests deep in the mountains, bringing common medicines along with them, so that the villagers would at least not go short of basic healthcare. Most of those villages were separated from the outside by endlessly deep mountain ranges, and some communities had gone into such decline that only two or three dozen households were left, and they hardly made it out of the mountains more often than once every few years.

Li Yi's suggestion excited me, but I asked him, hesitantly, if we would have to walk back at night.

Li Yi laughed and told me no, we would not, because it was such a remote place – it would definitely be an overnight trip.

THE NEXT DAY, as dawn broke, Li Yi and I took a rickety minibus at the mouth of the gorge, heading up into the huge, boundless mountains.

The roads were inaccessible from the outside, full of cracks and potholes, and the ride was extremely bumpy. Most of the time we were snaking through forests and arrived at Meiyou Plain just before noon. The plain was situated in a basin, surrounded on most sides by high cliffs, but thankfully reachable by an access road. The hundred or so huts that made up the village were scattered across the mountain slopes, most of them built from yellow mud bricks, and had roofs thatched with sogon grass.

As Li Yi and I entered the village, I noticed that whenever a villager saw him, they walked around him, or regarded him with contempt in their eyes. We came to a very old house, the style of which looked at least a century old. In front of the house was a courtyard, whose walls, I could just make out, bore slogans from the 1960s and '70s, mottled with age. On a cable pole in the courtyard, there were two old-fashioned loudspeakers.

Entering the courtyard with Li Yi, I was dumbstruck, and remembered his conversation with Auntie Zhu.

There was a group of people in the yard, all women, between one or two dozen, old and young. Most of them had their eyes closed, but the ones that had them open wore a glazed, unfocused look that lacked consciousness. Half of them had thick steel needles piercing their cheeks, the ends of which protruded far from their heads. The sight horrified me, and I had no idea what was going on.

Their bodies were shaking, their arms swinging, whether they were sitting or standing. After a while, those who were standing began to spin round and round on the spot, then those that were sitting began rolling around on the ground.

A young man, about our age, was holding a very thick steel needle, about a foot long. He walked up to one of the women and began babbling in an unintelligible language.

"Xianghua!" Li Yi shouted. "What the fuck are you up to now?"

The young man turned towards us and froze in surprise, though he seemed to know Li Yi. His pause lasted only a moment, before he plunged the needle into the face of the woman in front of him, in through the right cheek and out through the left.

The woman's expression drooped, and she acted as though she were unable to feel the pain at all. What stunned me even more, though, was that no blood came from the wound, not one drop.

The woman wandered back into the group, the giant needle firmly lodged through her mouth. Li Yi shouted,

"Xianghua, why are you doing these things, you good-for-nothing pillock?"

Xianghua did not reply, but the group of women turned their heads as one and looked towards Li Yi and me.

Looking at their needle-pierced faces, I felt my insides prickle.

One of the women, who did not have a needle through her face, yelled, "It's here, it's here again…" She fell to the ground and began rolling around, scratching at the dirt with her hands. Xianghua picked up a broken bowl, drank a mouthful of the liquid it contained – I don't know if it was wine or something else – and sprayed it out over the possessed woman.

The woman quietened down immediately.

Li Yi darted towards Xianghua, grabbing him by the lapels. "You promised you wouldn't do this sort of thing again."

Not in the least affected by Li Yi's interrogation, Xianghua pointed a hand towards the crowd. "Then what should I do? You tell me what I should do!"

Li Yi yelled at Xianghua, "Where's the medicine I gave you? Did you administer it to them? Why don't you listen to me?"

Xianghua refuted him. "How much did you give me? How could I have split it between all of them?"

Those 'possessed' women knelt on the floor and began to sob. "It's here, it's here again…"

These sights and sounds made my hairs bristle and my bones shudder.

Xianghua ran into the house, and shortly, his voice came through the loudspeakers: "Take your guests and women home now, there's nothing more I can do today. Come and take your people away."

In a few moments, many villagers hastened into the courtyard, all men. They began leading their family members away, and after a few moments more, the crowd had dispersed.

I stood and watched, in utter disbelief.

We went inside what seemed to be Xianghua's home, and all sat down together.

"How long have they been sick? Why didn't you inform our hospital?" Li Yi shot Xianghua a quick-fire succession of questions.

Xianghua replied, "All the vi- vi- villagers think this is possession. They believe that Scarface d- d- Dou has come back to make trouble." Xianghua had a stutter and bad diction.

"That's horse shit! What possession? Scarface Dou died decades ago. Besides, groups of women are apparently very susceptible to mass hysteria," Li Yi said. "You've been to med school for a few years, haven't you?"

"So what if I went to med school? I'm a shengun now, like my dad, just a witch doctor."

"Come back with me tomorrow, and you can bring back the medication that will actually help them," Li Yi urged. "The hospital just received a supply of Seroquel, so bring that back here."

Xianghua sighed. "Fine, you're the doctor, what you say goes." And then he busied himself cooking for us.

I looked around the house, which epitomised the meaning of jiatu sibi – nothing but the four walls, apart from a few broken chairs and a baxian table[9]. The other room was in darkness, and I couldn't tell if it was occupied.

---

9 Baxian table 八仙桌, traditional Chinese square wooden table, that comes with wooden benches that could hold two people on each side, hence the name "Table of the Eight Immortals".

Before we began to eat, Xianghua went into that darkened side room, and came out carrying an old woman, whom he placed by the baxian table. This paralysed figure was introduced to us as Xianghua's mother. We began to eat. When I was reaching over to a dish with my chopsticks, I happened to glance up at her, and found her staring venomously at Li Yi, with hatred in her eyes. Shocked, I quickly lowered my gaze, and continued to eat.

We ate dinner very early, and the sky was still light.

Li Yi said to Xianghua, "Can you take me over to Tian Jiarun's? I heard that her dad has been very sick."

Xianghua looked at Li Yi, startled from some unknown thought. He cleared up the dishes and carried his mother back into the side room. I heard her cursing in a soft, low voice.

After settling her, Xianghua came out, and led us to the other side of the village, to a house of yellow earth.

"Doctor Li, you're here at last." Turning towards the voice, I recognised Auntie Zhu from her visit into town.

Li Yi said, "Yes, I heard you say that Uncle's condition has got worse, so I've come to take a look."

"Jiarun," Auntie Zhu called, "Li Yi's here."

There was no answer, and Auntie Zhu turned to Li Yi to say, "She must have gone to find feed for the pigs."

Li Yi said nothing, but headed inside.

I saw the patient. A man of well over fifty, propped up against the headboard of the bed, in so much pain that his body was doubled over, and he was groaning softly for his mother and father. Seeing Li Yi, he wanted to greet him, but could not say anything, his face growing even paler as sweat drops trickled down from it.

"It's been getting worse over the past two days," Auntie whispered to Li Yi. "He wasn't in anything like this much pain yesterday."

Li Yi asked, "Have you finished the painkillers and antibiotics?"

Xianghua said, "Those ran out ages ago."

Li Yi asked no more questions, but took out the painkillers he was carrying and shook some out for the man to take. Then, carefully, he pressed the patient's abdomen, and examined his face and tongue.

"Uncle, you must come with me right now to the town hospital – you need an operation."

"What?" Auntie Zhu, who had been standing nearby, said in shock. "Is it so serious? Where do we get the money for an operation?"

"Uncle's gallbladder is already very serious. I said last time, the longer we put it off, the more trouble this condition can bring. The only thing we can do now is to cut him open and remove it."

This sent Auntie Zhu into a panic. "What to do? What to do?"

Seeing the wretched state the man was in, I felt incredibly sorry for him.

Li Yi turned towards Xianghua. "Go and get the driver of the minibus and tell him he needs to take us away tonight."

Xianghua obliged and ducked out immediately.

A pretty young woman entered, and taking in the scene, began asking repeatedly, "Dad, is it hurting again?" until she saw Li Yi. She seemed surprised, and mumbled, "Oh, you're here."

Li Yi's voice sounded heavy and stuffy. "The inflammation around Uncle's gallbladder has reached a dangerous point. He needs an operation."

The man seemed to back up Li Yi's words, unable to stifle his loud moaning. First, high-pitched, then low.

Auntie Zhu said pressingly, "Then it can't wait – take da'ge[10] to the hospital quickly, while I get your second uncle to come and help."

And out she rushed.

I could not take my eyes off the beautiful woman. So, this was the Tian Jiarun that Li Yi had spoken of. They seemed to know each other very well indeed.

Everyone scrambled around in chaos, trying to get ready to take Tian Jiarun's father out of the mountains. After a while, Xianghua returned, with a pained expression. "The driver says he can't leave."

"Why not?" Auntie Zhu barked at Xianghua.

"You know why, there's rules here! Don't you remember what date it is today?"

"What year is it?" Li Yi shouted frustratedly. "And you still believe in these ghostly tricks! Take me to the driver."

With that, Li Yi grabbed Xianghua and dragged him away to find the driver. I was about to follow, but Li Yi stopped me. "Fengfeng, stay and help wrap things up here."

I did not know Tian Jiarun and felt awkward being there with her.

She asked me, while packing, "Are you Li Yi's colleague?"

"No, no." I felt inexplicably nervous. "I was his classmate at university. We shared a dorm for three years."

"Oh, I see, that's why I haven't met you before." Tian Jiarun smiled at me, two deep dimples showing on her face.

The scene I had witnessed earlier, of Xianghua skewering the cheeks of the village women, floated into my head, and instantly those dimples looked somewhat sinister.

I asked her, "Why doesn't anyone in the village like Li Yi?"

---

10 Da'ge 大哥 – term for referring to "oldest brother" or "eldest brother". In this case, it means the latter.

Tian Jiarun laughed wryly. "He doesn't believe that Scarface Dou's soul comes back here. The villagers are not educated people, and felt that his words offended Scarface, and brought the evil possessions down on their womenfolk."

"What about you?" I asked. "Who do you believe?"

"I believe Li Yi, of course." She blushed.

"What kind of monster is this Scarface?" Tian Jiarun frowned at me harshly, as if to indicate I had said something inappropriate.

Li Yi and Xianghua had returned with the minibus driver in tow. Li Yi was still chastising him, even though he already looked utterly defeated, apologising profusely, and saying a lot of ingratiating words. It was good being a doctor – no one dared to get on the wrong side of you.

As soon as Li Yi came back in, he had us roll Uncle Tian onto a bed board. The four of us lifted it and began to move it out. Meanwhile, Auntie Zhu was dragging a man over by his ears, scolding him as she went. "Why don't you swill some more down? All you do is drink that horse piss! Da'ge is so ill he's dying, and you're still out drinking!"

This man must have been Tian Jiarun's second uncle, who was so drunk he could not tell his Peking opera from his Cantonese. He could not even walk straight. As soon as they entered, he collapsed into a chair.

"Tian Changnian! Wake up this instant!" Auntie Zhu roared at Tian Jiarun's second uncle. "Go and help get your big brother to the hospital, NOW!"

This seemed to wake Tian Changnian up a little, at least enough for his mouth to work. "Can't go anywhere today. How can we go anywhere today, Scar—"

Auntie Zhu slapped her hand across his mouth. "Shut up!"

The roads in the village were barely paths, so the minibus had to park up at the entrance. Carrying Uncle Tian, we hurried towards it, but before we'd even got to the van, we had to stop.

There was someone lying across the road: Xianghua's paralysed mother. No one knew how she had crawled out of the house, but Xianghua and Li Yi went to her. Still holding the makeshift stretcher, I watched them argue from a distance while we waited.

Xianghua's mother croaked, "No one can go anywhere today. Xianghua, what are you playing at?"

"Uncle Tian is going to die if we don't get him to hospital. We need to go," Xianghua said to his mother.

"No, nobody leaves today," the old lady wailed. "It's not like you don't all know that the mountain road won't take you anywhere… tonight."

"I don't care, I am a doctor, I'm here to save people." Li Yi pointed at Uncle Tian.

"Not tonight! There is too much evil out there. Listen to me, I'm not trying to harm you," Xianghua's mother urged. "Tonight is the night of Scarface Dou's huanhun, the roads are too fierce. If you really must go, please, just don't drag my son along with you!"

As that plea left the mother's mouth, a great clap of thunder rang out, sounding like an explosion just above our heads. Everybody ducked. Including Li Yi.

Everyone, except Li Yi and Tian Jiarun, shuffled hesitantly. Even I began to believe that the old woman's warnings were more than just the wind blowing around an empty cave. The heavens opened and rain began to pour down around us. Li Yi said to Xianghua resolutely, "I simply do not believe in this evil. Xianghua, if you don't want to go, go home."

"If you don't listen to me, you will all die in the mountains... that year, Hua's dad insisted on going out on this day, and we still haven't found his corpse! Have you all forgotten about this?" Xianghua's mother began to sob anxious tears.

My innards were already knotted by fear. It seemed the old woman was not lying after all.

However, a life was on the line, and Li Yi was not going to give up on taking Uncle Tian away, just because of a few words. Auntie Zhu helped Xianghua's mother off the road while the rest of us piled into the rickety bus. Li Yi urged the driver to hurry.

The driver was hesitant again, but could not withstand the repeated pressure Li Yi was exerting, so he got into the driving seat and started the engine.

"Hua, get out of there now!" his mother bawled at him. "If they want to head towards their deaths, you don't have to follow... get out."

Xianghua, who was sitting restlessly in the van, looked like he wanted to leap out, but casting a glance at Li Yi and Tian Jiarun, he called out of the window, "Mum, it's going to be fine."

Li Yi screamed to the driver, "Let's go, what are you waiting for?"

The driver stepped on the gas, driving down the gravel road leading out of the mountains.

Rain fell as if it were ladled from the skies.

Through the windows, Xianghua heard his mother's howling and weeping, distinct and clear even in the downpour.

The driver could just about put a cigarette to his mouth, but his hand was trembling so much that he could not light it, so I went over and lit it for him.

He nodded his thanks towards me and said, between gulps

of smoke, "Tonight is a really bad time to travel."

I did not know if he was talking to me, or himself.

The minibus drove on towards the mountains. Behind us, I saw the road disappearing into the sinister craggy rocks, and turning to look at the road ahead, saw it cloaked in a cage of torrential rain, which completely blurred the landscape.

I thought about Xianghua's mother and her dire words, before glancing at the nervous driver, his hands shaking on the wheel. I could not help but feel anxious. I looked towards Xianghua, who was trembling even more violently. Li Yi kept checking on Uncle Tian. Only Tian Changnian was relaxed. Having slid down his seat, he was now lying on the floor of the van, leaning against Uncle Tian's bed board and making indistinct whining noises.

It was already dusk, and dark clouds pressed heavily in from the skies, forcing it to darken early.

The car took a couple of sharp corners, following the course of the mountains, speeding towards the valley floor. The raindrops striking the car sounded like firecrackers.

"This rain is just too much, isn't it?" Xianghua said, a rictus grin plastered across his face.

We were all on alert, listening carefully for any noise, watching for any movement.

"Stop the bus!" Li Yi yelled.

The driver slammed the brakes on. *PONK*, something fell heavily onto the roof, leaving a deep indent, followed by a *PIKIPAKA* and *PONK, THUNK* as something showered over the roof.

Rocks were falling from the mountain. Stones of different sizes, previously balanced precariously on the mountaintops, had been loosened by the gale, and swept down by the torrential rain, came tumbling into the valley one after another. I looked out through the side window, and saw a rockslide, moving down the steep mountain cliffs to either side of us.

I was stupefied.

A great deafening roar came from the road ahead, the sound of giant rocks crumbling. We were all shaken by the violence of this phenomenon, and even Tian Changnian, who had been in a state of inebriation mere moments before, was now awake, his face ashen. We all looked at each other, staring into each other's faces for answers. Xianghua pointed a torch through the windshield.

There was a landslide about twenty metres ahead.

Not only was there a wall of mud and rocks, but a figure, lying stiffly across the road, in front of the bus, face down in the mud.

We fell silent, staring at the figure.

The rain died away suddenly, though flashes of light still penetrated the dark clouds. In those brief lightning strikes, we saw that the head of the figure on the ground had been split open, and bright red gore flowed from it onto the churning ground, along with the rainwater. He must have been killed by the falling rocks.

"He's dead," Li Yi said softly, then, glancing at the driver, added, "There's no way forward. Let's head back."

The driver seemed to be relieved of a great burden, like a condemned man who had just received a pardon. Nodding profusely, he got back into his seat, and turned the bus around.

Li Yi spoke again. "We should collect the body before we go."

The driver and Xianghua picked up the corpse, managing to fit it onto the floor of the bus.

Tian Jiarun said nothing, and just watched her father,

who had stopped groaning and whose spirits seemed greatly improved after leaving the village.

We drove on for a quarter hour or so, before coming to a break in the mountain wall, where Li Yi again called to stop. "We'll get off here."

Xianghua said, "Didn't you say we were going back?"

"We're going to walk out of the mountains," Li Yi said. "Uncle Tian must get to the hospital."

Xianghua looked at Tian Jiarun for a long moment, before helping Li Yi move Uncle Tian out of the van. I was amused to realise that Xianghua had come out with us, not because of Li Yi, but Jiarun. He loved her.

"We're taking the small road out via Horse Hoof Hollow," Li Yi said.

Xianghua's face turned a chalky white. "Horse Hoof Hollow, as in where Scarface Dou and his gang were executed?"

Li Yi rebuffed him. "It's not like we've never taken that road before."

"But last time wasn't the day of his huanhun."

Li Yi was determined. "Don't pull that crap with me again. Do you want to watch Uncle Tian die?"

Saving the patient came first, and nothing much else was said, everyone following Li Yi's arrangements. I saw Tian Jiarun and Li Yi stealthily exchange a look, and then very quickly avoid each other's gaze. My mind could not help but fill in all sorts of blanks. What did Li Yi have to do with this woman? He had a girlfriend back in the village, who was also very pretty, and worked at the electricity plant, so had very good prospects.

I looked at Xianghua. Even with his body in tremors, he had still agreed to Li Yi's request. The three of them would have been classmates at middle school. They must have both fallen for Tian Jiarun, but for some reason, she had apparently chosen someone else. And then another thought hit me. Li Yi had told me she was married, but why wasn't Tian Jiarun's husband around?

Tian Changnian seemed to have sobered up a little, and said to Uncle Tian, "Da'ge, let me carry you." Wobbling slightly from side to side, he picked up his big brother and seated him across his back.

We walked in a single line towards the small road in the hollow.

The driver did not seem happy with this. "Hey, you can't just leave me here! There's a dead body on the bus."

"He's dead, so what are you scared of? Hurry back to Meiyou Plain," Li Yi said.

The driver thought about it for a moment, plucked up his courage, and started the engine.

"I almost forgot." He pulled out a few emergency torches and tossed them out to us. "You be careful. That road isn't easy to walk at night. If you're going through Horse Hoof Hollow, that means you're going around in a big circle. It'll take you at least six or seven hours to get to town." And with that, he drove off.

We formed a single file, Li Yi at the front with one torch, and Xianghua at the rear with another. I carried the other torches, while Tian Changnian carried his brother, with Tian Jiarun next to him assisting.

Li Yi called out to me from the front as we walked, "Fengfeng, I'm sorry. I never meant for you to come out on a night walk with me."

I reassured him, "Don't worry about it," but then I saw the mountain peak. If we were climbing this mountain during the day, I would have been more than happy to. But now...

I turned to Xianghua, who was directly behind me, and

asked softly, "This Scarface you've all been talking about… what's his deal?" This was the question I had been bursting to ask for hours.

"Scar- Scarface Dou was a bandit leader in Xingshan and Shennong's Ladder before the Liberation. Sixty years ago, he and his gang fell into a trap in Horse Hoof Hollow. They were arrested, and the whole gang were immediately put to death. There were over a hundred of them and blood flowed like a river."

The image made me shudder. "So, if he died in this hollow, why are the people in your village scared to come out?"

"Scarface Dou was from Meiyou Plain. I heard from my dad, he- he…"

Xianghua's stammer grew stronger until he was unable to speak but still, I could not wait to hear the rest of the tale.

"Xianghua!" Li Yi bellowed from the front. "What hokum are you trying to scare him with now?"

Xianghua could not finish his sentence. "He- he- he…" but he faded away.

At least I now knew this much. We were going to be walking across Horse Hoof Hollow, in the middle of the night, on the night this place was haunted. My scalp began tingling, and the hairs rose on the back of my neck.

At last, we arrived at the mountain's peak. We followed the ridge, finding that it was now a lot brighter in front of me, and that even without the torch, I could see the stones and scrub from several metres away. I looked into the sky and saw the moon had found its way out from behind the dark clouds, and not only was it bright, but it had gained a fuzzy halo. My field of vision opened up and I saw, ahead of us, a mountainous structure. Round mounds on either side joined in the middle to make a "U" shape. No introduction was necessary, I knew that this was Horse Hoof Hollow.

Xianghua had also looked up at the moon, and started chanting, almost on autopilot: "Yueliang changmao, huoren nantao." A hairy moon means certain doom.

Li Yi harrumphed.

Xianghua added, "Last time we took a night walk together, it was the day that Jia- Jiarun got married."

Li Yi spun round, and Xianghua clapped his hand over his mouth.

I had guessed that Li Yi and Xianghua had walked through this hollow on some other night and must have run into something so terrifying that Xianghua could not help but stammer whenever it was mentioned.

I FOUND IT harder and harder to walk, and without really noticing, had fallen behind, becoming the last in line. I hated it. I had heard somewhere that when walking at night, never be the last one. If the person in front of you doesn't turn to check in on you regularly, no one would even know if you disappeared. The more I thought about it like that, the more I began to feel that, in the deep darkness behind me, something was hiding, stalking me.

My body was bristling all over, but I dared not look back. I fixed my eyes on Xianghua in front of me. He had walked across Horse Hoof Hollow with Li Yi, like we were doing tonight, but why was he so terrified, and Li Yi so indifferent?

I whispered my thoughts to Xianghua.

He paused for a moment, as if to calm himself, before replying, "That night, he was anxious and miserable, so I stayed with him, and I saw them all..."

"Who are 'them'?"

"Them... they..." Xianghua said, "...are the ghosts of Horse Hoof Hollow."

"You mean Scarface Dou?" I spurred him on. "But you walked this route before, and nothing happened."

"Who said no- no- nothing happened?" Xianghua's stuttering grew worse. "My dad was worried something would happen to us, so came up to Horse Hoof Hollow to find us. He's been missing ever since. There's not even a trace of a body."

I understood. Xianghua's father was a witch doctor, and, worried that his son would be in trouble going into the hollow because of Li Yi, he mysteriously disappeared whilst trying to save his son. No wonder Xianghua's mother had cursed Li Yi as soon as she had seen him.

"You don't hate Li Yi?" I continued to press him. "For causing your dad's disappearance?"

"Why? Why would I blame him? It was me who told Li Yi that Jiarun was getting married. It was m- m- my fault."

"Doesn't Li Yi feel guilty he dragged you both into this?"

Xianghua said, "It's why he never set foot in Meiyou Plain again, not until he became a doctor."

Li Yi must have been wracked with guilt over Xianghua's father, all this time.

"What did you see back then? Was it as bad as today?"

"I only know that Sc- Sc- Scarface Dou's huanhun is always on a full moon," Xianghua muttered.

I thought I saw a blood red hue spread across the full moon, and my whole body jolted. From the direction of Horse Hoof Hollow drifted rousing revolutionary music from the 1960s: "The golden sun rises from the East, shining over ten thousand fathoms…"

I thought at first that I was imagining the sound, but everyone stopped walking, rooted to the spot, so I knew they had all heard it.

"Xinhua News reports…" said a male voice in the distinct

tones of the Revolutionary Era.

"Xinhua News reports…" A corresponding female voice.

"…the East Wind blows ten thousand li, fresh flowers are blooming, the red flags are waving like the sea. Great teacher, wise leader, beloved…" came the words to the background music of "The East is Red".

The female voice rattled off a news briefing: "The People's Daily reports… the people of Asia… setting off a wave of volunteer resistance against America and solidarity with Vietnam…"

The loudspeaker crackled, and then stopped.

My mind exploded. Why was this broadcast playing in the mountains, in the twenty-first century?

"What the hell is this broadcast?" I shouted ahead of me. "What's going on here?"

Li Yi replied dismissively from the front of the group, "People in Horse Hoof Hollow are playing an old broadcast, what's odd about that?"

Xianghua retorted, "Who still lives in Horse Hoof Hollow? The workers from the tea farm were fired years ago."

"*KSSHHKLK, KSSHHKLK,*" the broadcast resumed. "The Great Proletarian Cultural Revolution… has already… attained a great and glorious victory…" The background music had changed to "You Need Good Helmsmen to Sail the Seas".

At this time, in this place, hearing broadcasts from decades ago… The uncanny atmosphere had reached an extreme.

The broadcast continued for a while, and then suddenly went dead. The silence made my body shake uncontrollably.

Tian Jiarun's father tried to struggle down from his little brother's back. "I can walk by myself, I'll walk by myself."

At last, we passed this stretch of the mountain's spine and

reached the peak of one side of the Horse Hoof.

"We can just walk round the ridge to the other mountainside," Xianghua suggested. "We don't need to go through Horse Hoof Hollow. Please?"

"No, if we do that, we'll be walking till dawn," Li Yi said.

Tian Jiarun's father interjected with feeble tones, "Let's just walk round the mountaintops, follow the horse hoof... ahh, hnggg... sssshhhtttt... I can't drag you kids down with me." He seemed to be sinking back into extreme pain.

Li Yi checked on him and said, "We haven't got time to go round the mountaintops, we have to just push through the hollow, and we have to go now."

"It's the huanhun of Scarface Dou and his band, they're vicious!" Tian Jiarun's father moaned.

"Don't worry, Uncle, there's no such thing as ghosts," Li Yi said. "Don't scare yourself." And with that, he pushed forward, towards the hollow.

WALKING IN SINGLE file down the mountain path was even harder than walking up. The winding track twisted and turned, and since no one had walked it for a month, it had become overgrown with weeds as tall as a person, blocking most of it. As we walked, we had to push them aside. I thought that the drunkard Tian Changnian would end up toppling both his brother and himself into the bushes. Fortunately, Tian Jiarun had taken a torch from me, and was guiding the brothers along the route.

I walked slowly, worried that if I lost concentration, I would fall. Xianghua saw that I had slowed and stopped from time to time to wait for me. This meant our line lengthened, with Li Yi striding ahead, over a dozen metres away from me.

I was praying that those broadcasts would not start up again, and actually, a complete absence of weirdness would be great, but just as I was forming these thoughts in my head, I heard the crisp, clear sound of a firecracker exploding. Just one, but the sound echoed interminably.

Xianghua froze, and turned his head sideways, listening intently.

"Who's so bored they're setting off firecrackers now?" I asked.

"That's not a firecracker." Xianghua turned his head towards me, his face taut. "It's a gunshot."

"This isn't a warzone, why would there be gunshots?"

Then, as if to mock my words, another crisp and clear crack sounded in the hollow. *PTANGGGggg*. The echo rang out, unwilling to disperse.

"Is it hunting season?" I asked, hoping for an affirmative from Xianghua.

But my hopes fell as he shook his head.

"No," Xianghua stammered. "It's Scarface, and his g- g- gang."

"They're dead, so how can they be shooting?"

I shut up as Xianghua lifted his trembling hand and pointed it into the hollow.

I looked along the line he was indicating. In the moonlight, where the riverbanks were less overgrown, I saw shadows of flitting figures, but when I tried to focus on them, I could see nothing.

"Kids," Uncle Tian mumbled, "Scarface Dou has come to block our progress."

Li Yi shouted back, annoyed, "This is a scientific phenomenon, there's minerals in the grounds of Horse Hoof Hollow. Stormy weather just ignites it... that's what the geological team said back then – you know that,

Jiarun. Jiarun…"

Li Yi clammed up abruptly.

Xianghua sighed. And then Uncle Tian burst into tears. "I'm sorry, I'm so sorry… It's my fault, Jiarun. I should never have talked Guangping into joining that research team."

Tian's sobbing words muddled my head. So, Guangping must have been Jiarun's husband?

In the darkness, I thought I heard the scream of someone in the throes of death.

Xianghua began to mumble, "I should explain this. Li Yi, Jiarun and I used to be classmates, and good friends. Li Yi and Jiarun were in love, but Uncle Tian was in poor health, and wanted an heir, so they arranged a husband who would marry into the bride's family. At the time, Li Yi was still at university, so how could he come back to the mountains for the daochamen[11]? So, Jiarun had to marry someone else."

From what Xianghua had said about Li Yi's state at the time, I realised that was why he had stormed into the hollow that night, because he had found out about Jiarun's marriage, and I understood why Li Yi had been trying so hard to save Uncle Tian, even at the cost of everything else. Because in his mind, Uncle Tian was family.

I asked Xianghua one more thing: "So, how come I didn't meet Tian Jiarun's husband? Where is he?"

Xianghua smiled bitterly. "Jiarun's husband, Guangping, is dead. A few years ago, a geological survey team came to investigate the terrain of Horse Hoof Hollow. They said

11 Daochamen, 倒插门 – "going back through one's own door", in historical times, well-to-do families with no male heir sometimes arranged marriages in which a poorer man was willing to move in with the woman's family and take on their surname. In this case, wedding rituals were arranged differently than the norm. The bride would go and stay with her grandparents, and during the ceremony the groom would proceed from her family home, to usher her back in through the threshold.

the iron in the hollow was very good quality, and they wanted to blast the mountains open and start a mine. The group recruited locals, offering a very good thirty yuan a day. None of our people would dare go into the pass, though, except for Guangping."

In a roundabout way, it looked like all the heartache in the village came down to Horse Hoof Hollow.

Xianghua continued, "Guangping died a strange death. During that day, he said he'd got hit in the head by a piece of debris from the blasting. It didn't look like a deep wound, so they patched it up, and he went on working. In the evening, he returned to camp and slept as usual, but in the middle of the night, his colleague got up for a piss, and found the ground covered with blood. Then, he saw Tian Jiarun's husband. Just lying there, with a bloody bullet hole through his head, long dead.

"Some people say that anyone from the Meiyou Plain who strays into Horse Hoof Hollow is guaranteed to die. Later, the company paid out a compensation of two thousand yuan." My heart tightened, but Xianghua continued, "They say that when Scarface Dou was executed, he was shot in the head, in exactly the same way."

After this story, I was beginning to doubt that Li Yi's determination would bring the protection I had hoped for.

We were already halfway down the mountain, and the path was now neatly lined with rows of tea trees. Ahead of us, lines of bungalows had been built. This looked like the tea plantation Xianghua had mentioned. The houses were pitch dark and hollow. As we moved nearer, I could see that they had fallen into total dereliction, with the window glass all missing. But one house at the end had the light on, and Li Yi was already knocking at its door.

The old man who opened the door said he was the caretaker of the plantation, but Xianghua had just told us that there was no one left in Horse Hoof Hollow.

The old man was enthusiastically hospitable. "It's so late, but you're still out – today is really not the day to go out into the mountains."

"My uncle is sick" – Li Yi pointed to Uncle Tian – "but the big road has been blocked off by flooding. So we've had to detour through here by the small road."

"You're from Meiyou Plain." The old man furrowed his brow.

We all sat down to rest for a while. I found myself carefully observing the old man's shadow under the light. He did not look like a ghost. I breathed a sigh of relief.

Li Yi checked his watch, then checked Uncle Tian. "Uncle, how are you doing?"

"I'm fine, fine," Uncle Tian said, but seeing the cold sweat on his forehead, we knew he was not telling the truth.

"Once we clear Horse Hoof Hollow, we'll be practically in the town. Just hang on, Uncle."

The old caretaker went to the table in the corner of the room, picked up a teacup, and asked if I wanted a drink. I was thirsty and went to take the cup from him. This was when I noticed that he had only three fingers left on one hand, the fourth and little fingers missing, with the scar from the stump extending all the way up to his wrist. My heart thumped, and my eyes shot to his other hand, but it was tucked inside his sleeve, and not visible.

The old man picked up the teapot with his diminished hand and poured me some tea. I took the cup and regarded the liquid within. It looked like a strong hongcha, with a dark red, gore-like tint.

Li Yi blurted out, "Did we hear a broadcast from the '60s just then, in the hollow?"

The old man seemed surprised. "You heard it today? Why didn't I? I must be getting deaf in my old age."

The old man's answer caused more confusion, and nobody seemed to want to muddy the waters with more questions.

Having rested for about ten minutes, we thanked the old man, and prepared to leave.

At the last minute, the old man rushed to the door and said, "If you didn't have someone so sick with you, I would never let you leave."

We left the row of bungalows behind, and descended further down the mountain till we reached the riverbank at its foot, a stream to the right of it. The terrain of Horse Hoof Hollow really was quite unique. There was no river feeding the stream, and that day's torrential rain had raised the river's level by no more than a couple of inches. On the far side was a lush forest, into which the road disappeared. In the distance beyond the trees, some buildings were faintly visible.

We followed the path into the woods. The moonlight seemed to be blocked out by the dense foliage, with not a thread of light passing through. Now, we could only rely on the torches to see ahead of us. The thin cones of light from the others walking ahead of us looked as though they were swaying in the dark. I looked at the edges of my own beam and saw that it was wrapped in a curling, heavy haze. I figured out that the real reason why we could see so little in these woods was the heavy miasma of mist which hung between the trees, wrapping itself around them.

I held the torch out at eye level, and thought I saw it flash over a human face, ashen grey, with twisted features. I froze, horrified, but convinced myself it must have just been a shape of the fog, reflecting the torchlight, and the trick of the human mind to see faces in anything.

After this sudden lurch, I managed to steady my nerves somewhat, and continued to walk on slowly, but my heart continued to pound in my chest, so loudly I could hear it. I also became aware of how it had grown deathly quiet around me. Not even the chirping of insects, or the rustle of nesting birds. Did this thick, heavy fog block out the whole world?

I could not even hear Li Yi and the others in front of me.

"Li Yi! Xianghua! Xianghua!" I shouted into the darkness, flashing my torch around at random, hoping to catch sight of one of them, but no one answered. I stood there, petrified, not knowing how to act.

I must have fallen behind, I reasoned. They must have just gone too far ahead to hear me.

I could not even get my bearings now. The darkness was intensified by the fog, and I was trapped, somewhere within. Terror, catalysed by the feeling of isolation, engulfed me and seized my mind. I felt as if the space around me was filled with horrible things and beings. In this dense fog, in this dark night, I was blind and could not see them, but they could see me.

A line of poetry entered my head. "That slobber blood through wetted fangs." The fear in my heart had surged to a peak. Scarface's soul was returning tonight. They were bandits, capable of every imaginable atrocity. "And slaughter men like chopping hemp."

I cursed myself. *Stop reciting these dreadful lines. Stop with all this, "Hostile ones who guard it become leopards and wolves"* [12]. *Stop it! Don't even think about it!* I bashed

---

12 These lines are from "The Way on Shudao is Hard" (蜀道难) by romantic Tang Dynasty poet Li Bai (701-62). The Shudao roads were a system of pathways that connected the

my head with my own hand.

"The silver-haired fisherman by the riverbanks, to whom the changing seasons, fading and passing times are but fleeting and familiar"[13]. *Yes! Good lines! Continue to think about this poem.*

"At dawn one flees from angry tigers, at dusk one flees from giant snakes." I bellowed at myself: "STOP RECITING THIS BLOODY POEM!"

But there was nothing I could do. I could not drive the fear from my mind, no matter how hard I tried. My body felt damp as the creeping fog slowly seeped in through my clothes and onto my flesh.

I waved the torch around me desperately in all directions, like a weapon, hoping to find the way I had come. There should have been footprints on the ground. It was wet earth, so there must have been footprints.

But my attempt at being methodical was useless, because the light of the torch, impeded by the fog, could not even reach the ground. I could only see as far down as my knees. So, I crouched down, and shone the torch on the forest floor. I would have been better not to, because what I saw turned my stomach.

The ground was covered with fat maggots, wriggling earthworms and centipedes that curled round in a sickening mess. These were underground things, but after the rain, they had crawled up out of the filth.

My stomach churned, when I heard sound and movement above me.

I shot up immediately, twitching the torch left and right,

central province of Shaanxi and the western province of Sichuan. Here Li writes about the lofty and unpredictable harshness of the roads that are full of hazards for the traveller.

13 From "Celestial By the River: The Rolling Waters of the Yangtze Flow Eastwards" (linjiang xian: gungun changjiang dong shi shui) by Yang Shen (1488-1557), Ming Dynasty poet.

shouting, "Li Yi! Xianghua! Is that you?"

No answer came, and I began to panic, swinging the torch in all directions, and found someone standing above me.

No! Not standing. *Hanging*. Hanging dead from the branch of a tree right above my head. As I looked up, their shoes were not an inch from the tip of my nose.

I screamed, and backed away a few steps, tripping over my own feet, and landing with a bump on a mound of soft earth. I placed my hands down to prop myself up, and my palms sank into something supple, soft and moist. Slippery and smooth, the object felt almost pleasant against my fingers.

"Fengfeng, are you there!?" I heard Li Yi's voice calling from ahead.

"I'm here! I'm here!" I shouted frantically.

Two clouds of light came bobbing towards me, and then Li Yi and Xianghua stood before me. Li Yi was berating Xianghua. "Why didn't you stay behind him? He's never walked in the mountains before! Why didn't you keep a close eye on him?"

Xianghua said sheepishly, "I had no idea when we lost him."

They shone their torches down over me. "Why are you sitting on a grave?"

I looked down, and realised what the mound actually was. Pulling my hands into the light, I nearly screamed again. My hands seemed to have pushed into the corpse of some unknown creature, which must have already half rotted through, which was why it felt slippery and soft, against a pile of rotten guts. Countless maggots were making their way across my hands. I swung them wildly, but the maggots that were already well up my wrist continued to hold on and crawl further. I scraped my hand against some nearby scrub, feeling utterly disgusted. At least it had taken my mind off sitting on the grave.

"There are no graveyards in Horse Hoof Hollow." Xianghua was confused. "So why has a grave mound suddenly appeared?"

"There's a hanging corpse up there!" I pointed up at the tree.

Xianghua and Li Yi moved their torches closer and found a scarecrow hanging from the branches.

"Looks like the work of some prankster cowherd, or their kid." Li Yi tutted.

Neither Xianghua nor I contradicted him, both understanding very well that there would be no cowherd, let alone a child, in a place like Horse Hoof Hollow. I had clearly seen shoes on the hanged figure just now, and there were none on that dummy.

Horse Hoof Hollow really was haunted!

STILL SHAKEN, WE emerged from the woods. I saw the Tian family waiting for us at the tree line, with what must be the houses of the old hollow village behind them. I guessed Li Yi had got out of the woods, noticed I was missing, and had then come back to find me. Having taken up everyone's time, I felt incredibly guilty.

We walked into the crumbling original village of Horse Hoof Hollow. The houses were built in pre-Liberation days, mostly period style buildings two storeys high, made of wood. A diaojiaolou[14] caught my attention. It had been

---

14 Diaojiaolou, 吊脚楼, style of wooden houses mainly adopted by ethnic groups and other inhabitants of the south-western, southern central and western regions of China. Usually found by rivers, these houses are built on wooden stilts that lift them up above the water.

a shop, and still had its sign hanging. I could not make out the characters painted on it, noticing it only because the wind was rocking it to and fro. Horse Hoof Hollow must have once been a prosperous town, but now it was desolate and deserted, with only one old inhabitant left.

Creeaak, Creeeaaak... I watched the shop sign as it swayed in the wind and felt a ringing in my ears. It continued for a few moments, but when it cleared, I heard Jiarun say, "Dad, I think I can see Guangping. Do you see him?"

Uncle Tian did not answer, but shook his head and called out, "Hua! Hua! Get over here."

Xianghua hastened to his side.

With his face full of dread, Uncle Tian turned to him. "It- it- it is here. Did you bring the thing?"

Xianghua motioned to Uncle Tian to keep his voice down and drew out one of those damned steel needles I had seen him use that first afternoon. Tian Jiarun seemed to have heard, but not listened to the conversation between her father and Xianghua – was she possessed, too?

"The twelve core ideologies are centred around... adhere to the path of Chinese-style socialism... oppose complete Westernization..."

That sinister broadcast had started up again, seemingly from right above our heads. It was the female voice this time.

"How are you going to explain this away?" I whispered to Li Yi after scuttling over to his side. "Also, after we got here, something seems wrong with Jiarun, like something happened to her."

Li Yi whispered back, "Did Xianghua bring his needle?"

That now-familiar broadcaster's voice piped up next to our ears: "The seventh set of group exercises now begins...

Third part... stretching exercise... one two three four, two two three four..."

That music was so familiar, but here, it filled me with dread.

Everyone was quiet. We all listened in absolute silence.

I noticed Uncle Tian tugging at the shoulder of his younger brother, so tightly that he pulled the fabric of his coat taut. I could not tell if he was suffering extreme pain, or extreme fear.

After two looping clicks, the broadcast fell silent, but the magnetic hum of the live speaker had not disappeared. My ears began to hum again, and then... just the cold, empty, eerie streets, without even the slightest hint of a breeze. Everything was still, so unquestionably still. Everyone grew uneasy, and the strangeness in the air grew heavy.

"Dad! I can see my dad!" Xianghua shouted, and before anyone could react, Xianghua had run off towards a small sideroad that branched off from the main street, disappearing into it.

I was stunned, but Li Yi shook me. "Fengfeng, keep an eye on them and wait for me here," he said, before dashing down the dark alley.

"Hua! Come back! Hua!"

I went to Uncle Tian, whom Changnian had put down on the ground. He was holding his abdomen with both hands, sweat running down his face and rolling off it, but Tian Jiarun was oblivious. Her eyes were dull, her face slack, and her mouth mumbling something inaudible.

Alcohol seemed to have washed over Tian Changnian's head again – he twisted his head to the right and slurred, "Littlest lass from the Lius, why aren't you out feeding the pigs? Hang on, didn't Scarface Dou get you at his huanhun back in '73?"

There was nobody to Tian Changnian's right. He was talking to thin air.

My body felt barbed, as if parts of it were being rolled in thorns. I looked towards Tian Jiarun again, who was pestering her father with the same question: "Dad, Dad, did you see Guangping?" Those dimples appeared again, sinking deeper and deeper into her face.

Uncle Tian said nothing – he couldn't even if he wanted to, so bad was the pain.

Tian Jiarun's behaviour was growing wilder and wilder. She gave up speaking to her father, and stared into the nothingness towards the riverbank, calling, "Guangping, what are you doing over there? Does your head hurt? Why did you leave me behind all by myself?"

Uncle Tian could not speak but managed to point at his daughter, with an anxious expression plastered across his face.

"Haha," Tian Changnian chuckled. "Nephew-in-law's here, too."

I listened in abject horror.

Luckily, Li Yi returned with Xianghua just in time. Xianghua had been dragged back by the hair, and was still kicking and struggling, screaming, "I need to find my dad! Get your hands off me!"

Li Yi looked towards the river, where Uncle Tian was pointing, and saw Tian Jiarun's frail figure running towards it.

"Have you had enough of your hokum yet?" Li Yi shook Xianghua by the head. "Jiarun is running into the river!"

This seemed to break Xianghua out of his trance-like state. "Don't let her go! She's possessed! We have to stop her."

Uncle Tian struggled to speak. "Go. I'm fine. Hua, use the needle, the needle."

We darted through the weeds and reached the riverbank. The slipway was covered with pebbles, and I nearly rolled my ankle a few times. We got to the middle of the sprawl just as Jiarun reached the water's edge. She had squatted down and was drawing something in the water with her finger. Li Yi, the most anxious of us all, ran the fastest. I tried to keep up with him, but I stepped into a patch of sand and tumbled onto my knees. As I pulled myself up, I saw that the stones under me were a bright red ochre.

Li Yi and Xianghua stood on either side of Tian Jiarun.

She was not doing anything dangerous, but what she was doing seemed so out of place.

Jiarun was humming a song. "We sit on the high, high piles of grain, listening to mama speak of the past…[15]" With her left hand, she was pulling weeds from the water, and laying them on a large flat stone. With her right, she held up a piece of driftwood like a club, and began beating the grass on the stone, over and over.

She was washing clothes. From time to time, she scooped up water from the river and poured it over the stone, as if the pondweed were really cloth.

"Jiarun, please wake up," Li Yi said, tenderly.

Jiarun lifted her head slowly, and turned towards us, wearing a smile on her face. "I'm washing my husband's clothes." Then she began beating the stone again with the stick. Thump… Thump… the sound spread far, far out into the night.

"Jiarun! Don't act like this!" Xianghua dropped to her side, pulling out that long needle from behind his back, and with a single swooping motion, strung it through both of Jiarun's dimpled cheeks.

---

15 Popular children's song "Listening to Mama Speak of the Past", composed by Qu Xixian, lyrics by Guan Hua, first released 1957.

Jiarun yelped, but did at least wake up, unsure why she was kneeling by the river. Looking up at Li Yi, her tears began to fall, like rain.

The night sky had become much brighter; the now blood-red moon had doubled in size and hung right over our heads. When I lowered my head, the reflection in the river was not my own.

They were there. A long row of figures, their postures indicated they were kneeling. "Execute!" I seemed to be really hearing this voice, but felt as if it were my hallucination.

I heard a series of gunshots, and the reflections of the figures tumbled into the water, one by one.

I leapt back, pointing at the water. "They're dead, AHHH, dead." Reflecting the moonlight, the river turned a dark red, and churned with chaotic waves.

Half crawling, half rolling, I desperately dragged myself from the river. Li Yi was holding Tian Jiarun, and slowly edging her away.

I grabbed Xianghua. "After Scarface Dou was killed at Horse Hoof Hollow, what happened?"

"What else?" Xianghua grimaced. "They say that Scarface Dou's huanhun was the worst during the years of the Wudou16. There was a big tea harvest at Horse Hoof Hollow, and a lot of people at Meiyou were brought in to help. Suddenly, the Rebel Faction, who'd come down from the county, went crazy. They started attacking anyone they came across. A few people were killed, my mum was maimed. Their leader was Tian Changnian, but we all knew that he and his group were possessed by Scarface Dou's gang. From then on, people began to move out of

---

16 Wudou 武斗, 1966-9, a period during the Cultural Revolution in which armed political factions fought against each other.

the tea plantation. I have no idea who is doing the planting now." I remembered Xianghua's mother lying there, weeping in the rain.

Xianghua continued, "That night, when Tian Changnian was leading the Rebel Faction and beating people, they said he was snorting with laughter as he did it, and picking his nose throughout. Just like Scarface had acted whenever he was on a rampage."

We walked back to the village and froze. Both the old Tian brothers had gone.

"WHERE ARE THEY?" Li Yi roared at Xianghua like a madman. Tian Jiarun collapsed to the ground, her hands scraping the earth. The needle through her cheeks prevented her from talking, but a constant growling rumble came from her throat.

"The government promises everyone that we are moving towards stability, moving towards prosperity. Migrate during the development, and develop during migration..."

The broadcast overhead had started up again.

Cursing loudly, Xianghua climbed up an earthen terrace, and then a persimmon tree. I saw two old-fashioned speakers hanging from its branches, moments before he ripped them out viciously, and threw them to the ground.

Descending from the tree, he was still seething. "Let's see you fucking squawk now." Xianghua furiously brought his boots down on the speakers hard. "Squawk now, you fucker!"

The speakers lay in shards, the voices silenced.

We were glad for quietness and clarity, and glad the creepy broadcasts had, at last, been taken off the air for good. But still, Horse Hoof Hollow had not seen human habitation for a long time. Where did the electricity come from? The old man at the tea plantation was using a rig that ran off a couple of car batteries.

I was still thinking about this question, when…

A harsh and severe voice sounded in the air.

"The anti-government militant faction led by Dou Fucang… crimes of tremendous evil… today… was the time to pay back blood with blood… carry out the execution…"

This voice was clearly not issuing from any loudspeaker.

I whipped around looking for the source of the voice, and when I found it, it pushed my already strained nerves to the absolute edge of breakdown.

Tian Changnian had found a log splitter, which he was holding up high. Below him was Tian Jiarun's father, kneeling on the floor.

"Second uncle!" Tian Jiarun pulled the needle from her mouth, leaving fresh blood pouring down her cheeks. "What are you doing?"

Li Yi bolted over, leapt up and tackled Tian Changnian to the ground. The two of them grappled. I rushed in and kicked the fallen weapon into a corner, far away from the fight.

Tian Jiarun threw herself over her father, shielding him and holding his head. She began to weep out loud.

"Jiarun… I'm so, so sorry… I can't burden you anymore," Uncle Tian said to his daughter, stroking her hair.

On the other side, Li Yi and Tian Changnian had stopped fighting. They stood, Tian Changnian having fully sobered up again. "What happened to me? What was I just doing?

Was it Scarface? Did Scarface Dou come back? I need a drink, has anyone got anything?"

The blood moon slowly hid itself behind the dark clouds, and the pitch-black night sky gradually returned, invading Horse Hoof Hollow. A gust of wind blew through the village, and we all shivered. Not because it was particularly cold, but because carried in the air were the vague hints of low, heavy whimpering and furious hissing.

Tian Changnian bent down, picked up an old black bottle, and shook it. He was about to take a swig, before Li Yi knocked it away with a swipe. The drunk had mistaken an old bottle of fertiliser for alcohol. Meanwhile, Xianghua seemed to enter a trance again, shouting into thin air, "Dad, Dad…"

When I turned back, I witnessed another horrible scene. I had not seen Li Yi pick up the log splitter, but he now held it, a horrid smile on his face, and the forefinger of his other hand was buried to the knuckle up his nose. He fixed his eyes on the close-to-death Uncle Tian, and step by step, he stalked closer. Tian Jiarun, her face lined with blood, looked up at Li Yi.

Li Yi raised the axe.

A new voice rang out. "Brother Dou! Da'ge! It's not that I'm meddling, but what happened is all in the past. Let it go. So many years have gone by. Let go, all the brothers are keeping you company, and so am I. I'm here. Let it go."

None of us had noticed that the old caretaker from the tea farm had crept up.

I listened to the old man's hoarse plea, and I understood. He had been one of Scarface Dou's gang of bandits, the little fish that had slipped through the net. But in the end, he had decided to return and reunite with his brothers. It was his own form of honour.

Li Yi dropped his raised arm, and his face gradually returned to normal. I could clearly see a shadow behind Li Yi, which steadily melted into the wind, until nothing remained.

In the end, with the old bandit as a guide, we made it out

of Horse Hoof Hollow, alive. Just a little bridge to cross, and we would be on the paved road, two hours' walk from town.

"Back then, Dou da'ge was desperate, and had nowhere to turn to, so he went back home to the Plain of Enchanted Plums. It's the people in your village who ratted him out. It made sense. Before he was executed, he said he had spent his life killing people like cutting hemp, and so if he got cut down in turn, he couldn't complain. The people he held a grudge against were the villagers of Meiyou Plain, his own kinsfolk, who'd betrayed him." The old man continued, "He had been a bandit for decades, but never lifted a finger against anybody from Meiyou Plain, but in the end, what led to his downfall was the village he trusted the most."

The old man stopped walking, and we thanked him. Around midnight, we finally reached the town hospital.

IN THE END, Uncle Tian did not survive. I heard later from Li Yi, when he visited me in Changyi, Uncle Tian's gallstone had been inflamed, which was hiding a more serious problem, late-stage cancer of the liver.

When Li Yi got married, he invited me to Xingshan, to attend the festivities. I did not go.

I had finally found a job and could not get the time off. I could not help but wonder, though, if Tian Jiarun would go to the wedding, and, if the road was blocked, whether she would try Horse Hoof Hollow.

NOTES

KNOWING THAT THIS was going to be such a key work in

introducing contemporary Chinese horror, I wanted to feature a broad mix of stories, including those with a more traditional feel, and was delighted to find one as excellently crafted as this novelette. One element of uniqueness in Chinese horror stories seems to be how regional they are, with China's many mountains being an infinite source of fascination, wonder and exoticism. The more mountain-bound a region is, the more it lends itself to the setting for strange peoples, creatures and events. Apart from the iconic horror location of Xiangxi in Hunan, there are few regions more shrouded and mountainous than Hubei, right in the heart of China.

This story grew from She Cong Ge's youthful experience, when he had to make a long trek at night through wild mountain passes, on a route which took him through several small village graveyards. He remembers being terrified by the growls and howls of the mountain's nocturnal residents, and any modern scepticism evaporating as he was seized by traditional Chinese worldviews of ghosts, gods, and witchcraft, convinced that vengeful ligui ghosts were hiding in the desolate wilderness, ready to pounce on unsuspecting travellers, snatch away their minds and leave them to die on the mountainside.

From these unchecked fears, we can see the roots of the bizarre shamanism in the story, as well as the abject terror Xianghua and the superstitious villagers feel towards the spectral Scarface Dou. Not even our intelligent and observant protagonist can escape losing his wits in the miasmic forest. Whilst he tries to make rational deductions, his inner frame of reference keeps serving him the traditional Chinese fare, ancient poetry and supernatural beliefs. The introduction has that great traditional feeling of the horror film narration, where warnings are issued, rules are outlined, and we, as the audience, know that each and every one of those taboos are about to be broken.

This story blends local and national history, as well as regional culture such as the tea plantations and unique architecture. It is clear that China, as a nation, is still coming to terms with the traumas of war and internal revolution from the last century. This novelette deals with them so evocatively, adeptly illustrating how the lives of generations were torn apart and haunted by these events. People remember, and so do places. We are at a point in time when these things are considered 'the past', but our perception of time is skewed by the sheer weight of the present. The fact that we meet a still-living member of Scarface Dou's party is a creeping reminder that for many, the eras of nation making and hardship in China are still a period of living memory. This story is beset by conflicts, between the living and the dead, the rural and the urban, Nature and Industry. Whilst you will remember the supernatural threats in this piece, it's worth noting that the only death that occurs in this story is from the very real problem of providing modern medicine and support across a country as vast, and as geographically diverse, as China.

Like many in this generation of online writers, She Cong Ge took up writing as a hobby, turning to fiction at the relatively late age of thirty-four, as a way of relaxing from his busy work. It was not until his discovery of Lianpeng Guihua (Lotus Pod Horror), an online forum that serialised horror fiction, that he began his path as a professional writer.

THE YIN YANG POT

鴛鴦鍋

Chuan Ge

WHEN YOU GO for a hotpot, do you ever order the Yuanyang pot? You know, the one that has a clear white guodi soup base in one half, and a spicy red soup base in the other.

Someone once told me that in the Bashu regions, experienced folks would never order this. Because another name for the Yuanyang, or Mandarin Ducks Pot, is "Yin Yang Pot", and you never know who, or what, you will end up sharing the table with.

1

WHEN I WAS at university, I had a girlfriend from Chongqing, named Qiao Qian. I was a Zhejiang boy who never touched anything spicy, but in order to keep her company, I had ninety-nine hotpots in four years – luckily, this Yuanyang dish was an option. Later, other friends from Chongqing told me that if a Chongqinger is willing to share a Yuanyang pot with you, it indicates a kind of devotion that is equal to breaking one's principles.

We were going to celebrate our anniversary with our

hundredth hotpot, but then we broke up, and this total has forever stuck at ninety-nine.

Three years after graduation, I went to Chongqing on a business trip. I got hungry in the night and went out to find some xiaoye. After walking for a while along the dimly lit streets, I realised not a single shop was open, and then as I walked further, a sudden xian fragrance of fresh meats and Sichuan peppers floated towards me. I took a deeper sniff and picked up my pace, following the scent, turning a few corners as the delicious smell became intense.

Winding round an area of unlit dark alleys, fiery hot and spicy steam assaulted my face, billowing from a nearby hotpot restaurant. A cacophony of voices, bear-chested blokes and sassy Chongqing girls chatted and laughed heartily amidst the dense, humid pot mist, devouring large pieces of food.

This was a dongzi huoguo, "cave hotpot".

It is said that during the Occupation, Jiang Jieshi mobilised the entire population of Chongqing to carry out a large-scale operation, digging a complex tangle of caves, the world's largest system of air raid shelters. The war ended, but those shelters were heavy with Yin, so impossible to use as homes. But the industrious Chongqing people carved out another path for themselves, using the spicy hot qi of hotpot and the yang of happy patrons to bring the spaces back into balance, and set up a network of dongzi hotpot, which became a speciality of Chongqing.

Qiao Qian had been the one to tell me this story, and now, thinking of her, my mind darkened. I shook my head to break that chain of thought, lowered it, and was about to dive into the restaurant.

All of a sudden, the restaurant keeper, who had been busying himself, stepped out and blocked my way with an extended arm. This middle-aged man, whose hands were covered in soot and grease, seemed unimportant in his appearance, but was obviously managing the entire restaurant almost single-handedly.

"What, don't you want the custom?" I asked, a little angry, but still keeping my calm.

The restaurant keeper looked me up and down. "You're not from here, are you?" Seeing that I nodded, he twitched his mouth, and pointed towards the altar by the door. "Pay your respects before you come in."

That was a bronze sculpture about the size of an open hand. It was unlike the statues of Caishen and Guanyin that these places usually venerated. This one was a sword-brandishing general on horseback, whose eyes looked particularly alive, regarding me augustly, as if ready to strike me with his sword at any given time.

Seeing the confusion on my face, the restaurant keeper explained softly, "This is General Bamanzi, Arbiter of Yin and Yang, and Judge of Good and Evil."

"You mean, he's not a protector or a bringer of wealth?" I was puzzled, but felt this was not the time to enquire, so obediently, I bowed three times to the statue.

Seeing that I had paid my respects, the restaurant keeper breathed a sigh of relief and stepped aside to let me enter. "It's busy at the moment, so just sit anywhere you can, but be careful, and leave as soon as you're done eating."

I felt even more perplexed. What kind of business attitude was this, rushing the guests out the door?

Frowning, I turned a full circle to survey the restaurant floor, but there was not a single empty table. Did I really have to share a table with other customers? The way I'd shared hotpot before made it feel awkward, eating from the same pot as strangers.

Just as I was fretting about what to do, I heard a familiar voice: "Come and sit here, Chuan."

I turned, stunned.

That blossom-like smile, that exquisite face behind a wavering veil of misty steam – well, if it wasn't Qiao Qian...

2

NEVER MIND. IT was all in the past. *Let us be gracious and grown up about it,* or so I persuaded myself, as I took a deep breath, squeezed a smile onto my face and sat down.

"Qian, back then..."

"Cut the crap and order."

Seeing the cold indifference on Qiao Qian's face, I swallowed, and yelled on autopilot, "Hey boss, a Yuanyang pot, please."

As soon as the words had left my lips, the whole restaurant fell into silence, as if people had heard something incredible, and one after another, they cast their deep, questioning gazes towards us. It was a few seconds before they turned back and resumed their night snacking.

The restaurant keeper walked over, with a deep frown, and looked down at me, and then at Qiao Qian. "Young man, let me get you a red soup, I'll add as few chillies as I can."

I cheered up. "No worries, the Yuanyang pot will be fine. This is what my... friend and I used to eat together all the time."

Hearing this, the manager turned away, with his eyebrows raised and his lips pressed shut, and brought over a Yuanyang pot. Before retiring, he warned Qiao

Qian, "Don't make any trouble, General Ba is watching."

Watching the bubbling soup, I said curiously, "Qian, you Chongqingers are so weird. How come—"

Still seeming frosty and detached, Qiao Qian interrupted me again, "Just eat," and picked up a slice of lamb with her chopsticks, steeping it in the white soup.

Had she not always had the spicy side? Despite having questions, I had also been cut off twice that night, and felt my temper rising, so without asking her, I picked up a piece of bacon to dunk it in the white soup. Unexpectedly, Qiao Qian struck out her chopsticks and stopped me.

"Today, you get the red soup." She looked at me, her expression remaining the picture of icy indifference. "And don't touch any of the white."

Resentfully, I lowered my head. I was not sure why, but Qiao Qian's behaviour tonight was uncharacteristically snappy and rough, even a little frightening. Unthinkingly, I did as I was told.

The manager had said he would put fewer chillies in, but as soon as the chopsticks touched my mouth, my tongue felt like it was on fire. I had hardly taken a few bites before I had to stick out my tongue and try to fan away the spiciness.

"No way, it's too hot, I want to eat from the white side!" I shouted this, and immediately plucked up a piece of doufu to dunk in the other soup.

"Don't!" Without warning, Qiao Qian grabbed my hand. When our skin met, I felt an ice-cold shock that made me shiver all over.

For the first time, her face cracked into emotion, her eyes filling with tears. In an almost imploring tone, she said, "Chuan, do not eat anything in the white soup!"

Looking at her acting like this, an inexplicable fire rose

within me – it was that face! Back in the day, when I had pleaded desperately for her not to leave me, that expression had been on my face.

PAH. I shoved her hand away and stuffed the doufu into my mouth. "Well, I've eaten it now, so what next?"

As soon as the food entered my mouth, I froze. There was none of that familiar too-hot burning sensation. Instead, the doufu was stone cold.

I could tell that something was wrong, and automatically spat the food out. On Qiao Qian's face was a mix of contradictory emotions, pain and joy. With a look of despair, she fell back into the chair and closed her eyes, without saying another word.

Carefully, I moved over to ask her what the matter was. Now she was leaning back, I glimpsed her snow-white neck, which had previously been covered by her long hair. On her fine and luxurious skin was a row of small, densely packed stitches. It looked as though… she had been sewn up.

Suddenly aghast, I turned around and ran out of the restaurant, leaving Qiao Qian behind, and not even caring about the bill.

The restaurant keeper did not try to stop me, but as I dashed out past him, I thought I heard him make a vague sighing sound.

3

RUNNING BACK TO the hotel, I dove straight under the covers, and slept until the morning, before crawling out of bed, aching all over.

I sat in a stupor for a very long time before remembering

what had happened the night before. I hesitated, and reached for my mobile, dialling that familiar number from memory.

"Qian, last night..." I was already mentally prepared to be told off.

"Are you looking for Qiao Qian?" said a weary old female voice on the other end of the line.

"Are you her mother? Hello, Auntie, I'm Qiao Qian's... classmate from university. Could you please give me her mobile number?"

There was a long silence from the other end of the line, and then, in a hoarse voice: "Qianqian... passed away three years ago."

What? I was scared out of my skin, but I had clearly seen her the night before.

Having heard my account, Auntie Qiao seemed a little surprised, too, so I got her address, and hailed a cab to the Qiao family home.

That's right. Back then, Qiao Qian had ignored my pleading, and insisted on returning to her hometown, leaving me behind, but the day after she got back, she ended up in a major car accident. Her neck had apparently come into contact with a sheet of scrap iron, which had sliced her head clean off. Later, Auntie Qiao had gone to a lot of trouble in finding the best mortician she could, to sew her daughter's head back onto her body, so she could have a dignified funeral.

Hearing this, I felt that same shock of cold shoot straight up from my spine, all the way to my forehead. I remembered the line of stitching I had seen on Qiao Qian's neck. Trembling, I asked, "So, Auntie, what I saw last night...?"

Auntie Qiao rocked in her seat, unable to stop caressing

the portrait of Qiao Qian she held in her hands, and said tearfully, "That's my Qianqian coming back... I've missed her for three years, she's finally back... Where did you see her? Tell me!"

After struggling for half a day to remember, before I could give her even an approximate location, Auntie Qiao appeared contemplative for a while and then shook her head.

"I've lived in Chongqing for forty years, and never heard of this particular dongzi hotpot, but the Yuanyang pot..." She stared at me for a while, and then asked slowly and deliberately, "Chuān, you and Qian... weren't just classmates, were you?"

"You're... not wrong, Auntie, we'd been dating for some time." I rubbed the tip of my nose, feeling a little embarrassed.

"That makes sense," Auntie Qiao sighed. "Old folks here used to tell me a legend about this Yuanyang Pot, which is also called the Yin Yang Pot. In the old days, if you missed a deceased loved one, you would find a place with strong Yīn energy, and in the middle of the night, you would set up a Yuanyang Pot. If the deceased missed you, too, their spirit would be drawn to you. They would come and eat with you. The living must eat from the red soup, and the dead, from the white. After eating this dish, the two would no longer be separated by the boundaries between the Yang of the living world, and the Yin of the afterlife. They would be able to see each other for a brief length of time. After she died, I tried it. I wanted to see Qian again... but I never expected that the person she misses most would turn out to be you."

At this point, my hairs were already bristling as I came to the abrupt realisation of a horrible truth. I hastened to ask, "What if... the living eat from the white soup?"

"If the living eat from the white soup, it's the equivalent of making a Yin Yang betrothal to the dead. From then on, they would never be apart, in this world or the next. Like a pair of Mandarin ducks, always together. This is also called minghun, a ghost wedding." Then she also seemed to come to a sudden realisation, and began to ask in shock, "You didn't..."

Seeing my nodding, she sighed, hesitated, and finally said, "Of course, from a mother's point of view, I would do anything to see my daughter, but nobody who's made a Yin Yang pact has ever lived for more than seven days."

Inside, the chill in my body became arctic, but I forced myself to appear in good cheer.

"That's just legend and hearsay – it's wind in an empty cave, nothing to it! What a thing to think in modern times. I don't believe any of it. Yesterday was probably just a strange dream. Auntie, I'm really sorry to have disturbed you."

With my mouth spilling out these words, my body turned and carried me out of the Qiao family home, as if it were running for its life.

4

BY THE TIME I got back to the hotel, my whole back was already drenched in sweat.

Outside, it was growing dark, but I didn't even have the presence of mind to eat dinner. Whipping out my mobile, I booked the earliest flight the next day. I had to get out of Chongqing!

The moment the confirmation came through, I sighed with relief and collapsed on the bed. My shameful stomach began growling, and sitting up straight, I decided to order room service.

Just as I was thinking about what to get, there was a knock on the door. "Sir, your meal."

Wow, this hotel was good, so considerate of my needs. I was getting ready to lavish my praise, but, opening the door, I saw only one thing on the trolley that the waiter was pushing into the room. A simple Yuanyang pot.

My hairs rose on end again, and I shivered. "Why... why are you delivering this?"

The waiter looked confused. "Didn't your wife just ring down to the front desk to order?"

My... wife? Drops of sweat began to bead on my forehead, but I did not have the wherewithal to wipe them. Gritting my teeth, I answered the waiter, "That's right, sorry I got confused just then. Please leave it here, and you can go."

The second the door clicked shut, I could not hold it in any longer. I exploded hysterically, calling to an empty room: "Qiao Qian! Come the fuck out! If you're already dead, then you should stay in the netherworld, like a good little ghost! Why the fuck have you come back to harass me?"

I scattered and smashed and vented, but got no response whatsoever. Panting, I sat down on the bed, gasping, and was just about to throw myself back on it, when the swishing sound of running water came suddenly from the closed bathroom, accompanied by a familiar female voice, humming a tune softly, as if enjoying a shower.

This was Qiao Qian's favourite song! I rushed over, yanked the bathroom door open, and saw a graceful, seductive form silhouetted faintly behind the frosted glass. My mind returned to those nights with Qiao Qian, in the motel just off campus, during my university days...

With clenched fists, I ran into the bathroom, and pounced on nothing – the shower was spouting hot water, but there was no one for it to fall on.

A soft puk came from outside, as if something had broken. Stony-faced, I returned to the trolley, and saw fragments of a broken porcelain spoon on the floor, in the white soup of the Yuanyang pot. Some food was cooking, and a pair of chopsticks lay by the pot, as if they had just been used.

Anger rose within me again, but this time, I was done with throwing a fit. I walked over to the table, blanched a few pieces of meat in the red soup, and ate them with a blank face, even though they were so hot they sent streams of tears and snot running down my face. I put up with the discomfort, and shouted, "Fine, I've eaten the Yuanyang pot! Are you happy now? What else do you want?"

Things seemed to subside, and from that point to when I finally fell asleep, nothing else remarkable happened.

In the night, when I was fuzzy with sleep, I vaguely felt my nose itching, as if it were being tickled by someone's hair.

"Stop that!" I waved my hand in annoyance. A lock of silky hair swept over my fingertips, and then suddenly, I woke up. I sat bolt upright, catching a string of laughter like silver bells drifting away into the distance – towards the direction of the window, a window on the eighteenth floor!

At this point, how could I have dared go back to sleep? I downloaded a Great Compassion Mantra app on my phone, and let it play on loop until the morning.

Qiao Qian, have you really latched onto me?

With a wretched laugh, I hailed a cab, and decided to pay that dongzi hotpot another visit.

5

IN THE EARLY Chongqing morning, there were few people on the streets. The slow and leisurely pace of this city gave out a relaxed, almost comforting vibe.

But I did not have the heart to enjoy the atmosphere. Stepping out of the car, I ran towards that dongzi hotpot, and again, its manager happened to be standing at the entrance, blocking my way.

He had changed into day clothes, locked up, and was respectfully bringing down the general's statue from the altar. I took a few steps closer and tapped his shoulder.

I'd done some research on the story of General Bamanzi. Legend says he lived in the Ba Kingdom during the Zhou Dynasty, and was loyal and trustworthy, loved by the people. Ever since his death, he had enjoyed incense and veneration from the people of the Bashu region and could be considered part of the local faith.

The sun had just come up, and a ray of the early morning sunlight fell upon the blade of the idol's sword, reflecting the severe beam piercingly into my eyes. Automatically I raised my hand to block it. As it shone onto my hand, I felt the centre of my palm heat up, and then my whole body lightened, as if some burden had been lifted from it. A weak scream broke near my ear, speeding into the distance.

The restaurant keeper seemed to notice this, turning his head to look at me as I stood, rooted to the spot. He smiled. "Any trouble?"

Hearing this after the experience I had just had, it felt like I had grabbed hold of a lifeline. I pleaded profusely,

"Boss, please save me!"

The manager did not reply. He just wrapped the god statue in a red cloth, and carefully placed it in his bag. Only then did he beckon me with his hand. "Come with me."

I followed the man down a good length of road before we came to a teahouse in an alley. The teahouse looked like it had just opened for business; a silver-haired, energetic and healthy-looking old man was polishing the tea bowls.

The manager seemed to know the place well, picking a seat by the window. "A pot of Laoyin, please."

Maybe because there was not a lot of business that early, after the old man delivered the tea, he did not leave, but sat to one side and gawked at me for some time. "Young man, what happened to the girl from two days ago?"

I was startled by this question, but fixed a dumb smile on my face. Observing him carefully, I suddenly realised that, on the night at the restaurant, this old man had been sitting at the table next to us, eating with a group of other old men.

I turned to face them both and rushed to pour out my story of what had happened with Qiao Qian.

The restaurant keeper frowned. "Young man, the way I look at it, you have nobody else to blame in this matter." He paused for a mouthful of tea. "You have bowed to the statue of General Ba, so no matter what kind of yao mo gui guai, or where they come from, they wouldn't dare cause mischief. But you did order this Yin Yang pot of your own free will. You ignored the warnings and ate from the white side. The expression 'zishi qiguo'? Eating the bitter fruit you planted yourself? This is it."

I laughed nervously. "Boss, don't make fun of me. You had the balls to open a restaurant like this, you must have some powers here. Please guide me down the right path."

The restaurant keeper shook his head. "What powers could I have? This dongzi opens at night and shuts in the day. If the customers aren't old gods, spirits, ghosts or demons, then they're witches and sorcerers. It's all up to General Ba to keep the peace. I saw that you had ordered the Yan Yang pot without a care in the world and seemed to know the female ghost sitting across from you. I thought you were some experienced master occultist from out of town, who had come to take care of business in the trade. I never expected you'd turn out to be just some naive kid."

I turned my imploring gaze and fixed it upon the old man. "Old master, if you were eating in that restaurant, you must be no ordinary person either, right?"

Before the old man could reply, the restaurant keeper had already cracked into a snort. "Him? He just knows how to brew a good pot of anhun tea to calm the soul. That's why everyone in the city, whether dead or alive, gives him a bit of face. He doesn't even have that long to live."

Smiling at this, the old man did not show a jot of anger, as if the person being taunted was some stranger.

The restaurant keeper sighed. "Just then, you borrowed General Ba's energy, and temporarily cast out the thing that has been following you around, but if she comes back tonight, because you have eaten the Yin Yang pot with her, this is beyond General Ba's jurisdiction. If you want my advice, wrap things up in this world. When you're under, you're both welcome to come to my restaurant!"

Was there really no hope? I lowered my head, feeling grim and speechless. Just as all my thoughts seemed to turn to ashes, the old man brought me a cup of tea.

"Rest assured, the boat that reaches the bridge will straighten itself. Young man, drink this bowl of soul-calming tea to regain your spiritual energy. Otherwise, you'll die of exhaustion before the wronged soul even comes to claim you."

As soon as the tea entered my mouth, its light fragrance seemed to refresh my mind, completely expelling my tiredness from a whole night's lack of sleep.

"Tonight, you're going to help Zhang at the dongzi, just stay there. Every master of the three faiths and nine disciplines, every practitioner and cultivator of the occult loves the hotpot at his place. You'll have no problem trying to find a master to help you there, will you?"

This made perfect sense! Hearing the old man's words, I felt my hopes rise. That's right, to untie the knot, I needed someone who knew how to tie it. A problem that came from the dongzi hotpot could very well be resolved there, too!

6

I WAS A graduate from a prestigious university, so how hard would it be to help out at a restaurant? I never thought I would end up such a hindrance to Manager Zhang, reducing his efficiency and eventually getting shooed off to one side.

Sitting on the front steps of the restaurant, I whiled away my boredom flicking through Weibo, watching the skies darken, and watching Manager Zhang prepare his tables.

"What are you doing?" A wave of sweet fragrance floated along with the soft voice from behind me.

"Doom scrolling," I blurted out, and suddenly froze, that familiar cold sweat forming on my forehead. Carefully, I turned my head, and with the very edge of my vision, tentatively spied the pretty figure behind me, or should I say, the shadow of it...

I leapt up nervously and hid behind Manager Zhang. Shaking, I pointed in the direction of the shadow. "Qiao... Qiao Qian..."

Manager Zhang put down the vegetables he'd been washing, wiping his hands on his apron. "I don't care what's going on between you two, but General Ba's territory is a neutral zone."

Emerging from the darkness, Qiao Qian revealed her face, which was streaked with angry tears. "Chuan, I never forced you to do it... the Yuanyang Pot, you can't blame me."

Before I could marshal myself, I yelled at her, "Then go away! For my sake, just fuck off!"

Zhang lost his temper and dragged me out from behind him. "The will of heaven's order, it wasn't up to her, either. You're a bloody man, can't you take some responsibility!"

Bringing over a Yuanyang Pot, he set it on the table with a bang. "You two talk this over – I have to finish setting up. Don't forget to pay the bill this time."

With timorous caution, I sat down, watching Qiao Qian emerge from the night, floating elegantly across to sit opposite me.

"Chuan, please don't be scared, I won't hurt you," Qiao Qian said in a low voice, picking up a piece of huanghou offal with chopsticks, steeping it in the boiling red soup, before rinsing it with tea and putting it in my bowl.

The scene sent me into a haze of memories. I remembered

the first time I went out to a hotpot with her, when I insisted on braving the red soup, and the spice nearly killed me. In order for me to taste the authentic flavour of Chongqing hotpot, Qiao Qian would cook the food in the burning soup, and then rinse it, piece by piece in the white. Huanghou offal was my favourite delicacy…

This familiar scene also rinsed away my terror. I picked up the huanghou and ate it. I hesitated for a few seconds, then picked up a piece of lamb, swished it in the white soup, and placed it in her bowl.

"In the past, I always had the white side and you the red. I never expected we would be swapping over now." I tried hard to smile, but my face must have ended up looking ghastly.

Qiao Qian did not eat, but instead dropped her head, letting her tears fall. "Chuan, how have you been these past few years?"

"Not good." I shook my head. "That year, when you insisted on leaving, I was depressed for a long time. I missed the recruitment season at college, really struggled to find a job, it took me three years to get back on the right track… and now you've ruined me again."

"I'm sorry," Qiao Qian sobbed. "Back then, my mother forced me to return, even saying that if I didn't, she'd kill herself. I really didn't have a choice—"

"It's OK," I interrupted, gazing into her eyes sincerely. "Since it's all in the past, let's just release each other? Can you let me go?"

Qiao Qian shook her head. "There's nothing I can do. I'm now tied to your side, and I can't move away… And I've been slowly absorbing your Yang energy – this can't be changed."

"And there was me thinking it was some catastrophe,

but it's just a Yin Yang Lock," said a shrill voice.

I turned and saw a heavily made-up old woman sitting to one side, legs crossed, smoking an old-fashioned yanqiang, looking sideways at us. Next to her stood a few old men, one of whom was the man from the teahouse.

He gave me a smile, pointing at the old woman, and said, "This is Granny Yan of Guanyin Bridge, adept at affairs of the red and the white; if there's one person who can pick the Yin Yang Lock, it would be her."

Granny Yan harrumphed. "Now you've got the sense to flatter me? Where was that fifty years ago?"

The teahouse grandpa smiled, shuffling coyly. "Shufen, there's people here, it's not the time to bring up those things. We're not young anymore, why do you keep bringing them up?"

Granny Yan rolled her eyes. "Fine, go and reminisce with your bunch of old devils, leave this with me."

The old man waved at me and went off to sit with his companions.

I bowed to the granny with a hand salute of the highest respect. "Madam, Granny Yan, are you really able to help me?"

"Someone's already done the bragging. I have to help you now, even if I don't think I could." Granny Yan looked towards the old men, and said, with a dissatisfied manner, "Besides, he'd rather sit with those old devils night after night, rather than come and keep me company."

"Old devils?" I felt a bit awkward – was this not the sort of jibing you would save for an ex-lover?

Granny Yan seemed to have read my mind and giggled. "Those are his old war buddies, whom he can only see at night in this cave now. I call them old devils, because that's what they are. Don't you go thinking filthy thoughts."

I contemplated her words, too afraid to ask any more questions. Drawing in my neck, I shrank away from the direction of the old men, as if to show my deference.

Granny Yan took a look at Qiao Qian, knocking some ashes out of her pipe onto the table. "This matter between you... you could say it's a hard one to sort, but you could also say, it's quite simple..."

7

I HAD, FOR better or worse, worked through red tape for a few years, and could tell what tunes the strings were playing. I emptied my wallet, handing over every fen I had. "So, Granny Yan, where should we begin?"

Granny Yan accepted the notes, counting them deftly with a satisfied little smile, and straightened up. "There are two ways to open this Yin Yang Lock. One of these is something I once heard: some years ago, there was a lass in Chengdu, who became a widow after a month. Missing her husband to distraction, she summoned his spirit with the Yin Yang pot, but then she regretted it, and had to go all the way to Wuhou Temple before the problem could be fixed."

Hearing this, I immediately perked up. Who has not heard of the great Zhuge Wuhou[17]? This method was surely sound!

"Find a place with the full Bagua, then set up another hotpot. Yidu gongdu, it takes poison to cure poison... Can you guess what kind of pot should you make up?" Infuriatingly, she began to grow cryptic.

---

17 Zhuge Wuhou 诸葛武侯 - Zhuge Liang (Kong Ming), celebrated 181-234 military advisor to Liu Bei who founded the Shu Han Dynasty, a period of history famously fictionalised in the Romance of the Three Kingdoms. Wuhóu is a posthumous title granted to Zhuge.

I concentrated on my thoughts. "Wuhou... Bagua... could it be the..."

"Correct!" Granny Yan slapped her thigh. "This soup base is indeed the 'jiugongge', Nine Squares." These words stunned me. I could not help but look around, and see that in this restaurant alone, there were at least seven or eight jiugongge pots simmering away. Was it really this simple?

Granny Yan continued, "Of course, this particular jiugongge isn't simple. First of all, the soup base must contain shegu, hujin, baotai – nine rare medicines in all. When boiling it, nine powerful occult masters must be summoned, and the Navagraha such as the Rahu and Ketu alerted–"

"Stop, stop, stop," I hurriedly interrupted her. "All this hocus pocus, are we making the xiandan elixir here? Where could I acquire all this stuff?"

"What did you think it would take?" Granny Yan scowled at me. "You're planning on snatching a soul back from Yanwang, the King of Hell..."

Qiao Qian mumbled, "Chuan, I've still got some savings at home, why don't...?"

I waved my hand. "I've been to your home, so I can tell your mother doesn't have much money; besides, a few thousand kuai won't help with all that. Granny Yan, please tell us, what is the second option?"

At this point, Granny Yan snapped her lips together, as if reluctant to go on, finally pushing the words out between the gaps in her gritted teeth. "The second one is that if the clash of Yīn and Yáng harms you, then you need to make Yin and Yang converge..."

I could hardly contain myself from shouting and swearing. "What the f... does that mean? Are you suggesting I turn myself into a ghost?"

But Qiao Qian got her meaning. "Chuan, what Granny Yan means is for me to return to the Yang."

What? Of all the horrible things that had happened today, this shook me more than all of them combined. Qiao Qian had been dead for three years, her ashes were buried in the cemetery, so how could she come back from the dead?

Granny Yan narrowed her eyes, which glinted with a hint of danger. "Have you ever heard of returning the soul to a borrowed corpse?"

I hesitated for a while, but ultimately could not resist the temptation, and inquired, "You mean, find a corpse that has just died and get Qian–"

"No, a corpse won't do, it needs to be a young woman who is alive and well, one who trusts you completely, who will enter the pact willingly..." As soon as she said this, Granny Yan took up her pipe, and stopped talking.

A young woman... who trusts me? Where could I find one of those right now? I felt my anxiety rising again.

Suddenly, I heard my phone ping with a WeChat message from my university classmate.

"Xuezhang[18], I won a flight to Chongqing in a raffle. I'm flying out tomorrow. I heard that you are in Chongqing, do you want to meet up for a meal?" She signed off with a bright smiley emoji.

I took a deep breath and looked from the calm and collected Granny Yán, to the poor, suffering Qiao Qian.

"You've only got five days left," Granny Yan reminded me, bluntly.

---

18 Xuezhang 学长 – a term referring to a male graduate who attended the same institution as oneself, who was either senior in age or grade/academic level.

Gritting my teeth, I set my resolve, and replied, "Sure, it's a date, xuemei[19]!"

Typing these few characters, I sank into the chair, exhausted and drained.

8

"XUEZHANG, YOU'RE BEING very mysterious, what amazing place are you taking me to eat?"

Gu Liang followed behind me good-naturedly. Perceiving my silence and the heaviness on my face, she tugged at my sleeve very gently.

I half turned, keeping my face blank – because I had no idea what expression I should wear to face my xuémèi. I admit, I am not a good person, but I could not bring myself to send someone who trusts me into the abyss with a smile on my face.

"It's just a little further ahead. This is the most authentic dongzi hotpot in Chongqing, it wasn't easy to find."

"Heehee." Even with my back towards her, I could hear the big grin in Gu Liang's voice. "I think any restaurant that Xuezhang picks must be super delicious, Xuezhang is the best."

By the entrance to the hotpot place, Manager Zhang noticed me, and putting down the task in hand, took a look at Gu Liang, and frowned. "Chuan, who's this?"

My heart pounded – oh no, Manager Zhang had seen me.

According to Granny Yan, this place was the only place, in the whole of this mountain city, whose fengshu was

---

19 Xuemèi 学妹 – a term referring to a female graduate who attended the same institution as oneself, who was either junior in age or grade/academic level.

suitable for doing this business, which was why Old Zhang had opened a hotpot shop here in the first place. But what we were about to do, ultimately harming an innocent... I had no idea whether General Ba would permit it. To prevent any unwanted complications, I had hoped to "set the rice to boil" before Old Zhang ever found out what we intended.

Starting to sweat again, I stammered a reply, "This is my... friend, who's come all the way from another province."

Unexpectedly, Old Zhang actually waved her through. "If the young miss is from the outside, then there's no need to bow to General Ba. Our Dao differ, and it's better that our paths don't clash."

Confused, I dragged Gu Liang into the restaurant, and then it dawned on me that Boss Zhang probably thought she was the fengshui master I had recruited to deal with my problem!

As Gu Liang and I took our seats, I looked around surreptitiously. Granny Yan and the teahouse grandpa were sitting at a neighbouring table, nodding at me subtly.

But even before I spoke, Gu Liang had launched into conversation. "Wow, Xuezhang, this place really does do hotpot, and it's so busy, even at midnight. I thought you were finding an excuse to stall me..."

"Stall you?" I wondered. "Why would I want to keep you out at night, unless..."

I realised I had misspoken, and shut my mouth, wishing I could hide under the table, but Gu Liang had flushed so bright red that she lowered her face.

The hotpot came, and to ease the atmosphere, I quickly began talking about the food. "Here, taste the most authentic hotpot in Chongqing. I know you don't like spicy food, so I asked especially for this kind of guodi."

The hotpot arrangement in front of us looked like two concentric circles. The bigger one contained red soup, but in the smaller ring within, a small patch of white soup simmered. This kind of arrangement, sometimes referred to by uneducated hotpot places as the 'Yuanyang Pot', is in fact, more accurately, the Zimu, Mother and Child Pot.

This was what, according to Granny Yan, would solve the problem. If eating the Yin Yang pot means "always be together", then eating the Zimu Pot would mean "I live within you".

Salivating, Gu Liang rushed to pick up a piece of doufu and was about to dip it in, when I stopped her in her tracks: "Not yet! There's someone I'd like you to meet."

Qiao Qian stepped out from the darkness, and sat, facing Gu Liang, giving her a rueful and apologetic smile. "Hi, my name is Qiao Qian. I'm Chuan's... girlfriend."

Immediately, Gu Liang's countenance changed, and the piece of doufu she had picked up fell to the table. She fumbled to grab it, but I stopped her. "Don't worry, it doesn't matter."

Gu Liang lifted her head, forcing herself to show a smile, dredged with disappointment. "Xuejie[20], you're so pretty... you make such a good match with Xuezhang."

Qiao Qian seemed to have worked something out from Gu Liang's smile, so turned and glared at me. "Thank you, xuémei, for your praise. Look, I'm a local here, and you've travelled so far; come, let me treat you to some Chongqing delicacies..."

She steeped two pieces of meat in the white soup

---

20 Xuejie 学姐 – a term referring to a female graduate who attended the same institution as oneself, who is senior in age or grade/academic level.

and shared them with Gu Liang. I put on a brave face and began to blanch vegetables in the red soup, eating wordlessly.

Seeing that Gu Liang had eaten the chilly piece of meat, Qiao Qian suddenly stood up, and bowed to her. "Meimei, I am so sorry... from now on, please guide me."

As if Gu Liang had thought something through, she snatched a beer bottle off the table, threw back her head and drank it down in one go, and then said to us loudly, "Xuezhang, Xuejie, I wish you happiness. You don't need guidance from me. I don't want to disturb you for no reason."

She stood up, wiped her eyes, and walked towards the exit. "Xuezhang, I'm sorry, I have some urgent business, and have to go. Xuejie, look after xuézhang for me..."

Watching her figure shrink away as she walked off, I smiled bitterly. *Stupid girl, what you and Qiao Qian were talking about were entirely different things.*

Granny Yan nodded solemnly, Qiao Qian sighed, and floated away in the direction in which Gu Liang had disappeared.

9

THAT NIGHT, EVEN though there was no Qiao Qian to haunt me, I still could not sleep peacefully, worrying the whole night whether or not things would go smoothly.

In the morning, I received a phone call from Gu Liang.

"Xuemei, what can I do for you?"

"Chuan, it's me." Gu Liang's voice at the other end of the line was the same, but its timbre gave me a totally different feeling. "It worked; I'm coming over to you now."

In the hotel lobby, I saw Gu Liang… or rather, Qiao Qian.

The long dress, the type Qiao Qian preferred, looked awkward draped over Gu Liang, whose body was more athletic. It made me feel a little out of sorts, but also brought a strange kind of familiarity. I dared not quite believe it, so I probed, "You are?"

She smiled tenderly and brushed some hair over my temples. "Come home with me for once. I haven't seen my mother in three years."

It worked! My life was saved, and Qiao Qian had also been returned to me!

On the way to the Qiao family home, I could not help but ask Qian, "How are you feeling right now?"

Qiao Qian replied, brimming with joy, "I feel great. I'm not very coordinated in this body yet, but I'm already very satisfied… All of Gu Liang's memories are now in my head, so dealing with her family shouldn't be a problem… but in case they spot anything amiss, I'm going to slowly distance myself from them."

"So, is Gu Liang already…" I spluttered.

"She… she's still here," Qiao Qian sighed. "She's also inside this body, just not in control of it. Everything that I see and hear, she can, too. She is going to be watching, eyes wide open, as I live with her identity, communicating with her friends and relatives, but there's nothing she can do about it."

We saw Auntie Qiao, who looked at us doubtfully. Qiao Qian stepped forwards, pulled her aside, and told her some things that only the mother and daughter knew. Within moments, they held each other and wept.

Auntie Qiao wiped her tears with one hand and gripped Qiao Qian tightly with the other. "Qianqian, you've come back at last... I have missed you so much I could have died. It was all my fault – if I hadn't forced you to come back, you wouldn't have... but I didn't know what else to do. Your dad died early, and I really couldn't bear to be apart from you. Even the few years you were away at university nearly drove me mad..."

Choking with sobs, Qiao Qian consoled her mother. "It's OK, Mum, I don't blame you. See, I'm back, aren't I...?"

I did not speak, I just sat back quietly, letting the two of them enjoy their reunion. It was not until the skies darkened, and they calmed down, that I spoke. "Auntie, in a few days, Qiao Qian has to go back with me. She's using someone else's body after all, and to prevent suspicion, we need to go back for a few years, until things die down, then we can come back to Chongqing, or have you move to us, and settle down. It can all be arranged."

"Yes, yes, yes!" Auntie Qiao nodded non-stop. "Just remember to come back, I won't interfere with your lives."

"Qian." I stood up. "Stay here with Auntie, I'm going back to the dongzi hotpot. This is all thanks to Granny Yan, and I need to thank them properly."

10

As I ENTER the restaurant, Manager Zhang casts me a glare, but doesn't speak to me. It feels off, but as I am the guilty party, I dare not broach it, so head straight for Granny Yan.

She seems to have already been there for a while with the gentleman from the teahouse. She keeps beckoning me to sit, the table sumptuously laden with dishes.

"Did everything work out?" Granny Yan smiles

complacently.

"It worked, smooth as anything. Anyi[21]!" I hold up my thumb to her, lifting the wine cup. "Let me toast you!"

I drain my cup, pour a fresh one, and turn towards the teahouse grandpa. "Old master, this was all thanks to you. I ran into you by chance, but you helped me so much, without asking for a reward. There's nothing else to say, ganbei!"

The teahouse grandpa looks a little guilty. He turns away slightly and does not accept my toast. "An old devil like me… can't say I want nothing in return…"

Oh? That piques my curiosity, but before I have the chance to ask, my phone rings.

"Chuan, your stomach's not in a great state, try not to drink too much, do you hear?"

"Don't worry, Qian, I'm not an idiot." Hanging up, I smile at everyone apologetically. "You see? She's only just come back and is already bossing me around – the days ahead are going to be tough."

Manager Zhang brings over the hotpot. "Here, in case you've lost your taste for the Yuanyang, I swapped it. Go right ahead and eat all you like!"

"What can I say, you're a man of honour!" I laugh, sloshing the meat in the white soup. "I haven't eaten properly in days, but now I can finally relax and have a hearty meal."

When I am well fed, and half drowning in wine, I ask a question that has puzzled me for ages. "I've been wondering, when I first came here, running into Qiao Qian straight away, was it by pure chance?"

---

21 Anyi! 安逸! – usually means "at ease, comfortable". In the Sichuanese and other south-western regional languages, it's a colloquialism used to express that one is very satisfied and happy about something.

Granny Yan smiles, and points to the furniture in the restaurant. "Young man, you see this arrangement of the tables and chairs, there's a lot to it. This is a Feng Shui formation, set up by none other than your Granny Yan... especially to draw the living and the dead who miss each other but are separated by the boundaries Yīn and Yáng... and they come, as if it was dictated by fate."

I'm jolted. "This... Granny Yan, what did you set up this formation for?"

The teahouse grandpa sighed. "If it wasn't for me... I... recently I developed a brain tumour and could have dropped dead at any time. So, Shufen, worried that my decrepit old soul would be lost to her, set this up especially, to ensure that we would be able to see each other again."

I ask curiously, "Granny Yan, you clearly have great powers, so why can't you predict which day the old master would leave this world?"

As soon as I say this, I realise how wrong that is, and I want to slap myself – how can you ask anyone what day they are going to die?

Unexpectedly, Granny Yan does not seem to mind at all. "Of course I can! It's the third of lunar June."

I slide my finger over my phone screen, open the lunar calendar app, and see the date. I freeze.

Today is the fourth.

Shuddering, I make myself bend, and look under the table – under the chair on which the teahouse grandpa sits. Where there should be a pair of legs, it is completely empty.

Seeing me checking, he sighs. "That's right, kid, I'm dead."

I do not know what to say, but rack my brain for something to diffuse this awkwardness, when Granny Yan says something that shakes me to my bones.

"Thank you, young man. I didn't even know if this Zímu Pot technique would work, but after you'd tested it for me, I felt pretty confident…"

I begin to get a sinking sensation.

I force out a smile and stand up. "Um, look, you two, my girlfriend is pretty strict, I really should be heading home now."

As I try to take a step, I feel my head spinning.

Granny Yan grins, revealing a large gold tooth. "Young man, this Zimu Pot, was it tasty?"

The teahouse ghost sighs, says, "Sorry", and begins to drift towards me.

I start to yell towards the entrance of the shop: "Manager Zhang, help! Get the general over here, quick!"

But Old Zhang has his back to me and is covering the god statue with its red cloth. He turns, casting a chilling glance at me.

They were all in this together…

Without the protection of the idol, the old man of the teahouse no longer hesitates, and lunges for me.

11

WHO… AM I?

Oh yes, I'm Chuan. Hahaha, from now on, I… am… Chuan.

This young and strong body feels great.

Shufen turns her caring gaze towards me. "How are you doing?"

"Anyi!" I smile, picking up her pipe and taking a long puff. "I've got almost all the memories, too."

Old Zhang comes over, rubbing his hands. "So, the

golden cicada has shed its skin. It worked! From now on, the three of us have an escape plan, and can live like immortals!"

"Right, tidy up, in case anyone spots anything suspicious."

I take out this smartphone thing in my pocket, operating it clumsily. "Let me have a go with that young lass for a while... Shufen, once you've worked out how much time you've got left, I'll bring her back here when you're ready."

"Qian, it's Chuan here. Let's leave Chongqing tomorrow..."

NOTES

FOR THE CHINESE, food culture is immensely important, and I felt it was only right for the collection to feature one story that centres around a meal.

The inspiration for this story came when the author Chuan Ge visited Chongqing with a friend one year during the Spring Festival. The city's famous hotpot left a deep impression on them, as did the local customs they witnessed during the new year festivities. He wanted to create a horror story that combined urban legend, traditional culture and the regional uniqueness of Chongqing. Taking rituals that involve the hotpot meal, Chuan Ge created a myth surrounding the Yuanyang Pot, inventing the terrible taboo for the sake of the story, where truly, the worst thing that could happen is making the white soup pink. Much to his amusement, after the story was published, he found more and more comments from the public stating that this was a true superstition, or repeating it as local lore, or that waiters had physically restrained someone from inviting the curse. This is how urban legends are born.

The blending in of these elements only fuelled the gripping, relentless sense of dread I felt, reading it for the first time. Just when you think the protagonist has escaped hellish plight, the devastating denouement arrives, where, amidst the horror, you actually have some schadenfreude, with him suffering the same fate as he has inflicted on others. Chuan Ge lives up to his self-proclaimed title of 'story gravedigger'. This new generation of horror writers also seem to be voicing an honest sense of exasperation at the emotional blackmailing that Chinese parents widely resort to, often to the complete destruction of their children's individuality, and adult lives. I appreciate the courage entailed to write works that confront certain fears, even if they are caused by socially accepted norms.

Chuan Ge worked as a journalist for some time before making a career change. However, still feeling the need to express himself through words, he turned to fiction writing. He began publishing stories online in his spare time, which were very well received. This encouraged him to continue. He now writes pretty much full time.

Working on this story really made me long for Sichuan hotpot, and I am sure that despite the threats of possession, curses, and ghostly betrothals, many of you will still be hankering to share those thin slices of spicy lamb and fragrant mushrooms with friends. Just be careful of what soup you order.

THE SHAXIAO

山魈

Goodnight, Xiaoqing

HAVE YOU EVER been to Xiaoshan? If not, let me give you a word of advice: never ever set foot in those mountains.

Despite being named 'The Laughing Mountain', it is a vast forest of endless horrors, with huge trees, giant, ancient vines – even the toadstools grow large. This abundance of life, though, leads to its opposite. The plants drip with murderous qi, eight hundred li[22] of garish vitality, suffuse greenish death above your head and beneath your feet, like falling into the rolling dark bile of some monster's stomach.

So many years have passed, yet every time I dream of that forest, I wake from the shock with a body shaking in cold sweat, and swear that in all my remaining years, I shall never go within a hundred li of that place, even though my remaining years number very few.

Ahhh, I have visited Xiaoshan only once in my life, and that was forty... fifty years ago? Back then I was but a naive youth, who did not know how high the sky was, nor how thick the earth. I had read some books, learnt a few basic skills of gongfu, but I fancied myself a rare breed, unequalled as both a scholar and swordsman. Off I rode, on my bony donkey, wishing to roam *jianghu* like those *xiake* of the romances, adventuring, dispensing swashbuckling justice; and surely, there would be dalliances? The women in the

22 Li 里, Chinese term of measurement, roughly equivalent to five hundred metres.

stories were as wildly amorous as they were beautiful, full of legendary airs. When I found her, she would be my love.

The love in the stories had nothing to do with the smoke of the hearth and the grease of the kitchen, nor was it ordinary or mundane. It was ardent, fierce, abiding till death, heart-rending, lung tearing, and so forth. Chanting such poems, I sauntered around aimlessly for over a year. I did not know where all these women of the stories who would die for love had gone, but before entering Xiaoshan, I had not even glimpsed the shadow of one.

The villagers at the foot of the mountain said that there were man-eating monsters in the forests above and tried to persuade me to think reasonably. But back then, none of this could have dismayed me. I pressed on, dragging my donkey, and leaving them with a most

memorable view of my handsome back and shoulders. Monsters? I had been dying to meet one.

I hoped the monster would be holding a maiden in its jaws, and she would be very pretty, and helpless, and on the cusp of death. I would, of course, save her, and this would be how love began. As I trudged through the thorns and brambles, I stroked the scabbard at my waist, impatient to unsheathe my sword.

To this day, I still cannot remember whether I was able to use a single technique of swordplay that day, as by the time the monster really reared its head, the act of hacking a path through the dense mass of worm-green bushes had already blunted and notched my blade.

The books would never have told of such an embarrassing wandering *youxia* like me. As the monster leapt towards me from the steep cliff edge, my instincts were to tumble off my donkey and curl up into a ball, arse in the air.

I had imagined that, before the monster appeared, there

would be a demoniac cloud, or strange drifting mists. But it just crashed down from on high, howling and leaping at me like a great ape. It had no grandeur or style whatsoever. I crawled under the belly of my donkey, despising the intruder. It had not even the decency to wait for me to strike a dramatic counter-stance when I was showered with a stinking downpour of gore.

The poor old donkey had been ripped in two. I was too petrified to even wipe away the donkey guts splattered across my face. Through the nauseating veil of blood, I saw the strange, black-furred beast throw the two halves aside, as he leapt onto an ancient cedar tree, crouching on a fork in its branches, a few dozen feet high. It began to grind its teeth, readying itself to strike again. Its body was dark, and bulkier than a black bear, but its speed and ferocity excelled that of the hunting leopard.

Unfolding two long arms, its claws descended over my head, latching on with ten hooklike fingers. At that point, all time came to a halt, amidst the dense leaves that rippled like thunder and whose lurid green flashed like lightning, I saw the face of an inhuman human, a long, blood-red nose, on either side of which indigo blue skin was stretched over bulging cheeks. Malevolent as a demon... it bared a row of crooked three-inch fangs that flashed like knives as they advanced towards me. I screamed wretchedly, flailing with the long sword swinging about me, in some vague hope of shielding the front of my head.

The black-furred beast launched itself at me. I toppled backwards, falling limp on the ground, watching as the ghoulish face, more horrific in its near humanity, drew nearer and nearer, despite my wildly waving sword... and then it lifted a corner of its lips.

I had never heard such deafening and unnerving laughter.

It sounded entirely human, but no human could have filled their laugh with such malicious insanity. Heaven and earth were all transformed into that giant mouth, pressing in and closing around me.

"There was a beast in the deep mountains, with long arms, a human face, and a furry black body. It likes to laugh when it sees people, it devours flesh, indiscriminate of the source"[23]. I remembered reading that in the books.

I had run into a *shanxiao* – and with that final realisation, I lost the strength to even close my eyes.

Suddenly, a white feather arrow pierced the black clouds like a ray of lightning, fleeting past like the cry of a crane and hitting the *shanxiao* squarely in its hind leg. It flipped its body up high in the air and fell to the ground a dozen feet away from me. With a prowess at odds with its bestial manner, the *shanxiao* seized the arrow and worked it out of its flesh. I thought it would fly into a rage, but the monster limped to one side, turning its head in the direction whence the arrow had come, and struck up its laughing again, louder than before. Its maw stretched so wide, I could almost see its vibrating tonsils. That mass of crimson flesh was twitching, and from it issued a hoarse cacophony that echoed throughout the pass. I was suddenly brought back to the time when, roaming the yellow earth plateaus, I'd happened across a bridal procession of suona[24] players belting out crude tunes of joy as loud as they could, with no regard of key, be it gong, shang, jiao, wei or yu[25], so each added to the great cloud of atonal chaos, shaking heaven

---

23 The Classic of Mountains and Seas 山海经 (Shānhǎi Jīng), China's oldest collection of mythology, which appeared as early as the fourth century BCE.

24 Suona 唢呐, a double-reed woodwind instrument widely used in China since the 14th century. Its shrill and penetrating sound lends itself to ceremonies and processions.

25 Gong, shang, jue, zhi, yu 宫商角微羽, the five notes in the pentatonic wuyin traditional Chinese music.

and earth. This evil, heartless shrieking called out mirth, madness, grief and sorrow.

Flipping onto my belly, I followed the shanxiao's gaze. At the edge of its vision, about a dozen feet beyond the hill, stood a delicate and slender form.

Raven hair fell from under a dark douli[26], her fine form perched atop the green mountains like a black feather, so light that a gust of wind would carry it away. Only the arrowhead in her hand shone with a determined light.

She raised the bow to her chest and knocked a second arrow. The shanxiao began jumping and beating its chest, comical little movements totally at odds with its horrific laugh. This seemed to intimidate the archer, who backed away a few steps, but in a flash, a shadow loomed up behind her.

A giant hairy shadow on all fours – another shanxiao! I wanted to call out a warning, but quickly saw that the beast had no intention of attacking; it came close, butting against her leg, before drawing itself up into a human-like stance. Beating its chest, it began its own mad laugh.

I have heard that sometimes, hunters in the mountains would capture ferocious beasts which, if they could be tamed, would become loyal pets and assistants. There had been plenty of wolves, bears, tigers, leopards and so forth that had been tamed in this manner, so was it so strange for this goddess-like stranger before me to possess a *shanxiao* as her hunting beast?

It was my eighteenth year, and in my youthful eyes, though I could not even see her face clearly, the lady was a goddess. Because she appeared like a figure of legend, because she was so far away and yet I could sense her mysterious and

---

26 Douli 斗笠, a conical hat made of bamboo or palm fiber worn in Asia as a shield against the sun and rain, sometimes worn with a veil over it.

powerful beauty, because to me, her pure black douli looked more dazzling than the rainbow.

The monster almost held me in its jaws, and I was on the cusp of death. She had saved me, and this is how love begins… even if it had varied somewhat from the anticipated plot.

The *shanxiao* by her side began to leap higher and higher, its laughter now sounding like an unbridled challenge, whereas the beast by my side had begun to foam with bloody spittle. I knew that the shot had hit it hard – its blue eyes burned with a phantasmic fire of deep vengeance. It lowered its head, charging forward.

As I understood it, now was the point in the story for the hunting beast to enter the arena. The archer should be ordering her beast into battle, but once again, I was wrong.

The *shanxiao* beside her let out a long howl, and stepped back, rather than forward. Its owner, though, seemed to be under some sort of invisible but strict command, for she sprang up and leapt down the mountain. The veil over her douli swept back, revealing her long, flowing black hair that floated as if dancing. She was like a goddess of war in the books, sweeping over the battlefield, over paths of thorns, with her long, athletic legs, copper breastplate, and the ornamental buttons on her boots… this dazzling vision of beauty drew her bow to the full, aiming at that shanxiao. The arrow whistled as it flew.

If my memory stands, the second arrow burrowed into the shanxiao's abdomen. The girl's archery was God-like, a scourge to any ferocious monster.

But the shanxiao, twice struck, still howled its call. Its laughter, now fading far, now drawing near. As I lost consciousness, that strange laughter continued to ring, murky in its joy or tragedy.

When I awoke, I discovered she had saved me, and taken me home. What? You're laughing at this tired old plot... yes, a lot of books tell this sort of story.

In the books, the mysterious hunter who lives alone in the mountains usually makes their home somewhere shrouded in mystery, such as a cave. My encounter was no exception. I woke up in an unearthly green grotto, with the musky scent of plants wafting in the air, the daylight seeping dimly through the vines that hung from all directions. I felt the walls around me, and found they were not mossy stone, as I assumed, but I was in fact in the heart of an ancient tree that had been hollowed out over many years by the rain and the insects. A natural treehouse. I dared not imagine how large the tree actually was.

It was too damp there, the ice-cold moisture boring into the cracks of my bones. I was very grateful that she had made up a fire next to me. I sat with my hands up to the flames, trying to dry my fingertips, which had become coated with a slippery moss, before I opened my mouth, trying to speak as calmly as I could.

"Thank you for the kindness of saving my life, my lady." I edged a little towards the fire, suppressing the trembling chill that ran through me. "May I have the pleasure of your company by the fire?"

She was sitting on the other side of the cave, very far from the fire, both feet curled up on the stone that served as a stool, crouching like a wild animal. This was really a very inelegant posture, but, assumed by a girl with such a slender waist, and such long legs, revealed beneath her short, leopard-skin skirt, there was even a kind of wild beauty to her – an untamed loveliness, distinct from conventional ideals.

She was the mysterious and primal beauty of legends.

I had found her at last. Her dark wood bow and quiver lay by her feet. Having heard my question, she seemed to shift uneasily. Her feet, wrapped in deerskin, twitched vigorously, knocking her arrows to the floor...

Her glossy brown skin. The powerful muscles undulating in her thighs. I was suddenly aware my mouth and tongue felt hot and parched.

She had kept her head hung low all this time. Her long hair fell over her face, cascading over her hands, with only her glinting chest armour blossoming like a bronze flower on my heart.

"Madam, why do you live here alone? ... Your archery is excellent, the most wonderful I have seen, mythical... Where is that *shanxiao* now? I think your arrows must have finished it off?"

No matter how I coaxed, she would not talk. And then, I had the thought, she might not understand my speech. Perhaps she had lived alone in the mountains all her life, with wild beasts for companions, and never seeing another human... but if that were so, where had the clothes and weapons come from? She really was like an enigma – the more silent she remained, the more enticing she became. It almost felt like an enchantment.

I was considering how I could possibly commune with her, when suddenly, something furry moved across my back, causing me to leap up with shock. The creature shot aside. It was the *shanxiao* she had been keeping.

It jumped up onto the stone bed on which I had been lying, and cosily began to warm itself. It seemed to have been well tamed, losing even the fear of fire commonly shared by wild beasts. Its ugly blue face with the bulbous nose looked down at me over the fire, even gaining an arrogant air as the light illuminated it from below.

Of course, wild beasts do not have such expressions – it must have been an illusion on my part. Plucking up the courage, I held out my hand to play with it, and to my surprise it did not even bare its teeth, only twisted its face and gave a few snorts, as if to express a mild disdain.

"This *shanxiao* is quite adorable, really." I smiled at its owner, but she had already turned her back, and was now facing the wall, the rise and fall of her shoulders showing her to be busy with something. Maybe repairing her bow or her arrows? I gazed at her back and found I could wait no longer.

"My lady, it does not matter if you can understand me or not, I… have fallen in love with you!" I burst out, whilst scrambling towards her, fearing that if I hesitated for a moment, I would lose my courage. Ahhh, such delicate, yet strong shoulders… I felt my head grow dizzy as I stumbled forward, holding out my hand to stroke them.

Abruptly, she spun around and bounded back, a strange scream emanating from her. I felt every drop of blood in my body congeal – that was no human sound!

Exactly as I had imagined, she was stunningly beautiful, with a tanned, almond-shaped face, long lashes, and full and luscious lips… but she had been chewing a piece of raw meat, her mouth now saturated with blood, which had spilled down her chin and stained her chest. She was still clutching a lump of some animal in her hand, and as she nervously edged away, she stuffed it into her mouth, as if she were afraid I would snatch her food away.

Yes, this beautiful maiden had taken to all fours, and was leaping like an ape. She bounded some distance away before she stopped, turned, and began growling, low and viciously at me.

This must be a dream.

"I knew that any man who caught a glimpse of her would be amorous."

This hoarse mocking had come from the shanxiao's mouth. With the way things had been unfolding, I was beyond shocked. It all just felt like a single nightmare. Unsure whether I was acting calmly or numbly, I approached the black-furred beast as it crouched by the fire like an old man, not even bothering to look up at me. It blathered on to itself, in its rough, cackling voice.

"Ahhhh, you are not to blame. When I first saw her twenty years ago, I was the same. I was about your age then, and didn't even know her name, yet still I fell in love with her at first sight. She appeared to me, just as she did today…"

The girl had now finished her meat and slunk back to the entrance to crouch. The deep green of the tree branches offsetting her silhouette and douli, she still looked splendid and beautiful regardless, like a devotional statue of obsidian jade laid over green velvet.

"I came to Xiaoshan on my travels. I was young then, and afraid of nothing. I was making my way through the thicket and saw her pursuing a herd of wild boars. Her archery was outstanding, and those little brutes were struck down one by one. Not one of them could even touch the tip of her robes. The way she looked, holding her bow, I have never been able to forget, even now. So soft and fragile, yet so courageous, the wind blowing her long hair… she was the queen of the forest. Stern and proud in her absolute beauty, making you want to kneel and worship at her feet.

"Stumbling and tripping, I ran towards her. I wanted to ask her name, wanted to tell her I would be hers for the rest of my life, but suddenly, two *shanxiao* leapt out from behind her. You know how terrifying those beasts are. Everything happened so quickly, and I couldn't get there to save her.

"In one moment, she was alive, and in the next... right in front of me, they tore her in two. Such beauty, ripped in half by the monsters!"

Heart-rending rancour rumbled from deep in the shanxiao's throat. I gazed at the woman who had died so tragically twenty years ago, unable to comprehend.

"Wait... so what are you?" I mumbled.

"Oh, I'm a human, of course," said the shanxiao, dismissively, "I was a *shushi*[27]. Whilst I was young, I was also adept in many cultivational techniques. It was just that everything happened so quickly... I had no time to use my skills."

It let its body slump, and exhaled a few low, suppressed moans which, I believed, were the closest it could manage to human sobbing.

"So you killed the *shanxiao* to avenge her?"

"Why kill it? They were a pair of beasts. I captured the female one first, who'd been the actual murderer. And then I employed all the powers I could muster with my knowledge and skill, to perform a little spell on it.

"I transmuted it to look like her." Looking towards the silhouette at the mouth of the grotto, a sinister smile spread across its – or rather, 'his' face.

"It will never be able to change back, and its movements are controlled by me. Whatever I tell it to do, it will do. Have you ever seen a *kuilei*? It's just like a puppet in my hands." He fluttered his furry black claws. "Even if I tell it to loose an arrow into its mate. It makes an excellent archer, doesn't it?"

"The other one, her mate... is it dead?"

"It has taken countless arrows over these twenty years, but it's still alive and well, isn't it? Hahaha, it must be lovely

27 Shushi, see page 37 in Those Who Walk At Night.

to be wounded by your own wife's hand! I put a lot of care into steering the puppet. This is the punishment that murderers deserve, they killed my woman, so... they must pay me back with one!

"Mixing beasts and man... that's breaking the taboo of heaven. The price of wielding this dark magic was that I must take the form of the being I had cast the spell upon, for all eternity. But I can't regret it."

I had never seen such a wicked and unhinged look on any face. The ghostly blue face of the *shanxiao* bore the kind of hatred that could not be found even in hell. The girl sat at the mouth of the cave, staring blankly at the light of the sky beyond the vines, motionless. A bizarre roar seemed to roll in from afar, and then rang out nearer and then further once again. Was it a wail of anguish, or a cry of longing? Yet the *shanxiao* were supposedly beasts that could only make that inhuman laughing call.

Silently, I sat there with them, until the light of the new day was beginning to break, and the mournful hollering had completely subsided.

"The *shanxiao* will not come out at dawn. Leave," he grunted distractedly, "and never come back."

I pushed aside the heavy vines and exited the hollow, the sunlight almost blinding me.

Under the fierce white light, I saw the girl I had left in the dark, her beautiful face wearing a wooden, vacant expression, a tear slowly rolling down her cheek. The vines fell, obscuring her.

"You brute, do not think you can run away! Sparing your life was my will! Death is what a murderer like you deserves, demon! Ahhhh, my goddess, you are so beautiful, I shall kneel at your feet, will you stay with me, always? Yes! Always, for eternity..."

Even when I had walked for an age, I could still hear the hoarse roaring from that rotten tree. The *shushi* wrathfully cursed and reviled his prisoner, again and again, before descending into maniacal ravings. Love… this was a deranged nightmare.

And then, he began to laugh the strange call of the shanxiao, louder and louder, as if it were drawing the very life blood out of him. I will never be able to forget that hysterical, horrible laughter.

It sounded like mad joy.

NOTES

THE TERM "SHĀNXIÀO" refers to two things. In modern culture, this is the term used for the mandrill, the largest of all monkeys that is native only to the rainforests of equatorial Africa.

Shanxiao is also the name of a well-known mountain monster from the Shanhaijing, The Classic of Mountains and Seas, China's oldest compilation of strange creatures, plants and peoples. The creatures in this story, despite sharing many features with the mandrill, are most certainly the mythic monsters, though some of the descriptions may lead to confusion. It is probably safer to think that the modern use of the term is down to these similarities. Goodnight, Xiaoqing's reimagining of this creature certainly captures all these qualities, their strange beauty and mad murderousness, in a tale that blends mad, twisted passion with horror and Xianxia genres.

This piece came about when the editor of *Qihuan World: Flying* sent Goodnight, Xiaoqing an image they were going to use for the cover of an issue and asked her to write an accompanying story. The image featured a young female archer and a shanxiao, lurking in a cave. At the time, the author had been engrossed in the video game World of Warcraft, and the image immediately reminded her of the Hunter Pets in the game. What if the dynamic between hunter and pet were reversed? Seized by this idea, she followed it and wrote the story, even showing it to her guild friends in WoW, knowing full well that it would result in her being griefed on, next time she was online.

Goodnight, Xiaoqing's first foray into creative writing had been purely accidental, back when she was first learning to use the internet. One day, roaming aimlessly around the web, she came across a website called rongshuxia.com (China's first online publishing platform), where she found a whole community who were publishing their writing and exchanging feedback online. For a net newbie, this virtual space had opened up a whole new world for her. She started writing fantasy stories on the site, and received positive and encouraging responses, which convinced her to continue. Through the years, she has formed lasting friendships with kindred spirits within the community, including editors who eventually guided her to become a full-time writer. I have written about how online publishing platforms have removed much of the traditional gatekeeping from the publishing world, providing nurturing environments for potential female writers. It makes my heart swell to hear just such an experience first-hand from a Chinese writer, and hope that there will be many more who follow in her wake, and I will always be glad to bring them to an international audience.

HAVE YOU HEARD OF 'ANCIENT GLORY'?

你知道是古辉楼吗？

Zhou Dedong

1

THE LONELINESS OF APARTMENT 801

AT LAST, WE managed to buy somewhere!

The neighbourhood was located in the western suburbs of V City in Hebei. Block 4, Unit 2, number 801. The day we moved in, my partner and I were both ridiculously excited, and kept grinning at each other. As we walked round and round our new home, we just couldn't get enough of it. It was only 87 square metres, but we had literally walked a few miles in it.

In the early evening, we made chive dumplings together, hiding a lucky coin among them, like it was Chinese New Year, and then we opened two bottles of beer, and drank them with our arms linked.

Oh, yeah. My partner is called Xuanxuan – she is a couple of years older than me, and I cherish her more than anything. I have secretly sworn that in this life, I will do anything to protect what we have together.

That night, we both had great appetites, and polished off the whole batch of dumplings. When I was gathering the dishes to wash up, Xuanxuan suddenly exclaimed,

"Where's that coin?"

The question hit me, too. "Oh yeah."

Xuanxuan asked, "Did you swallow it?"

I grumbled, "Am I that stupid?"

"Are you sure you put it in one of the dumplings?"

"I'm certain," I confirmed.

"Then what happened to it?"

I was puzzled, too, I just couldn't fathom it. I could only say, "Maybe I did eat it…"

"You pillock," Xuanxuan teased.

If a strange thing happens, then a second and a third will follow, which, in itself, is a strange thing.

We took a shower together, and then went to bed and… well, I won't give you the details. Afterwards, Xuanxuan fell fast asleep.

I slid out quietly and went for a smoke on the balcony. I immediately discovered a problem – the entire area was blanketed in darkness, not a single light shining in a single window; everything seemed to have stopped. Only the aircraft warning light shone, blinking on the rooftop like a pair of bloodshot eyes, their eyelids drooping before abruptly twitching open, again and again. Oh, and there were also dim streetlamps, which only lit up the pavements, leaving the wider green areas lost in blackness. I could practically feel the Yin energy waxing, and the Yang waning. The fewer people there are, the more space there is for… other things. Were those streetlamps not lit for the benefit of the living?

I checked my phone: it wasn't even ten o'clock.

Why was there no one in this xiaoqu[28]? Hadn't the estate agent said that most of the flats had been sold? Or was

---

28 Xiaoqu 小区 - prevalent across cities in China, large residential areas with an independent living environment, and facilities such as services, shops and schools.

that just a sales tactic?

The entire neighbourhood was so deserted, it seemed to emanate loneliness. That's when the show started. First, one of the streetlamps below our building flickered a couple of times and went out. A moment later, a new light appeared in the distance; it must have been a lamp on strike, which for some reason, had started its work again.

I stubbed out my cigarette and crept back inside.

In actual fact, our yangtai faces north, hardly catches any sun. This balcony should really be called a "yin"-tai," but our restrictive funds had us trapped in our options.

I returned to the bedroom and lay down gently. The bedroom was also in complete darkness, with only the sound of Xuanxuan's snoring, sounding so clear, and occasional lorries driving past in the distance. With no ambient noise, they both seemed loud and abrupt.

I could not sleep, and my thoughts were firing off like a firework display. There were fifteen floors in this block, seven above us, seven below. I wasn't sure how many apartments there were on each, but I felt as though there was an ear glued to the door of every single one of them, listening with interest to every move that Xuanxuan and I made.

I turned to look at Xuanxuan. She lay on her back, her chin raised high, and her mouth slightly open, her habitual sleeping position.

Then I began to think about this xiaoqu.

I'd seen an advert for it by the motorway – "Just south of Beijing, 31 minutes by car. You could be home for dinner."

At the time, I'd nearly laughed out loud.

I worked in Beijing and was only too familiar with the journey: there was a full 180 miles between V City and the Sixth Ring Road of Beijing. If you drove through that in 31 minutes, your wheels wouldn't even be touching the ground.

There were two possibilities: one, they were basing their calculations on a race car. Or two, they were measuring by the most southerly point still classified as 'Beijing', like Stone Buddha Village in Daxing; if you could drive across the Yongding River, then maybe you could get to Gu'An in Hebei.

The most canny thing was that odd one minute, which made it seem so believable.

But, once a piece of information has been embedded in your brain, it always has some sort of impact, however small, and I made a mental note of the name of this xiaoqu.

I desperately needed a home.

Xuanxuan and I had been at the same university in Beijing, she in the year above me. After graduation, she'd returned to V City and passed the exams for an office job at the Forestry Bureau, while I stayed in Beijing and went into IT. We had been together for nearly three years, we had already registered for a wedding licence, and we were planning to get married on the 9th of September, for the lucky pun on the date, "changchang jiujiu", always and forever. But I wasn't entitled to buy a home in Beijing, and even if I were, I would have to save for fifty years, giving up luxuries like eating or drinking. Xuanxuan's job was secure, so she would never come to Beijing with me anyway. We had agreed, long ago, that we would buy our marital home in V City.

At the weekend, I drove down to V City again, and I mentioned the xiaoqu to Xuanxuan. Compared to the other new builds we'd looked at, it was much cheaper, and if Xuanxuan and I worked hard, we could just about afford it, which was the most important thing.

So, Xuanxuan and I drove to the western suburbs and found this neighbourhood. It had just been built, and the plots across the road were still a wasteland.

In the end, we finally settled on a two-bedroom suite that we liked, and with family from both sides pooling their resources, we managed to pay the deposit. On the 1st of March, we finally got the keys.

The flat was pre-decorated, so all Xuanxuan and I needed to do was run around purchasing the big appliances and such, and very quickly we'd furnished our new home, and moved in.

Everything went so smoothly, but how did I fail to consider the problem of the low number of residents that only these villas seem to have?

Something seemed off with Xuanxuan's snoring – it sounded as if she had a piece of candy in her mouth. I nudged her gently, and she went completely quiet. I closed my eyes for a moment, but I couldn't stop worrying. Sitting up carefully, I peered into her slightly parted lips, and thought I saw something against her tongue. I turned on my phone's torch, and shone it into her mouth, where to my shock, I saw a coin glinting!

My heart froze, while my mind went straight to thoughts of hankou, an ancient burial rite. It was believed that the dead could not carry anything into the next world in their hands, or over the shoulders, but could hold a coin in their mouths, with which they could pay the ferryman to cross the nether river.

Had she actually swallowed this coin, and thrown it back up while she was sleeping?

I was afraid to startle her, in case the coin got stuck in her windpipe, so with great care, I put two fingers into her mouth, seized the coin and whisked it out and onto the floor in one swift movement.

Xuanxuan still woke up, and with an irate voice asked, "What are you doing?"

"That coin was in your mouth, so I got it out," I replied.

As anger turned into confusion, she asked, "Why would it be in my mouth?"

"How should I know?"

She grabbed a tissue and wiped her mouth, muttering, "This place is evil." But then, tilting her head back, she shut her eyes and fell back into sleep.

She started to snore again, but her words had sunk into my heart, soaking through it like drops of ink. I twisted my head to see that the clock on the nightstand said 10:31.

I pulled on my clothes and tiptoed out.

There were four flats on this floor, so I checked each of the other three doors. They all had an identical black doormat in front of them, only we had a red one. Were they cousins that also happened to be neighbours?

I decided to take the lift all the way to the top and check out the floors one by one. I found that in front of every door, there was the same black rug, exactly like the ones of our immediate neighbours. There was only one rug on the twelfth or thirteenth floor which was dark grey, with a few white letters on it, but even that was a dour decoration.

The other thing was that I could smell something burning on every floor.

I walked out of the lobby and went quickly to the main gates of the xiaoqū, where a security guard was standing. He was very short, with a wide chin, and wore a black trainee uniform. He looked like an honest person. He was staring out across the road towards the wasteland, so I went over and asked him, "Excuse me, can you tell me how many people live in this xiaoqu?"

He looked at me sideways and said, "Most people have been moved in."

I turned back and regarded the buildings. The blocks looked like large dark mountains against the night sky. I asked, "How come there's no lights on?"

Without looking round, the guard said casually, "Isn't there a light on the roof?"

"Mate, that's the aviation warning light!" I said.

He didn't argue with me. "Maybe people in this neighbourhood like to be in the dark."

What annoyed me was his lack of attention. I took a step forward to stand right in front of him and stared into his eyes. "Are you serious?"

This guard stared at me quietly for a moment. "Go home and go back to sleep. If your eyes are closed, you won't mind the dark."

For our entire conversation, he had not uttered a single earnest word, yet I somehow felt he knew everything, but didn't want to tell me the truth.

The next day, Xuanxuan woke up first, and elbowed me roughly. Without waiting for me to wake up properly, she asked, "Last night you said that coin was in my mouth, or did I just dream that?"

Speaking on autopilot, I said, "Er, I think you must have been dreaming."

We ate a simple breakfast and went down to the car park. The huge lot was empty, with only my car parked there, but there were plants growing in the flower beds, and it looked lovely. Driving out of the car park, I looked up at all the buildings, and found another major peculiarity – every single window had the curtains pulled shut. My suspicions rose again, but I didn't say anything to Xuanxuan. It had been so hard for us to buy somewhere, I didn't want her to feel despondent.

So, I drove Xuanxuan to the door of her danwei, before going back to Beijing.

As she got out of the car, she mentioned, "It's nearly the Qingming holidays, how many days off have you got?"

"Three, I think," I answered.

"OK, till then, I think I'll go back to stay with my mum for a few days."

"Why?"

"I had a lot of nightmares last night. I dreamt there was someone lying in each of the flats in our building, and every single one of them had a coin in their mouths – it was terrifying."

"Alright then, sure."

On the day of Qingming, I drove down to V City from Beijing, picked up Xuanxuan from her family home, and together, we returned to our new home in the western suburbs.

It was precisely on this day that the curtains over the secret were torn open with a 'whoosh'. As soon as we approached the xiaoqu, we found that the place had become full of life all of a sudden. Lots of cars were parked outside, and observing them closely, I saw that nearly all of them had Beijing licence plates.

I drove slowly into the xiaoqu, and saw groups of people, in twos and threes. Nearly all of them were wearing white clothes, many of them holding bunches of yellow chrysanthemums. Even with the car windows rolled up, the smell of burning incense attacked my nostrils, as if I'd walked into the city temple. So much white paper money had been scattered across the road, it looked like it had just snowed.

Lost for words, Xuanxuan looked at me, and I glanced

back at her, equally stupefied.

In that instant, we understood the whole thing. These people hadn't bought the properties here for themselves, but to house the ashes of their dead relatives.

Everything was on fire. The filament of the sun burnt out, and the world plunged into darkness.

This is how the news reported it:

ZHANG BOUGHT A property in X City, Hebei, in preparation for his forthcoming marriage, but found there was something strange about this particular xiaoqu. He could not see a single soul during the day, nor a light on during the night. On the day of Qingming, however, things suddenly livened up, as flocks of Beijingers drove over for jìbài, the rituals of commemorating the dead. It turns out that with cemeteries in Beijing becoming prohibitively expensive, many people had bought flats here instead, to safely store their loved one's ashes. A similar situation has occurred in Shanghai. Burial grounds have become too expensive in First Tier cities, rising to the rate of tens of thousands of RMB per square metre, whilst in neighbouring cities, this amount of money could buy an apartment. The rights to a cemetery plot are limited to twenty years, whilst the leasehold for an apartment is seventy. Moreover, should a cemetery plot be reclaimed by the government, there is no reimbursement, but the relocation of homes is at least backed by some compensation. Therefore, this has created the societal abnormality of the yinzhai, or Ghost Apartment. Some estate agencies are even putting out semi-concealed campaigns such as – "find your lost loved ones a good home…"

Yes, that "Zhang" in the news? That was me.

2
WHAT THE ESTATE AGENT SAID.

AFTER I HAD read this news on the internet, I travelled to V City especially, to interview Xiao Zhang[29].

By "I", I mean the fictional 'Mr Zhou', but also, me.

Guhui Lou, does this name not sound a little strange? The word I refer to means "Ancient Glory", but it is a code name I have given it which implies a different homonymous word, meaning "ashes of the dead". For the same reason, I have said 'V' and 'X' City. If I had used the area's real name, there would certainly have been trouble with lawsuits.

Maybe I was a ham-fisted driver, but it took me a good three hours to get from Beijing to V City. Around three o'clock in the afternoon, I met with Xiao Zhang at a café. Xuanxuan did not appear. This place was only a 'café' as far as its name. It was still selling bowls of beef noodles, which we ordered, and which were brought to us, steaming hot. Xiao Zhang and I sank into a booth, and slowly got chatting.

Xiao Zhang was an orphan. Brought up by his grandfather, he longed passionately for a home of his own. To this end, he had poured almost everything he had into the purchase, never expecting to fall into a graveyard.

After he had finished recounting his experience of buying the property, he took out the promotional advert from Ancient Glory Apartments at the time, his deposit receipt, buyer's contract, proof of mortgage from the bank,

---

29 Xiao Zhang – "xiao", meaning little, or young, is an affectionate prefix referring to a young person, or someone junior to oneself in age.

and a bundle of photos he had taken on the day of Qingming Festival.

He told me that in the past six months, he had been negotiating with the estate agent, hoping to cancel his purchase. And having gone through all these torments, Xuanxuan had developed depression, and had already resigned from the Forestry Bureau.

He then told me about the situation with the family's elderly from both sides, especially his grandfather, who is now over seventy, but who still goes out daily to clear sewers for people, putting all the money from his hard work into this property for his grandson.

"Did the estate agent agree to the cancellation?" I asked Xiao Zhang.

He shook his head.

"Then what do you plan to do?"

"Well, go to court."

Upon hearing this, I could not help but feel half a chill in my heart for him. If he took them to court, his wedding with Xuanxuan would be changchang jiujiu", always and forever. Always and forever out of their reach.

After the interview, as I was about to leave, Xiao Zhang looked at me with a most pleading expression, and said, "Zhou laoshi[30], I'm much obliged to you!"

The problems he had gone through had already knocked him into a state of misery, his complexion waxy and sallow, his eyes dazed and lacking focus. He was clearly in a lamentable predicament, and hoped that in writing about this incident, I could bring it to many eyes, and the property developers would be forced to return his deposit or face public disgrace.

---

30 Laoshi 老师 – meaning "teacher", often used to refer to someone one defers to, or as a term of respect.

I held his gaze and nodded solemnly.

After that, I drove out to the western suburbs, and found the Ancient Glory Apartments. This neighbourhood was ringed by white walls that looked a little higher than normal, and the sunlight that shone on them took on a harsh quality. On the wasteland across the road grew a few slanted and gnarled trees, on one of which I spotted a big bird's nest that resembled a basket, definitely a penthouse apartment. Next to it was a smaller bird's nest, positioned lower – it seemed quite humble. That was the hierarchy for you, among the bird species.

It was really very quiet around here; I circled the neighbourhood once, and only passed one trike making its 'put-put' sound.

Usually, the front gates of these xiaoqu have electric gates, but here, there were a pair of large black ironwork doors, tightly closed and solidly fastened. At the entrance was a security guard, short, with a wide chin.

I had just pulled up when he extended an arm to block my way. "Who are you looking for?"

I rolled the window down and said to him, "Would it be OK to come in and see what the neighbourhood is like?"

He immediately shook his head.

So I turned the car around and went straight to the sales office of Ancient Glory. This kind of place is always open, and usually can't wait to get a body in through the door. There were seven or eight customers inside the office, most of whom were middle-aged, and the salespeople were attending to them individually.

I went to take a look at the architectural model near the window. This neighbourhood was much bigger than I had imagined. Looking at the whole plot from this elevation, the groups of buildings seemed to make up the character

奠, dian, as in settling the dead. A salesgirl approached me. She was about twenty-seven or so, and bucktoothed. Before she opened her mouth, I intercepted her spiel: "I'm here to see manager Liu."

Xiao Zhang had told me that the person in charge here was called Liu Aocai.

The salesgirl said straight away, "Oh, then please follow me."

She led me to a very narrow office, where a man of around thirty years of age stood up at once from his computer. He was wearing a set of navy-blue workman's clothes, had a side parting in his hair, and a pair of quick little eyes. He said, piling on the smiles, "Sir, how can I help you?"

"I'd like to purchase an apartment, but I wanted to talk to you in person," I replied.

Liu Aocai purred, "Not a problem, please sit down."

If you wanted to find out if someone was a pusher, you should present yourself as an addict. Of course, this analogy was not entirely appropriate.

The salesgirl left the room, and I sat down on the sofa. Liu Aocai poured me tea, and asked, "Have you come out from Beijing?"

I nodded. "My mother passed away, and I wanted to find a place to put her to rest."

Liu Aocai became silent all of a sudden.

His guarded silence at once made me realise I had strayed into a taboo area. The secret of Ancient Glory must have been an unspoken rule that no real buyer would be this obvious about.

I pressed on anyway: "Isn't that why people come to buy from your neighbourhood?"

His eyeballs slid sideways, and very cautiously, he replied,

"All we guarantee is to provide you with the best housing – as for how you use it, we don't have the right to know."

I decided I would lay my cards on the table. "Are you acquainted with Zhang Jili?"

Xiao Zhang's proper name was Zhang Jili, the word for "Lucky".

Liu Aocai seemed to have figured something out. He sighed dramatically, and then answered, "You're from the media, aren't you?" Before waiting for me to reply, he added, "There's nothing wrong with our neighbourhood, the problem is with him."

I narrowed my eyes and waited for him to continue.

He carried on, "His girlfriend died, which was a great trauma to him..."

My ears rang. Xiao Zhang's worn face appeared in my mind's eye, his eyes appearing to have severed their communications with his brain, and kept flitting back and forth, unable to focus. And then I remembered a detail he had mentioned – when she was sleeping, his girlfriend had held a coin in her mouth...My belief switched to Liu Aocai now.

Liu Aocai continued, "He bought a suite from our office, put his girlfriend's ashes in there, and keeps it company all the time. He thinks that she's still alive, and every weekend he hurries back from Beijing to 'spend time' with her, good god."

It was an age before I could speak again. "How did you know?"

"What do you mean, how did I know?"

"How did you know he had bought the apartment for storing her ashes?"

"He put two people on the registry, but the neighbours have only ever seen him come and go. Always him, never his girlfriend. During Qingming, his neighbours smelled burning coming from his flat, and thought it was a fire, so rang the superintendent's office. The super went to knock on his door, and Zhang said the flat wasn't warm enough, his girlfriend was complaining it was too cold, and he was lighting a fire to help her warm up. The caretaker looked past him through the gap at the door, and what he saw gave him goosebumps – there was a large altar table in the living room, on which stood the yixiang, the mourning portrait of a girl, with an urn positioned below it. There were even four incense sticks, and a very large copper basin on the floor, in which paper money was burning. The whole flat was filled with smoke."

"How did his girlfriend die?" I asked.

"Wang Xuan? Car accident, I think; I don't know the details," Liu Aocai answered.

I asked another question: "Then why has he been shouting 'catch the thief' all over the internet?"

"Perhaps in his subconscious, he believes it's normal for him and his girlfriend to be the only people in the entire neighbourhood, and that no one else exists."

I had come to X City to investigate and experience a phenomenon of social horror, but I had never expected it to turn out to be such a sorrowful tragedy.

After leaving the sales office, I rang the Forestry Bureau of V City, to confirm the information about Wang Xuan. Sure enough, the people from the bureau told me that Wang Xuan had been one of their employees, but had passed away after a car accident a year earlier.

I hung up, leaned back into the car seat, and thought about it from the beginning to the end.

In actual fact, no formal media entity had reported on the so-called inside workings of Ancient Glory. From the very start it had been Xiao Zhang who had exposed the incident on the internet, and was reposted by a 'Blue Tick', which was why the case had garnered a lot of attention, including mine. And then, very quickly, for unknown reasons, that celebrity account deleted their repost.

I was reluctant to walk away, and sent Xiao Zhang a WeChat message: Xiao Zhang, I'd like to have a look at the apartment you bought, is that okay?

He replied, but seemed a little guarded: What do you want to see?

I wrote: I'd like to take a few photos, to post with the article.

He replied, but not immediately: It's pointless photographing my place, you should take some of the other flats.

I did not push any further: Can we meet up again then?

Sure.

This time I'd like to meet your girlfriend, can she come along?

No problem.

WE MET AGAIN at the same café; the time was 21:30.

I had eaten a couple of donkey meat huoshao buns at a stall, and drunk some lamb broth, before heading to the café. It was well past dinner time, and with no one ordering beef noodles, the air in the café became fresh and clear.

Lucky Zhang arrived on time, but alone. After sitting down, he ordered a pot of tea, and then softly poured two cups. Feigning nonchalance, I asked him, "So where's your girlfriend?"

He seemed unfazed, and merely said, "She's got some

things to take care of, but she'll be here by 10:30."

An hour later.

Suddenly, I did not know what to say to him.

The two of us sat there in silence for a while. Eventually, he asked, "Did you have any other questions?"

So I asked, "How is your girlfriend's condition?"

Xiao Zhang replied, "She is unhappy all the time, and doesn't even leave the flat."

After a pause, I asked another question: "What kind of a person is she?"

At once, a happy smile blossomed on Xiao Zhang's face. "If there was one word I could use to describe her, that would be – accommodating."

"What does that mean?"

"She doesn't argue or cause drama, doesn't nag... she's a serene person."

The word "serene" struck a nerve in me.

Evidently, Xiao Zhang had noticed I'd become quiet, so he continued the conversation. "I met her during the second year of university, at the time our department was organising a party. We both volunteered, and she asked me to look after the cloakroom, but I ended up drinking with a classmate and got blind drunk. A few days later, I bumped into her in the sportsground, and she asked me, "Do you have weixin at all?" I said, well, I'm on WeChat, I'll add you there, but she just turned away immediately and stomped off. I realised that she had been interrogating me. She wasn't referring to the social media platform, but weixin, as in 'sense of trustworthiness'."

Xiao Zhang was immersed in his memories, and while he was, I could not help but check the time: it was way past 22:30.

I reminded him: "Is she still coming over?"

Xiao Zhang had a look at his phone. "Let me check with her."

I stared at his phone screen. He really did send somebody a message, and after a while, he picked up his phone, took a look and said, "Really sorry, she'll be here a little later."

"How much later?" I asked.

Xiao Zhang replied, "Around 11:30." And then he added: "She always does everything slowly and without hurry."

Right. Another hour passed. My instincts were telling me that I was probably not going to see this "Xuanxuan".

Apart from the two of us, the café was empty. Even the wait staff seemed to have disappeared into the back room.

Xiao Zhang seemed worried that I might lose my patience, so asked me, "So what's life like for writers like you?"

"Like this, really," I replied. "Occasionally going out for an interview, but most of the time writing at home."

"What will happen when this article is published?"

I shook my head. "It's hard to say."

He sighed softly. "Looks like the fish dies when the net is torn. I'll have to go down with them."

I was not sure why I blurted out, "Do you really have to move out?"

Xiao Zhang gazed at me with a strange expression, as if I had suddenly turned on him, and then he lowered his voice. "There's not one person in the entire neighbourhood, and a cremation casket in every room. If it were you, would you not be scared?"

These words, coming from someone who had placed an urn in his own home, sounded especially sinister. So, I changed the subject, and began chatting to him about

Beijing, but he did not seem inclined to talk, growing increasingly distracted.

At last, the waitress appeared, hovering a few feet away. "Gentlemen, we need to start closing up at half past eleven, I'm sorry," she said apologetically.

Xiao Zhang checked his phone, and grumbled, "Why isn't she here yet?" and then went to settle the bill, saying to me, "Let's go and wait outside."

It was mainly clothing and shoe shops on that street, which were all closed, and only the streetlamps were lit. As I walked out with him, he pointed to the entrance of a hutong, saying, "Let's go there for a smoke."

"Why do we need to go in there?" I asked.

"Her family home's just on the other side, so she'll definitely come through there."

Hesitantly, I went to the entrance of the small alley with him, casting a look inside; everything was murky and dark. I felt the situation was getting stranger and stranger. We lit our cigarettes separately, leant against the wall, and began to smoke. I could no longer see his face.

It was like this for a long time. He did not talk, nor did I.

It grew close to midnight, and I became more and more anxious. Just as I was planning on leaving, he suddenly checked his phone, and shouted, "Fuck!"

"What is it?" I asked him pressingly.

"She's been hit by a car on the way here…"

And then he no longer bothered with me. Turning to go, he shouted back, "Sorry, Zhou Laoshi, I have to get over there immediately."

Just like that, without even a goodbye, he dashed urgently into the depths of the pitch-dark hutong and disappeared.

A car accident, just like the man from the sales office had said.

3
HOW IT WENT IN THE WORLD
OF LUCKY ZHANG.

ON WEDNESDAY AFTERNOON, Lucky Zhang requested time off from his lingdao, and drove back to V City.

In the morning, Xuanxuan had called him, saying she was too frightened to stay in the suite at Ancient Glory alone, and just could not sleep. Xuanxuan was not a woman who employed girly wiles, and unless she really could not help it, she would not disrupt Zhang Jili while he was at work.

On his way back to the xiaoqu, Zhang Jili had made a detour to the florist to buy some white periwinkles and put them on the back seat.

By the time he had driven his car through the gates, the skies were already getting dark.

He took the lift up, entered the code, and opened the door to his home. It was in complete darkness, and he called out softly, "Xuanxuan?"

From the blackness came Xuanxuan's voice: "You're back?"

He said, "Mm." He had to feel the wall for the light switch before he could see Xuanxuan sitting on the sofa, the curtains tightly shut. He asked, "Why don't you switch on the light?"

"We're the only window in the whole xiaoqu with the light on, it's too conspicuous," Xuanxuan replied.

Zhang Jili did not want to continue the conversation, so he held up the bouquet of periwinkles. "For you, darling."

Xuanxuan walked over, took the flowers and smelled them. Happiness reclaimed her face, and she said, softly, "Love you."

Zhang Jili reached into his bag and pulled out a large stack of red bank notes, gently laying them on the table. "Love me times two."

Xuanxuan was a little confused. "Your salary? Who pays in cash these days?"

"This is hongbao from the lingdao," Zhang Jili replied proudly.

Xuanxuan put down the flowers, picked up the wad of money, counted it and shoved it into the coffee table drawer.

Lucky Zhang reached into his bag again and pulled out four thick incense sticks. Xuanxuan burst out, "What did you get these for?"

Zhang whispered, "There are boxes of dead people's ashes all over the building, so we need to light some incense to ward off any spirits." Lighting them as he spoke, he placed them on the candle holders on the table.

Through the winding smoke, Xuanxuan's face seemed pallid. She had not slept well for the past few days.

Once he'd finished busying himself, Zhang Jili sat down on the sofa and held Xuanxuan, saying with deliberate casualness, "So, have you taken a walk around and got to know the neighbourhood over the last few days?"

"No. I'm not going out. This is the only place that smells like ours. This is the only place that feels like home."

"Let's be patient. Didn't that writer Zhou come over a few days ago? I've told him everything about our situation. He'll make more people aware of Ancient Glory's dirty secret. Tomorrow, I'm going to the sales office to speak to them again."

When the two of them lay down for the night, the whole world became dead silent.

A night light glowed in the bedroom, but through the door, the living room was velvet black, the bunch of white periwinkles decorating the table in quiet bloom. The four incense sticks burnt silently, their embers glowing and flickering, somehow mimicking the aviation warning lights outside. In the drawer of the table, the pile of banknotes, now free from their long journey and compression, started to curl up slightly at the corners…

Zhang pricked up his ears, alertly listening for any movement in the building, but there was only Xuanxuan's snoring. He turned softly and looked at her, lying on her back as usual, with her chin high and her mouth slightly open.

Lucky Zhang closed his eyes. Without trying, his breathing began to match that of Xuanxuan's. He realised that hers was very slow, and while he followed it for a while, he felt a little suffocated, and opened his mouth to gasp a few mouthfuls of air.

The next morning, Xuanxuan slept on, so Zhang Jili went downstairs by himself, and drove to the sales office, which had just opened for the day.

Two other cars with Beijing licence plates appeared at the door.

He did not go in, but squatted down by the door, lit a cigarette, and smoked while he waited.

About half an hour later, an old grey BMW approached, which Zhang Jili recognised as Manager Liu's car.

Manager Liu was all too familiar with Zhang Jili, and after parking his car, he got out, and with a smile, waved at Lucky Zhang. "Xiao Zhang! Here so early?"

Zhang Jili stubbed out his cigarette immediately and stood up. "I've come again about my apartment."

Manager Liu walked over, patting his shoulders sympathetically, and said, "Your circumstances are very unusual. We have reported it to the group, and we are all waiting to hear back."

Lucky Zhang was not buying this. "It's not me that's unusual, it's this neighbourhood that you developed. On the last two visits you asked me to wait. Do I have to keep on waiting seventy years till my leasehold runs out?"

"There has to be a procedure, isn't that right? How much authority do you think I've got?"

"I bought the property from your hands, so I can only look to you."

Manager Liu looked back helplessly. "Does this neighbourhood not have a mortgage licence? Is there a problem with the quality of the flat? Are there any discrepancies with the size? Has the planning been altered? Did we not deliver the property on time?" After this string of rhetorical questions, he patted Lucky Zhang's shoulders again. "Young man, we need to be reasonable."

And with that, he began to walk away.

Lucky Zhang said loudly, "I don't want to cancel the mortgage now. I have already informed all the major media outlets. I'll let the whole country know about the inner workings of this xiaoqu. You just wait for your stinking reputation to spread!"

Manager Liu stopped in his tracks, turned to look at Lucky Zhang, and retraced his steps.

Warily, Zhang Jili stepped back.

Manager Liu said smoothly, "Don't get so fired up, there are ways to resolve this."

Zhang Jili was not inclined to trust him. "What ways?"

"Why do so many people come from Beijing to buy property? This kind of apartment doesn't suit your needs, but meets theirs. So what you have to do, is remortgage the property to them."

"But how do I find buyers?"

"I happen to have a client from Beijing – his mother passed away last week, he is in urgent need of a two bedroom, you could have a chat."

Lucky Zhang felt as though he had grabbed hold of the rope to a lifeboat. "So can you please help me get in touch?"

Manager Liu was highly efficient. The Beijinger drove over that same afternoon, and, seeing Zhang Jili's apartment, said it would be perfect for his mother, and closed the deal right there, even paying the deposit in cash. After that, under the arrangement of the property developer, the two parties signed the contract, agreeing that the remainder of the payment would be made in a lump sum, one month later.

The dark and oppressive days had at last brightened up for Lucky Zhang and Xuanxuan.

The new owner gave Lucky Zhang one day to move out.

Zhang Jili hired a moving company straight away, taking all the furniture temporarily to Xuanxuan's parents' house. At dusk, he paid a final visit to Ancient Glory. There was only some tableware left in the flat, but since it was a cherished set, he was worried the movers might break it, so decided to transport it in his own car.

After he drove into the xiaoqū, he found that the street lighting did not turn on, and the place remained dark and eerie. He was just about to call maintenance, but remembered that he was no longer a resident, and put his phone away. It made sense. The only people who were actually living there had been he and Xuanxuan, so now that management knew that they had sold their flat, they did not even bother switching the lighting on.

He switched on his high beams and drove on like he was in some abandoned village.

In fact, he had only lived in the neighbourhood for a few nights and was far from familiar with the place. Between that and the poor visibility, he drove round and round for far too long, trying to find block number four. After parking the car, he got out and raised his head to look up at the balcony of his former home. There was no sign of anyone there.

He wasn't sure what kind of psychology had motivated him to switch on the torch to check his car, but he found that he had parked across two spaces. He got back in to nudge it, got out for another look, and well, now it was parked straight and square. And then, he had another strange thought. If he could drive whilst lying on his stomach on the roof of the car, he would be able to see everything, and would never get a parking fine...

He walked quickly to the rear entrance of the building, took the lift to floor eight, entered his code, and walked in, but just as he closed the door, something made him freeze.

There, hanging in the dark, was a strange smell. A bit like very old rouge. He sniffed, and then reached out to switch on the light. He looked round, and saw their vacated flat, already emptied, although there was something left behind in the middle of the living room – placed neatly, aligned square with the centre of the room, was an urn.

His heart lurched.

The new owner had been desperately eager, moving the

ashes in already.

After a few seconds, he walked over slowly, and squatted down in front of the box. It was a casket made of black jade, so large it almost resembled a small coffin. The lid was inlaid with a colour photograph, and the woman it showed was not particularly old, perhaps around sixty, so perhaps it had been taken a few years before her death.

Thinking about it, he came to understand the other party better. He had been in such a hurry to buy, in order to find somewhere to store this reliquary, because he could not keep the ashes in his home. It would frighten his wife and children...

No matter what, Zhang Jili no longer had anything to do with this flat anymore. Right now, he just wanted to get his tableware, and leave.

He stood, bowed towards the casket, and then went to the kitchen.

Just as he was packing the last of the cutlery, he heard the sudden sound of coughing from the living room. The clatter of colliding plates and bowls had been so prominent, though, he could not be sure if it was something he had imagined, so he stopped still, and focused on listening.

He waited for three minutes, without a single noise from around the flat. Just as he was about to resume, there came another cough from the living room. This time he had heard it, clear and sharp. His whole body prickled with goosebumps.

He slowly straightened up, and shuffled step by step towards the kitchen door. There was a figure standing in the middle of the living room – the old woman from the photo was on the casket! Her face was devoid of expression, but her eyes were piercing, and they were looking straight at Zhang.

He nearly fainted.

He threw himself back against the kitchen wall in a flash, not daring to move a muscle. The old woman did not follow him in, but Lucky Zhang could not see what she was doing. After the longest time, he slid out his phone with trembling hands, and sent Xuanxuan a WeChat: A casket has appeared in the flat. The old woman from the photo has come out. Call the police.

And then, he put his phone on silent.

He had no idea how much time had passed before he could venture out to look back into the living room, but the old woman had gone.

He shook his head hard – had that been a hallucination?

He picked up the heaviest serving plate to use as a weapon, and slowly made his way out of the kitchen. The living room was now completely empty, and he cast an automatic glance at the urn. The photograph was gone! He walked quickly to the door and turned the handle, but it was locked, from the outside!

At that moment, another cough came from behind him. He spun round and saw the old woman standing in the doorway of the bedroom, staring at him, her eyes gleaming brightly.

Zhang stared into her face, realising he had no way to escape. Despite the utter strangeness of the encounter in this apartment, he opened his mouth. "Hello..."

The old woman did not answer, but began to move towards him, step by step, stooping slightly and focusing on the plate in his hands, alarm spreading across her face. Then she spoke, with a surprisingly airy voice, "Careful now, don't break it."

Zhang Jili was shaking all over. "Why are you here?"

But the old woman's eyes were firmly focused on the

plate in his hand, as if she knew how to speak only the one sentence, repeating, "Careful now, don't break it."

The old woman came closer and closer. Zhang pressed himself tightly against the wall. "What are you going to do?"

The old woman was still staring at the plate, slowly holding out her arms, as if reaching out for something, repeating and repeating, "Careful now, don't break it."

Lucky Zhang knew she was coming for him. He dropped the plate and ran straight towards the balcony door, which strangely, was wide open. Zhang did not have the time to ponder why it was open, just that in his panic, it was his only escape route.

He reached the balcony, and kept going to the edge, and leapt. At last, he managed to get away...

Had he not straightened his car, he would have fallen on the hard tarmac, but now, his fall was broken as he landed squarely on his stomach, across the roof of his car.

Luckily, the plate had not broken.

4

THE NOVEL AS DEPOSITION

THINKING BACK, THE night of Xiao Zhang's accident, I had been drinking with a dancing girl in a bar in Tongzhou, with all kinds of unspeakably wicked thoughts in my head, and totally unaware of what had happened in X City, "31 minutes" drive south of Beijing.

A few days later, I sent a WeChat message to Xiao Zhang, asking about the situation, but he did not reply. I rang him, but his phone was off. I went back to his Weibo and sent him a couple of private messages.

Unexpectedly, he replied, saying: Something has happened, please come.

I got in the car and drove down at once. At the appointed time, I arrived at that café.

It was the afternoon, and the café was filled with steam from the beef noodles. I had just sat down, when a girl came towards me. "Are you Zhou Laoshi?"

I looked at her, and asked, "And you are…?"

She sat down facing me, and replied, "I'm Zhang Jili's girlfriend, my name is Xuanxuan."

I felt like I was watching a suspense drama – the constant plot twists were making my head spin. Frankly speaking, Xuanxuan was not well-matched with Xiao Zhang, looks-wise. Xuanxuan looked older than her age, but Xiao Zhang was a shuaige. Then I said something very stupid. "You… really exist?"

"Why wouldn't I exist?" she snapped.

"I rang your office at the Forestry Bureau, they said you had passed away. Is your name Wang Xuan?"

"My name is Han Yaxuan. Wang Xuan was my colleague, who did pass away in a car accident. Why did you think I was Wang Xuan?"

It seemed I had underestimated Liu Aocai, who had dosed me with a bowl of mihuntang, that brain-wiping soup.

I repeated what Liu Aocai had told me, and hatred burst out of Xuanxuan. "They're all liars, and they killed my boyfriend."

I felt my heart could not take any more of this. "Xiao Zhang? Is dead?"

Xuanxuan closed her eyes, squeezing them shut, as if steeling herself. At this very moment the serving staff came over. "Would you like anything else?"

I waved them away impatiently, and then asked Xuanxuan, "What on earth happened?"

Xuanxuan began telling me. That night, she had been staying with her parents, and Lucky Zhang had gone to fetch the last of their things. Not long after he had gone, Xuanxuan suddenly received his WeChat...

Xuanxuan showed me that message, the last two words of which were "Cuddle please", which she later realised had to be an autocorrect, because Zhang Jili must have been terrified when he was trying to type "Call the police".

After receiving the WeChat message, Xuanxuan had rung Zhang, but there was no answer. She'd taken a taxi to Ancient Glory, and quickly found her boyfriend lying face down on the roof of his car, stone dead, before she could even call the police.

This means that the story in chapter three was true, and not just Lucky Zhang's imagination.

As for what exactly happened when he went to fetch the tableware, nobody knows – those descriptions were merely my own musings.

Throughout this case, there have been several coincidences that have confused matters. The first day that Lucky Zhang and Xuanxuan moved into their new flat, they did indeed put a coin in their dumplings, and when Xuanxuan fell asleep, the coin did somehow turn up in her mouth; Liu Aocai claimed that Xuanxuan had died in a car accident, and on the day that I asked to see her, she really had run into a motor trike, but it was only a scratch; when Zhang Jili returned to X City to spend time with Xuanxuan, he had indeed bought the white flowers, incense, and the huge pile of bank notes he had just been rewarded with, and these objects had somehow been seen as the paraphernalia of funeral rituals.

"What did the police say?" I asked Xuanxuan.

"They're still investigating. I told them the murderer was the estate developer, but they say there was only an old woman in the flat at the time. She was the mother of the new owner, and already over sixty years old. She was tidying the place for her son, and gave a statement that my boyfriend came in, acting like he was possessed. He dashed towards the balcony and then jumped. It nearly gave her a heart attack. The police have inspected the crime scene, and found no signs of any struggle, so for now, they can't even confirm it was a murder. They need to find more evidence."

"You'd already sold the flat," I pointed out. "If this was all the schemes of the developers, what would be their motive?"

"It's all a scam. The day after Zhang was killed, the buyer raised a request to cancel the purchase, then I saw a clause in the contract – if the buyer discovers that the property was a xiongzhai, a place where a suicide or murder has taken place, then the agreement can be terminated, and the seller must return the deposit. When we signed the contract, we didn't think much of this, since the property was a new build, so of course no one had died in it. We never thought that after signing the contract, they would push my boyfriend to his death from it."

Considering it from this viewpoint, this clause did indeed seem too suspicious.

I tried to sound sensible. "Then let's wait for the result of the investigation – the police should be able to find the truth."

"I have already returned the deposit to the buyer, and the

apartment is mine again. I put my boyfriend's urn in there. From today onwards, this apartment is his resting place."

When she got to this point in her story, Xuanxuan's face turned grim. "I will pursue them through the courts to the bitter end, and I won't rest until I bring this company down, even if I am dead."

I felt a little sorry for this waif of a girl. "Xiao Zhang told me that you've become depressed, so why don't you rest and recover? You can pick this up when you've recuperated."

Xuanxuan laughed mirthlessly. "When your life has become an endless string of tragedies, you don't know what it's like to suffer depression. It's just how you feel all the time."

Looking out of the window, I noticed the sun was already heading west, and I had to return to Beijing.

After some thought, I said to Xuanxuan, "I will write your experiences into a story, and try to get it published on Zhihu."

She looked at me blankly, as if she did not see any silver lining in my words.

I added, "If you really do go to court with them, you can use this story as your preparatory statement. There might be no precedent for this, but it could move the hearts of the jury, and impress the judge. No matter what, I believe that you and Zhang Jili were telling the truth."

She looked at me for a moment, and her eyes grew wet with tears.

I recognised those tears – they were the tears of the vulnerable and the oppressed.

NOTES

"HAVE YOU HEARD of Ancient Glory?" is a prime example of China's social horror, which has really grown over the last decade, both in film and in literature. Throughout much of the 20th century, war and political conflicts have made real life horrific enough for those living in China, and it's only in this era of relative stability that the social issues symptomatic of a developing nation and a burgeoning consumerist society are surfacing in China, leading to some utterly bizarre stories, not only in literature, but also in the daily news. Abductions, ingredient tampering, and all kinds of abuses of power are regularly reported. The prevalence of social media and smartphones has removed the distance between these very often regional problems and provided the ordinary citizen with a voice.

The author, Zhou Dedong, was inspired to write this story after reading about real life events reported in the news around 2019, where a legal loophole was being exploited, to use cheap apartments in failing complexes on the outskirts of big cities like Beijing and Shanghai to house the remains of the dead. I had already written about China's changing burial customs, due to a mixture of ecological awareness and skyrocketing land prices, but reading this story made me realise quite how unique a situation this is in China, simultaneously wanting to house your departed relatives somewhere fitting where they can be visited often, but absolutely not wishing to have the remains in your own home. In the past, wealthy families may have had an ancestral altar or shrine separate from their living quarters, and even till quite recently, certain government officials and military heroes had ashes stored in large reliquaries, where family members could visit, and occasionally retrieve the casket of ashes to perform ceremonial offerings. It has always been seen as culturally inappropriate to have the ashes of even one's closest family or loved ones in your home. This comes from an ingrained belief in an afterlife, and a reverential fear of the dead, who would only bother the living if angered. The living do not mix, or interfere, with the spaces of the dead, outside set culturally appropriate times, such as Qingming. Hopefully, this insight gives a little more understanding of the heightened state of all concerned in this story. This creeping threat may not bring the traditional thrills of a haunted village, nor the jump scares of a gorefest, but these kinds of stories have their firm place in Chinese horror, with the slow dismantling of prospects, homes, and sanity.

Zhou Dedong began his writing career in the 1990s and had been considered one of the country's best essayists, before moving into fictional works of horror in the 2000s. I had known Zhou's work for a while, and perhaps it is because he was used to people contacting him with strange and unusual requests, that he responded so quickly. I was delighted to be able to get in touch, and for him to be so open to the idea of a horror anthology, where others were reticent.

Zhou is known for his more traditional novels of psychological, paranormal and historical mystery horror, but the dynamism of his style and subject matter can still be found in his shorter fiction, where he plays more with ideas of ecology, the impact of technology on privacy, as well as more genre-normal subjects from extra-terrestrial life to extreme dystopian nightmares. "Ancient Glory" combines fiction with reportage, presenting a shattered mirror of events from which the horrific truth is finally pieced together. It was first published on zhihu.com, a Chinese Q&A website similar to Quora, which added further to its 'Found Footage' feeling. In the original text, that is what the journalist promised to do. Now that the story has been translated and published internationally, we thought it only fair that he lay claim to that as his intention.

RECORDS OF XIANGXI

怪九心之湘西注子

Nanpai Sanshu

PROLOGUE

WHEN MY GRANDFATHER spoke to me of the past, he would always avoid the heavy subjects and tend towards the light. It was just like any ordinary family, when the seniors tell you stories – what they impart is one version, and the chatter of those around them forms another. The truth can only be determined by weaving the two together. I still remember that, after Grandfather's passing, and during the mourning arrangements, Grandmother was sometimes calm, and sometimes overwhelmed by grief. During the night vigils, in a broken fashion, she told her grandchildren much. However, the things that Grandmother said, what Grandfather wrote in his notes, and the stories he told us throughout his life, varied greatly.

I could say that they were different, but it was rather the way my grandmother told it that made The Nine Gates appear more human, and not like the characters in the huaben novels. Most of what came out of Grandfather's mouth were stories of how The Nine Gates defied the world, how they were founded in their youth, how Zhang Qishan and February Red first met, and unveiled the golden age of the Changsha Nine Gates, how Old Six came to Hunan, how Number Four became a disciple of February Red, and how Fifth Master Old Dog Wu and Ninth Master once led the clan. In his heart, Grandfather had hoped that The Nine Gates he knew would remain the household legend of Changsha, instead of turning into a bunch of exhausted and obligated parties just muddling through the torrents of the time.

I began to understand The Nine Gates. Because of reasons stated above, there were at first segments, rather than whole stories. These segments being relatively independent of each other, we had no immediate way of piecing together what had happened between them, but from the fine and broken fragments of the past, I began the long process of trying to do so, and over time, the atmosphere of The Nine Gates era swept through me like a current. I could not help but feel the leap in my heart and the yearning in my spirits. Doubtless, it was a time overflowing with Romanticism, a time when desires ran deep, and a time when one had no choice.

Human beings are such that, in any era, if they could face their fate with Romanticism, then no matter the outcome, they should consider themselves fortunate. I hope that you, too, can experience all that I have felt.

1

THE EIGHTY-TWO STRONGHOLD

THE RELATIONSHIP BETWEEN Zhang Qishan and The Eighty-Two Stronghold began with that of February Red and the chief tusi. In that year, February Red had gone underground among the Miao villages, to avoid assassination attempts. After a chance meeting with Iron Mouth Qi, they were both captured by the chief tusi, and forced to be part of the burial procession for her son, who had just died prematurely. The village's hufa had already made preparations for a coup against their superior. After entering the Ghost Valley, the accompanying guards would kill the Han footmen, gouge out both of the chief tusi's eyes before dragging her into the depths of the Valley of the Dead, cut her corpse into pieces, and return to the entourage with the story that her child had risen to claim her life.

The chief tusi's world had turned to ashes, but none of the villains knew that among the coffin bearers were the Second and Eighth Masters of the Changsha Nine Gates. By a reed pond, February Red quickly put down the traitors among the attendants and brought the chief tusi safely back to the zhai fortress. The chief tusi had already developed feelings for him, but alas, Second Master had just lost his wife, and could hardly bring himself to reciprocate. Their relationship was thus interrupted, and once the moment had passed, it could never be found again. Later, with the aid of February Red, Yixin brought Buddha Zhang into hiding in the Miao villages, thus beginning the entanglement between Zhang Qishan and Eighty-Two Stronghold.

These are the stories of generations past, recounted fleetingly. The Battle of Changsha dyed the River Xiang red, most members of The Nine Gates had perished in the fight. The Japanese army forced Old Dog Wu to send his beloved dogs into fields of landmines to clear them, which Wu used as an opportunity to lure the enemy soldiers in. He had resigned himself to die in this act of revenge, never expecting that the pack he had raised would all leap onto him in unison in the instant before the series of explosions, saving his life.

As for Zhang Qishan, he had followed the Japanese army, during a battle, into the mountains, and continued to fight them alongside the Eighty-Two Stronghold. At the time, Hunan had already become the core region for the War for Resistance, with a long battlefront, rendering the historical environment and geographical location of this story exceptionally unique. This all happened in the brief months of calm between two major campaigns and involved almost all of Hunan.

Three or four zhai villages out of the Eighty-Two Stronghold were under the jurisdiction of the chief tusi. Even though this extended across more than a dozen mountains, it was still just a small part of the entire Eighty-Two Stronghold, which was run by seven tusi chiefs, with thirty-six jisi under them... a complicated system.

At the time, the fight was ceaseless, with Japanese spies infiltrating the region on many occasions to carry out 'disintegration initiatives', hoping to gain the support of a section of the people in the stronghold, in order to sever the intelligence and supply networks that spread like capillaries throughout Hunan. The key figure in this struggle was an old man whose real name I am unable to use here, so I shall call him the Touling of the Eighty-Two Stronghold. The title he held was of extremely high status in Miao Mythology, and even though he did not take care of the actual affairs of the Stronghold, he possessed supreme authority.

In order to gain his support, it was said that Zhang Qishan and this Touling spent three days in a secret chamber, negotiating. During this time, they reached an agreement, and after making this pact, Zhang led his troops into the mountains, where they stayed for over two months.

Later legends say that Zhang Qishan himself held this title, having completed some great task in the mountains, for which he gained the complete support of the Eighty-Two Stronghold. Nobody knew for sure quite what the terms of this agreement were.

The story was so submerged in the magnificent Republican legends of The Nine Gates, that no one really knew how important it was, or that it was one of the key pieces in the puzzle that is the history of The Nine Gates.

Here are the few known details.

Before Zhang Qishan set off into the mountains, the Touling was practically blind. Because there was no record of his age, no one knew exactly how old he was, but many had said that they had never seen anyone as old as the Touling of the Stronghold.

The stranger thing was, this Head did not sleep. Each night, he would sit facing the deep mountains, and gaze at them with sightless eyes until sunrise. Year after year, nobody had seen him sleep. People interpreted his behaviour as an act of patience. He seemed to have been waiting for someone to come out of the mountains all along, and was said to have been performing this vigil for over half a century.

Combined with the fact that Zhang Qishan's mission took him into those mountains, the two parts seemed connected. Did the Touling feel he was reaching the end of his life, and wanted Zhang to help him find something in the mountains?

As I investigated the matter, events seemed to take a further turn.

After Zhang Qishan came back from the mountains, the old man shut himself away, while Zhang sent his people to stand guard outside his door. Rumours spread among the villagers that Zhang was attempting to usurp power. The children in the village, who were extremely naughty, and never submitted to discipline, went to spy on them. Crowding around the guards one night, some of them snuck round to the window, where they saw no lights whatsoever in the Touling's room. Relying solely on the light of the moon, they saw a giant mound of earth piled in the middle of the room, in which something was moving. The colour of the soil showed that it was not from the village or its surroundings. It had a peculiar kind of greenish-grey hue. The locals called it Qiqiao Linglong Tu, Enlightened and Exquisite Earth.

The Miao have legends about the Earth Maidens. It was said that these women lived in the earth, only emerging from time to time, appearing as stark-naked corpses. They seduced travelling merchants that passed by, dragging them into the earth, eating their flesh and drinking their blood. There are records in Xiangxi of decomposing female corpses washed up in landslides, with scraps of human bone and fingernails found in their stomachs. These were recorded as unfortunate village women who were killed in natural disasters, but others say these were Earth Maidens crushed to death by falling stones and collapsing mountain faces.

Rumours began spreading around the village that the Touling was hiding an Earth Maiden in his room. A month later, when he finally emerged from that room, the pile of earth had disappeared. And Zhang Qishan was henceforth considered an honoured guest.

What exactly did Zhang do for the Touling? What was

in the mountains? And where had the earth come from?

Inspired by an event recorded in the Xiangxi county journals, I went on to uncover more of the truth.

2

CORPSE SWITCHING HERB

THE COUNTY RECORDERS who wrote these Xiangxi journals were mischievous. Many traders and visitors crossed paths here, bringing news from everywhere they had been, so they collected it all in the journals, providing some very entertaining reading.

In a group of zhai villages along the Xi River, on the border with Burma, there was a secret herb found in the village of Ten Holes, called the Huanshicao, Corpse Switching Herb. There were two varieties of this herb, one with horizontal roots, and one with vertical. Consuming it within the first three months of pregnancy could change the baby's gender. Ten Holes was a very mysterious village which hardly communicated with outsiders, and near-kin marriages brought problems. In the past, they traded this herb for a living. The Huanshicao was relatively rare, could only be picked in the deep mountains, and must be processed by cabalistic herbalists, who passed their skills down only to women, and not men. The local population's ratio of men and women was almost exactly one to one, and seemed to prove the efficacy of this herb.

Later, it was said that this frighteningly balanced ratio had come about because of a horrific "hoax", where the herb was used as a local convention to hide behind. When the ratio dropped out of balance, to maintain the myth of the herb, the locals would drown babies in wine, to establish the new balance of the sexes.

The hoax was uncovered by an official's attempt to get to the bottom of "two lost years". The official discovered that the age gaps between children in the households of Ten Hole was highly unusual. Many families had offspring who were born three or four years apart, but the locals did not use any contraception. Theoretically, the age gaps between their children would be much smaller. The official surmised that between the youngest and eldest children of these families, there must have been another child who had gone missing, and in the case of some families, perhaps even two.

Where did these missing children go? According to the official's research, the village shaman would have drowned them in shaojiu, as soon as they were born. It was believed that those who were drowned in shaojiu suffered less pain.

Whether it was the cruel practice of infanticide, or magical medicine, no real evidence could be found either way, so no definite conclusion has been recorded, even to this day.

What is certain is that no bodies of any drowned children were ever found in Ten Hole. According to the rumours, children's corpses were taken into the deep mountains, where they were put into the care of the Shan Niangniang, the mountain goddess.

This Shan Niangniang was a deity who shared considerable similarities with the Earth Maidens of Xiangxi. Again, she lived within the earth.

Another entry in the journals recounted another story. In the deep mountains beyond the Eighty-Two Stronghold, there were bandits who threw the bodies of the people they had killed into a sinkhole, where the corpses piled up high. Later, they were pursued by officials tasked with ending their reign and jumped into the sinkhole to evade capture. They found that the corpses they had previously tossed in were nowhere to be seen, with only portions of white bone protruding slightly from the earth. They seemed to have all been dragged into the ground, where all the blood and meat had been sucked clean off. They realised that this was the lair of an Earth Maiden. Amidst the peppering of bones lay an infant girl on the verge of death, reeking of wine. They rescued the child, at first thinking she was an Earth Maiden in infant form, who would eat them when she grew up, so they planned to sell her in the city when she matured. They never expected the girl to become more and more adorable, or that they would grow more and more attached to her. When she reached adulthood, the girl was an exceptional beauty. She became 'The Blossom Bandit', famous across the region. Having inherited all the skills of her adoptive fathers combined, she was cruel beyond compare, cutting down victims like hemp, but still acting so innocent and carefree.

The bandits later deduced that this girl must have been one of the child corpses thrown into the mountains. Maybe there were some travellers from Ten Holes who had come here trading Huanshicao and found themselves needing to enact their cruel balance on the road. The girl happened to be exceptionally fit, with good lungs, and so had not quite perished from being drowned in the shaojiu. This may also be the reason she now had an excellent tolerance to alcohol.

When the girl grew up, she naturally wanted to find her real parents, so with a band of twelve other bandits in tow, she came to Ten Holes, but for some undisclosed reason, slaughtered every single villager and razed the place to the ground. It is not known what the girl had discovered in Ten Holes that had induced her to commit such extreme acts.

Later, the girl came to Xiangxi, and formed her troops around the thirteen bandit leaders. They fought and carved out a territory of eighty-two zhai villages. This was the origin of the Eighty-Two Stronghold. These events took place over six hundred years ago.

These thirteen bandits were the original thirteen tusi of Eighty-Two Stronghold. Its structure changed many times over the years through the infighting and annexation, but the girl herself did not have any descendants. This left the descendants of the twelve to rule, all the way down to the Touling of this generation, the last descendant of the original twelve. Because of the relative stability of the Stronghold, their whole history had been recorded in full.

Aside from this story, there were several facts, which were related to the whole matter.

Firstly, where the Earth Maidens had been found, was also where the Corpse Switching Herb grew. Secondly, the leaders of Eighty-Two Stronghold, who had passed down their hereditary titles for generation after generation, all venerated something within the mountains. This mysterious place, and the female infant of unknown origin from six hundred years ago, were also all connected.

3

GOD HUNTING

IT WAS SUMMER when I visited the location of the Eighty-

Two Stronghold, and Xiangxi was oppressively hot and humid. The entity of the Stronghold had long disappeared, along with the tusi, but the villages among that dense chain of mountains remained.

I sought out many scholars of local customs; some of whom were even writing papers or books on Xiangxi-related subjects, but none of them had looked at the history of the Eighty-Two Stronghold. During its time, it had been an intensely guarded secret among the Miao people. However, when I carried out interviews with centenarians, I discovered that some of these elderly people still remembered such people in the village. Later, I altered

course, and researched the areas of religion and mythology, and discovered that a large part of Eighty-Two Stronghold was within the jurisdiction of Guizhou. The region was much larger than I had thought.

There was a distinct legend about the part in Guizhou, and the leaders of the so-called 'black villages', which secretly venerated monsters in the mountains, and in doing so were able to extend their lifespans. Yet, every time they solicited the mountain god's blessing, the leaders must offer up something from their own body. Usually it was eyes, fingers, or a piece of flesh.

When February Red escorted the chief tusi into the Valley of the Dead in Xiangxi, it may have been for such a ceremony, to offer up the deceased child to the mountain god. A child counts as a piece of flesh, indicating that this legend potentially had a widespread, cross-regional foundation.

Was the mysterious entity that the Head of the Eighty-Two Stronghold seemed to worship, in fact, Shanshen, the mountain god? What was the bargain between them?

And what offerings did the Head give Zhang Qishan with which to enter the mountains? What did he bring back in return?

Collating all the background information, I pinpointed a story from my grandfather's "Graverobber's Notes". In fact, it was the one I had loved most when I was little, which my yeye usually told me in the form of a fable. The protagonist of this story, Ye Fuda, was a military official. Because so many details from this story were eerily similar to what I had discovered in my own investigations into the Eighty-Two Stronghold, I had long suspected that this story had something to do with Zhang Qishan.

It wasn't until later that my friend Chunk pointed out to me that it was not "ye fu da", but "da fo ye", meaning Big Buddha, which had been Zhang's nickname. It was then that I came to the realisation that these were almost certainly the same story.

In this story, the chief tusi of the Miao villages, in reality the Touling, had hoped that Ye Fuda would bring a child into the mountains, and offer it to the Shanshen, in exchange for fifty years of safety for his villages.

There is another local legend. Six hundred years ago, a mysterious young woman came to the zhai villages, where she fell in love. She was not, in fact, human, and once she reached the age of forty, she began to change, so she decided to leave the village. Before she went away, she demanded that every year, everyone who had been part of her life provide her a piece of human flesh, to allow her to keep living on in the mountains. If they failed to do this, she would come to hunt the villagers. At the same time, she promised that if she received her tribute each year, she would grant the rulers of the villages a longer life. According to historical records, there were chiefs that resisted, and during those years, almost all the newborn infants were taken by some monster. In the end, people grew so scared they no longer dared mention the matter.

Six hundred years later, Zhang Qishan would have heard this legend when he was in hiding. The specifics of how he came across it are unknown. One could only deduce that he would have heard it directly from the Touling, as they described how terrifying Shanshen was. Judging by Zhang Qishan's personality, he would not have believed this kind of people-eating-mountain-god story, and would have dismissed it as a kind of blind belief in the antiquated. I made a bold assumption as to what happened, and Zhang Qishan agreed, that he would 'deliver this offering' in exchange for the longevity of the Touling, but must have also thought it was time to challenge the rule of the mountain god.

So Zhang Qishan led his men into the mountains, to hunt this Shanshen down.

For a born rebel like me, who thought that rules were there to be broken, this kind of god-hunting story about Big Buddha Zhang brought me the greatest of pleasures.

What boldness. When I was little, I often used to play at riding into the mountains to hunt a god. It also taught me to think that there was nothing in the world that could not be challenged.

Having expended all this ink to clearly plot the course of this dragon, I shall now faithfully record the entire story of Buddha Zhang's hunt for the gods. Every time he told it, yeye would take around two hours, not too long, nor too short, all the fantastical details affording the younger me the rarest of bedtime stories. Though if

I had known how real they were, I may never have slept.

4

INTO THE MOUNTAINS

THE MEN THAT Zhang Qishan had brought into the mountains were the elite troops. His family army, every single one sharing his name, dressed in sharp uniforms, toting submachine guns, and German-made pistols. They had two horses to every rider as, whilst mules may have been better on the mountains, mules could only carry weight. When it came to the hunt, they would need a horse's ability to charge.

There used to be some official roads built through the Xiangxi mountains, but through countless battles, they had long disappeared, so the Touling set them off on the right track himself. At this time, still unaware of Zhang Qishan's god-hunting intentions, he handed him the baby.

"This is a child from the village," the Touling said to him. "I'm too old, and I offered up my eyes long ago. After these years of war and strife, I can no longer find the path that leads towards Shanshen. If you can complete this task for me, I will grant you your request."

Zhang Qishan looked at the child, a boy with the deep-set facial features particular to the locals, who was sure to become a heroic Miao warrior when he grew up.

Behind them stood the boy's parents, the father's eyes full of enforced apathy. For the men in Eighty-Two Stronghold, too many people had died over those years, whether it was in disorderly fights among warlords, power struggles between tusi, or for the Resistance. The mother, though, was unable to suppress the pain in her heart, and could not stop her bitter tears.

Nodding a farewell, Zhang Qishan set off with his thirty men, heading into the mountains. Leading from the villages to the foothills was a small dirt path, usually used by trappers, down which they had to travel for a week, before reaching the truly deep mountains.

The captain of Zhang's guard, Zhang Xiaoyu, felt awkward carrying the baby. The accompanying entourage followed for a few miles before they fell back, until eventually we could no longer see them. Xiaoyu asked Zhang Qishan, "It seems rash to put such an important matter into the hands of outsiders like us. Do you think the Eighty-Two Stronghold really trusts us?"

"I've asked around. Those who venture into the mountains never return. Whenever an envoy goes to perform the offering, only the Touling returns. So, clearly the child isn't the only offering," Zhang Qishan said. "This time, we've pushed the Touling too hard. I guess he's sending us into the mouth of Shanshen and doesn't expect us to return."

"Ha, what the hell? How can we let them pull this on us?" Xiaoyu mused. "Relations between us and the Eighty-Two have always been good. How come they're going for the kill all of a sudden?"

"The environment has grown too harsh, especially recently. The good and evil in men's hearts, what's right and wrong, changes drastically with what's going on around them. The Touling bears tremendous responsibilities towards the people of the stronghold. In their sense of good and evil, we're expendable." Looking at the primaeval forest ahead of them, Zhang Qishan could already make out two towering and wild-looking mountains, the canyon between them bearing the name

"The Gate of the Black Skies".

Within the canyon, there would be no clear paths, the routes would wind in complex patterns, and only the best of warriors could hunt there.

Beyond that, there would be more beasts roaming wild, and even that was still not the territory of the Shanshen. Xiaoyu made a hand sign, signalling the guards to be on extreme alert.

Xiaoyu patted the baby strapped to his back. The child was alive, but had been plied into a heavy sleep. When he woke up and found he'd been separated from his mum, he would probably bawl his lungs out, drawing whatever monsters, ghosts and demons there happened to be straight to them. "I've been thinking…"

Zhang Xiaoyu continued in a low voice, "Chief, what do you think this mountain god is?"

"Just treat it as prey," Zhang Qishan replied. "In all these years, have you ever seen anything more ferocious than us?"

A quiet, trembling voice replied from behind Zhang Qishan: "Buddha, 'know your enemy as well as yourself, and win every war'. You mustn't underestimate these things. They say it's lived for over six hundred years – during all that time there must have been fierce hunters wanting to bring it down before, but none succeeded. Whatever it is, it's stood the test of time, and probably learned the lessons of history."

"I fucking hate things that don't know when to die." Zhang Qishan turned his head, just in time to see Iron Mouth Qi shrinking back into line, gripping his Nambu 14 firmly in both hands.

"Take care that the Bastard Box doesn't misfire and hurt someone," said Zhang Xiaoyu.

Iron Mouth Qi chuckled, stuffing his pistol back into its holster. "Don't you worry, I made a forecast before we set off. Shocks, but no dangers on this campaign. There'll even be a romance. Who knows, maybe when we get back to the villages, one of those nice Miao women will show her appreciation, and the Qi family will have an heir."

"Did you know that to marry into a Miao family, you need to lie on a bamboo bed, whilst all the women from your betrothed's side of the family get to pinch you with their nails, until you're black and blue all over? That's so all the hardships their daughter will suffer with you will be punished in advance," said Zhang Xiaoyu.

"Oh no, no, no. My little Miao girl will take pity on me, and we'll run away together to Changsha." Iron Mouth Qi pushed his glasses up and surveyed the surrounding terrain. "This Xiangxi area is covered in corpse-preserving earth. Buddha, do you think that this Shanshen would turn out to be an old corpse in some ancient tomb in the valley, who just looks fresh due to the minerals in the Linglong Soil?"

Looking around him, Zhang Qishan did not reply. The fēngshui of these mountains was cryptic and changeable. Depending on the angle of viewing, there were three or four ways of reading it, all different in contradictory ways. It was akin to witchcraft. No wonder there were so many strange stories to come out of Xiangxi.

They continued to press ahead. In short, seven days after crossing the Gate of Black Skies, the troop had already reached the jungle. Their horses were intelligent, and would trot ahead by themselves, actively finding the clearest routes. It was only when they got to places with denser shrubbery that they came to a stop and waited for the soldiers to open up the path.

During one such clearance, the trailbreakers dashed back, reporting the sounds of flies swarming ahead of them. Zhang Qishan spurred his horse on to push through the last few feet of undergrowth, and, entering a gully beyond, saw a hunter's corpse, which had been skinned and strung up low on a vine. Above, the jungle canopy was so dense that the foliage blocked out the skies.

The man had been dead for six or seven days, and flies were already taking their fill, swarming so thickly that they covered the entire body. Even though it had been strung up from the vine, the corpse had its head buried in the ground. However, the spot where the head was buried had a patch of earth which looked very different from the soil around it.

5

THE CORPSE

ZHANG XIAOYU WAS about to dismount when Zhang Qishan stopped him, pointing to the ground. In a situation like this, the danger may very well come from the ground itself, and at least on horseback, one would have some buffer. Craning his neck, Zhang Qishan nudged his horse to head towards the corpse.

The brush was high, and the horse made its way uncomfortably forward; unable to advance in a straight line, it searched for openings. As Zhang Qishan rode around the corpse, approaching it in a spiralling fashion, startled flies began to leave the feast. He gestured to one of the soldiers, who cut a branch about the length of a person and threw it to him.

With the branch, Zhang pushed away the soil around the head of the corpse, and found no skin or flesh left whatsoever, just a perfectly clean skull with a large hole in the back.

"All the brains have been sucked out," Zhang Qishan called over. "Mr Qi, what have we got?"

"The Book of Inner Sea North of the Shanhaijing: there the Taoquan lives. Green, and resembling a dog, it devours people from the head. The Qiongqi is shaped like a tiger, with wings, and also devours people from the head first. Qiongqi lives north of the Taoquan. Some say that the Qiongqi eats people from the feet," Iron Mouth Qi said. "It says in the Classic of Mountains and Seas, that both the Taoquan and the Qiongqi eat people from the head first."

Zhang Qishan turned from him, revealing a snippet of his Qiongqi tattoo. "You're saying that my pet ate it."

"It might have been the Taoquan," said Iron Mouth Qi sheepishly, hiding himself behind Zhang Xiaoyu.

Zhang Qishan cut the vine with one swing of his sabre, letting the corpse drop to the ground. Iron Mouth Qi continued, "There's also a monster from Liaozhai. I only know that it's shaped like a wild dog and sucks out people's brains."

"Why is only the skin gone? Does it only eat skin, and not the meat?" Zhang Qishan mused.

"Often the skin is taken for wearing, rather than eating," Iron Mouth Qi pointed out. "We need to be careful. What we're hunting might be wearing human skin to look like a person."

"Maybe it's your fiancé," Xiaoyu teased, smiling. "Please Master Qi, you shouldn't be too picky, she is a mountain god after all..."

All this was still a long way away from the area the Touling had told them about. Zhang Qishan thought it odd to find scenes of the Shanshen so far down the mountain, unless so many years of fighting and disruption had drawn the mountain god out of hiding, bringing them down to hunt nearer the villages.

While he was considering this, a splash of liquid fell on his face. He looked up and saw blood dripping from above. Following the trail, he found that all the branches overhead were splattered with blood, a trail crossing over the vines. Clearly, the corpse had been dragged along by something in the canopy and lowered to its final resting spot.

Zhang Qishan tracked the blood trail and followed it forwards, waving to draw the others' attention to it. He was puzzled. One moment, the corpse seemed to have been attacked by some creature in the ground, the next, assaulted by something in the canopy. Why would these two trails strangely lead to the same body?

"Get me some of that soil." Iron Mouth Qi gestured to Xiaoyu. "It doesn't look like it's from around here. After that, we'll continue on."

Before they had gone a hundred steps, Zhang Qishan stopped again.

In front of him hung another corpse, skinned and teeming with flies.

But this thing did not look human. Approaching it slowly, Zhang found that it was not a big cat, or an ape, either. He had never seen a creature like it. It seemed to have two arms, but its body just continued on.

He threw a glance at Iron Mouth Qi, whose face also showed his astonishment. Slowly, he approached Zhang

Qishan, who was leaning forward on his horse, his face tense and heavy. This was a monster.

Gazing at the corpse, Iron Mouth Qi said, with less than absolute confidence, "If I'm not mistaken, Buddha, this is an Erfu. It's a kind of snake."

"It has a human face."

"This thing is very malignant, eats people's brains, and lives underground. The corpse we came upon before was probably its prey. But how come…" Iron Mouth Qi was puzzled. "…How come it's dead, too?"

6
THE BAIT

ZHANG QISHAN TURNED to Iron Mouth Qi, grimacing. "What? Can you say that again?"

"Buddha, this is a monster. An Erfu. It's a snake with arms and a human face, which eats brains. That dead hunter was its prey, so if it's dead too, then there must be an even stronger monster somewhere in the mountains," said Iron Mouth Qi.

Zhang Qishan beckoned him over. "Come here."

Iron Mouth Qi saw the unfriendly expression on Zhang Qishan's face and shook his head. "No, I don't want to."

Zhang Qishan threw a look at Xiaoyu, who nodded back, then slapped the hindquarters of Qi's horse. It dutifully trotted forwards, bringing its rider to Zhang Qishan's side, no matter how he tried to rein it back.

Zhang gave him a superior smile, and, sighing, Iron Mouth Qi put his hand over his nose and mouth, leaning in to inspect the corpse of the Erfu, twisting his neck back as much as he could. Suddenly, he realised why Zhang

Qishan had asked him to come closer.

This was not the corpse of an Erfu, but a human torso, somehow attached to the body of an immense snake.

Iron Mouth Qi gave Zhang Qishan an embarrassed smile, and then, darkening, he feigned confusion. "But why do this? What is gained by joining a human corpse with a snake's?"

They were now significantly far from the villages. Was it the – Tuzhu?

There were many different populations in this region, including indigenous peoples who had remained isolated. The Tuzhu tribes were odd: some of them were quite developed, whilst others were practically primitive, living almost as slaves, with their clothes made of hemp.

When the German visitors had tried to study them, they found that some of the tribes had a custom of hunting heads, and that each tribe had their own unique religious ceremonies. Putting these corpses together was obviously a work of some skill, and the Tuzhu were a very suitable explanation.

Zhang Qishan observed the corpse quietly, but did not vocalise any conclusions. Spurring his horse on, he signalled to the party. The well-trained troops dismounted, and speedily concealed the horses. Bullets were loaded, bayonets were fixed at the ready. Zhang Qishan addressed his men: "This thing is a killer. We don't know what it is, but it's naughty, and likes to play with the corpses. The most savage people I've seen in this world, who mess with the dead, treated them like they were alive. This thing does not."

Iron Mouth Qi instantly understood Zhang Qishan's words, turning to look at the corpse-made 'Erfu'. This murderous thing played with corpses as if they were inanimate clay. In other words, this thing did not possess any worldly humanity.

The whole team pulled on camouflage doupeng cloaks made of leaves, concealing themselves almost entirely against the jungle. Zhang Xiaoyu whispered, "This is still pretty far from our destination, so we can't stop here for too long. When night falls, we'll carry out a carpet search."

"Will we find it?" Iron Mouth Qi asked.

"That thing is nearby." Zhang Qishan looked into the jungle that surrounded them, the air moist and heavy, a thin fog floating everywhere. A little sunlight came through, but the jungle seemed to swallow it up. "It won't stray far from its toys, so it's probably watching us right now."

Iron Mouth Li said, almost to reassure himself, "Even when there are so many of us? Even tigers would run away. Besides, there's always you, chief. What sort of thing would dare stalk you?"

Iron Mouth Qi looked up at Zhang Qishan, whose blood seemed so active within his body, and who exuded such strong qi that even the miasma parted around him, like a layer of clarity hanging around his body.

Zhang Qishan gazed back at Iron Mouth Qi, and said in contemplation, "What you said makes sense, so let's change the strategy a little. Xiaoyu, let's set Master Qi here apart from the team tonight, as bait. We'll follow from behind."

Iron Mouth Qi's eyes bulged out of his head. "Buddha, you're toying with human life?"

Zhang Qishan said, "Don't you worry – 'shocks, but no danger', you said. You've done the forecast." The whole team started to snigger, as Iron Mouth Qi pulled out his coins and began to make another forecast. Zhang Qishan said to Zhang Xiaoyu, "Xiaoyu, prep that thing so our

Bagua master can set out soon."

"What thing?" Iron Mouth Qi asked, and was shocked as Zhang Xiaoyu brought over the child, and dropped it into his arms, teasing him. "The Zhang's secret weapon, a mystic tool for battle, you'll love it. Buddha, this child—"

"This child barely cries. He's going to be unstoppable in the future, so take good care of him." Zhang Qishan played with the child's face, before noticing the child's attention drawn to the trees above them. A feeling of alarm was born in Zhang Qishan, who stared up into the leaves, but there was nothing there.

7
THE CRYING

IRON MOUTH QI had a chainmail-like vest buckled over him, onto which clusters of grenades were strapped.

The night was deep, and the jungle filled with the hooting of owls and the chirruping of all kinds of bugs. The humidity grew heavier, and almost everyone was soaked through. The mosquitos were not too bothersome – few mosquitos bothered the Zhang family.

Watching Zhang Xiaoyu fiddle with his helmet, Iron Mouth Qi pleaded, "Don't you think Buddha is picking on me?"

"There must be a reason why Buddha is doing this – he would never rashly put you in danger, so he must be totally confident."

"If he were absolutely sure, then I wouldn't need the grenades. There's about a dozen corn cobs in my bag, can you swap out the grenades for those?"

"Buddha said, if the monster drags you away into the

brush, it would probably be too hard to rescue you, but if you pull the pins, you'll be remembered by the Eighty-Two Stronghold for your efforts."

"Now I understand what Buddha was absolutely sure about."

"Buddha said you made the predictions yourself, so you would face it with an open heart. I'm putting the cords for the grenades in your hands."

"I shan't pull it, I shall shout for help until the last moment, and then scream in agony, so that Zhang Qishan will regret it for the rest of his life."

"We'll all feel remorse, rest assured, Mr Qi." Xiaoyu jammed the helmet on and handed Iron Mouth Qi a storm lantern. The lantern hung from a special rod inserted into the vest; it was suspended high over Iron Mouth Qi's head, so they would not lose him in the dark.

The rest of the entourage withdrew into the darkness, until suddenly, Iron Mouth Qi could see none of them, as if he were alone in the jungle.

"You'll all feel guilty! Guilty! You'll meet the devil lying!" Iron Mouth Qi calmed down and resigned himself to the situation. This was it. Indeed, just as Zhang Qishan had said, he was totally confident in his own divination, he thought, beginning to swagger through the trees. As he walked, he hummed, "Buddha Zhang treats lives like weeds, he's got no conscience... I wielded the steel whip; I struck him with it... but I could not beat him."

Iron Mouth Qi sang his lament as a Shaoxing Opera, the heavy southern accent of which he hoped would be hard for the northerners to understand. Having walked for half an hour, he had encountered... nothing. So he went round and round in circles. As he walked, he began to feel fear, because there was not even a whisper of movement from behind him. He began imagining things. Was he lost? Maybe there had never been a group of soldiers behind him with a bunch of machine guns.

"Buddha, if yōu're with me, can you give me a sign?" Iron Mouth Qi spoke to the underbrush around him.

No one answered. After taking a few steps more, he asked again. Still there was no answer. Iron Mouth Qi began to feel his hair rise. "Buddha, stop mucking about. Even if you just throw out a stone, you've got to let me know!"

There was still no response whatsoever, and all of a sudden Iron Mouth Qi realised that all the birdsong and bug sound had died away. There was not a single sound in the entire jungle, other than moist air congealing on the branches and droplets falling, making a tiny dripping sound.

"Don't you tell me that the thing is right next to me," Iron Mouth Qi said, feeling for the grenade's pull string straight away, and at the same time, drawing his pistol.

Abruptly, a baby's crying rang out behind him. He spun round instantly. The wailing sounded as if it was six or seven feet away in the shrubbery.

Iron Mouth Qi breathed a sigh of relief and was about to let out a second when he halted. The crying child meant that Zhang Qishan and his men were only six or seven feet away from him, but once the child started crying, they were exposed.

The child's crying grew louder and louder. Qi was a little unsure of what to do. Little by little, he realised the cries were getting closer.

Iron Mouth Qi suddenly felt that something was wrong. Was Zhang Xiaoyu crawling towards him with the baby on his back? Then why was there no movement in the brush?

Just as he was wondering, to his left came the sound of another baby wailing.

How could there be two babies? Iron Mouth Qi was stunned. It was ridiculous enough for them to bring one child into this jungle, so how could there be another?

Did it just grow up out of the ground?

The two babies crying simultaneously gave Iron Mouth the chance to realise that the baby on the left was the one they had brought from the village. The other cry was just a perfunctory noise.

But then what was crawling towards him? The sound of that cry was now next to Iron Mouth Qi's face. He held up the pistol, already prepared for a monster to jump out from the dark. Without warning, the baby's cry vanished, leaving only the real wailing of the child with Zhang Xiaoyu, which seemed to be moving further and further away.

Iron Mouth Qi held up the gun, sweat beading on his brow as he saw the shadow thing shoot up in front of him. Iron Mouth Qi jumped, but realised almost immediately that it was Zhang Qishan, who had taken a flying leap into the darkness in front of him and seemed to have caught something.

"So, Buddha was always at my side, protecting me," Qi realised, and Zhang Qishan had never been more than three steps away. His heart warmed with this total certainty, but he had also been farting freely and nervously for the past twenty minutes. Buddha would certainly have... Suddenly, a protracted, blood-curdling child's scream rose from the darkness ahead, and after that, everything was still.

Zhang Qishan walked out of the dark, carrying a

strange ball-shaped lump, which Iron Mouth Qi realised straight away was the head of some creature. Zhang leant in close to Iron Mouth Qi and asked, "What the hell did you have for dinner last night?"

8
THE MUTANT

THE WHOLE TEAM were crouched in the clearing, all storm lanterns and torches lit. The monster Zhang Qishan had killed lay stretched out on the ground. It was over two metres long, with stubby arms and legs, but an elongated body. It was completely hairless, its pallid skin moist.

The head had been wrenched off, its neck presumably having been broken before the head was ripped off by brute force. Turning the head around, its bloated face became visible, looking like that of a drowned corpse, with no hair, and tiny eyes.

"Is this a wawayu?" Iron Mouth Qi searched his memory, putting the baby cry he'd heard together with this two-metre-long salamander thing.

Zhang Qishan prised open the jaw, and saw a mouth filled with rotten teeth, densely packed around the gums. Those were not fish teeth, but human teeth. Human teeth were very easy to discern.

"This is a person," Zhang Qishan said. "A freak. For a person" – he pressed the flesh on the corpse – "to develop muscles like this would take at least a decade. So this thing is over ten years old. Judging by the skin, it must be amphibious."

The soldiers looked at each other, while Iron Mouth Qi glanced at Zhang Qishan. "Why would there be a human salamander in the deep mountains? Are there any tribes with strange offspring that we aren't aware of?"

Zhang Qishan lifted his head and looked around, his expression full of doubt.

Iron Mouth Qi asked, "Buddha, this freak isn't the mountain god, is it? As the proverb goes, two tigers can't share a mountain. If there was a deity in this mountain, as well as a monster, that would be one too many."

Zhang Qishan still said nothing, but looking at his face, Iron Mouth Qi knew that he had already come to his own conclusions. Assuming they shared the same thought, he continued, "I think I was making sense. If this is the mountain god, then we have now completed our task, and my prediction of a shock, but no danger has come true." He thought for a moment more, and added, "But why is Shanshen a mutant? Was he a child abandoned by the village, who grew up here and became this beast? Buddha, you Zhangs have seen much and know more – have you ever seen deformations like this before?"

Zhang Qishan did not engage with Iron Mouth Qi, but stood up, patted him on the shoulder, and called to his men: "Take the Bagua master over to that tree, and let him tell some new fortunes in peace."

Iron Mouth Qi stood there, surprised, but the soldier next to him had already stepped up, and with a determined air, began to frogmarch him away.

Zhang Qishan felt the quietness flow back around him, and, sighing, continued to inspect the surrounding terrain. Another of his guards came over, and asked, "Buddha, is this really the Shanshen?"

"Probably not. Nothing under heaven comes that

easily," Zhang Qishan replied. "According to legend, the mountain deity has been around for hundreds of years, and had made a firm agreement with humans, showing that it possessed a clear, functional intelligence. Shanshen lives in the mountains, indicating that they keep to their word. But this thing that plays with human corpses, and joins them with snakes, has a low, infantile intelligence, and is obviously still a child. It has left the deep mountains and appeared on the more populated borders. None of this fits the description, so why would I think it's the mountain god? But as of now, we don't have enough information, so this isn't the right time to make random guesses. Keep the brothers on high alert. The situation in these mountains is more complicated than I thought. Let's camp here tonight."

On the other side, Iron Mouth Qi had just taken out his turtle shells and coins, when he saw all the Zhang guards starting to shovel up weeds and turn the soil. He sighed. "Just tell me if you find me a nuisance." Grumbling, he made his cast, and watched the coins roll to the ground with a clatter. Looking at the pattern, Iron Mouth Qi froze, before bending down to take a closer look. He turned a cadaverous shade of white and collapsed onto the ground.

The soldier next to him asked, "Well, Master Qi, more news about your upcoming marriage?"

Iron Mouth Qi stood up, looking around him, utterly at a loss.

The seasoned soldier grew nervous. "What's wrong?"

"There's something wrong with the divination."

"You said, 'shocks, but no danger'?"

"The Zhen Trigram indicates 'Thunder'. Zhen in both the upper and lower trigams means "a hundred li of thunder, yet unyielding". Hence, 'shocks, but no real danger'. This cast is the same, but see for yourself."

The soldier moved in closer and, straight away, spotted that one of the coins had not landed flat on the ground, but was propped at a high angle against a small stone.

"Well, we're not on flat ground, so these things happen. Don't be so superstitious, Master Qi."

"If I wasn't, there'd be no point in Buddha bringing me along. That's what I'm here for, the superstitions!" Iron Mouth Qi was angry. "This is the Lei Di Yu, the transformation hexagram of the Zhen, indicating that there is a change to the divination pattern. My original divination was already unstable. If it was shocks and no danger before, the energy from the Yù Hexagram is destabilising it even further. Things can only go sour, and we're going to suffer some losses."

"Divination patterns can change? What are we going to lose?"

"I was casting for safety, so what do you think we're going to lose? Money? We're going to lose men." Iron Mouth Qi craned his neck and looked around. "Quick, see if anyone's missing!"

Clearly convinced by Qi, the soldier, too, stuck out his head, the two of them counting the troops. In an instant, the diviner and the soldier both remembered the same thing and yelled out simultaneously, "The child!"

Just then, the baby had started to cry, and Zhang Xiaoyu sped away, carrying the boy with him. A quick glance over the entire team was enough to determine that he and the child were the only ones missing.

Iron Mouth Qi rushed to Zhang Qishan and relayed the situation. Zhang immediately got someone to do a roll call, and sure enough, Zhang Xiaoyu did not answer. Zhang Qishan turned to Iron Mouth Qi. "What does it say?"

"The pattern says there will be misfortune on the people, but it is yet to stabilise, so they could still be saved. This cast probably relates to Zhang Xiaoyu."

Zhang Qishan ordered the team into patrols, to take up ammunition, and begin searching for Zhang Xiaoyu. Iron Mouth Qi watched the Zhangs, who formed into trines in a flash, and disappeared group by group into the jungle. In less than a minute, only he and the horses were left in the camp, wide-eyed and open mouthed.

Iron Mouth Qi looked around, stunned at being the only man left behind. Suddenly he felt a cold gust in the wind. Quietly, he returned to the spot where he had sat divining and squatted down. Looking at the coins again, he did not know why there was such a sense of disquiet in his soul, as though he might have missed something. He rarely felt this way, he did not underestimate the enemy, nor was he careless. Still, he felt as if there was something he had omitted.

Picking up the three coins, he discovered that it was not a stone lying beneath them, but something pearlescent that resembled white jade.

He picked it up and examined it, terror seeping from him as he realised he was holding a tooth. A human tooth, if this human were three times larger than normal.

The tooth must have been there from long ago, its surface having dried out and cracked. Taking a deep breath, he returned to the corpse of the 'salamander', and, holding his breath, struggled to prise its mouth open, comparing the giant tooth against it.

The mouth smelt thoroughly repugnant, the reek nearly bringing tears to Qi's eyes. He saw that the tooth he had picked up was far bigger than any of the salamander's.

And then, far in the darkness, he felt something in the

treetops move.

Iron Mouth Qi looked in the direction of the movement and realised that what he had thought to be a tree in the distance was, in fact, some other thing.

He swallowed, listening for any movement all around him. The Zhangs had not returned. He cursed internally. "I wonder if the lost man is going to be me. At any moment Zhang Xiaoyu will wander back, carrying the child, and find me lying here, dead."

He dared not take his eyes away from that murky point, but slowly, he shrank behind a tree. Although his eyesight was poor, he had already fully understood that not only was the thing not a tree, but it was some giant creature.

Iron Mouth Qi was the last in a line of single heirs, but not even that low birth rate had extinguished the family line. The Qis had their own natural tendency for survival. Taking a few deep breaths, he lay down very slowly, flat on his stomach, and began to cover himself with fallen leaves.

Beneath the leaves was black mud and litter, and into this, Iron Mouth Qi silently buried himself, leaving only his nostrils at the surface.

Calming himself as much as possible, slowly he felt the ground vibrate. With his ears below the pooling mud, he could not hear the creature, but he could sense its giant form, slowly approaching the area where he was hidden.

9

THE SEVERED HAND

HALF A LI westwards, Zhang Qishan and his men found Zhang Xiaoyu's trail.

The weather was close. Their first sign had been the

sound of gathering flies, and then, they'd found the trail of blood across the brush.

The trail was thick; whatever was bleeding must have had a serious wound to leave a trail like that. The area was overgrown, and the trail of blood stretched over a dozen metres of ferns and bushes, either thick blood, or swarming flies.

Following the blood trail, they focused their search, and soon began to hear the baby's cry. All torches swung towards it, but they could see nothing clearly, except the cloud of flying insects. Zhang Qishan walked over, and from under a thick shrub, brought out a baby, covered in gore.

It was the child that Zhang Xiaoyu had run off with, and under their body was a severed hand, still clutching the child with a deadly grip.

It was Zhang Xiaoyu's hand, which looked as though it had been torn right off.

Zhang Qishan cricked his neck, his eyes growing dark and stormy. As he moved, the tattoo under his collar was exposed briefly.

This was where the blood trail ended, but after carefully checking the leaves, Zhang Qishan found the point where the trail should have led upwards. So, with a roll of his body, he leaped onto the tree, and sure enough, found more signs of blood, but still nothing more of Zhang Xiaoyu.

"He was attacked under the tree and then dragged up into the branches," he said.

A soldier under the tree asked, "Was it a wild beast?"

Looking at the blood on the tree, Zhang Qishan had seen a giant handprint, which, putting his own hand over it, he guessed to be about three times the size of a normal person's.

"Use the bat whistle to summon the troops. We're retreating immediately. This thing is not done yet. There's another one of those 'salamanders' here." Zhang Qishan dropped out of the tree.

"Another one?"

"Yes, three times bigger than the last one. It attacked Zhang Xiaoyu."

"Shouldn't we carry on looking for it?" The soldiers were showing their fear – did Buddha think Zhang Xiaoyu was already dead?

"Zhang Xiaoyu's gongfu isn't bad. If he couldn't get away, that means this monster is powerful. When the little one attacked Master Qi, it concealed itself in the bushes. If we're scattered like this, not only are we unlikely to find this thing, but any one group of us might be ambushed. First, we regroup, then we burn this place down. Lighting it up raises our chances of winning." Zhang Qishan made a gesture for them to stop their questions, and the teams headed back with speed.

When they reached the clearing where they had left Iron Mouth Qi and the horses, there was an overwhelming metallic stench of blood.

The horses were gone, the thick jungle painted red with gore, which also dripped from overhead. Looking up, Zhang Qishan saw that the horses hung limp and broken from the high branches, their heads torn off and missing, letting blood and innards gush freely out of their bodies, raining down on the undergrowth.

"Shit," Zhang Qishan spat. Looking around him, he suddenly began yelling, "Qi!"

No answer.

"Did anyone see the Bagua Master?"

The soldiers all shook their heads. Looking from face to

face, Zhang Qishan glanced at the baby one of them had been holding. His eyes were locked, staring dead straight at a point in the distance, to the left of him. In the near pitch darkness, he could vaguely make out the shadow of a tree.

As he stared at the trunk, a gurgling laugh came out of the baby, and Qishan realised that it was no tree.

10

THE CHASE

ZHANG QISHAN LOOKED at the black, treelike shadow.

The only reason he realised it was not a tree, was because of the way the baby had looked at it. This child's eyes seemed peculiar, picking things out in conditions that rendered his men's eyes nearly useless. But once he had looked, he saw the shadow's outline was very similar to that of the wawayu-like freak he had just killed.

It hung back in the foliage, its long body seeming very much like just another tree trunk.

An ordinary human would not have been able to spot the monster in this darkness, even if they had been trained to do so. They would still need to be pointed in the right direction and would have to know what to look for.

Zhang Qishan made a gesture with his hand, and the troops focused their attention on the spot.

"Are you Shanshen?" he asked.

The 'tree' did not move. Zhang Qishan shone his torch on it and was about to order his men to open fire, when he heard Zhang Xiaoyu's voice ring out from it.

"Buddha, don't shoot! You can't... can't shoot!" Zhang Xiaoyu called.

Zhang Qishan tried to search for Zhang Xiaoyu with his torch, but the 'tree' shifted back, retreating into the darkness. Xiaoyu's voice also sounded further away: "This... really... is... the mountain god, you can't shoot."

The voice drifted further and further away, till eventually, it could no longer be heard. The subordinates prepared to give chase, but Zhang Qishan stopped them.

"But Master Zhang...!" the soldiers cried anxiously.

Zhang Qishan said, "It's baiting us."

"But Lieutenant Xiaoyu is..."

"It's not a wild beast, don't underestimate it." Zhang Qishan gazed at the infant, who in turn, gazed in the direction in which the Shanshen had gone. "Let's find Master Qi first. He's the only one who can explain this matter."

When Iron Mouth Qi was found, and dug out of his den, he was black from head to toe, coughing incessantly, and spitting out black ditch water. He was covered in all manner of slugs and leeches.

Zhang Qishan held a flaming torch to them, forcing them off one by one. Iron Mouth Qi said, "Buddha, promise me in the future, when you all go off, can you let me know? There's not much point putting me in charge of the camp by myself, I can't beat up any intruders."

Zhang Qishan ignored his complaint. "How do you explain this?"

Iron Mouth Qi asked in turn, "Did you see that thing?"

Zhang Qishan said, "Zhang Xiaoyu is in harm's way, so don't pad this out."

Iron Mouth Qi said, "Are we sure that this creature is actually the mountain god? This thing is so big, the several dozen mountains around here could all be its territory. So it's unlikely other Shanshen will want to fight it."

A soldier called out: "Lieutenant Xiaoyu said that that

thing was the mountain god!"

Zhang Qishan knotted his brow and focused his thoughts, considering Xiaoyu's words.

He knew Xiaoyu's background very well. He was not some able-bodied villager who had been forcibly conscripted, he was one of the brothers who had followed him out of Dongbei. The north-eastern Zhangs exercised very strict discipline among family members. None of them would jump to rash conclusions, unless they had seen irrefutable evidence.

Therefore, if Xiaoyu had said this was the real Shānshén, that they must not shoot, then he must have found very solid proof. What kind of proof could a person see that would make him think a creature was a god?

If this thing was the mountain god, then things would be easy. Staring at Iron Mouth Qi, he asked, "Have you got anything constructive to add?"

The miasma pervaded, and the rest of the troops had gathered around them. Still looking at Iron Mouth Qi, Zhang Qishan asked the others to check their ammo, at the same time gesturing to the mountains on either side of the canyon. It was easy to lose track of the target in the canyon. With the monster hiding in the thick foliage, you could simply walk right past it without even realising. It was best to track it up on the mountainside, where the view was clearer, and you could keep an eye on each other.

Iron Mouth Qi said, "You'll need to let me study what that corpse is, before I can tell you what it might possibly be."

Zhang Qishan threw the head of the "little wawayu" over to Qi. "Take it with you and study it as we go, we need to get moving. When we get back, I promise I'll spread the word about your inaccurate divinations."

Iron Mouth Qi held the head with a great deal of distaste, answering, "My casting was definitely accurate, which means there is only one possibility where this kind of situation could occur."

"What's that?"

"Buddha, it could be that our opponent is not ruled or guided by the Five Elements. Maybe the Shanshen is not something from our world. Perhaps it truly is a god."

Zhang Qishan looked at the baby, who was starting to wriggle. Once the monster had moved out of sight, there was nothing left to stimulate his attention, and he was feeling sorry for himself.

Zhang Qishan was still trying to figure out why Zhang Xiaoyu was convinced that this was the mountain deity. He must have seen something, but there was no time to think about the details. He said to Iron Mouth Qi, "If this thing is outside of the Five Elements, can we still kill it?"

The question seemed to stump Iron Mouth Qi, so Zhang Qishan patted him on the back and grinned. "Let's make a bet? If we can kill it, you stand guard outside my office for a month."

Having said that, Zhang Qishan went about things in his own fashion. He sent Iron Mouth Qi off to the right with half the team, while he took the baby and the rest of his men to the left and began to climb the ridge.

As soon as they were separated from Iron Mouth Qi, his subordinates began to ask why he'd decided to put Qi in a separate group. Zhang Qishan explained, "Master Qi is shit at a lot of things, but he's from a long line of survivors, and he's an expert in not getting killed. Besides, without him here, we can move more quickly."

Soon, Zhang Qishan's team had scaled midway up the mountain. The trees were still dense, and the view of the canyon was more or less obscured. They had to climb to the treetops just to gaze out into it.

Under the moonlight, the bottom of the canyon looked like a sea of treetops. The valley base was flat, like a small plain trapped between the two mountains. At first, at the centre of the canyon, they could see the treetops shaking, as if some giant beast was pushing away the trees while advancing.

Zhang Qishan mumbled, "Shanshen…" then ordered his men to slowly head in the direction of the disturbance.

After following it for a while, the canyon grew wider, the distance between the two mountains drawing in until the shaking treetops were no longer visible. It was only by the fluttering of startled birds that they could still tell something was on the move.

After two hours of tracking, there were no more startled birds, so they brought the baby up to the treetop. He fixed his stare straight at one point on the canyon floor.

Odds were the monster would return to its lair, and probably feed. Zhang Qishan knew he could wait no longer. He turned to look up at the mountain across from him, but because it was too far away, he could not see Iron Mouth Qi's team, nor any sign of their lamps or torches. If he read Qi's skill correctly, their walking speed would be half of his own, so they should still be where he had been an hour ago.

11

WAITING FOR WHAT?

THE NIGHTTIME FOG was thick, and the temperature had dropped. Iron Mouth Qi had been advancing for over two hours with his temporary troop. Judging by eye, they did not seem to have made much progress, but Iron Mouth Qi was already exhausted, and the Zhang fighters under him were growing impatient. "At this speed, we'll be lagging behind Buddha by ten thousand li."

Despite their moaning, they dared not leave him behind. Qi was trying his best. When they took the first break, he was pinching his lip while his eyes were rolling back, and was so tired he actually fainted. The team could only wait for him to come round. When they started to march on, they planned on resting every two hours, and then every half an hour, and in the end, they had to stop every few steps. The soldiers gave up the idea of being ready at any moment to provide backup for Zhang Qishan's squad, but what else could they do? They had no clue. After all, they were not travelling fast, nor did Iron Mouth Qi issue any orders. So everyone slipped into a state of bewilderment, and morale fell, weighing them down.

Iron Mouth Qi understood the situation, but did not have the physical strength to solve the problem, so he pretended not to notice.

When they took another break, one of the soldiers could not help but ask him, "Master Qi, your physical condition is totally unsuited to fighting or the army life. Why does Buddha bring you every time? Can you really make accurate divinations? Buddha almost never listens to them."

Iron Mouth Qi glared at him. "The relationship between Buddha and I, is it something that you junior initiates could understand?"

Another soldier said, "I heard from someone in The Nine Gates that Buddha brings you every time because he's worried that when he's not in Changsha, you'll get beaten to death on the street."

Iron Mouth Qi's entire face flushed red. He snapped

back angrily, "Nonsense! When Buddha's not there, there's Second Master, and Fifth Master. I wouldn't be in such a sorry state as to be beaten to death."

Even though he was speaking this way, Iron Mouth Qi knew full well that he possessed expert knowledge and proficiency in all manner of esoteric lore, folk customs, paranormal practices, knew of every sprite, demon, goblin and monster in existence, as well as the complete fengshui and fortunes of Changsha. Zhang Qishan brought him along mainly for his encyclopaedic knowledge. Besides, it was not that Zhang did not believe him – he could not, or he would never have accomplished half his fate-defying feats.

There were certain people whose fortunes Iron Mouth Qi avoided telling. Foreigners, conspiracists, and of course anyone with a qilin tattoo, because it was said that they were no longer bound by the Five Elements. Among everyone's threads of destiny in this world, only theirs were not fixed, so their destinies could not be foretold. Zhang Qishan's birth chart was almost illegible. His tattoo was of a Qiongqi, so this man's fate was not impossible to divine. Iron Mouth Qi had tried to tell his fortune on many occasions. Sometimes he was accurate, other times wholly wrong – it was strange.

Some of the soldiers were now openly showing their contempt. Iron Mouth Qi said, "Buddha is the master warrior, so he fights at the head. I am the master strategist. The strategist uses his brains. Buddha didn't ask me to lead this team in order to slow you down. It's because Buddha is wise, and knew he'd have to move too fast for me to keep up with, but he's on an urgent rescue mission, so he would have been unable to keep an eye on the troops at the back. Therefore, he lets us take our time, so I can think, and when he has completed the rescue ahead, and I have reached a better understanding of the situation, we can reunite, and put practice together with theory, and then, and only then, can we resolve things once and for all."

The soldiers at least acted like they understood Qi's words. One of them asked, "So... have you come to a better understanding, then? Seeing as we aren't going anywhere at the moment, perhaps you can explain it to us, so we can learn more about it, too?"

Iron Mouth Qi stared at the soldier and cleared his throat. "You little shits, if I don't show you a trick or two, you'll go running off to Buddha and badmouth me. So listen carefully. According to my analysis, after we came into the mountains, we encountered two monsters, which were mother and child. The small one is about three metres tall; the mother is about seven metres. On our way, I carefully examined the head, and Buddha was right, it is, in some way, basically human. Why do I say 'mother and child', not 'father and child'? That's because when I was hiding under the leaves, the mother came close to me, and she had that uniquely female smell of thick blood. You won't understand that."

A younger soldier looked up curiously at this and asked, "What's so female about thick blood?"

Iron Mouth Qi rapped him on the head. "Whatever it is, is that important to the mission?"

"Right, right, sorry for my rudeness, please continue." The soldiers laughed mockingly.

"At that moment, I was praying, I daren't move. It was female, so think about it, the child is here, the mother is here... where is the father?"

Everyone looked at each other, not daring to have any ideas.

Iron Mouth Qi continued, "OK, let's cast our minds back to before we set out. Do you remember that village Touling?

He's lost his sight in both eyes, but he's always looking in the direction of the mountains, as if he's waiting for someone to come out. Every year, it's he who takes the babies into the mountains, to offer them to the mountain god. It is said that a lot of chiefs have made exchanges with Shanshen using their organs, so what do you think he got in exchange for giving the deity his eyes?"

Everyone felt horrified and dared not interject.

"Think hard. For a man to be looking at the mountains day in, day out, for dozens of years, waiting and expecting, what do you think could possibly be the reason?"

A soldier suddenly cried out, "Someone in the mountains owes him money!"

Iron Mouth Qi said, "Bollocks they do! I can tell from one look at you you're still wet behind the ears. For a man to act like that, the only reason is a woman. But where would the women be in these mountains? There aren't any, are there? When I was marching, I was trying to figure this out, until I realised I had seen one. Seven metres tall, mutated, but definitely female."

The soldiers, as one, sucked in a hiss of cold air over their teeth.

"Master Qi, are you nuts? That village Head must be, too, waiting year after year for a woman like that. He really must be all kinds of special."

Iron Mouth Qi replied, "Let me tell you, from my experience, there can't be two tigers on one mountain. There can only be one top predator. But up till now, we've already seen two monsters. If you tell me that neither of them are the mountain god, I'd find that hard to believe. So, the story would have had to go like this.

"The Shanshen to whom the Touling made offerings was this strange, giant woman. She was not only physically freakish, but mentally. She liked to eat children. But for some reason, the Touling fell in love with her, and so, one time, after making an offering, they have... time together... and she bore his child. Afterwards, the Touling returns to the villages. Because he had lost his eyes, he could no longer go into the mountains to make the sacrifices, but still he yearned for this woman in his soul, and so every day, he looked towards the mountains, longing for her.

"This woman gave birth to her child alone in the mountains, but it was even more of a monster. Originally, the wild prey in the mountains was enough for this goddess, but now there's a child to feed, and she had to expand her hunting ground, and began to come into conflict with the villagers. Having discovered that deaths among hunters had increased, the Touling realises that his lover and child must be coming nearer the villages. Worrying that they don't have enough to eat, he summoned us. That is the big secret! We are the tasty delicacies that the Touling is sending to his wife and child."

No one spoke. After the longest silence, the youngest soldier raised his hand. "If one of them is just under six foot, and the other is seven metres long... how do you reckon they fucked?"

12
THE EARTH MAIDENS

IRON MOUTH QI pondered. "This is the biggest hole in my deductions."

Another soldier said, "Isn't that hole a bit too big?"

Iron Mouth Qi continued, "Do you remember what the villagers believed to be Shanshen's origin? They said that the mountain god was the founder of the villages, the so-called Earth Maiden of those days. That woman was as stunning as a celestial, the best of the beauties in all the villages... But this seven-metre-long monster is a world apart. So let me try and fill that hole. Think about it, what if, when the Touling saw it, it was yet to become a monster, and was still the beautiful goddess-like Earth Maiden? If his eyes were later taken by the mountain god, he would have kept that impression of her, and the most wonderful sight he could recollect of the world would have been that of the Earth Maiden. Now do you think he would be capable of carnal relations, or yearning for her with all his soul?"

Everyone slid into silence. After a while, someone asked, "Do you think that the Earth Woman got pregnant first, and then became a monster?"

Iron Mouth Qi nodded.

"Master Qi, how sure are you of that hypothesis?"

Iron Mouth Qi ignored him and continued, "Let me now tell you what the Earth Maiden is, and you'll see how my deductions are mostly along the right lines."

Iron Mouth Qi's version of the Earth Maiden legend was a lot fuller than I had managed to collect. The Earth Maidens were indeed the dead naked women found in the landslides I mentioned. At first, the public thought they were victims of natural disasters. But when court coroners were processing the corpses, some of whom had already begun to decompose and break down internally, they found human fingers and teeth in the guts. In other words, these women had lived on human flesh.

The layers of earth in which the bodies were found were all from very deep repositories in the ground. Those uninitiated believed that when these landslides occurred, these creatures had been hiding, deep. Because these bodies were found mostly in the winter months, it was assumed that like frogs and snakes, they were hibernating in the depths of the soil. When these disasters took place, whole mountainsides were displaced, and they were caught in the enormous rushing force which crushed them in their sleep and carried them to the place where they were found.

In later legends, the Earth Maidens became beings that lived in the soil, and lured hunters with their beauty and sexual appeal, dragging them into the ground to feed on. In his recount, Iron Mouth Qi mentioned one thing: it was discovered that, in the muds and stones where the Earth Maidens were found, there was usually also a unique type of soil.

This was earth made up of seven different minerals, only found several hundred metres deep in the ground. Legend said that the Earth Maidens would burrow deep into the ground, to obtain this Qiqiao Linglong Tu – "Seven Opening Enlightened Exquisite Earth" – to make their nest. The nest was very large, weighing over a dozen tonnes. When the landslides ended, they exposed shifting hues under the sun, a very impressive sight.

"Legend says that this soil was extraordinarily valuable and had enormous medicinal worth. So, in the past, there were people who went digging for it in the winter, in order to sell it. Due to the removal of the soil, the Earth Maidens froze to death," Iron Mouth Qi recounted as the soldiers resumed their march. "When Earth Maidens who were fortunate enough to survive found that their nest soil had been stolen, they would be enraged, and if they were unable to find replacement soil within a short time, they would expose themselves to the air, turn into giant monsters, and attack the villages. One by one, they would drag every child and lone villager either underwater or underground, and devour them."

"Master, that last bit… you made that up? Right?" The soldiers looked doubtful, and Iron Mouth Qi chuckled, but did not reply. He knew he now had these cadets hooked. The youngest soldier asked suddenly, "Master Qi, you're saying that the Earth Maidens look like humans at the beginning, and then turn into seven-metre-long salamanders, because their Linglong soil was stolen?"

Iron Mouth Qi replied, as if getting to the true core of his meaning, "Correct! Now, who do you think stole this one's soil?"

The soldiers were intrigued. "Who?"

Iron Mouth Qi sagged. "I still don't know."

Naturally, he had his ideas, but no evidence. Even this story of the Linglong soil had many parts where he had to stretch the facts to fit his hypothesis. All he knew for sure was that in Records of the Strange[31] there was a monster that hid in special soil, whose form resembled the human, and when it was away from the soil for too long, it turned into a monster.

Naturally, he felt that this monster bore some relation to the Legend of the Earth Maidens.

Mountain deities fell for mortals, and the Earth Maidens had their nests stolen and were made pregnant with unwanted children. In all these cases, the most terrible monsters were actually men, but that seemed to be the case with most things in this world.

Disillusioned by the anticlimax of Iron Mouth Qi's lecture, they no longer pressed him to talk, and left him to continue his deductions. Struggling to push aside the

---

31 Records of the Strange 述异记, Southern Dynasty collection of strange tales of the supernatural, mythology, folklore and folk customs by Liang Renfang.

shrubbery, Iron Mouth Qi knew in his heart that what he really needed to think about was not this convoluted history, but the real reason why the Touling had asked them to go into the mountains.

Perhaps this man had lied to the Shanshen, and realised that the god was seeking vengeance, so wanted The Nine Gates to prevent her from taking it. Perhaps he did not believe in Zhang Qishan's ability to hunt gods, and hoped the mountain god would fill up, eat their entire team, and retreat back to the mountains. Before they left, the Touling's expression made him very uneasy, as if he were masking some unknown intent.

Iron Mouth Qi then remembered Zhang Xiaoyu's words: "It really is the Shanshen."

There was bound to be some ulterior motive behind this. He only hoped that Zhang Qishan could adapt to the situation. The hexagram in his second divination was loose and shifting, which meant that somewhere along the chain of events, one of the links must be weak, and subject to change from something outside of the Five Elements. Therefore, he could not foretell its influence. It was only now that the clues were beginning to appear. The most fatal situation was just beginning to unravel.

13
THE GREAT BANYAN TREE

ZHANG QISHAN AND his men raced into the canyon's jungle sea, towards the point in which the baby had locked his gaze.

No other troop could coordinate as well as the Zhang army. It was almost like a needle threading through the weft.

The trees and brush were dense, concentrated, and almost impenetrable. The trees wound around each other's roots and crossed branches, the vines hung as if woven together, extending across space in every direction, yet Zhang Qishan moved like water between them. Rapidly running and leaping without hesitation, traversing the gaps, or simply clambering over the obstacles. He quickly realised how the monster had disappeared, because beneath the dense canopy of trees, was now a marsh.

This canyon had, of course, collected the mountain rain into this swamp. Before, the monster would have been travelling through the treetops, like an arboreal snake. But upon reaching the marsh, it would have immediately sunk into it, swimming at speed, only needing to surface to take a fresh breath of air.

Its surfacing was probably what had startled the birds into breaking the tree cover.

Zhang Qishan hoped that Xiaoyu, whose name meant 'little fish', could survive the swim.

As they converged, a deathly silence surrounded them. The whole jungle seemed to have gone silent. No living thing made a sound.

Zhang Qishan realised they must be getting near to their quarry, because they had entered a new area of the jungle. The plants here were different to those outside, and the trees in this place the monster had chosen to rest were all banyans. To his knowledge, the whole copse of banyan trees was made up of offshoots of just one plant. A single tree forming a whole forest. In the centre of this cluster must be something he had never seen in his life. The Mother Tree.

Banyan trees were powerful water-fixers, and in this climate, each one would house an incredible number of mosquitoes, more per tree than most places would have per forest.

They saw the insects almost filling every single gap in the bark, hanging in clouds, but none of them made a hint of a sound. It was as if the organisms around here had evolved the ability to remain noiseless.

One of Zhang's guards plucked one from the air. Unable to see it clearly in the dim moonlight, he popped it into his mouth and chewed a little. He reported, "Tastes like blood, so it's feeding on blood, but it doesn't taste like mosquitos."

A keen sense of taste for water, and bugs, was a specialist skill of the Zhangs. Many a time, when the situation did not afford a good field of vision, there was a need to rely heavily on taste and sense of smell to assess the situation.

Zhang Qishan and his men began to scale the trees, walking along the branches, in order to avoid contact with the marsh. There were aerial roots everywhere, swaying in the silent breeze like curtains, severely hampering their view. As they advanced further, Zhang Qishan saw the Mother Tree.

It was an enormous banyan tree. With no visible trunk, its body consisted of the gathering of countless matured roots, which alone were already thicker than the trunks of the thickest trees they had passed, the gaps between them so narrow, they looked like a single entity.

How big was it? To Zhang Qishan, this tree was like a wall in the forest. He flicked out his fingers and dipped his wrist, as a sign for his men to spread themselves flat on their stomachs, then began to crawl ahead on the branches.

Almost all the branches of the banyan tree were connected, their dense coverage of vines and moss making for good camouflage. In the middle of the tree cluster, it was pitch black.

Lowering his head, Zhang Qishan looked at the baby,

who now had his eyes set on the pitch-black interior among the trees, as if it had some sort of connection with the mountain god. *The monster is in there?* he thought. *Right.*

He could wait no longer, and with another wave of his hand, everybody started crawling carefully towards the cluster of trunks.

Just as they were entering the hollow, Zhang Qishan heard a sound rumbling out of the innermost depths. In the dark, they felt their way ahead on all fours, advancing slowly. The darkness around them was impenetrable, the moonlight that shone on the treetops unable to pierce the heart of the banyan grove and having no effect on what was below.

The rumbling noise was unnatural. It sounded like some great beast rapidly gulping down its own spit. It made their hairs spike up in primaeval alertness.

Zhang Qishan cricked his neck, pleading in his head, *please don't let Zhang Xiaoyu get eaten before I can reach him.*

As they crawled towards the rumbling noise, they found that the banyan trunks were covered in holes, which looked as if they'd been dug out by claws. These holes were filled with bones. Zhang Qishan could not see them clearly, but by touch he could recognise both human and animal bones, strung together by rough ropes of woven hemp.

Some of the larger bones had been broken into pieces, and strung together with rod-like objects, as if to make ornaments. Peering further in, he noticed something ahead of them. Flames.

Zhang Qishan checked on his men, who were concealed in the dark around him. He had no idea if any of them had become separated. With the utmost care, he continued to crawl in, finding that the 'trunk' of this giant tree, or rather this mass of trailing roots and branches, had been hollowed out. About four or five giant roots were severed, leaving the most primal trunk of the Mother Tree. It was so huge that it would have taken over thirty people to surround it. Countless branches shot off from it.

The flames were coming from a storm lantern, hanging from another branch of the Mother Tree. It was hung full of them, presumably left by the people the monster had eaten. They had all been meticulously collected there, though only one of them was lit. On a much thicker branch, directly below it, that giant monster was sprawled out, and lying motionless atop the creature's stomach was Zhang Xiaoyu.

14
GOD ASSASSINATING

ONE STORM LANTERN is not particularly bright. Under its reddish glow the monster resembled a giant axolotl or an immense human embryo, yet to mature, but which has endlessly multiplied in size. Its white skin looked unusually sickly, its distended body about six metres long, its arms even longer. Even at this distance, it was capable of reaching out and grasping Zhang Qishan.

In another dark corner, one of his men stuck out his head and, using hand signals, asked Zhang Qishan if they should make a move.

Zhang Qishan waved his hand. He was exhausting his field-trained observation skills, trying to observe Zhang Xiaoyu's condition, and he realised there was a kind of creepy symbiosis between Zhang Xiaoyu and this giant axolotl.

This pose, if he was reading it correctly, indicated that the monster was nursing Zhang

Xiaoyu on its milk.

Zhang Qishan looked at the area where Zhang Xiaoyu was lying. There was a protrusion on the monster's chest, its breast. Taking a more focused look, he could pick out light hair on the monster's head and body, but could still not make out Zhang Xiaoyu's expression. He seemed to be unconscious, or fully absorbed in his feeding.

Zhang Qishan surveyed his surroundings. It was too quiet here – if he tried to creep nearer, the monster would almost certainly notice him.

But at this distance, if he leaped in and rushed the thing, made to drive his bayonet into the monster's head, he believed that, under such dim light, no monster would be able to react in the three or four seconds it would take.

In his careful examination of the monster's body, he found no signs of 'godliness'. He was still unable to understand why Zhang Xiaoyu had said what he did. Did he sense superhuman powers when he'd fought it? Zhang Xiaoyu's gongfu was well honed. Among the officers, he would rank third, so if this monster could hurt him, it really should not be underestimated.

Besides, what kind of monster was it? How did it come about? This thing had a lot of human traits.

While he was thinking, Zhang Xiaoyu began to cough. When the monster lifted him up, Zhang Qishan saw that its milk was black, and the monster's claws were firmly lodged into Zhang Xiaoyu's head, digging deeply into his scalp.

There was no time to think further. Zhang Qishan made three moves. First, he signalled his intent for his men to attack. Secondly, he ordered them to, once he had wounded the target, lay down covering fire to prevent reprisal. Thirdly, he indicated that if his attack failed, everyone should break cover, distract the Shanshen, and provide him with another opportunity.

After conveying these signals, he stretched his joints, slid out his bayonet, and settled it into a backhand grip.

The monster's head was huge, and its skull would be thick. The blade would need to be absolutely buried to make it count. With this in mind, he climbed out into the mesh of branches, examined the positions of a few roots and burrs, and propelled himself forward.

Using the great explosive energy of his first leap, he sent himself almost halfway to the target, landing on a branch jutting into the middle of the space, from which he sprinted forward a dozen steps or so.

The monster turned in an instant, and glared towards Zhang Qishan, who had already begun his second leap. He landed on the monster's neck in an instant. He instantly shifted to strike with his bayonet, but almost simultaneously, Zhang Xiaoyu's body moved like a phantom, slipping into the bayonet's path so that Zhang Qishan almost stabbed him.

Zhang Qishan reacted with animal speed, at once somersaulting back through the air, and landing on the monster's body, which was slick, doused with its oily black milk. He slipped, and the bayonet pierced the monster in the ribs. The obstruction saved Zhang Qishan from sliding into the darkness below. The monster opened its mouth, but did not cry out, though its twisted expression showed the extreme pain it felt. It threw Zhang Qishan off at once.

Zhang Qishan regulated his posture and dove safely into the marsh. Just as he hit the water, he heard gunfire from all directions, as the Zhang guards opened fire.

15
WHO THE HELL ARE YOU?

ZHANG QISHAN PULLED himself out of the swamp, and, grabbing one of the trailing roots, he quickly climbed back onto a branch. In an instant, the gunshots above died away. He could not concern himself with that right now, as he scaled up to the monster's nest. He had just

steadied himself, before Zhang Xiaoyu's face floated towards him from the darkness.

The monster had grabbed hold of Xiaoyu's head with a single hand and was suspending him over the gap between them. Zhang Qishan was just about to shoot, when he heard Zhang Xiaoyu speak.

"Who are you?"

Shocked, Zhang Qishan felt that something was very wrong. Zhang Xiaoyu's eyes had rolled totally back in his head, until only the whites were showing. He did not seem to be conscious at all.

Who was speaking to him through Zhang Xiaoyu? The monster?

"Are you the mountain god?"

"Why did you kill my child?"

The monster's face came out of the dark, revealing a mouth full of teeth.

This thing had a dozen rows of them, all growing haphazardly, and now the sides of its mouth were full of blood.

"Do you eat people?"

"People taste good," said the monster, through Zhang

Xiaoyu. The movements of Xiaoyu's mouth mirrored those of the monster, a disturbing vision.

"Then you must die," Zhang Qishan said.

"I don't want to."

"Not your choice." Now at short range, Zhang Qishan drew his gun and aimed at the monster's head. Immediately, the monster moved Xiaoyu in front of itself.

Zhang Qishan could not shoot. The creature was enormous, but it was also exceptionally fast. Every time Zhang changed his aim, it would shift Xiaoyu to block him a fraction before he had steadied his aim. Zhang Xiaoyu began to 'laugh' – every time they shifted, he would emit a few gurgling chuckles.

Zhang Qishan was furious, not at the monster teasing and goading him, but because it was treating Zhang Xiaoyu like a rag doll. Suddenly, he lashed out, hurling the gun towards the skies, and with a leap, powered up towards it. Zhang Xiaoyu swung at him head on, but like a mudfish, Zhang Qishan burrowed in under his armpit.

This was a human tactic, closing the distance to the enemy and moving both bodies with full strength. It was usually employed in close combat, and the monster obviously had not expected Zhang to make such a move, and when it looked up, found itself face to face with the bayonet. Zhang Qishan did not drive it into the monster's head, but reversed the blade in his hand and stabbed it into the creature's elbow joint.

Zhang Qishan aimed at the cartilage in the joint, and the bayonet slid straight through. The monster tried to retract its hand, but found the joint locked. Unable to move freely, it smashed its arm into the trunk, and Zhang Xiaoyu slid from its hand, and fell.

They were still high up, and Zhang Qishan's heart leapt,

but the monster held out its other hand, and plucked Zhang Xiaoyu mid-fall.

Meanwhile, Zhang Qishan's pistol had begun its descent, and just as deftly, Qishan caught it and pressed the muzzle directly against the monster's head.

Zhang Xiaoyu's voice rang out, without warning: "I will kill him, if you shoot."

But Zhang Qishan had shot. He squeezed the trigger so rapidly that in an instant, he had emptied every chamber into the monster's head. The bloated thing collapsed against the branches, and stopped moving, brains and blood flowing out, spreading over the branches.

With a standoff, the more hesitation, the more danger the hostages are in.

Zhang Qishan unslung the machine gun, and emptied it into the monster's skull, reducing it to a pulp.

And then he went to retrieve Zhang Xiaoyu, who was still hanging from the monster's hand.

The monster's talons had penetrated Zhang Xiaoyu's skull, sinking deep into his brain. They were incredibly long and thin, like needles, inserted into the exact spots to control his speech. He carefully snapped each one from the monster's hand and extracted them from Xiaoyu's head.

Zhang Xiaoyu's whole scalp was already a wretched, unbearable mess of blood and bone.

Zhang Qishan laid him on the branches and felt his chest. The heart was still beating, but the eyes were rolled back. Qishan had seen this state before, usually when people had been shot in the head.

He had no idea whether Xiaoyu could be saved, he could only try to staunch the bleeding. With a series of speedy flips, Zhang Qishan reached the collection of storm lanterns, and signalled into the darkness.

Not one soldier responded.

One by one, he lit all the lanterns, and spread them out on different branches, to give some brighter light to the situation.

Blood was splattered across everything. Guns had fallen onto the branches, some had been broken, others had fallen into the water. Not one person could be seen.

Zhang Qishan felt a chill in his heart: was it possible that, in that short instance, everyone had been slaughtered? The monster did not seem that powerful, yet why would they sustain such a huge loss of life?

And then he heard a baby's cry, coming from above his head.

Slowly moving away from the glow of the lanterns, Zhang Qishan felt his way towards the direction of the crying. He had torn off the monster's head and hung it near the lanterns. Zhang Xiaoyu was still lying in the same spot, unresponsive. Zhang Qishan slowly realised that, across the nest, the baby had been standing by itself, on a branch, dully mimicking its own cries.

Whilst making a crying sound, its face remained placidly calm, its deadly gaze fixed firmly on Zhang Qishan. Not only was it observing him, it was doing so very closely.

"Who the hell are you?" he asked.

It did not reply, but started toddling towards Zhang Qishan, swaying gently from side to side, holding its arms outstretched, as if wanting a hug.

16
THE QILIN TATTOO

WHAT ZHANG QISHAN did not know was that Iron Mouth

Qi's team had almost reached the banyan grove. However, they did not continue their approach. From a treetop in the distance, Iron Mouth Qi gazed out anxiously.

"Master Qi, why don't we just head over there?"

"That's a banyan tree, correct? An especially large specimen?" Iron Mouth Qi asked.

The soldier nodded. "We've just scouted ahead – it is a banyan tree. Master Buddha has already gone in. We should hurry and follow."

"Wait a moment." Iron Mouth Qi looked around him, and saw that where they were now situated was a high point in the canyon. The trees here were different from the rest of the plain and set much further apart. The soldier pressed him. "What's the matter, Master? We mustn't hesitate."

Iron Mouth Qi replied, "This is the Coiling Dragon Standing on Pillar formation. The surrounding mountains are shaped like a dragon, but the dragon's head is pointing down. In common Fengshui this is called Zuilong, Sinful Dragon. This dragon has sinned, so it's trapped here. That's why this tree could grow to such an enormous size. In the formation, the dragon is coiling around the tree, which must have a huge system of roots, locking the dragon here. If Shānshén lives here, then it could only live within that grove, because this canyon is otherwise plagued with a semi-toxic miasma, and the air is only fresh inside this tree. If that banyan tree ahead of us is the mountain god's nest, then it is also the best location to make an offering. Look, you can see the work that has been done to these trees – this is obviously an altar."

Everyone looked around them, finding that the fallen leaves were much thicker than elsewhere.

Iron Mouth Qi carefully surveyed their position,

ordering everyone to wait patiently, and sweep aside the fallen leaves on the ground. They found that buried under the litter were small ancient stone statues.

One of the Zhang guards recognised it, yelling, "This is a Shanpo statue!"

Iron Mouth Qi asked, "Which one? Granny Mountain was just a general term for all the mountain gods hereabouts. The locals were quite smart, working out that the deity is female."

Iron Mouth Qi was just remarking at the basicness of the sacrificial altar, when someone shouted, "There's a lot of tie-dye cloths here."

When they swept away more of the fallen leaves, they found, submerged in the black mud beneath, copious amounts of tie-dye cloth, some of which had almost totally rotted away, others kept in good condition. The Miao in these parts had a custom of writing their wishes on these tie-dye cloths and tying them to trees. It looked like the past generations of wish cloths had fallen and been gathered here.

Indeed, this was where the chiefs had made their offerings, Iron Mouth Qi thought.

He asked the soldiers to clear away all the fallen leaves, revealing an area of over a dozen square metres, packed densely with the now faded wish cloths.

One of the soldiers picked up a piece that had been kept in relatively good condition, the writing on it still visible.

Taking the scrap, Iron Mouth Qi scrutinised the writing. "This is written in Baitang Miao script, which dates back several decades. Do you see these ones below? Most of them are in ancient Miao, which was so rarely passed down within the ethnic group that outsiders thought its written form had gone extinct."

The soldiers asked Iron Mouth Qi, "So the one in the thingy tang script, what does it say?"

Iron Mouth Qi read the text, and went very pale, then read out loud: "I make the tribute of an infant, may Shanpo wield her shugu magic, and move the life from the sacrifice to the one who makes the offering."

Iron Mouth Qi looked contemplative, and the soldiers dared not disturb him further, they simply looked at him in silence. Suddenly, Qi ran back to the lookout point from which he had considered the banyan grove, gasped and slapped his thigh. "I've got it."

The soldiers broke out yelling: "Tell us, Master Qi, the suspense is killing us."

Iron Mouth Qi said, "You see that banyan tree? That is not a tree, it is a vessel, a gu. The Miao peoples worshipped the Mountain Granny, because she was the mountain deity who could do powerful magic. This wondrous Shanshen nest served as the vessel that housed her magic. Within the tree, the mountain goddess could transfer the life from one person into another. Do you remember when we first arrived at the Stronghold, the Touling looked so old and frail? As though he had lived for centuries. Perhaps he has really lived for a few hundred years. When the Touling requested that Buddha bring the baby into the mountains, we thought the sacrifice was the baby, but it's Buddha himself!"

The soldiers all knew about Zhang Qishan's longevity, and the unique physique that set him apart from normal people, but still they gasped at Iron Mouth Qi's words. This Touling was trying for immortality.

Iron Mouth Qi wiped his forehead. "You must think of a way to inform Buddha, so he can get out of here as quickly as possible."

"Master Qi, didn't you say that your divination meant

we'll be safe this time round?"

"This compulsion is not of the human world, nor that of the spirits. I cannot guarantee the accuracy of my predictions, but I never thought they'd be out by this much. There must be another force at work, but what?"

After a whole journey of thinking, he was still unable to solve the last parts of the puzzle. Iron Mouth Qi felt the urge to slap himself. What was he neglecting to consider? He took stock once more. He avoided telling the fortunes of foreigners, conspiracy theorists, and people with qilin tattoos. Zhang Qishan had a Qióngqí tattoo, so whilst telling his fortune was difficult, it was not impossible for him. There were no foreigners in the team. And as for conspiracists, it was not that he could not tell their fortunes, but rather that it was inauspicious, and invited calamity.

Iron Mouth Qi pondered the question, staring into the jungle. Was it possible that someone with a qilin tattoo had intervened in this event, but had not yet made themselves known?

Iron Mouth Qi saw that none of the soldiers reacted, so he silently offered up some prayers. Worrying about the safety of Zhang Qishan, he continued on towards the banyan grove. The soldiers followed suit immediately. Qi understood that, unless they were specifically ordered to do so, they would not move under their own steam.

Although Iron Mouth Qi was a skilled tactician, he knew about battle formations, and was aware that he was playing with human lives. It was in some people's birth charts that they were destined to put people's lives on the chessboard, and act against popular feeling for the cause of righteousness. But very few of these people were infallible.

When he thought about it, he could hardly take command of a ball. If a poor command or an ill-considered threat led people to their deaths, not only would he never be able to come to terms with his failure, but the weight on his karma would also be too great to bear.

It was best if he treated everyone as if they were him. He issued a command, ordering everyone behind him to get down in single file like a caterpillar, so they could inch their way towards the banyan grove.

17

THE BABY

IN THE INTERIORS of the banyan cluster, Zhang Qishan was not in the least thinking about leaving. He fixed his eyes on the baby, whose deadly black eyes were as firmly fixed on him.

"What the hell are you?" Zhang Qishan asked.

The baby began a high-pitched giggle, stopping thirty paces from Zhang. Zhang lifted his pistol and pointed it at him. Surprised, its expression became malignant.

At this time of their lives, babies did sometimes look malevolent, sometimes adorable, and sometimes shifted from one to the other. It was said that Mengpo's soul-cleansing soup had not quite worked its magic, and they were still being affected by memories of their past lives.

Zhang Qishan understood, though, that the baby in front of him was no ordinary infant. During their staring competition, he was certain that the baby was forming deep thoughts. So he pressed on. "Cut the crap! You're no baby, so what the fuck are you?"

But the baby was looking lost again, his attention now caught by the mosquitoes, as if his previous behaviour just then was a mere accident.

Zhang Qishan dared not be dismissive, and carefully observed the baby for a while. He really seemed to have turned back to an ordinary child. With suspicion still in his mind, Zhang edged up, on tiptoes, behind the boy.

He was, honestly, not afraid of the baby suddenly attacking him, because physically it was no different from any other baby. A simple glance told Zhang that its physique had not developed enough to hurt people. Yet some of the expressions he had seen pass its face resembled those of a mercenary adult.

Holstering his pistol, Zhang Qishan snapped a thinner branch from the banyan wall, to use in the manner of a cat toy. It was something his father had done when he was a child, and one of the few toys he remembered playing with.

He flicked the stick above the baby's head, and, being quickly attracted to movement, he was drawn to the dancing end above his head. He relaxed, and even began to laugh. Zhang Qishan edged over and picked him up again.

At this moment, the baby's face suddenly reverted to a malevolent stare, but this gaze was not directed at Zhang, rather something behind him. His mouth moved, as if saying, "Watch out."

Zhang Qishan spun around, and saw the monster crawling towards him, the remnants of its head dangling, and with a swat of its great arm, it knocked Zhang off the nest.

Twisting his body in midair, Zhang Qishan fell smoothly into the marsh below, keeping the baby above the waterline. The great monster leaped down from the web of branches, arms spread, and Zhang saw that under one of them was another human face.

Conjoined twins.

That smaller head was positioned at the monster's breast. Zhang Qishan realised that Zhang Xiaoyu must not have been nursing, but – kissing that thing?

The tiny head had an eye that did not open and was not in the most natural of locations, so Zhang Qishan was able to smoothly avoid the first blind strike. Turning, he spotted one of the machine guns that had caught on a burr in the banyan wall. He instantly made a dash for it, child in one hand, while he scooped up the weapon with the other.

The barrel was bent. Dodging another blow, he threw the child up into the air, and used his temporarily free other hand to force it back straight.

The monster's attention was drawn by the child, and it swiped at him with its claws. Zhang Qishan sent sweeping rounds of lead across its front, forcing the fiend to withdraw.

Zhang leapt to catch the child, and the monster fled to the darkness between draping roots. Zhang Qishan watched the child's eyes, and wherever the child looked, he sprayed machine gun fire. The monster twisted and lunged in the dark, but the stream of glowing lead followed it, like an offensive stream of piss.

The clip was emptied in a moment, and when the monster burst out of the darkness, it was riddled with bullet holes.

Zhang Qishan noticed that this face's control of the body was not as smooth as the other one. Suddenly, he leaped onto the main trunk, hanging the child on a branch, before kicking off and rushing the creature.

The monster tried to slap him away, but he twisted away midair, and when the hand almost grazed his chin, he made a grab for it, and swung with the arm until he could land and then charge back at the Shanshen.

The thing leant down. Its legs were sinking into the swamp mud, which slowed its movement, whilst Zhang Qishan, on the other hand, had reached his peak speed, and in an instant stood toe-to-toe with his foe. He only came up to the monster's pelvis, and as it curled its body around him, trying to crush him to death, he pressed himself through the gap, as he had done to bypass the puppet Zhang Xiaoyu. Zhang Qishan shifted quickly against the monster's body, swinging and flipping onto its back. He stabbed his flattened hand, again and again, into the monster's soft back, until eventually, with both hands buried either side of its spine, he stomped hard with both feet. Letting out an almighty roar, he pulled with every drop of strength he had.

Half of the monster's spine was ripped free, with an explosion of spinal fluid and twitching nerves. The whole bloated body spasmed and collapsed into the marsh.

Zhang Qishan fell, too, but scrambling out of the stagnant water, he sped to the face wrapped round the monster's side, and pulling free the bayonet lodged in its elbow, he drove it cleanly through the bulging head, and out the other side.

This head did not have the protection of a skull, and so drained like a punctured catheter bag, its brains pouring out into the swamp like soft scrambled doufu.

The monster lay completely motionless. Zhang Qishan panted for breath, with six or seven wounds dotting his body. He had no idea how he had acquired them, but none were too serious.

Staring down at the monster, he said to himself, "Still just a mortal."

He climbed back up to the branch where he had hung up the baby and retrieved it. Since the monster had stopped moving, it no longer held the child's interest.

"You can talk, right? How old are you, really?" Zhang Qishan looked at the baby. He'd heard of some people who never physically grew after birth, meaning they still looked like a child, despite being fully grown adults. He suspected this was the case with this baby. Or perhaps some mysterious power was hiding within the consciousness of the boy, spying on him from time to time through the infant's eyes. Whatever the case, the Touling must have given him this particular baby for a purpose other than sacrifice.

To his surprise, he found that the baby, once again, had fixed his gaze at a point in the darkness.

Still not over? he asked himself, carrying the baby back up to where he had laid Zhang Xiaoyu, whose condition seemed to be stable. He took up one of the storm lanterns, and quickly spun, hurling it towards the point the baby had locked onto.

The lantern flew up and shattered against the treetops. The kerosene ignited and lit up that dark corner. Zhang Qishan saw a giant brass-bound coffin in the twisted limbs, almost entirely integrated into the wall of banyan roots, vines completely coiled around it. He could see in the firelight that it was set with a rainbow of gemstones; though their hues were dimmed by the dust accumulated over the ages, they still emitted a halo-like glow. The baby kept its eyes fixed on the coffin.

"What's this? what now?" Zhang Qishan asked him.

The baby clapped and gurgled, as if happy to see the coffin. He held out his hands, making grabby gestures, as if he wanted Zhang to carry him over to it.

Zhang did not move straight away, well aware that this was yet another trial he'd have to face.

18

THE BRASS-BOUND COFFIN

ZHANG QISHAN COULD find no sign of his soldiers

anywhere, nor their corpses. He sliced open the belly of the monster, and found it stuffed with mashed meat, and mixed in with that were the remnants of the Zhang army uniforms, buttons and belt buckles.

They had all been devoured and ground to a mash.

He stood in front of the monster's corpse for a long time, unable to speak.

Death was death, painful or not; these men all had been alive and well, not an hour ago.

Staring at the meat gruel, Zhang Qishan saw a flare gun. Pulling it from the mess, he climbed up above the canopy, and shot it into the sky.

This was how fate worked. Everyone who had followed Zhang Qishan, apart from Zhang Xiaoyu, who was ironically the first to be wounded, had wound up dead. Yet everyone who was with Iron Mouth Qi was still alive. It was often what happened, and the loyal people he had brought out with him from Dongbei were reduced further and further in numbers. Not all of them were Zhangs, but it was growing rarer to hear the language of home, and he could not help but feel emotional.

But he did not let himself dwell on it.

It was not long before Iron Mouth Qi's whistle sounded from the edge of the woods, and Zhang responded, the two converging.

Looking at the tragic conditions of their fellows, the troops were silent. Someone began bandaging Zhang Xiaoyu with care, and another saw to the baby. Looking at Zhang Qishan, Iron Mouth Qi patted him, and shared with him all his deductions. He was hoping for some corroborations from Qishan, but he did not seem to care, turning back to the matter of the baby. One of the soldiers sat down opposite them with the baby on his lap, whilst the pair sat side by side. Zhang Qishan told Iron Mouth Qi about the baby's strangeness and abnormal behaviours in detail.

Resting his chin on his hand, Iron Mouth Qi ruminated, while Zhang Qishan demanded explanations. At the time, the baby was acting perfectly normally, apart from lifting his head to glance at the coffin from time to time. There was no abnormality.

They were also unsure of what impact the monster's skull-piercing would have on Zhang Xiaoyu's brain. The manner and deftness of control had seemed magical.

"When Zhang Xiaoyu wakes up, should we tell him what happened?" Iron Mouth Qi asked.

"Telling him what we saw, that's only half of it. If he can accept it and move on, then that will be the end of it."

"Buddha, that isn't going to be easy."

"Nothing that is truly painful in this world is easy, but it will pass."

"Ordinary people get old, but you–"

"This is just the reality of it. We're not blaming the heavens, nor anyone else." Zhang Qishan threw Iron Mouth Qi a look, before the pair climbed up to the coffin.

Zhang asked for Qi's opinion.

"Well, I see copper, which to the ancients was as rare as gold, and certainly brass was used in the same manner as gold. I think this is probably from the Han Dynasty. Why is it up a tree?"

"That's exactly what I asked you."

Iron Mouth Qi took another long, careful look, before saying, "You see that vine? It's grown out from the coffin and has coiled around the banyan tree. I have never seen it before. The scholarship in my family includes medicinal theory, which requires the distinction of all existing herbs. If it were from another region, there's a chance I wouldn't recognise it. I wasn't great at medicine, but just look at it! Have you ever seen anything like this?"

Taking a more considered look, Zhang Qishan could see what he meant. The vine did indeed seem to grow out from the coffin, its leaves resembling nails. All of them were tightly curled, clearly distinct and incompatible with the flora they had seen around here before.

"This is an ancient coffin, and you see this vine has come out through this hole here" – Iron Mouth Qi pointed to a deliberate portal in the metal – "as if it was planned. Someone had placed the body in the coffin, knowing that something would grow out of the corpse."

"But it could also be seeds that had just fallen into the coffin."

"Look here." Iron Mouth Qi pointed to the bucolic relief sculpture carved into the coffin. It was a vine, exactly like the one that had grown out of it, like a tongue extending out of the coffin. The detail had been carved in with tiny augers, each line traced and carved thousands of times, in order that each groove would be deep enough to stand the trials of time and corrosion.

So, this is a pénzai potted plant, Zhang Qishan said internally.

"What kind of vine is it?" Iron Mouth Qi shone his torch onto the leaves. "And does it have any bearing on the Shanshen?"

"Call the men up here, and let's open the coffin," Zhang Qishan ordered. "Whatever is in here must have something to do with the mountain god. According to your deduction, the villages offer up a baby every year in exchange for longevity. These are all parts of the mystery.

Let's open the box and see if we can figure this all out."

19
OPENING THE COFFIN

As the Zhang army climbed up to the golden coffin, all were filled with sorrow for their fallen comrades. They stood in solemn silence for a while, before their expressions eased. This was a ceremony of all battlefields, grief coming too thick and fast – there was often no time for people to immerse themselves in mourning. These brief few minutes of sorrow were the periods of grief that they had become accustomed to.

One soldier brought the baby up with him and placed it next to the coffin.

Before they opened it, Zhang Qishan wanted to see if there had been any changes to the baby.

The infant's gaze remained fixed on the coffin, his eyes full of narrow curiosity. Zhang Qishan leaned in and asked, "OK, you little devil, why did you point this out to us?"

The baby gave absolutely no response.

The scene was comical. Zhang Qishan glanced at Iron Mouth Qi with a self-mocking smile, and waved his hand, signalling his men to open the coffin. Some soldiers took out crowbars, some sprayed shaojiu, and some lit incense. They watched the smoke to see if it was absorbed by whatever was in the coffin. This was a unique coffin-opening ceremony of the Zhangs. If the smoke was sucked into the coffin, it meant something of very low pressure or temperature was in there, which usually indicated the yao.

"You said this thing was old, which part of the Han Dynasty?" As Zhang watched his men in their preparations, he quizzed Iron Mouth Qi.

"Buddha, you can't tell? I'm not really surprised. This isn't a standard item. Brass-cornered copper-lined coffins were used during the late Han period, for transporting jiāngshī. But I've only seen ones made of cedarwood, with gold paint and copper foil on the corners, not ones entirely lined with metal," Iron Mouth Qi said. "They would find a huashidi to bury it, a place where a corpse would rot down into bloody water within three months, thus preventing the jiangshi from hurting anyone. But huashidi are usually located downslope, where the waters pool, and can wash away the soil. This is why they are painted in gold, so if they do become uncovered, people can see them glinting in the sun from a dozen li away and avoid coming too close."

Iron Mouth Qi touched his hand to the coffin. Whilst it had a skin of grey rust and black dirt, those with the knowledge could tell that the body of the coffin was real metal.

"But the coffin is so big – if it were entirely metal, there's no way the tree could support it." Iron Mouth Qi pursued his thoughts. "Therefore, I deduce that the coffin is plated. Be careful when you open it, everyone. The interiors could be wood, and would already have rotted, so if the brass corners have not been well cast, the whole thing could disintegrate as soon as you apply some pressure."

With that fresh warning, several pry bars were inserted through the gap in the coffin, and once secured, with a quick lift, the lid was pried open.

Because of the hole in the top of the coffin, it was not an airtight seal, so opening it did not produce the usual assault of foul smells. However, there was clearly a mass of plants in the coffin, which were joined at the roots, so it took several attempts to fully open it. The coffin lid was slid to one side, and a storm lantern brought over. Under the dim light, gasps of astonishment escaped from the whole party.

The inside of the coffin was neither metal nor wood, but ivory. Each segment of it had yellowed, overgrown with roots, from which a host of startled and scattering bugs emerged.

This was a particularly rare ivory, according to the records. The material used to make the interior of this coffin were fossilised mammoth tusk. This kind of giant bone fossil is now being used to carve artwork and ornaments.

Even more shocking was that inside this coffin, there was another smaller one, made to fit perfectly into the bigger, brass-cornered one. This smaller coffin was made of translucent stone, crafted in a simple, archaic style, like something from the Stone Age. Under the light of the flames, a liquid could be seen within the coffin, with multiple figures submerged within.

"What is this?" a soldier asked.

The first instant they saw the floating figures, everyone had the same thought – those floating shadows looked like babies.

The plants around this smaller coffin had wrapped their roots firmly around the semi-clear stone, with their finer tendrils penetrating through the gaps, as if absorbing nutrients from the liquid within.

"What do you think this is?" Zhang Qishan asked Iron Mouth Qi.

"It seems to be some kind of ancient, botanic alchemy. The bodies submerged within all seem to be children, and then the corpse water is nourishing these plants."

Zhang Qishan made a signal for his subordinate to bring over the baby. Zhang Qishan looked at the baby, who was gazing at the figures in the stone coffin. Suddenly, he let out a strange call. It was a complex sound, and not one that such a young thing could make. A baby's tongue would not be so agile, and since nobody except Qishan had expected real language from the boy, they were not sure if they had really heard it or not.

But the three words uttered sent Iron Mouth Qi into a cold sweat. The baby had said, "Corpse Switching Herb."

They waited for the baby to make more sounds, looking to each other for confirmation of what their own ears had told them, but it just stared at the coffin, and then, with no subtle transition, fell into a slumber, so quickly it felt like a deliberate exit.

Zhang Qishan reached out, and was handed a crowbar, with which he rushed over, inserting it into the seam of the smaller coffin. The roots were wound about the stone coffin extremely tightly, as if tying it up with a hundred loops of string. Zhang Qishan had to pry as if his life depended on it, before he could open it. In an instant, a thick fragrance attacked him, and, holding his breath, he pulled the lid aside.

The sea-glass coffin was indeed full of baby corpses. Many of them had turned black from soaking in the liquid, some were cloudy masses of decay, already indistinguishable pieces of flesh. The corpses were packed close together within the liquid which, from its thick fragrance, was almost certainly some sort of alcohol and herbs. The root system had inveigled itself into the coffin and had grown into the flesh of the child corpses. On some corpses, which retained their distinct shape, the skin was marked in wrinkles, making them seem nothing like babies at all.

Iron Mouth Qi moved over, his hand over his nose, took one look and stated, "You see, some of these babies have tattoos on their bodies. A custom from centuries ago. Nowadays, babies no longer get tattooed at birth, so these corpses would have been from very distant times."

"Did every baby that was sacrificed through the centuries end up here?" Zhang Qishan asked.

Iron Mouth Qi could not tell. He moved the storm lantern closer and examined one wrinkled child. "Why would the skin be like this? It was an infant, yet its skin appears so aged."

"Corpse Switching Herb." Zhang Qishan looked at the tree and sighed a long sigh.

"This is very ancient sorcery, Buddha. They did indeed place the babies in this vessel. It looks like the baby's life would be absorbed by the corpse switching herb, and then, by a certain method, the life within the herb would be transferred over to the chiefs. This is why these babies are so aged. The Huanshicao not only had the power to change sex, but to transfer life."

Zhang Qishan was silent. Iron Mouth Qi asked himself, had Zhang Qishan not prevailed, would he have been placed in this coffin? With his vitality, would this strange tree have grown as tall as the heavens?

He turned to look at the baby, who was sleeping soundly. He seemed to at last have some inkling of what it might be. He took the child and turned to Iron Mouth Qi. "You said that people with qílín tattoos can negate the accuracy of your divinations, right?"

Iron Mouth Qi nodded. Zhang Qishan pushed the child's clothes apart and put his hand over the child's chest. The tattoo near Zhang Qishan's collar flashed, and Iron Mouth Qi saw the veins on Zhang's hand swell, as with heat. Slowly, Qi saw that on the child's chest, under that steaming body heat, rose a fragment of a newborn's luck tattoo. The scale tattoo was obviously unfinished, but it was evident which beast this scale was from.

Friends, the ending you take away from this depends on how deeply you want to dig into the details. There is no need to overthink it, but those that feel the need can dive in deeper.

20
ENDING 1

FOR A CHILD from the Zhang family to have ended up suffering as a sacrifice, the exact mechanics are still unknown, but here a child from the clan had somehow fallen into the hands of the Touling, before their qílín tattoo was finished.

If it were really possible to obtain other people's lives through the Huanshicao, consider the combined potential of the Zhang child with the qilin tattoo, and that of Zhang Qishan, this Touling's greed for life would make one's skin crawl.

Of course, Zhang Qishan also thought that maybe the Touling had misunderstood, and thought that every Zhang with a legendary tattoo was long-lived.

It was eternity he wanted.

But that was not the way of it. Only Zhang Qishan himself knew enough about this detail. Those Zhangs who gained immortality did not get it purely from the power of the qílín.

For those who do not require in-depth notes, here is a brief account of what happened next.

The investigation of the Mother Tree lasted for three days. I shall not go into the superfluous details here. The number of children who had been sacrificed were recorded.

They carried out a more detailed survey of the coffin, especially when in full daylight, when Iron Mouth Qi discovered that the ivory panels were full of dense carvings, resembling pictograms. He used the ritual paper and incense he had with him to take charcoal rubbings of them. Surprisingly, these were all included in the records I have been studying.

Those carved pictograms were similar to Mayan script, containing an astonishing amount of information.

These records of the coffin's origin clarified the connection between the Earth Maidens and the stone sarcophagus.

Additionally, Buddha Zhang thought that the baby had a special ability to seek out the Earth Maidens. The relief carvings seemed to also record the Earth Maidens' ability to ascend into human form using the Línglóng soil, as well as cure diseases, wounds and pains.

This information was too complicated to be included in this tale, but for those who are interested, I will try to provide a simple explanation. This has been a fascinating story, although many will feel it is far-fetched and illogical. Nevertheless, I hope that in the way I have recorded it here, it will be a pleasure to read, and I hope I shall come across more of its ilk, to enrich my historical research.

21
ENDING 2

ACCORDING TO THE relief texts seen by Buddha and Master Qi, I believe I have pieced together the history of the relic buried deep underground in Xiangxi. This relic, found several hundred times deeper than the deepest tomb, we can be sure was never part of any human burial rite, nor sunken ancient city.

It is the remnant of the habitat of the Earth Maidens, which would have been totally submerged in Qiqiao Linglong soil, which was to these creatures as air to humans. They could breathe in it. They spent most of their lives in the dark. The biological structure of the Earth Maiden was very similar to those of humans, so they ought to be classified as a subspecies of homo sapiens, and their reproductive systems were compatible with those of humans.

How did this artefact come to light? The only possibility was that someone had dug deep into the ground, in an attempt to build a place habitable for humans. According to the murals, the Earth Maidens' habitat very much resembled an ant's nest. In certain seasons, they would venture above ground with their Linglong soil, looking for food. At the moment, we are not yet certain of the existence of a queen that lived at the core, or if these maidens brought the food back underground, to feed the Her. What we can be sure of, is that beneath the Mother Banyan Tree was a passage that led deep underground and into this hive, and that at the connection point with the hive, the trees would always grow especially verdant.

However, it was not possible for humans to descend into the underground network, which astonished me most, as the Earth Maidens' ant-like ecosystem seemed to have been constructed by humans, as proven by that brass-cornered coffin, which came from the hive, and, since it dates back to the late Han era, suggests that the hive was created during that dynasty.

It also appears that these Earth Maidens had a custom of placing their children overground, where they would be mistaken for abandoned infants and raised by humans. The founder of the Eighty-Two Stronghold was an Earth Maiden. She had appeared in the jungle, was brought up by bandits, and at a certain point in her life, she must have encountered an emissary from the colony, who informed her of her identity. So, she founded the Stronghold, and started the annual tradition of child sacrifice.

According to historic records, after this tradition was established, the incidents of child theft across Xiangxi greatly reduced in number. Was this proof that the stolen infants from across the province were largely the actions of the Earth Maidens? As theft became annual offerings, the people above ground and those below reached a kind of harmony. They would drag the children underneath. In other words, into the hive, where, perhaps, there was some creature or process which could turn human babies into Earth Maidens?

Because there was no requirement on the gender of the offering, there needed to be a technique within the remnant (for example, the Corpse Switching Herb) that could change the sex of the baby. (This is totally my own assumption, which I do not believe, but have mentioned as a possibility just in case.) Or else, perhaps there were Earth Bachelors, living in the hive, but never making it to the surface.

The Huanshicao would have been the key in the transferring of human life in this vessel, but the specifics have been lost, and were nowhere to be found within the records. The Earth Maidens used this method of attaining longevity to trade with people in the villages. However, the stronghold's Touling and an Earth Maiden did indeed fall for each other, and I even suspect that his loss of sight was to do with the Earth Maiden's special method of *enabling him to enter and exist within the underground structure. The ending of the story was missing a great deal of information. We only knew that Zhang Qishan brought back a large pile of Linglong soil, which, even thinking with one's toes, clearly contained the body of an Earth Maiden.*

When Zhang Qishan went into the swamp, he did not find Linglong soil there, but must have gone to further trouble to acquire it. From the relief sculptures, we can tell that when the Earth Maidens returned to the soil, they would return to human form. I do not know whether the Earth Woman he had brought back was a fresh one that he had newly caught, or the monster he had killed, which was revived gradually in the life-giving soil, thus reuniting the Touling with his lover. Either way, Zhang Qishan completed his part of the bargain.

What still haunts my dreams, though, is the ancient habitat that was built during the Han Dynasty so deep underground, at a depth beyond the Nine Springs, that was documented in classical novels. I began to contemplate the possibility that the so-called underworld might not be an imagined construct, but a real place, constructed by the ancients within certain unique cultural systems, which were forgotten because they were too deep underground, and it was not possible for them to be discovered by everyday engineering. Then why? What was the purpose of this architecture? And why did the Earth Maidens live within them?

I will add to this account if I make any progress.

NOTES

THERE IS A particular genre of adventure story in China, Daomu, which could best be described as tomb raiding, or grave-robbing fiction. These tend to straddle the line between action and horror, with creatures from mythology, lost civilisations, cursed objects and ancient threats often rearing their ugly heads. The absolute master of this genre is Nanpai Sanshu ("Third Uncle of the Southern Sect"), whose interconnected stories tell of particular clans of tomb raiders and their adventures. This is the first short work the author has produced surrounding his characters and the organisations that feature in "The Grave Robber Chronicles", but we felt it worked well as a stand-alone horror story.

When you start a tale with a group of hardened fighters or elite troops going off on a mysterious mission into the jungle, full of bravado and boasting that nothing in the trees is deadlier than them, it is with a mixture of trepidation and schadenfreude that we wait for them to be slowly picked off, to descend into abject terror, or to otherwise end up seriously out of their depth. Having a well-prepared set of protagonists gives the writer justification to indulge in overt violence, gore, and creating threat and suspense by conjuring the most intelligent and vicious of monsters. This story, however, offers so much more. Set in the mountainous southern region of Hunan, with its rich diversity of ethnic cultures, the story weaves in national and regional history, local mythologies and folklore, beliefs and rituals, as well as exploring how these interact. Records of Xiangxi is, in the end, the story of a scholar trying to piece together his family history, of a loyal clan following their leaders into the unknown for the sake of protecting their country, an inter-species tragedy, and a contemplation of mankind's worldview.

This is a manifold horror story. There are the horrors of war, the horrors of the unfathomable, the horrors of human greed and lust for power, and horrors of the monstrous. There were some interesting elements I needed to approach in this piece, certain words which would mechanically be replaced with "deformed", "twisted" or "misshapen". There are creatures, there are monsters, and there are humans who have been contorted and changed into inhuman things. There are prejudiced voices and scholars who are following ancient legends with very set views about monsters. I have tried my best to encapsulate all these things, without falling into the usual cart tracks of 'Looks Different = Evil', even when certain characters find themselves challenged by the uncanny.

This is also the most action-packed of the stories, which again had me leaning on my video-game-playing friends for firearms terms, and using action figures on my desk to act out complex fights. While many pieces in this book revolve around horror leaking into the everyday, this novella has the appeal of bringing in misfits and brigands, those who live on the periphery of society and whose eccentricities lend themselves to adventuring, where normal rules can be bent.

The Chinese title may more directly be translated as "Memories of Xiangxi", but because of the investigative framework in which the story is presented, and the interloping between narration and the scholar's voice, I have translated it as "Records". This short piece has much of the flavour of the longer daomu adventures, which I have tended to describe to Western friends by invoking the excitement of Indiana Jones, or Tomb Raider. However, it is a very important distinction that whilst both of those franchises indulge in exotic, foreign locations, daomu stories are almost entirely centred around remarkable explorations of the rich lore surrounding China's great ancient tombs, and the equally exciting secret clans, sects and strange creatures from its lost cultures and those of its near neighbours.

THE GHOST WEDDING

远结冤缘

Yimei Tangguo

PRELUDE

THE BALLOON ARCH is pasted with four red characters, xi jie liang yuan, a happy union of serendipity, just adding to the scene, and makes the atmosphere even more joyous and exciting. The banquet in the tent has been laid out in a long row. Within the tent can be seen the rustic smiling faces of the whole village, joy flowing between the clinking of wine cups, the consuming of large pieces of deep-fried pork and chicken, as well as sea urchin, turtle and the latest trend, baby abalone. Everyone is full of compliments for the fancy delicacies of this banquet, which will probably be the talk of the village for the next month.

The groom's parents have taken a huge financial hit in order to welcome the bride. After all, arranging a decent wedding for their son is the duty of good parents. The bride's mother, however, still seems aloof, with her manners frosty. Director Zhang, of the county police bureau, sits on one of the special tables, courtesy of the bride's family, apparently to add weight to the occasion.

The bride's father is getting a little teary, but slowly seems to be coming round to the fact his daughter is going to become someone else's. The dowry was a three hundred square-metre apartment, exquisitely furnished. There was also an Audi, some gold and jade, a large amount of clothes, shoes and bags. The groom's family cannot help but keep nodding with satisfaction – such a good girl, there is nothing else to be said.

It is about to snow, and the dishes are coming out of the kitchen faster and faster. Ninety-nine percent of Ox Head villages are drinking Wuliangye for the first time. Great stuff, and at six or seven hundred kuai a bottle, it'd be a shame to throw it up. So they gulp the vomit back down as though their lives depend on it. Who knows when they'll get the chance to go to such a high-class banquet again, or if they'll still be alive to enjoy it.

The ceremony is about to start, and the children, gnawing at chicken drumsticks, have been keeping their heads raised and their eyes glued to the stage at the front of the tent, anticipating the entrance of the bride and groom, which apparently will be accompanied by the throwing out of a lot of sweets.

Not far from this, Little Guapi shudders. He hears the rolling of the drums and gongs, and can smell the scent of roasting meats, and his stomach is growling.

He is also very aware of the woman lying next to him. It is cold on the mountains, and whilst everyone else is enjoying the wine and the wedding banquet, he has been landed with this thankless task.

Under the blue plastic tarp, she lies wrapped in bright red cotton bed linen, in a shallow pit filled with lime. The curve of her stomach rises and falls rhythmically, as if she is breathing.

But it is only the wind.

Curious, Little Guapi lifts a corner of the plastic and

takes a peek. The face of the corpse bride has already turned green, with her eyes tightly shut. She is dead to the marrow. A red cord has been tied around her head, because there is a big crack in it, while the right corner of her mouth slants upwards, as if deliberately forming a ghastly smirk.

Outside, the sheep are grazing, their bellies full and round, and soon, it will get dark.

THE START OF IT

XUE SHUANGXI WAS having a meal with her classmates, flash-cooking lamb and maodu tripe over a steaming hot pot, everyone's eyes watering from the spices. She raised her wine glass, its body filled with red liquid. She had brought the wine from home; it was a few thousand kuai a bottle, and one bottle stood on each of the four tables, in addition to bottomless beers. This was how Xue Shuangxi played hostess.

Even this short separation had brought Xue Shuangxi feelings of long emptiness. As she swiped her bank card, and got ready to head home, she thought about how all her classmates were either going abroad or returning to their hometowns for the winter break.

Outside, the bustling traffic snaked off into the distance, and the cold was invasive, but home was as warm as spring, with fresh, blossoming lilies and roses set on the dining table. Xue Shuangxi began the tedium of her winter holidays. Mother had rung again from abroad and said she had transferred her new year hongbao into Shuangxi's account, as she would not be back from Australia until the end of Spring Festival. Shuangxi was to stay at home, be good, NOT to get in touch with Qu Xiangtian, and definitely not even THINK about seeing her father.

"Also, don't just live on instant noodles all the time, they're not good for you, Xixi dear. Mummy loves you, and I'll call you again when I'm free." Feng Jingshui's current husband was an American, and "love you" had become one of her catchphrases. But what was wrong with seeing Qu Xiangtian? People cannot choose the family they are born into. Not unless they could acquire the skills of reincarnation.

Xue Shuangxi nodded obediently at the other end of the phone. Feng Jingshui did love her. She was her mother. Why else would she have exhausted her efforts, wealth and power in relocating Shuangxi all the way from a rural district, whose only ability to place in a league table was to win top five poorest villages in the country, to the Modu metropolis.

Xue Shuangxi had been given designer clothes, make-up, bags, shoes, an apartment with underfloor heating, and more food than she could ever eat... but before she'd started high school, her memories of her mother had been a total blank.

In the deep of the night, Shuangxi took a can of soda from the fridge, opened it, and began to think about her stupid but not entirely 'special' dad, who was still familiar, despite being all the way back in that poor, distant village of Ox Head...

"Go to school, even if I have to sell the wok for scrap – you gotta get an education." Xue 'Get Rich' Fugui had placed all his hopes on his precious daughter, even though his wife had run away before the child had even grown past breastfeeding. At least the kid was still with him.

"From primary to middle school, my daughter's always

been number two at school. Number two. Who's top of the class? Old Qu's son, Qu Xiangtian. Little shit. One day I'll do him in, and my daughter can be number one. But at least the two little sods were school friends, and Qu Dajun did me a big favour at my wedding, so I can't really do that."

Qu Xiangtian's name had come from that poem quxiang xiangtian ge[32], which was the sole poem that Qu Dajun, who had only completed primary school level education, could recite. So, he had named his son Qu Xiangtian.

Xue Fugui's family had little money, and what they did have, they spent on trying to get him a wife. The whole village was as poor as a ghost town. It suffered drought one year and floods the next. Nothing except corn and potatoes would grow in the thin soil, and the nearest town was several dozen kilometres away, only accessible by foot. The walk involved climbing over a mountain via a tiny narrow path, on which multiple motorcyclists had tumbled to their deaths. Naturally, men with hunger in their bones do not make attractive matches. If they were really desperate, they would trade their own sisters for wives with the neighbouring villages. But Xue Fugui was in luck – Gua Pi's old man came back from Fujian and had brought wife material with him. Her fresh, shining eyes were so helpless, pleading with him as she knelt on the floor, kowtowing as if her life depended on it. "Da'ge[33], I beg you, if you can just let me go home, I'll do whatever you ask. My family will give you a lot of money, you'll

---

32 Quxing xiangtian ge 曲项向天歌, a line from the famous Tang poem by Luo Binwang, Eulogy of Geese, that is taught in the primary school curriculum and which, therefore, everyone knows by heart. This line describes the activities of a flock of geese by the river. Hence Qu Xiangtian's name, "neck arched towards the sky".

33 Da'ge (see note in Those Who Walk At Night), traditionally the Chinese address everyone in familial terms. Here it's a term of respect for someone male who is not related.

never want for anything for the rest of your life."

Xue Fugui harrumphed down his nose. "Don't even think about it, I gave Guapi three thousand RMB two years ago, and I have waited day and night for you. I don't want money, I want you."

Feng Jingshui struggled and fought back with all the strength she could summon, but, like the strongest field mouse, she still could not break the grip of a much bigger predator.

The people in the village, who had crowded around for the spectacle, jabbed their fingers at her and gossiped. Feng Jingshui kowtowed to the villagers. "Please help me, I beg you. Call the police, I'll give you twenty thousand RMB! Twenty thousand RMB reward!"

A woman shouted, "You think you're so great just because you're rich, but now you've got to live here and serve the village. Fugui, fuck this city girl already, so we can get on with the wedding drinks."

Feng Jingshui's furious eyes swept past the face of every villager. "Do you not understand that kidnapping and trafficking women and children is against the law?"

The crowd all laughed and walked away.

Feng Jingshui kept on with her reproach. "You'll be punished for this! Your children will be punished for this! You're going to die painful deaths and your bloodlines are going to dry up and die out!"

After two backhand slaps across her face failed to quiet her, Xue Fugui dragged her by the arms to the pig pen that joined with the midden, and threw her in. Grabbing Feng's long hair, he forced her head down viciously into the bog full of faeces, old and new shit covering her hair and blouse. Those little elastic white devils burrowed into her nose and ears, crawling everywhere, dense and itching.

"AHHHH!" Feng Jingshui screamed desperately, before again being pressed into the filth, not being allowed to breathe, not being allowed to die. She would try to struggle whenever she was lifted, and was suppressed again, until at last, she drifted into unconsciousness.

When she woke up, she was in a barn, with a straw mat on the floor, and a bucket of water.

The door was locked, and whenever Feng Jingshui screamed or shouted for help, Xue Fugui would enter with a wooden club, and bring it down on her head. Before long, Feng Jingshui grew subdued. Starved to the point of death, her head was so swollen it looked like a papier mâché doll head from the new year shows.

She had no idea how many days had passed. One day, Feng Jingshui glimpsed through the crack of the door, and saw a piece of cured meat hanging outside the decrepit hut. It was black, stripy with fat, and covered in green-headed flies, which shimmered in the sunlight.

That night, Feng Jingshui did not cry out, but Xue Fugui still came in with the club.

"I want noodles."

"Strip," Xue Fugui ordered, oblivious to her demand.

Feng Jingshui looked at Xue Fugui, and woodenly nodded.

Ten minutes later, naked, and standing in the pen that joined with the midden, she swallowed a bowl of Tongyi instant noodles with cured meat. She had barely finished the noodles before Xue Fugui snatched the bowl away from her and gulped down the broth. "Out here, you only get to eat meat on your birthday. But if you're going to be my wife, consider the grass to be growing on your ancestors' graves[34]."

Ten days later, the banquet was held, although it was a little shabby, as all the money had gone to Gua Pi's old man. The three thousand RMB had just been a deposit, and a further five thousand had to be paid to make up the total. However, the village was always kind, and Xue Fugui received a lot of good wishes, gifts of white and red sugar, homemade mijiu rice wine, apples, and even Lux Soap. He reciprocated with two RMB packs of cigarettes. Cigarettes were the opium of the poor.

The bride Feng Jingshui was gracious and generous. When some of her white face powder fell on the borrowed red Western style suit, she refused to smile, in case more of it fell.

The journey from affluent university student to rural wife was long and tormented. There was only electricity for one hour a day, and the postman came once a week. Everyone in the village knew her now, and there was simply no way she could run. She had tried it once and was discovered by a villager who had dragged her back.

"I'll break your fucking legs." Xu Fugui could not contain his fury – he had treated her so well; how could she want to run away? But if she wanted to run, let's see her do it on broken legs.

Just as he lifted the rake, Feng Jingshui threw up.

"I have your baby in me. So just beat me to death." Feng Jingshui closed her eyes.

"Then you won't run off again? Say it!" Xu Fugui's voice grew calm.

---

34 Grass growing over your ancestor's graves – the Chinese hold different kinds of superstitions over how graves should be kept, one of these being that an overgrowth around the gravestone is an auspicious sign for the deceased's descendants. This may simply be down to the fact that the plants help to hold the soil in place, since a grave collapsing due to mudslides is definitely a bad sign.

"Won't run." Feng Jingshui rubbed her tummy bulge. It was two months old already.

From that day, Xu Fugui gave up his vice of wife-beating, and got a job moving bricks at a construction site in town. He came home once a week, bringing Feng Jingshui meat, powdered milk, fruit, and even a little bottle of something for her to put on her face. Honestly, he surrendered his wages to his wife. Everybody said that Xue Fugui was a good man to live a life with.

Feng Jingshui learned to dig potatoes and thresh corn by hand, to smoke with the other village women in the evenings, sticking out her big belly with practised ease, chatting about their little private matters, flashing a smile full of yellow teeth, and flirting with the village shopkeeper, mock-pinching him coquettishly and accepting a pinch back.

There was no environment that could not be adapted to, thought Feng Jingshui, whose name meant "still water". When her waters eventually broke, Xue Fugui was still off shifting bricks under the fierce sun, and when he returned on his day off, he saw a slightly plump Feng Jingshui half reclining on the bed, breast-feeding the child, a sweet smile on her face, gazing at the baby in her arms with boundless motherly love. A ray of sunshine happened to shine through a missing tile on the roof, in which dust motes danced quietly, setting the scene like a wonderful oil painting. Even though Xue Fugui had no idea what an oil painting was, he was now a father. The village midwife told him that, even though Feng Jingshui was a soft city woman, she had been strong, and it had not taken long for her to give birth smoothly, with only a little suffering.

Even though she had birthed a money-wasting daughter,

Xue Fugui was still moved to tears. Because she was the most beautiful baby he had ever seen in the entire village of Ox Head.

This most beautiful baby, Xue Shuangxi, meaning "double happiness", would be left motherless before her first birthday.

"I NEED MONEY quickly! I need to send it to the hospital! When the foreman hands over the compensation, I can pay you back double!"

Feng Jingshui rushed around with a face full of tears, to every household in the village.

"Shuangxi's dad has just had an accident at the construction site – his head's cracked open, not dead, but that bastard hospital won't even see him without getting paid."

To those who lent her money, she knelt and kowtowed. To those who did not, she rolled around the floor, curled into a ball, and then clung to their thighs, smearing them with snot and tears.

Xue Fugui was well liked, and she soon had a wad of fives and tens, with even a few tiny mao and fen in between. Feng Jingshui clambered onto the motorbike, and said to the driver, "Brother, please, drive quickly for me!"

At the entrance of the town hospital, the motorbike man asked if she wanted him to go in with her and beat the crap out of that doctor, boasting of his kung-fu. Feng Jingshui shook her head: there's no need, please go back.

The version that Xue Shuangxi was told of this story, was that her mother had gone to work in town and run away with a rich outsider. So she grew to hate her mother, until her second year at middle school, when, during English class, the teacher told her that her mother was there to see her.

Qu Xiangtian had been sitting by the window at the time. His eyes met those of Feng Jingshui, and he physically shuddered.

THE MIDDLE OF IT

QU XIANGTIAN LOOKED at Feng Jingshui. There was a hint of haughty disdain in this woman's eyes, yet her perfume smelled like lotus and fresh grass. Qu Xiangtian inhaled deeply.

What he did not know was that Feng Jingshui had held Xue Shuangxi in the corner of the school playground and wept for over half an hour, wept till she could not breathe. She told Xue Shuangxi everything, the whole truth.

Xue Shuangxi, however, did not weep.

A car was waiting for them at the school entrance.

"But Dad's waiting for me at home with dinner. Even if I go, I need to say goodbye first."

The mountain path had been widened, but was still too narrow for a car. Motorbikes had become common now, and riding with her mother holding her from behind, Xue Shuangxi's eyes felt hot and stinging, in the embrace of this familiar stranger.

On the table lay stir-fried eggs and vegetables, radish pickles, and a dish of cured meat that looked three days old. At first, Xue Fugui did not recognise her. He took another considered look, and saw it was the Feng Jingshui he had not seen for fifteen years, now with make-up, pale skin, and flowing, permed hair. In her fashionable clothes and shoes, she looked completely transformed, and there was a very nice smell about her, too.

He was shocked and happy, furious and nervous, and scared.

He wanted to tell her that he missed her, to tell her how hard it was for a man to bring up a daughter on his own, and that he would forgive her for the sake of a family reunion.

Feng Jingshui took out a pile of bank notes and handed it to Xue Shuangxi, who was completely at a loss as to what to do with it. To her former husband, she said only this, "In the future, you will not see her again. This is me returning the money you bought me with."

A dozen people had gathered in the front yard, including those who had taunted her all those years ago. Feng Jingshui held her daughter's hands and looked around icily. The bad people had grown old, the midden had already been filled in, but in her nightmares, where it still frequently appeared, it was still there, and the smell of shit and shame lingered over it.

This damned place. I shall never set foot in it again for the rest of my life, Feng Jingshui swore to herself.

There was another person Xue Shuangxi wanted to say goodbye to: Qu Xiangtian.

GAZING AT THE blue sky and white clouds from the aeroplane window, Xue Shuangxi felt very nervous; this was her first time on a plane, and she had no idea where the toilet was, and dare not ask Feng Jingshui, so she squeezed her legs together to hold it in, until a wave of turbulence hit the plane and hot yellow liquid streamed down her trousers.

It was the first time she had seen such tall buildings, such wide rivers, such pretty streets. It was the first time she had slept on such a big bed, the first time she had opened the fridge and seen so much to eat, the first time she had seen a blue-eyed and golden-haired man. Her stepfather, Thomas. Slowly, though, she learned. She learned how to switch on the air conditioner, how to use the water heater and the washing machine, how to listen to Modu people speak and make friends, how to gauge their speech and countenance, how to talk adroitly and express in turn with her own countenance, how to use a knife and fork to eat steak, and how to use iPhones and Alipay. Four years later, Xue Shuangxi was no longer the shy and self-conscious girl from the country, but the model of a graceful, educated and elegant debutante attending a prestigious university, with refined speech and impeccable taste in luxury goods, who could reel off nonchalant witticisms in English with aplomb.

Feng Jingshui would never have thought Xue Shuangxi would stay in touch with Qu Xiangtian all this time, at first by writing letters, and then via WeChat.

Xiangtian, do you remember the vows we made holding hands?
That one day, we will be together.
You'll study hard, get into university, and come to study in Modu.

Shuangxi, I don't know how you've been.
But I often dream of how you looked, sitting by my side, with your hair in two plaits.
I will study hard.
And oh, I received the new Cai Jun you sent me.

It's got my most favourite story, "The Night with the Wolf on White Reed Mountain". After I read it, I was so scared I couldn't go to the toilet at night!
Is this your favourite, too?

Xiangtian, the maths at high school is so hard.
If only you were in our class, then you could teach me Equilateral Triangular Calculations.
I've put on weight, will this put you off?
Also, how are your parents doing? If you've any spare time, please go and help my dad around the house.
You mentioned the second volume of The Longest Night: my favourite is "The Corpse Train".
People in the city feel so cold to me, I want to go back to the old days.
I don't like it here.

Shuangxi, congrats on getting into university.
Will there be lots of boys falling for you?
If so, then I'd be very nervous.
My parents are doing well.
This summer I'm going to be working at the kiln, making clay bricks.
One brick earns me fifty cents, so I can make fifty yuan a day, isn't that great?

Xiangtian, I heard you've been having a hard time at your job.
You're so skinny.
Remember to wear a straw hat, don't get heatstroke!

Shuangxi, I can't believe I'm going to see you again.
It feels like waiting to harvest wheat in the autumn.

Xiangtian, I miss you.

I think only of you.

Like wheat in the autumn that yearns to be harvested.

These two *naocanfen*, brain-damaged Cai Jun fans, were reunited at last. That evening, at the agreed time, Xue Shuangxi came out of her student halls, and saw, standing there, dusty from his travels, her former classmate Qu Xiangtian, who could fall asleep standing up. The pair had been separated for so long. His eyes were still so wide, but the sunken skin around them made her heart ache.

The little hotel felt like home to her, but Xiangtian was restless and anxious. "We're staying here? But isn't it pretty expensive?"

Shuangxi didn't answer. Once Xiangtian had washed up, she stroked his thin and fragile body. His scent, familiar and unfamiliar, stimulated her memories, as if she had returned to those happy and cloudless days in the village. They kissed awkwardly, and it felt like their clumsy attempts to catch grasshoppers together in the corn fields. Their energetic embrace felt like their united efforts to pull radishes up, when they had snuck into old Gua Pi's garden. Their lovemaking was as wild and joyous as their swim in the deep, cool reservoir at midnight, after taking part in the county's sports meet. It was then that Qu Xiangtian had saved Xue Shuangxi, nearly drowning himself in doing so. By the time he pulled her to shore, his belly was bloated with water, and when she pressed down on him to force it out, water even spewed from his ears.

"You still remember those times? I thought you'd forgotten them all," said Qu Xiangtian as Xue Shuangxi lay in his arms, smooth and shining like a fish.

She did not answer, but began to sing in a lovely voice,

Should auld acquaintance be forgot
And never brought to mind?
Should auld acquaintance be forgot
And auld lang syne?

"Shuangxi, will you marry me?" Qu Xiangtian said, solemnly.

"OK, but you'll need to make lots and lots of money first. The houses here are very expensive, and I don't want my mother to think you can't even afford to buy a house."

"I can skip university to go straight into work. Then, when you graduate in three years' time, I'll have enough money saved, and we can get married."

Xue Shuangxi smiled. She was a simple girl and did not even mind the parting. To her, parting now simply meant they could be reunited for longer, and no matter how far they were from their true love, they could always feel each other's heartbeat.

THE END OF IT

FENG JINGSHUI FOUND the hotel reservations in the credit card statements. Four times. Four! She could hardly believe it. Xue Shuangxi had no choice but to give up Qu Xiangtian's name.

Feng Jingshui's eyes reddened. When she had run away, almost escaped with Shuangxi in her belly, it had been Qu Xiangtian's father that had dragged her back.

"If you insist on being Qu Xiangtian's slut, I won't stop

you, I'll just die right now in front of you so you can spend the rest of your life in guilt."

Xue Shuangxi watched Feng Jingshui walk over to the balcony, and without hesitation, put one foot over so she straddled the railings, and started lifting the other...

Xiangtian, I am sorry, but I can never see you again, because my mother is extremely against it, and I cannot lose her.
I would rather lose you.
This is the last message I'll send.
The future does not belong to me, because my love is lost in the past.
I love you!

Shuangxi, it's OK.
You can choose your husband or wife, but you cannot choose your parents.
Sending a bracelet for you to remember me by.
I wasn't good enough for you in the first place.
Now that you've left, I don't have to worry about when I'll lose you anymore.
As long as you have me in your heart, you can see me there.
I wish you happiness!

Just like that, they were gone from each other's lives, without a trace. No more meetings, no more communications. It was as if everything had never happened, as if a tempest had washed away a bloodstain.

XUE SHUANGXI ONCE dreamed that she was getting married

to Qu Xiangtian, in the cornfield at the centre of the village. It was perfect, except for Qu Xiangtian's bloody stump for an arm, which was a shame...

Waking, shocked, she reached out and phoned him in the middle of the night, but his number had already been reassigned, and the woman who now had it answered the phone asking who the hell was calling at this hour.

UNHAPPY DAYS GREW ever more unhappy. Feng Jingshui darted abroad and back, arranging emigration papers for Xue Shuangxi, and in the end, decided she would just stay abroad this lunar new year to wait for the news.

QU DAJUN'S NIGHTMARES had become endless, ever since his son had died in the collapse of the black coal kiln the previous year. He had come to haunt his father in his dreams. His wife had been having the same nightmares. Did their son have some unfulfilled desire? Did they really need to find him a ghost bride?

Gua Pi's old man had taken the money, but his attitude was cool. "You can't even buy a leg bone for one hundred and fifty thousand yuan. Do you have any idea how expensive girls are these days? Let's call this a deposit. Hurry up and get another hundred thousand, in case there's any movement from my side. Don't worry, I have resources all over the country, I'm giving you a deal. We've been friends for so long."

The Qus pined and worried for a whole year, until at last, there was some good news.

An unknown girl had been found dead. She had laid unclaimed and unidentified for a month. And the mortuary was happy to see her moved on. Spending the additional hundred thousand seemed a fair price at this point. It was, luckily, the frozen heart of winter, so there would be no foul smells from the swaddled figure on the long bus ride.

They could not wait to see the goods that Gua Pi's old man had been boasting about. Peeling back the red bed linen, the girl looked kind of familiar, but they could not remember where they had seen her before. Qu Dajun's wife screamed. The corpse was wearing a little golden bracelet on her wrist, a family heirloom she had passed onto her son to give to his future wife. There was a character "Qu" carved on it.

And Qu Dajun remembered who she was.

XUE FUGUI HAMMERED his head against the wall until blood gushed out. Never in his wildest dreams could he have expected to be reunited with his daughter in this way.

"This pair had such misfortune in life – at least they can be together in death. 'When the bride is three more years old, then the marriage will be like gold.' What do you say, brother Fugui?" Qu Dajun consoled Xue Fugui. "Let's not lose any more time and get down to business."

SHE COULD HAVE bathed in the hot sun of Australia, bought perfumes in France, eaten hotdogs in America, or had her pick of Italy's young men.

She had been sitting on the balcony, downing cans of something called Four Loko, which had been left by her stepfather Thomas. It was fruity, and helped stave off sleep. She had been drinking them two at a time.

She glanced at Qu Xiangtian, waving at her from the street, but by the time she had thrown on some clothes and run down, he had gone.

He must have gone home – his hometown was my hometown. In our home, there is my childhood, my dad, my teachers and classmates. I can see them all now, waving at me, smiling at me. I am going home, no matter what, I am going back.

THE CAR CRASH had caused Xue Shuangxi's body to be thrown from her car, and over the motorway. Her body was found and temporarily placed at the Linzhou County Mortuary, waiting to be identified, lying alongside the other unknown corpses. Gua Pi's old man had arranged everything remotely, since the mortuary keeper was an old hand. After payment was received, transport was immediately arranged, and personnel booked for dispatch. It was a smooth chain of operations that any service industry would have taken pride in.

WHEN SHE GOT the call, Feng Jingshui had rushed to the village after all, crying herself dry, alone, on the long, arduous return trip.

THE LITTLE GUAPI who has been guarding the corpses is not really Guapi's son, but a penniless little waif whose parents have both died, and who has taken to calling Guapi 'Stepdad' in order to get fed. The firecrackers are sounding, the car coming to pick up Xue Shuangxi is on its way, and soon, he will be feasting at the banquet tables, too.

A giant coffin is carried by four men onto the stage, while a Buddhist monk is devoutly chanting sutras, and a Daoist priest performs spells on the altar. All that is left of Qu Xiangtian are his ashes, though Xue Shuangxi is still there in the flesh. They are laid side by side in the coffin. There isn't much of a conversation.

Family and relatives begin to approach, to toast the newlyweds in turn, weeping loudly, and exclaiming *daxi, daxi*. Great felicitations.

The lid is about to be placed over the coffin, and Feng Jingshui cannot help but burst into tears again. She wanted to take her daughter home, not leave her in this ugly, disgusting place forever to continue her own humiliation.

Director Zhang sees it is time to act. He flourishes a pair of handcuffs, and restrains Guapi's dad, who has been drinking at one of the tables, whilst three undercover officers who have been mingling with the crowd reveal their guns.

The villagers are enraged, and an old man, who is at least eighty years old, with a voice as bright as the flood bells, comes to stand before Director Zhang. "If we don't see this wedding through to the end, the spirits of these two kids will cause trouble, and put the whole village in danger. This is the law set down by our ancestors, and cannot be broken, without ending the world! You can have Guapi's old man – he's been kidnapping and selling women and children all his life, and should die for it – but you must not take Shuangxi away, unless it's over my dead body."

Everyone attending the banquet, some seventy or eighty villagers, Xue Fugui included, start to surround Director Zhang and his men, pressing and blocking them in over and over, each of them willing to die to protect Xue Shuangxi, who can no longer speak, nor breathe.

A gunshot! But it is no use. The poor are not afraid of death, they are afraid to die poor. The sound of a gun being fired only seems to excite the villagers – there has not been such a ruckus in the village for ages. On one side, they have the police surrounded and blockaded, on the other, preparations are underway to lower the coffin into the open grave. Money, houses, Audis, bags, shoes and clothes are being set alight, all made of paper. And then the incense, top quality coiled stuff and expensive sandalwood sticks lit in bunches. Offerings of pork, fish and doufu. A cockerel slaughtered for blood sacrifice. Firecrackers are set off whilst shovels begin to work.

Crying, Xue Fugui calls the Qus family.

Also crying, Qu Dajun calls the Xues family.

Feng Jingshui shouts to Director Zhang, "Let her stay here. I give up."

The snow is falling heavily. If they don't leave now, it'll be too late.

NOTES

THE GHOST WEDDING is a peculiarly traditional Chinese horror story. Whilst it has a modern setting, it still conveys a slow, inexorable descent into death and tragedy. Its creator, Yimei Tangguo, met one of her readers some years ago, who told her of his experience, quitting his office job to move to Sichuan as a zhijiao, a teacher specifically sent out to bring improved education to underdeveloped regions. The astounding poverty and isolation he saw was the inspiration for Ox Head Village, and the story of the crazed woman who had her legs broken to stop her from running away was part of the anecdote which left a deep impression on Tangguo. She imagined a happier and freer ending for this woman in the fictional character of Feng Jingshui, an ending that was also well-loved by her readers. Reality, however, is a sobering affair, and the crippled woman in the real village never escaped.

Tangguo also created the doomed relationship of Shuangxi and Xiangtian from inspiration she had found in her comfort characters in crime novels, deciding to add the further ingredient of an age-old matrimonial custom, the minghun (ghost wedding), which she finds detestable, spinning it all into a frightening tale of kidnapping, domestic abuse, human trafficking, and illegal mining operations. She hoped to fulfil her social role as a writer, and through the medium of horror, to encourage readers to reflect upon these very real social issues.

I came across Yimei Tangguo's work while first researching China's contemporary horror scene. Out of the dozen established names I cold contacted, she was one of the few who responded to the call from across the seas. Her public persona very much fits her pen name, which translates as "A Piece of Candy", or as her fans call her, "A Piece of Poisoned Candy". A creature of the web, she adroitly keeps her online fan community bubbling with regular content, including posts about her three cats, food, and her grandmother. Tangguo's flamboyant virtual presence is only one reason for her huge following. She writes with great flair, and switches effortlessly between gritty realism and romantic lyricism, between narrative perspectives and immediacy (sometimes all within a single sentence), seemingly unconstrained by conventional storytelling structures.

Tangguo cites Cai Jun as an influence, and here, also makes him the favourite author of Shuangxi and Xiangtian. As one of China's founding generation of contemporary horror writers, Cai was one of the first names I endeavoured to secure when I began this curation. It is truly wonderful to see the influence and interaction between generations of horror writers firsthand and include that within a single volume.

The idea of 'stolen women' is well known in China. The single child policy, and the traditional concepts of the favouring of sons, have led to a gender imbalance, especially in the rural areas. Many Chinese girls will have been 'warned' about gangs of kidnappers looking to take pretty girls away by force, as a tool to keep their behaviour in check and their attire modest. Whilst the threat is exaggerated for control, it is not unfounded. I have read plenty of cases about the abduction of women from cities and towns, many of whom are trafficked to rural villages and sold as brides. The sheer size of China, and the problems in policing the most remote locales, mean they are often lost in the murky structures of rural villages. Some do not reunite with their loved ones for years, while some never regain their freedom.

NIGHT CLIMB

夜攀

Chi Hui

"If you think you understand anything in this world, then you must be crazy."

— **Anon.**

THE SOUTHWEST SUMMER heat lingered on into September, but the nights brought traces of cool relief from the steamier heat of daytime, so the mountains had a lot more climbers at night.

There was more than one route to the Jinding peak of the Emei Mountains, and most people like me, with big, bulky frames, would have taken the cable car midway up, booked into one of the hotels there, and taken an hour's trek on foot the next day. But I had planned to watch the sunrise, and being a slow walker, I needed to set off deep in the night.

The yellow lamps along the mountain path formed dim ghostly rings of light, casting indistinct shadows flitting in the distance. Every so often, spaced out along the route, workers in hi-vis vests stood swinging their lanterns, yelling cautious warnings. Their cries got on my nerves.

"Please mind your step, do not approach the cliff edge, safety first, do not climb over the railings. Please mind your step, do not approach the cliff edge, safety first, do not climb over the railings. Please mind your step, do not approach the cliff edge, safety first, do not climb over the railings."

Again and again and again and again.

"Please mind your... please mind your hands..."

The yelling voices seemed to warp subtly. I turned my head and looked back. There was a row of people actually making their way up on all fours.

The night was thick, and their faces and clothing were obscured, just a row of taut, arched backs, one behind the other. The leader had his hands and feet all planted on the ground, shoulders lowered, neck craned up, like some kind of wild beast I had never seen before. All of them wore what looked like miners' helmets, with lamps on, which lit up the path before them but plunged their faces into sticky shadows beneath.

Silently, they crawled on.

Probably one of those fitness training groups, I guessed.

These climbers were far quicker than a chunk like me, and they overtook me, one by one, winding their way up the mountain path.

I could not tell which of them started it, but a deep and low chant began to emanate from the "climbers".

"Ohhh hay-oh – To live is to suffer – Ohhh hay-oh – To live is to suffer–"

It was then that I realised that the safety wardens had stopped yelling their warnings. They had let their tinny megaphones fall from their mouths, and, as if gripped by fear, they stood motionless, silently willing this group on their way.

The line of climbers was long. When the first of them

passed me, the sky was pitch black, but it had begun to lighten by the time the last of them overtook me.

It was another half hour's hard walk before I finally reached Jinding, huffing and panting. There was an expectant crowd bustling round the peak, all waiting for the moment the crimson sun would leap out of the sea of clouds, but none of them matched the strange train of climbers who had passed me.

At a nearby rest area, I found a pile of headlamps, along with gloves and knee pads which had been used for climbing, but no sign of that strange group. Coming down from the mountain, everyone had settled into pairs, or groups of three, all neatly dressed, chatting and laughing, strolling with a relaxed air. The September sun still scorched our faces a little as it beat down.

I ate plenty of jacket potatoes on the peak, took lots of photos, and even ran into a girl who was great fun to talk to. She looked to be in her early twenties, with a supple body; she exuded youth like sunshine and had a wonderful smile. The only reason she got talking to a fat guy like me was because we were both wearing superhero T-shirts. Superman and Batman.

We walked down the mountain together. The conversation went from American comics to monster movies and back again until, inevitably, I mentioned my encounter during the night's climb.

"Huh, were there really people like that?" the girl asked, somewhat curiously. "What were they singing?"

"Something about suffering and living…?"

"To live is to suffer – Ohhh hay-oh–"

The girl smiled as she sang, and the sound, so accurate and practiced, perfectly mimicked my memory of the night before.

Locking eyes with me, she bent backwards, assuming an elegant Yogic arch, planting her hands on the ground. She twisted round, like an animal righting itself, and leaving me behind, scuttled down the mountainside and into the treeline.

I never saw her again.

NOTES

THIS SHORT YET unique vignette came from a conversation the author, Chi Hui, had on QQ, about what kind of horror was the most horrific. She said that for her, it is the idea of some twisted thing suddenly appearing in a world where everything else is operating normally, and then just as suddenly disappearing. Fear arises from that which we do not understand, and there are plenty of things in this world that are incomprehensible.

Chi Hui is primarily known as a science fiction writer, although she has written some Qihuan (fantasy) works, too. I have loved Chi Hui's writing since I picked up Terminal Town 2030 in China a few years ago, and it was wonderful to include something by her. As a female writer who is keen to deal with the dark, gruesome and violent, her voice stood out to me at once. Her heroines are often socially isolated or marginalised, bearing the burden of a harsh and merciless world. This short piece is less dour in tone, but retains the sense of the Unheimlich that her writing evokes so well.

The Night Climb has so many interesting points of culture in it, from the ubiquitous mountain walks for health, and the ever-present security (where it is seen as a social duty to employ someone instead of putting up a camera) to the silent response to the strange. In the old works of Chinese mythology, there are short descriptions of strange peoples who exhibit bestial behaviours or physical abnormalities, and the Night Climbers could have been drawn verbatim from these works. The girl's lizard-like behaviour as she scurries off, and the fact that she and every other person at the peak seemed completely normal, reminds us that we never quite know where the monsters are hiding.

FORBIDDEN ROOMS

禁屋

Zhou Haohui

PROLOGUE

NOBODY CARES ABOUT you, because you never cared about anybody…

It had been a year since the incident, but Lin Na was still unable to forget that apartment.

She had tried many ways to do so. She had moved away from that xiaoqu, she had left behind every single one of her belongings, she had even broken up with her boyfriend, just because they had been together while she'd lived there.

She wanted to forsake everything connected to that part of her life to get away from those horrific memories, but she was drowning in the realisation that none of it worked.

She had worked like mad, and after work she would head to the gym to exhaust herself further. She had even started drinking, all in the hope of depriving herself of any time to think.

If you had no time to think, then how could you remember the past?

And nothing made the slightest difference.

There was one space that Lin Na had absolutely no

control over, the one in her sleep. No matter how much she exhausted herself, she could not stop herself from dreaming. So it was in this emotionally numb state that she found herself back in that apartment.

The dull grey floor tiles, the wretched, white walls, and the inescapable sound of a little boy wailing...

And then she saw the door being opened, and the boy's tiny, lifeless body rolling to the floor, with the softest thud. He was wearing a green T-shirt, his arms tucked in, but both hands splayed out, stiffened in the act of pressing his whole body flat against the locked door, by now resembling a huge frog. His eyes were bulging, too, like a frog's, the white parts distinct from the black, but neither holding a hint of life. The dilated pupils, soft like ink spots, exuded a chill that sent fear into the core of one's being.

The boy's eyes would meet Lin Na's for a moment, and then she would be awake, screaming, shivering and drenched in sweat. This scene repeated itself, night after night, torturing Lin Na's very soul, and gradually forcing her to the brink of a breakdown.

LIN NA KNOWS that the nightmare will never end. But one day, when she wakes from the familiar scene, she finds something even more terrifying.

She reaches out for the bedside lamp with clammy hands, the first thing she does every time, but finds nothing. Then, she hears the faint, mournful weeping of a child.

The dream has ended. The wailing continues.

Still sleep-dazed, Lin Na holds her breath. The night is as heavy and silent as death, and in it, the weeping becomes more and more distinct. It is continuous, and it does not sound very distant, nor very near. Just as Lin Na had once heard it.

She feels waves of pinpricks wash over her scalp, and she sits up on the bed like a Jack-in-the-box, her eyes widening in total terror – her surroundings are almost enough to make her scream.

The night is thick, and only the weakest shards of moonlight shine through the thin gauze curtains over the window, illuminating the room. In this cadaverous light, Lin Na makes out the familiar bed, the familiar wardrobe, desk, windows and walls. In an instant, everything around her feels familiar, so familiar it stops her breath.

Lin Na is back in that room. Back in the apartment where the nightmare began.

She feels a wave of dizziness and pinches her leg hard. There comes that spasm of pain.

This is not a dream, it is reality, a reality more nightmarish than the dreams.

Lin Na does not have time to work out what has happened. Her one thought is, "Run. Leave. Get out!" Trembling, she wriggles off the bed, and, not even bothering to put on shoes, strides straight for the door. When the door is opened, the boy's crying becomes even clearer.

Lin Na braces herself and steps out of the bedroom into the living room. In the haziness of the night, the floor tiles are a dull grey, and the walls a wretched white. Everything is the way it had appeared in her recurring dreams.

This is a two-bedroom apartment. The door to the room opposite is tightly shut, with the crying coming from within. Lin Na cannot, dares not, imagine what terrible things are taking place behind that door. The crying alone makes her hair stand on end. She hurls herself through the living room, towards the front door, and with trembling hands, reaches for the handle to open the heavy iron security door.

Once she's on the other side of this thick and heavy barrier, she will be able to run away, cast off the sounds of the child's crying that are wrapping themselves around her and clinging like a ghost. Leave this room, and its shroud of horror, far, far behind.

But the handle will not turn. The security door has clearly been double locked, and without the key, cannot be opened. Using all the energy she can muster, Lin Na tries to take on the door lock, only to find her spirits falling, further and further, with each round of defeat, down into despair. Finally, she gives up these futile actions, and withdraws, whimpering.

The boy's weeping continues. In this dark and locked apartment, fear presses in on this lonely, broken woman like an icy tide.

Suddenly, Lin Na remembers something, and dashes to the wall, flicking the switch next to the metal door. The fluorescent tubes flash a couple of times, before lighting up the room, diffusing some of the horrific ambience, and affording Lin Na's tense nerves a modicum of relief, and with that, she recovers her ability to think.

What the fuck is happening? Lin Na starts to search her memory. Slowly, she recalls some things.

Yesterday, after work, she had gone to a bar near the office. She had had a few drinks alone, not many, but she was beginning to lose her senses, and may have spilt her glass, which attracted a lot of bystanders. Amidst the chatter of the people who busied about her mopping up, there was a child's voice, crisp and clear. Then, she'd felt an unexplainable fear, and found herself slipping into that familiar dreamscape. When she'd woken up, she'd discovered herself in that room.

Yes, those memories all seem true. Lin Na glances down

at the clothes she is wearing. This purple camisole is the one she had changed into before going to the bar, but something else comes into focus. Something that gives her a jolt.

It is a red hebao pouch, embroidered with   in gold. Happiness. Lin Na remembered that the child had had a purse like this around his neck, apparently the only thing his mother had left him.

Now this pouch is around Lin Na's neck, leaving her to inevitably recall the horrific memory. Lin Na tears the hebao away and is about to hurl it as far from her as she can, when she suddenly feels something in her fist and pauses.

Something in the pouch! Hard, and long, it should be... the key!

Lin Na rips open the hebao, and sure enough, finds a stainless-steel key. Without a thought, she pulls out the key and jams it into the keyhole of the front door.

The key slides in easy enough, but will not turn. The excitement that Lin Na feels is immediately cooled, and abruptly, she comes to a realisation. That sense of extreme fear returns to grip and rend the tenderest part of her heart.

Slowly, as Lin Na withdraws the key with an uncontrollable, shaking hand, she turns her head towards the second bedroom, with wide, fearful eyes, and stares at the tightly locked door.

She begins to understand. She can't escape with this key, but she can use it to open that door.

The boy's sobbing is still coming from behind the door, just as it had a year ago.

If, back then, when Lin Na had first heard those tearful whimpers, she had opened this door, things would have been very different.

But of course, she hadn't.

So, will she do it this time?

Lin Na hesitates for a moment, before running back to the room she'd woken up in. She knows there is a window in that room, and even from the sixth floor, she could open it and shout down for help. She would rather be a crazy woman in hysterics at three o'clock in the morning than go back into that room with all its horrors.

When Lin Na eagerly yanks the curtains open, her heart sinks to an icy pit. Confronting her is a tightly packed cluster of wooden boards, almost entirely covering the window, save for a few cracks through which the light has filtered in from the outside.

Lin Na, now shivering, understands she never had any choice. For unknown reasons, she has been mysteriously returned to this apartment, and is now enduring these traumatic fears. But this time, she has no means of escape, of extricating herself from this predicament. The only thing she can do is open that door. Face what is behind it and confront the secrets within.

Everything has evidently been orchestrated well in advance. Lin Na has run for a year, but now, at last, someone has caught her and brought her back. Who could that be?

Lin Na steps out of her bedroom again, the boy's sobs piercing her heart like sharp needles. Slowly, she shifts towards that door, her movements stiff and awkward, like a lifeless puppet.

Perhaps she is a puppet, because it is clear this is all somebody's game, a terrifying game that she has entered, and is now being controlled by someone at every stage.

Lin Na stops in front of the door, but she still does not have the courage to open it.

"Is there anybody there? Who's in there?" she calls out in a trembling tone. In the quiet of the night, all she can hear is that wretched whimpering.

When she inserts the key into the lock and turns it, tears well up in her eyes, but she bites her lip hard, almost drawing blood.

At last, she gently turns the key, and with a soft click, the door is unlocked.

Lin Na does not need to push the door, which slowly glides open by itself, just as it did a year ago. She relives the scene clearly: the boy, tumbling forward from behind the door, as if he had pressed himself up against it, crying and crying, right up until the moment his life was extinguished.

But that horrific scene does not play out by the door. The room is completely bare, except for a large bed, from where the sobbing is emanating. Lin Na's first reaction is to feel the wall for the light switch, but when she presses it, the light does not come on.

Thankfully, some light pours in from the living room, and the window in this room has not been boarded up, meaning the moonlight which shines through is bright, even pleasant. By this illumination, Lin Na can see that there is a single quilt on the bed, which rises into a bump at the head of the bed, as if a small body is curled up beneath it.

The bedsheet is a ghastly white, and the quilt a gory red, fiercely contrasting under the nocturnal hues. Lin Na remembers that one year ago, an identical cover had been on the bed, and under it, reeking intensely, was a long-rotted corpse.

A decomposed corpse, a crying child... Lin Na cannot tell which would frighten her more to find.

Strangely, though, with the door now open, she feels her fear alleviating. Perhaps she has come to understand that there is no escape. No matter how far she runs, would she not just end up back here in her dreams anyway?

Now that there is no way out, she will face it bravely for

once! With these thoughts in mind, Lin Na walks into the room, and, step by step, makes her way towards the bed.

Despite the summer heatwave, when Lin Na stands at the head of the bed, she feels a bone-piercing chill surround her. Trying her hardest to keep calm, she holds out her hand to lift the blood-red cover.

A boy lies under the covers. His stomach and chest are pressed flat against the surface of the bed, but his head is turned one hundred and eighty degrees to face the ceiling; his eyes, like two black holes, are wide open, his mouth tightly shut, yet the crying still comes from inside him.

Lin Na feels the heat rush through her head, and her heart nearly jumps out of her throat. But this suffocating fear does not last long, as she discovers that this creepy child is a mannequin with a speaker in it.

The knowledge cannot undo the cold sweat which has broken out across Lin Na's neck and back. She calms her nerves a little, and grabs hold of the doll, searching for the sound box, and with the flick of a switch, the gut-wrenching sobbing finally comes to an end.

She breathes a sigh of relief, but has yet to process the whole thing. Suddenly, she feels a pressure around her right ankle, as if it is gripped fast by something. Astonished, she looks down, to find that that something is a pale human hand extending from under the valance. Lin Na feels her body go limp, and she collapses to the floor, screaming, instinctively kicking out with both feet.

In this flurry, Lin Na feels her feet repeatedly connect with something soft in the dark. At last, the hand lets go, and with the sheets thrown into disarray, they reveal what is under the bed.

Eyes stretched wide open, she ceases her kicking, and sees, huddled on the floor, a man trussed up like a zongzi, both his elbows and knees solidly hog-tied, so only his forearms are able to rotate within the confines of his bonds. His mouth has been sealed with duct tape, unable to make a sound.

She could imagine how this man must have writhed under the bed for a long time, struggling to rearrange his body, to reach out with his free hands, and grab hold of Lin Na's ankle. Right now, he is rocking his head, looking at her, pleading with his eyes for help.

Anxious and confused, Lin Na braces herself and moves over, removing the tape over the man's mouth. The man immediately takes in big gulps of air, clearly stifled from before.

"Who are you? And what is going on?" she asks him, calming herself as much as possible.

"How... how should I know?" The man is still recovering and talks with effort. He swallows, takes a rest, and, with an aggrieved and bewildered expression, asks, "Can you please untie me first? These ropes are killing me."

Lin Na doesn't know this man, but under the current circumstances, his appearance has helped to disperse much of her feelings of fear and helplessness. Without further hesitation, she drags the man out from under the bed, and proceeds to untie the ropes, knotted at his back.

"Where's the kid?" the man asks, suddenly.

Alarm catches Lin Na for a second, before she replies, "There is no kid."

A flash of confusion crosses the man's eyes. "But since I woke up, I've heard him crying. He was on the bed."

"A creepy doll with a recording," she explains, grabbing the doll to show the man.

He grumbles, angrily, "What the fuck is all this? You don't know either, do you?"

Lin Na shakes her head and looks at the man. In a baffled

voice, she explains, "I've just woken up, too, in the room across from this one. I don't even know how I got here."

With his limbs now free, he stumbles to stand, stretching his long-bound muscles and joints. Suddenly, he freezes. He stares at the bed beside him, and with a strange look on his face, he drags his eyes from the bed, and sweeps them around the room. That strangeness begins to dissolve into shock, and he stammers, "This... this room... this is..."

The corner of Lin Na's eye twitches sensitively. "You recognise this bed? This room?"

"Which fucker is doing this? What are they playing at?" The man's heart seems to have been jabbed in some painful place, and he suddenly grows agitated. Thrashing his hands around, his furious gesticulating is mingled with a deep, deep sense of sorrow.

Lin Na no longer pays any attention to the man's fluctuating mood, her eyes instead fixed on the small of his back.

"What? What is it?" the man asks, puzzled by Lin Na's gaze.

Lin Na holds out a hand, and plucks something from around his waist. Another hebao. Red, with a golden .

When Lin Na woke up, she was wearing an identical hebao. But she thought it had belonged to the boy who died a year ago.

The man's gaze shrinks, as if again something sharp has pierced him deep in the heart.

As Lin Na expected, there is something hidden in this hebao, too – opening the pouch, she finds a flip phone and a folded letter.

The man grabs the phone, checks it, and grumbles, "This isn't mine," and then immediately pats down his pockets. He cries out dramatically, "My phone! My wallet! They're gone! We've been robbed?"

Lin Na shakes her head slowly, a strong premonition telling her that the situation must be far more complex. She unfolds the letter, and seeing a dense chunk of text on it, walks briskly to the living room to read it in the light.

The man follows her, pestering her with impatient questions. "What does it say?"

Lin Na throws him a glance, and in return asks, "Is your name Liu Hong?"

The man is surprised. "How do you know?"

Lin Na waves the letter in her hand slightly. "This letter is addressed to the both of us, so your name's on it."

The man frowns and moves his head closer. As he reads the content of the letter, line by line, his face grows more and more sombre, as does Lin Na's, because the letter says:

Lin Na, Liu Hong,

When you read this letter, you will be in a state of confusion. How did you end up here?
Of course, I know the answer, but the answer itself is not the important part. What you need to be concerned with now is how you will get out.
Regarding this apartment, you both know very well what happened here a year ago: an old man and his grandson lived here, depending on each other – a man of well over sixty, and a three-year-old boy. In the heat of last summer, the old man's heart gave out. He lay down one night, and never got up again. The boy was left with nobody to care for him, confined to the room – he suffered the horrors of hunger, thirst and fear. He was too young to know what was happening. All he could do was weep. Weep until he was exhausted,

sleep, and when he woke up, weep again, until he had no strength left to even make a sound...

Back then, the boy had no means of self-preservation. Any hope of salvation and survival lay outside the bounds of that room.

Three years old was the age to be spoiled with cuddles in a father's arms, but where was this child's father? He had thrust the old man and the child into this concrete jungle, into this cold-hearted city, and did not even call them. When he was crying, the boy had called out 'Baba' countless times, but Liu Hong, you never appeared.

Despite this, the boy was not without another chance to be saved. There was a young woman who lived in the same split apartment. Under the same roof. Separated only by a small and narrow living room. Of course, this girl was you, Lin Na, and on those quiet and lonely nights, you must have heard the child crying. If you had only gone over and checked, this child's fate would have been totally different. But you did not.

In despair, the little boy expended the last of his life, little by little, like a young bud that was yet to bloom, withered in this cold, cruel and heartless world. In those last moments, the help he needed was so simple, like pouring a cup of water over dying flowers, but no one would spare him their cup of water.

Everybody lamented the boy's death so greatly, but who has seriously considered the reasons behind his death?

I hope to change people's minds, to make them feel truly shaken by this tragedy – starting with the two of you.

If anyone should pay the price for the boy's death, I can think of no two people more suitable. So, in the following days, you will fall into the predicament in which the boy found himself – this is the punishment I have arranged for you.

There are two doors leading to the outside from this apartment, one in the living room, and the other on the balcony. Both of these have now been upgraded to heavy-duty anti-intruder doors. Not only are they secure, but excellently soundproof. Lin Na, the window in your room has been permanently boarded up. It is impossible for you to pry out the nails without tools. As for the window leading to the balcony in the other room, although it has not been boarded up, I have changed the glazing to bulletproof glass, which has been embedded into the wall, so you have no escape route.

Your communications with the outside world have been more or less cut off. I have left you a mobile phone, but Liu Hong, since you never called a year ago, what reason would I have of letting you make calls now? I have desoldered the numeric keys on the phone, so whilst you can receive calls, you will not be able to dial out.

There is no food in the flat, and the water supply has been cut off. This is certainly a predicament you are in. So, the punishment begins. In the time you have remaining, you shall slowly experience the bitter taste of loneliness, helplessness and despair mingling into one.

Lin Na's hands are shaking, and she lifts her head, timidly glancing at the man next to her.

Liu Hong is also gazing at her, with an indescribable expression of shame on his face. After a long time, he smiles sourly, asking, "So you were that girl... the co-tenant." His voice sounds hoarse, as if squeezing his words out with difficulty.

Lin Na is struck by the grief in the other's tone. Her nose tingles, and tears well up.

"You heard the boy crying... but you didn't even go to take a look. In... in the end he died at the door!" Liu Hong's eyeballs are bulging with rage, bloodshot vessels on their underside exposed.

His reproach actually dissipates some of the guilt in Lin Na's heart. She stops crying, and shoots back indignantly, "You're blaming ME? What about you? You abandoned them here. I never saw you come and check on them."

"Of course I did!" Liu Hong retorts in agitation, raising his voice. "It must just have been when you weren't in!"

"If you'd phoned them on even one of those days, your son wouldn't have died!" Lin Na adds, coldly.

These words have clearly opened the most painful wound in Liu Hong's heart. He freezes for a moment, then starts barking out hysterically, "How could I have known this?! Both my father and son died tragically in this place! Do you have any idea how I feel? You don't know anything! I run around working so damn hard every day – who was that all for? What right do you have to criticise me?"

Seeing him flailing his limbs around in an uncontrolled state, Lin Na can't help but feel a little intimidated and takes a couple of steps back. Liu Hong presses forward, snatching the letter away from her with a swoop of his hand, tearing it to pieces, and then continues to roar, "Punish me? Who do you think you are? Who the hell are you to do that?"

Liu Hong lifts his head, his eyes sweeping the room

aimlessly, and then, as if unable to find a target for his ire, he becomes even more frenzied, and runs to the door of the living room. He starts pounding on the thick iron plate with his fists. "What kind of sick fuck are you? Punish me? Why don't you fucking punish yourselves!"

Against this, the terrified Lin Na retreats to the furthest corner, no longer daring to say another word, but Liu Hong has not vented enough, and starts to kick at the door. Like Lin Na, he had woken up barefooted, no socks or shoes. Now, his bare flesh connects hard with the immovable iron door. Whilst the kick is powerful, the sound it makes is light, and muffled.

As light and muffled as the sound is, the noise strikes heavily in Lin Na's heart. In sorrow and fear, she breaks down, sobbing, wanting to walk over and pull the man away, but not having the guts to do so.

Thankfully, Liu Hong eventually calms down by himself. Perhaps he is exhausted, perhaps he is in pain. He stops kicking the iron panel and collapses onto the floor in a dismal heap. He buries his head between his arms, his shoulders jerking, and from his throat come whimpering noises. She can hear them, but they are muffled, too.

Lin Na watches this man from her short distance, the fear in her eyes gradually melting into sympathy. She walks over slowly and squats down in front of him. Holding out her hand, she gives his arm a tentative squeeze.

First Liu Hong rubs his head into the crook of his arm, using his shirt to wipe away the tears. And then, lifting his head, he looks at Lin Na, who is biting her lip and saying nothing. The light from her eyes is bright, clear and calming.

Liu Hong takes a deep breath, his emotions apparently having returned to their normal state.

"Alright, we shouldn't point fingers, let's just try to get

out of here first." As he speaks, he holds onto the wall and slowly pulls himself up, a process which causes him to grimace and grit his teeth.

Lin Na notices that due to his deranged outburst before, his right foot is now swollen, and already blossoming into a yellow-green bruise. She cannot help but show concern. "Are you OK?"

Liu Hong shakes his head, looks around for a moment, and then, limping, heads into Lin Na's room.

Lin Na follows him in, reaching for the light switch, before mumbling her disappointment, "The lights are broken in here, too."

"That'd be part of the creep's plan." Liu Hong thinks for a moment, and spits out, "If we had light in either room, then we could send an SOS signal to the outside."

As he speaks, Liu Hong moves to the window, raising a hand to pull open the curtains, revealing the rows of densely packed wooden boards completely covering the glass on the window, obstructing the view between the inside and outside worlds.

"Shit. He's really blocked this window for good." Still cursing, Liu Hong tries to push and pull at the planks, his actions clearly futile. These wooden boards have been firmly nailed to the wall and are not moving an inch.

Liu Hong soon gives up. "Let's take a look over the other side," he says, dejection in his voice.

By the other side, he naturally means the other bedroom, where the tragedy took place a year ago. This room is a bit bigger than Lin Na's, and beyond it is a balcony. If they could just get out onto the balcony, the two of them would be able to make more than enough noise to get help from outside.

But as the note said, the exit onto the balcony has been

replaced with an identical heavy-duty door, which is firmly locked. The last glimmer of hope in the entire apartment now lies in the window that looks out onto the balcony.

This window is not boarded up, so through it they can see the rest of the world. It is the middle of the night, and the buildings across from them are blocks of pitch black. In her current mindset, Lin Na sees this view, and feels as if all the light in the whole world has gone out.

Quickly, though, she has a flash of inspiration, and says with some excitement, "If we just wait till the morning, maybe the people in the buildings across will see us!"

Standing at the window and looking into the distance, Liu Hong shakes his head dismissively. "It's too far. I'm afraid they won't be able to see us, and even if they did, what then? They wouldn't ever think that we are trapped here. We must think of a way to get out onto the balcony." He is already pushing to open the window.

It is an old-style window that pushes out from the bottom, but even with his full force against it, it gives no hint of loosening. Liu Hong squints to take a better look and finds that the iron frames of the windowpane, and its frame, have been welded together, rendering them impossible to open in the normal way.

Liu Hong makes a fist and knocks on the glass a couple of times with his knuckles. The sound is low and deadened. It feels tough and thick. Frowning, he says to the woman next to him, "Go and look around to see if you can find anything hard we can break the glass with."

Lin Na complies, sweeping around the apartment. After a while, Liu Hong hears her calling from the living room, "Can you come and take a look at this? I can't lift it."

Dragging his injured foot, Liu Hong hobbles into the living room, and sees the metal cube in the corner. It is a small safe. Although it is not a big box, it is made of cement and tungsten steel, and weighs a ton. Liu Hong needs to use all his strength to lift it. Lin Na moves in to help, and whilst she is not particularly strong, the two of them together lightens the load a little. They carry the box all the way to the window. Liu Hong pauses to catch his breath, before calling out, "On the count of three, we throw this at the glass."

Lin Na nods, and slowly, the two of them lift the weight, and on the count of three, they give the box their mightiest push. The solid metal case crashes into the window, causing it to resound with a dull note, but it bounces off. The glass wobbles a little, remaining unmarked.

The two of them leap back to avoid the safe as it flies back. It lands on the floor, smashing a thick groove into the wooden floor.

"It's useless." Lin Na shakes her head in utter disappointment. "He wasn't lying. That's bulletproof glass. We can't smash it."

Liu Hong's face sinks to an ashen grey. They look at each other for a while, and then at the same time, both start to look around them despondently. Deep and dark is the night, and the apartment is still and silent. A feeling of loneliness and dread pervades this calm, ruthlessly seeping under their skin.

The setup described in the letter has been demonstrated by their own examination. A new cruel, desperate reality.

Lin Na feels herself breaking into a cold sweat. Suddenly this sealed apartment seems to have gotten so hot and close that it might stop her from breathing. She licks her dry lips, and asks Liu Hong in an unsteady voice, "Is… is there really no way of getting out alive?"

Liu Hong does not reply, but throws himself onto the

bed. He picks up the phone from where he had cast it aside, randomly trying the keys, before petulantly throwing it back down on the bed. Lin Na hastens over to pick it up and, very quickly, comes to understand the reason for his irritation: except for the pick-up button, all the other keys on the mobile are useless, just like the letter said.

Liu Hong seems to recall something, and bearing the pain of his broken foot, quickly dives into the bathroom. Confused, Lin Na puts down the phone, and anxiously follows suit. When she reaches the door, she finds Liu Hong clutching the edge of the sink with both hands, and slowly turning to face her, his eyes bloodshot, his face the epitome of powerless dismay, a crowing, inhuman sound escapes from his throat. "No water, every sentence he wrote is true! There is no water in this flat... he– he wants us trapped here, and he wants us dead!"

Lin Na's heart plunges further, and the stifled feeling in her chest becomes more uncomfortable. Her throat is burning, as if it were being smoked. She clearly understands the meaning of Liu Hong's words: in this oppressive summer heat, without water, their lives are suspended on the edge of a precipice.

"Why?" There is a hint of tearfulness in Lin Na's tone. "Why is he doing this?"

"Punishment." Liu Hong stares at her, the muscles in his face contorting. "He already said, this is punishment... my son died of thirst, so we must face the same suffering."

"I didn't do anything, so why am I being treated like this?" Lin Na tears up, feeling wronged. "What kind of person does this?"

Liu Hong seems distracted for a moment, then he asks, without warning, "Were you living here all along?"

Lin Na lets out a grim laugh, shaking her head. "How

could I? I moved out the day of the incident. You know...
that scene was too horrible. I just wanted to get as far away
from there as possible, and never come back."

"Then how did you end up back here?" Liu Hong
pursues.

"I don't know." Again, Lin Na tries hard to think, but
still can't piece it together. "I think I got drunk after work,
and when I woke up, I was on my old bed in that room."

Liu Hong nods, appearing to think carefully. "I also
remember it was after work. I'd been working very late...
when I left the office it was already eleven o'clock. When
I was walking past an underpass, I heard urgent footsteps
behind me, but didn't have the chance to turn and take
a look before I was struck in the back of the head by
something heavy. I don't remember anything after that...
until you came into the room and rescued me from under
the bed. I looked at the time on the mobile phone just then
– it's three o'clock in the morning, which means we haven't
been out for long."

"This is all planned. You can tell by the arrangements
in this flat... and tracing our habits and movements. He
must have spent a long time preparing." Lin Na hugs her
own shoulders; the more she thinks about it, the more
frightened she feels. Opening her eyes wide, she looks at
Liu Hong somewhat forlornly. "Want to try again? Maybe
if we smash the same spot a few more times, that window
will break."

Liu Hong shakes his head resolutely. "No point." Just
as he says this, though, the corner of his eye twitches and
he speaks again, this time with excitement. "I have an idea
that might work!"

"What?" Lin Na presses him to speak more.

Liu Hong makes no reply, but leaves the bathroom,

returning to the big bedroom. He then lifts the safe up to about waist height, and suddenly lets go, causing the box to smash heavily onto the floor. Even Lin Na, who is two or three metres away, feels a slight wave of vibrations.

"What are you…"

"It's three, four in the morning, right? The people on the floor below won't be able to stand this, and they'll go find the caretaker, or come up and investigate, themselves." As he speaks, Liu Hong picks up the safe, and again lets it drop. "If either happens, there'll be a hope of getting help!"

"Yes!" Lin Na is excited by this idea, which is unfolding in her own mind. Seeing that the other prisoner is already out of breath from exertion, she rushes over to help him with his labour. The two of them lift the heavy safe, again and again, letting it smash onto the floor, and with each impact, create a series of dull thuds and vibrations.

But the box is so heavy that after seven or eight rounds, the pair of them have exhausted themselves. Lin Na's arms are aching, limp, and she can no longer lift the cabinet an inch off the floor. After several attempts and failures, she gives up, massaging her arms. "I… I can't, I really have no… no more energy."

Li Hong, also exhausted, throws himself on the bed, taking a few deep breaths. "Let's… let's take a break."

"The people below would have heard that by now, right?" Lin Na cannot help asking after a moment.

"Unless they're deaf, I'd say it was impossible not to." Liu Hong pauses, and adds, "But they might put up with a few knocks, and just curse about it. If we want to make them do something, I need to keep smashing, till they can't take it anymore!"

Lin Na nods, and is just about to say something else,

when the sound of music bursts into the room.

In the dead of night, the song sounds too loud, and they both jump. It's the tender voice of a young child, with bright and crisp string accompaniments: "Ding ding dang, ding ding dang, ding dang rings the bell…"

It's a Christmas tune with Chinese words that every child knows, jolly in tempo and mood, but playing right now, this happy tune introduces an inexpressible sense of the ominous. Both aghast, Liu Hong and Lin Na turn their heads towards the direction the music is coming from.

Simultaneously, they see the phone, lying on the bed.

The incoming caller display is flashing, looking particularly dazzling in the dark. Liu Hong dives over, snatching up the phone and flipping it open. "Hello?!"

"Is that Liu Hong?" A low, distorted male voice comes out of the speaker. In the silence of the apartment, Lin Na can clearly hear both parts of the conversation.

"And who are you?" Liu Hong volleys the question.

"You need not be concerned with who I am, because I will not be talking with you. Would you please hand the phone to the young lady next to you, Lin Na?" Despite the mysterious voice phrasing it as a question, and using the word "please", its tone does not suggest any room for negotiation.

"You little shit! It was you who locked us up in here, wasn't it? What the hell are you playing at?" Liu Hong loses control, screaming in agitation.

When Liu Hong ceases his bellowing, the voice on the other end states, coldly and calmly, "I will wait for ten seconds. If I don't hear Miss Lin Na's voice by then, I will hang up, and will not call again."

Stunned, Liu Hong throws a glance at Lin Na, who holds out her hand, and says softly but firmly, "Give me the phone."

Liu Hong swallows his resentment and passes the phone to the other occupant. Taking a deep breath, Lin Na steadies her nerves, before speaking to the person on the other end of the line: "Hello, I am Lin Na."

The other party does not respond immediately, appearing to be thinking. The room is as silent as the grave, and Lin Na can almost hear her own heartbeat. After a moment, she cannot resist another timid "Hello?" just as the deep voice starts to speak again.

"Nobody lives in the flat below you, so I suggest you save your strength. You'll need it for the game I have set up. Now, I shall set out the rules, which shall not be broken. First, all phone calls will be answered by you, Lin Na; secondly, you have the right to listen to what I say, but no right to ask questions or interject, or else…"

Hearing this, Lin Na cannot resist interrupting, "Who the hell are you?" But the effect is like placing a bamboo pole between her and the sun – the consequence is immediate shadow, and the caller disconnects.

Lin Na pursues with two more pointless greetings, but they are met only by the monotonous deadtone from the receiver.

"He's hung up?" Liu Hong stares at Lin Na anxiously, and before she can even answer, snatches the phone from her and puts it to his ear, and then frustratedly throws it onto the bed, grumbling, "You shouldn't have asked that question! You broke his rule! He knows what we are doing, he must have some kind of surveillance."

Liu Hong walks to the window, looking out, but finding nothing.

Feeling utterly desolate, Lin Na cannot be bothered to throw a retort back, and just asks helplessly, "So, what now?"

After pacing the room restlessly, Liu Hong seems to calm down. Stopping in his tracks, he looks over at Lin Na. "That was just a warning, he'll call us back."

Sure enough, as soon as he says this, that Ding Dang Bells song starts playing again.

They look at each other, with both excitement and worry in their eyes.

"You pick it up!" Liu Hong hands the phone to Lin Na, and at the same time, earnestly exhorts, "Remember, don't say anything, just listen to him."

Lin Na nods, bringing the phone up to her ear, and presses the pick-up button. "Hello?"

"I will only give you one chance to make a mistake. If you break the rules again, you will never hear from me again," says the icy voice on the line. "So, when I am talking, you do not have the right to open your mouth, do you understand?"

"I... understand," Lin Na replies in a very small voice, afraid that even this would offend.

Luckily, this time, the voice exhibits no disapproval, pausing only slightly before continuing to talk. "Very well, now listen to me, and listen carefully..."

Lin Na pricks up her ears, and Liu Hong leans in as closely as he can.

"You should know by now that this apartment has been completely sealed off. With your own strength, it is impossible for you to escape. You must seek help from the outside, but will those on the outside help you? One year ago, that child was in the same situation you find yourselves in now. In the end, the only thing he could do was die tragically in loneliness and fear. So, what will be your fate?

"Like the child, you will have some chances of getting out of here. What results these chances yield will depend on two factors. Whether people on the outside care about you, and the choices you make yourselves. Lin Na, a year ago, you made the wrong choice that led to the tragedy, so from now onwards, you will be the protagonist in this game, and all the choices shall be made by you – this is set by me, as a rule that cannot be broken.

"Liu Hong, a year ago, you abandoned your duties of caring for the elderly and the young, so your right to choose shall be removed. Whatever happens from now on, all your actions must be as per Lin Na's arrangement."

Liu Hong glares at Lin Na, resentment combining with powerlessness in his eyes. He licks his lips. The scorching weather and the strenuous attempts prior have left him parched; he tries to moisten the cracks in his lips with limited saliva, only to find it evaporating in an instant.

"You must be very thirsty now, right?" asks the voice on the phone in a mocking tone – he seems to know every stage of their predicament like a script. "In the overhead cupboard of this room, there is a bottle of water. You can access it very easily, but will you use this water to quench your thirst? You see, the security door is very solid, and utterly soundproof, but I have ground out some tiny gaps in the bottom corners of the door, so the seal is not wholly waterproof. Lin Na, this is the first choice you shall face. What you should do is up to you to decide."

As soon as he finishes speaking, the line goes dead. Lin Na and Liu Hong both look towards the cupboard simultaneously, their dry and rough throats constricting, the overwhelming impulse to drink welling up in their minds.

Liu Hong pushes the safe over to the cupboards, and steps onto it. Opening the highest cupboard door, he instantly cries out in an excited croak, "He was telling the truth! There's really water here!"

Lin Na tilts her head up and looks expectantly, watching Liu Hong take the container of water down in his arms. It is one of the four-litre jugs of mineral water usually sold in the convenience stores – although not a lot, it would be enough to eliminate their current thirst.

"Here, take it." Liu Hong puts the wide bottle into Lin Na's hands, but his eyes remain fixed on the inside of the cupboard. "There seems to be something else here."

Holding the bottle, Lin Na's mouth and tongue feel like they are burning even fiercer. Liu Hong jumps off the stool, holding something that looks like a plastic box in his right hand, and clutching a pair of headphones in his left.

"It's a… mini fridge?" Having tossed the headphones aside indifferently, Liu Hong is clasping the box, and guessing at its purpose.

Lin Na can see that it is indeed one of those electric coolers used in cars.

"Did that sicko leave this behind, too?" Lin Na's eyes light up as she suddenly thinks of something. "Is there any food inside?"

Liu Hong opens the fridge door to check, but disappointingly, it is bare. He tosses the fridge onto the bed hatefully. "For fuck's sake. What's the point of an empty fridge?"

"Let's have a drink first, I'm dying of thirst." Right now, Lin Na does not have the capacity to think about that question. She is profoundly tormented by the primal desire to survive.

"No…" Liu Hong snatches the bottle away from her, before giving it a few greedy strokes himself. A strong craving shines in his eyes, but this impulse is quickly suppressed by reason.

"We can't drink this bottle of water," he hissed. "We are

depending on it for our escape."

"What?" Lin Na can't equate the two, as her confounded expression indicates.

"Didn't you hear what he said? Water can get through the gaps in the door. He was giving us a clue! If we pour this water out, it will flow into the corridor and stairway. When someone sees it, they'll assume there's no one in the flat and there's a burst pipe or something. As long as they get in touch with the building's admin staff, who'll open the door, we'll be saved!" Liu Hong says all this in one breath, rushing along with the excitement of the idea.

Lin Na suddenly realises what the voice meant by "choice" in his phone call. To quench their thirst? Or pour it away in exchange for a chance to be rescued?

"What if nobody sees it, or doesn't inform maintenance?" A logical kind of concern arises in Lin Na's head.

"That is not something either of us could control." Liu Hong narrows his eyes at Lin Na. "All we can do is our best. Planning is down to mortals, but the outcome is up to the Heavens. However, we can't let this opportunity pass by."

Lin Na's eyes have still not left the water bottle. "Then you're saying…"

"No, it doesn't matter what I'm saying," Liu Hong interrupts Lin Na. "You have to make the decisions, that's the rule HE set, and we can't go against it."

Lin Na chuckles mirthlessly. She would rather that such a hard choice sat on her counterpart's shoulders, but the man on the phone was very clear. If his rules were disobeyed, then the two of them faced losing their only contact with the outside world.

"Can we not… drink a little… and then pour out the rest?" After a moment of hesitation, Lin Na comes up with a plan that seems to serve both goals.

Liu Hong sighs, shaking his head. "If too little water flows out, then there's no point to our plan, and since it's so hot, the water will evaporate pretty quickly, so understand this. Every mouthful we drink is a percentage of our hopes being lost. Besides, if no one comes to save us, there'll be no point in our having water to drink. Because the water will always run out, and we'll end up in the same situation as we were before, and when that time comes, you'll regret not taking this chance!"

Having finished talking, Liu Hong gazes at Lin Na with anticipation, waiting for his counterpart's final decision. But Lin Na is biting her lip. After a good long while, she finally nods. "Alright... let's pour all of the water out."

"Excellent! You've made the right choice." Liu Hong nods his approval. "Then let's wait till the morning when there are more people going up and down the building, before pouring the water out."

Lin Na turns her head, averting her eyes from the water bottle in her counterpart's arms, in order to fight her urge to grab it from him at all costs and take a big gulp. She walks to the bed and sits down, gazing out at the world through the window. The skies are already showing some hints of white, and a few rooms in the building across from them are now lit – early risers getting ready for a new day. Lin Na's eyes flash with envy, and at the same time, she smells the scent of hope.

Yes. The world outside seems so close, she can almost touch it. There is no way she would end up dying in this room, is there?

The freedom to come and go is such a basic, simple thing, but now it has become Lin Na's greatest wish. She begins to daydream of the time when she gets out, how happy she will be, but an anxiety that refuses to disperse gathers on her brows. What if they can't get out?

Myriad, complex and disordered thoughts spin through Lin Na's head, and then, she is assaulted by a wave of fatigue. This is understandable. Yesterday was Friday, the most tiring time of the week. Originally, she'd hoped to sleep in over the weekend. Of course, she never expected to be suffering in these bizarre trials. After a night of strained nerves, she feels mentally and physically exhausted.

Lin Na leans against the headboard and closes her eyes. She is just going to rest for a moment, but after that moment, her consciousness begins to grow fuzzy, and she finds herself entering a state of almost-sleep.

In this drowsy state, her thoughts gallop around like wild horses or clouds. In her daze, Lin Na thinks she sees her father, who is lying on the bed, looking withered. He is holding her hand, and saying something, but abruptly changes into another person, an old man.

Of course, Lin Na recognises the old man from the room across the way. When he was alive, she'd never really engaged with him. She didn't even know her flatmates' names. Every day, when she returned to her room, she would be in a state beyond exhaustion, and really didn't have the energy to care about the pair on the other side of the living room, who had nothing in common with her.

Yet the grandfather and the child were destined to live in her head, for eternity.

"Don't go minding other people's business," her father would tell her. But here, he is replaced by the old man, staring daggers at Lin Na with his murky, lifeless eyes, demanding in a lifeless voice, "Why did you leave us to die?"

Lin Na tries to move away, but finds her wrist in the solid grasp of the speaker's fingers, which are as dry and solid as gnarled branches. The fingers begin to rot, their decay spreading up his arm, until soon, it covers his entire body.

The old man withers into a decomposed corpse, just as Lin Na saw him a year ago, when the door was finally opened.

Of course, the crying terrifies her even more.

The weeping of the child.

The crying is coming from behind her. Lin Na turns her head, and sees the child pressed up against the door, beating it with his hands as he weeps. Because he is so frail, the noises he makes are soft and weak. He turns his head, so he is face to face with Lin Na. His eyes are big and black, but without any lustre of life whatsoever, nothing except for hair-raising, bone-chilling despair and fear.

Pierced by these eyes, Lin Na shudders, her body convulsing violently as she wakes out of her dream-state.

Daylight is breaking, and Lin Na stands up. Looking around her, she finds that Liu Hong is not in the room, so she hastens out to the living room, where she is confronted by a most disturbing sight.

Liu Hong is partially on his stomach next to the door, his head turned to one side, the left side of his face pressed firmly to the floor, his bum protruding up high, like a toad that has been half stepped on. Keeping this pose, he is completely still; even his bulging eyes are wide open and unblinking.

"What are you doing?" Lin Na is disturbed by the other's bizarre stance, and edging closer, she asks her question timidly.

Liu Hong does not reply immediately, but casts a glimpse at the phone in his right hand. After a moment, he sits up on the floor, and, absentmindedly rubbing the dust off his face, states, "Just now, four people have walked past the stairway in five minutes – it's time to pour out the water."

Lin Na figures out he has been pressing himself against the floor to listen to the footsteps outside. With the heavy iron door in the way, it really was the only way of detecting any movement outside.

The water bottle has been placed next to the door. Liu Hong tears off the plastic seal around the cap with his teeth, removes the stopper, and lifts the container. At this point, Lin Na squats close by, watching the other's every move.

Liu Hong tilts the bottle, and a clear pillar of water hangs down from its mouth, meeting the base of the iron door, which, whilst seeming impenetrable, cannot, in the end, prevent the water from freely seeping out.

The pillar of water sparkles, reflecting light in its curves and splashes, while the gurgling sound it makes is endlessly enticing. Both Liu Hong and Lin Na instinctively lick their lips, trying hard to repress their intense craving.

The water flows away very quickly. Most of it has seeped out under the door, following the shape of the floor, and should have formed a substantial pool in the passageway.

"Right. Now we pray to the heavens for a kind-hearted soul to pass and notice the water pooling outside." He throws the empty bottle to one side, and again presses his upper body against the floor, reassuming the squashed toad position.

Still staring at the bottle, Lin Na hesitates. Seeing that Liu Hong has his back towards her, she can no longer resist picking the bottle up and holding it high over her head. After a moment or two of being suspended upside down, a few drops of water fall, at last, slightly wetting her tongue.

"Someone's come over!" Liu Hong cries out in excitement as he spins around. Lin Na, who is in the middle of reaching out for the last half a drop of water in the bottle with her tongue, notices her counterpart's gaze, and at once halts her actions, blushing.

But Liu Hong does not mind too much, giving a dry laugh before hastening down to resume his monitoring of the outside.

Shyly, Lin Na imitates his posture, but hearing nothing, she moves closer, whispering with concern, "What's happening?"

Liu Hong places his index finger on his lips and Lin Na holds her breath for a while, only to see him get up and shake his head in disappointment. "He stopped for a while – but then quickly went up the stairs."

"Up the stairs? Then he must be going home…" Lin Na's heart contracts – this person clearly doesn't care about leaks in the building.

"Doesn't matter, someone else will see it," Liu Hong says soothingly to her, and again, gets down to his strange crawling stance by the door. This time he waits for over a minute, before excitement blazes in his eyes. Clearly there has been more movement.

"Has someone come over?" Lin Na asks eagerly. But this time, before Liu Hong can reply, the answer becomes evident.

Because the doorbell rings.

"Someone outside knows something is wrong!" Liu Hong shoots up like an arrow, yelling, "Hey! Help us, we're locked in!"

Lin Na snaps back to her senses, and reacts to the event, adding her voice to the other's calls: "Help! Save us!"

Yet no reply comes from the outside. The doorbell rings another two or three times.

Suddenly disheartened, Liu Hong shakes his head, and slightly hysterically tells Lin Na, "Stop yelling, it's no good. HE said this door is soundproof, so the people outside have no way of hearing us."

The doorbell has also now stopped ringing. Lin Na processes this, and asks in a panic, "Have they left?"

Liu Hong does not answer. Falling against the iron door, he lets his body slide down onto the floor, and closes his eyes, the epitome of helplessness and resignation.

"Don't go, save us, please!" Lin Na bangs and drums hard on the door – even though she knows it is futile, she is unable to stop herself.

The door is so thick that there is no way that the soft and insubstantial noises made by contact with the flesh will be able to pass through it.

Lin Na is quiet for a moment, and then, filled with sudden hope, asks, "Do you think he'll go to the caretaker?"

"Who knows?" Liu Hong stares into space and lets his vision wander, sighing a long, soft sigh. "Anyhow, all we can do is wait here. We can make choices, but we cannot determine our fate. Our lives lie in the hands of a stranger we have never met. That's the point of this game he's set up for us."

"Then we'll wait." Lin Na also sits down dejectedly. Neither of them, their backs to the metal door, have the heart to make conversation.

Time passes slowly. They are unsure how many other people have walked past them, down the passageway, separated only by that one door. Undoubtedly, they have all seen the puddle of water; they may find it strange, or worrying, some might even feel annoyed, but would any one of them reach out to offer a helping hand?

This kind person never appears to Liu Hong and Lin Na.

"Hmph." At last, Liu Hong breaks the heavy silence with a disillusioned huff. "The show's over – no one's coming to our aid."

A cloud of despair fleets over Lin Na's eyes, but she is still not ready to give up, so she starts to reason out loud: "Maybe they've already informed admin, but the caretaker is busy and doesn't have time to come up yet."

"Even if that were the case, it's still pointless." Liu Hong shakes his head. "The water outside will be nearly dry by now. When maintenance comes, they will assume that the occupants have resolved the problem, and there's no need to open up and check."

Startled, Lin Na turns to check the surface of the floor next to the door. Sure enough, the water stains on this side have now dried, so the situation on the other must be the same.

"So quickly?" Lin Na cries out in disappointment, and in an overtly whiney tone, groans, "We should never have poured the water out. This was always going to be useless. The time it lasted was always going to be too short, so there was never going to be anyone coming to save us!"

Lin Na's words seem to have ignited the wrath Liu Hong has been keeping in check. At once, he hits back hard: "Yes, no one will come, you're right. And only you can see this because all of those people are like you, not giving a damn about anyone else. Everyone out there is the same as you!"

Lin Na freezes in shock, and then smiles sadly. "I know

you hate me. You think I'm responsible for your son's death."

Liu Hong keeps his face taut, ironically choosing this moment to stop speaking.

Lin Na wraps her arms around her knees, lowers her head, and buries half her face in the nest of her arms. She locks her stare forwards, but her expression is wandering, as she is evidently thinking about other things. Thick crystal tears bubble up in her eyes, but she seems to be controlling her emotions, and trying hard not to let them fall.

The room falls into a heavy silence, punctuated only by Liu Hong's ragged, angry breathing.

After a while, Lin Na manages to collect her thoughts. She wipes the corners of her eyes with the back of her hand, and then says softly, "My father died when I was at primary school. Before he died, he gave me just one piece of advice. He said: 'Nana, don't go minding other people's business, because in this world, nobody else is going to mind yours.'"

Liu Hong is struck dumb – he did not expect her to have such a bleak past, nor does he understand why her father would bequeath her such harsh words. He focuses his attention on the woman next to him, with a little more concern now showing in his expression.

But Lin Na does not return his gaze, seeming to pay no attention to the key change in the other. She is absorbed in her own thoughts. In an indifferent yet slightly melancholic manner, she continues, "My father was a good person, everyone said so. When I was little, he loved me very much, and I thought I had the best father in the world. At the time, he told me that a person must have a warm heart, and if you see others in difficulty, one should offer help, because good things happen to good people. Right?

But then what happened? Things were nothing like he expected them to be."

Lin Na feels an irritation in her nose, and her eyes rim red again. She takes a deep breath, suppressing her stirred-up emotions, before carrying on: "That summer, when I was nine, Father was passing a riverbank on his way back from work. He saw a little boy struggling in the river and calling for help. Without hesitation, he dived into the water, not knowing that the water level was only about half a metre high. He hit his head badly on the riverbed and passed out straight away in the water. Even though the hospital did their best to save him, the damage and the oxygen starvation left him completely paralysed.

"It turned out the boy crying for help was just playing a prank. His parents brought him along to visit the hospital once, and we never saw them again. We couldn't afford the medical fees, even after draining all our savings, and in the end, we had to give up treatment. My father held onto his life for a year, before passing away."

"How could that happen?" Liu Hong is moved. "Wasn't there anyone to help you?"

"No. Not one person." Lin Na's detached tone feels like ice. "My mother appealed to the Foundation for Justice and Courage for aid, but they said, since my father didn't actually save anyone, it didn't count as an act of justice, or courage."

Liu Hong sighs, lost for words. He can imagine the mentality of Lin Na's father before he died – a warm-hearted person abandoned by a cruel society. No wonder he'd left her with those last words.

Once again, Lin Na's thoughts meandered to a year ago. There is a tremor in her voice as she says, "On those nights, when I heard the crying on and off... I didn't know what had happened – I was at work during the day, and when I got in, it was usually late, and the door to that room was locked. As a woman living on her own, I had to think of my own safety..."

Liu Hong throws back his head with another long sigh.

"Never mind. Enough of this..." Lin Na bites her lip, her tears at last rolling down her cheeks. "Whether you can forgive me or not, I would very much... very much like to say, I am truly sorry."

Having spoken between choking sobs, Lin Na gets up and returns to her room, lies down flat on her bed, and does not move for a long time.

Liu Hong remains, sitting with his back against the iron door, lost in thought. The stiff atmosphere continues, when the cheerful singing ringtone pipes up again. The sound of this tugs at the nerves of both people, making them jump simultaneously.

"Quick, get the phone, quick!" Liu Hong answers the phone, and plunges into Lin Na's room, summoning her with an urgent beckoning.

In the face of a common predicament, the previous unpleasantness has naturally been thrown to the back of their minds. Lin Na springs up from the bed, takes the phone and breathlessly answers: "Hello?"

"Do not interrupt, whatsoever. Listen closely." Again, the voice on the other end of the line emphasises his "rules", following this with a length of silence, before speaking again in an unhurried and methodical fashion. "It looks like your first escape plan didn't go so smoothly, but you may have another chance. In the building across from the big bedroom, there is a man who has a penchant for spying on people's private activities.

It is now the morning of the weekend, when he is most active in this pursuit. If you appear at the window now, he may see you. Of course, you cannot see him. But you may use another method to track his movements. I have installed a bug in his binoculars. If you put on the headphones and turn them on, you will get the signal from the device. What you do next is still up to you, Lin Na."

He barely finishes before the line goes dead. Lin Na puts away the phone carefully first, and then with wide eyes, asks Liu Hong: "Did you hear that?"

Liu Hong nods and mumbles to himself, "There is someone who can see us from the window... what should we do?"

"Let's see how the headphones work." As she speaks, Lin Na heads for the big bedroom, followed closely by Liu Hong. After a search, they quickly find the headphones that he had tossed on the bed. Being uncertain how they work, Lin Na once again puts them in Liu Hong's hands. "You take a look... How do you switch this thing on?"

Liu Hong finds a knob and gently turns it past the click. He puts the headphones on and listens for a moment.

"I can hear breathing... he's using the binoculars right now!" Liu Hong says excitedly, taking off the headphones and handing them to Lin Na. "You have a go, do you hear it?" Before he finishes talking, he is already approaching the window, and looking out at the opposite building.

Lin Na puts on the headphones and listens, nodding. "Yes, I can hear some sounds, but can he really see us?"

"Hey, take a look here, we are here!" Liu Hong waves his arms across the window, bellowing at the top of his lungs, actions which, at best, may make him feel better, but have no meaningful impact.

Lin Na also paces to the window, looking across aimlessly. Which room was this peeping tom in? What is he looking at right now? The morning sun is shining right at them through this window, so they would be concealed in the shadows, which makes this the best time for peeking.

The two of them stand by the window, with an unnatural hope of being spied upon.

After another moment, Lin Na blushes, and in a low voice, mumbles, "I think he… he's seen me."

Liu Hong turns to her eagerly. "How can you tell?"

"He is talking to himself and saying some… filthy things." Lin Na looks embarrassed, holding her hands tightly over the headphones, as if not wanting the sounds from them to leak into the ears of her counterpart.

This confuses Liu Hong, but quickly, he understands. For this voyeur, watching an attractive woman in the building across from him, talking dirty is probably part of their fun.

"What a pervert!" Liu Hong curses hatefully, and then strikes his hand on the glass, shouting at the top of his voice, "Don't just watch, you arsehole, think of a way to get us out of here!"

"It's no use doing this." Lin Na laughs wryly, giving Liu Hong's arm a tug. "Stop, he's cursing you."

"Cursing me?" Liu Hong grimaces ineffectually. Indeed, the other party wouldn't understand his meaning, and watching his movements, would probably just call him a stupid prick.

Liu Hong shakes his head grimly. "We can't make him understand the trap we're in. He's just going to spy on us for fun. He's never going to help us get out of it."

Lin Na is quiet for a moment, then says, "I have an

idea."

"What idea?"

"Hit me." Lin Na is gazing at Liu Hong with extreme solemnity. "Hit me hard."

Liu Hong understands her intention, but he frowns. "No... I've never hit a woman before."

"You have to beat the hell out of me. If he calls the police, then we'll be rescued – we can't let this chance pass us by." Lin Na's eyes are beaming with urgency and determination.

Liu Hong lifts his hand, which hesitates in mid-air, and finally falls, slapping Lin Na across the face, carefully aiming away from all the vital parts.

Lin Na hears a "Fucking hell!" from the headphones, but the tone is obviously full of schadenfreude.

"That's too soft!" Lin Na looks at Liu Hong impatiently. "You have to hit me hard, like you want to kill me, so we can freak that person out. You worthless prick." Lin Na's eyes change, and her tone turns malicious. "Just like your father, and your son, three generations of you – all the same trash, total losers!"

Horrified, Liu Hong freezes. "What did you say?"

"I said, you're all losers!" Lin Na continues with her malevolent insults. "They deserved to die here, and you can't do anything to stop yourself getting buried right alongside them."

True or not, these words stab at the most vulnerable places at the bottom of Liu Hong's heart, sending waves of white-hot fury exploding into his head. He glares at her.

"Come on and hit me, you loser!" Lin Na shrieks as she swings her hand, lashing Liu Hong viciously across the face. This slap triggers Liu Hong's eruption, and, roaring, he returns the attack, knocking Lin Na nearly off her feet with a backhanded slap.

Lin Na ignores the searing pain on her face, retreating to one side of the window. "Their deaths are all because of you! You are an unfilial son, and an even more disgraceful father!"

Liu Hong grunts like a wild beast, dashing forward with bloodshot eyes. He grips Lin Na's throat with his left hand, while his right hand administers blow after blow to her head and face. Lin Na does not cower, she continues to curse, kicking and clawing against him.

Liu Hong quickly gains the upper hand, and Lin Na gives up her resistance, leaning feebly against the window.

Liu Hong stops raining blows, but his left hand is still wrapped around her throat, forcing her to face him, and yelling in a voice dripping with indignation and pain, "It's not my fault..."

"It's... all... your... fault..." With her throat clenched in his grip, Lin Na struggles to form her words, but her attitude does not alter. "It was... it was you... who... killed your son..."

Liu Hong grits his teeth, a dark look overtaking his face, as he puts even more strength into his grip. Lin Na coughs desperately. She is already defenceless, unable to speak, her pretty face deep scarlet from lack of air, her eyeballs protruding from their sockets, radiating desperation and fear.

A moment later, two streams of tears glide down from the corners of Lin Na's eyes.

Liu Hong jolts back to his senses and loosens his grip, but Lin Na is no longer able to stand, and immediately crumples limply to the floor.

Liu Hong drops to his knees by Lin Na's side, picking her up and cradling her in his arms. "Lin Na... are you hurt?"

Lin Na keeps her eyes closed, her tears still streaming. After a moment of panting, she shakes her head painfully. "No, I'm fine… it's just… it's just we're still trapped here, he… he won't help us…"

Even during the fiercest moments of the fight, Lin Na was still keeping the headphones pressed close to her ears and had clearly heard some things.

Liu Hong takes the headphones from her head and puts them on. After listening for a few seconds, he frowns slightly. "There's no sound?"

Lin Na laughs bitterly. What had really brought her to tears was what she had heard through the bug.

First the man had exclaimed, *"Oh fuck! This is for real! Someone's going to get killed!"*

Then a woman's voice came through: *"You pervert, what are you watching now?"*

"Come and look, the fight's just getting good!"

"What's going on?" The sound change let Lin Na know the woman had taken over the binoculars.

"Isn't this too much? Should we call the police?"

"Police my arse! This is between them, why're you sticking your nose in? Do you feel sorry for your little tart?"

"What are you talking about?"

"Alright, I'm keeping these binoculars from now on. No more spying on random shit like that anymore."

After hearing Lin Na's account, Liu Hong looks utterly dispirited. "That woman took the binoculars away?"

Feebly, Lin Na nods. "So this plan isn't going to work, either."

Liu Hong throws back his head with a hard sigh, and it is hard to tell if he is dry-laughing or sobbing. Then he turns to Lin Na, filled with concern. "How are you doing?

I didn't hurt you, did I?"

The welts on Lin Na's neck have not yet faded and her cheeks have clearly swollen up, but she does not seem to mind any of this. Softly shaking her head, she suddenly realises she's lying in the arms of a man. She blushes, and struggles to sit up, while at the same time pushing Liu Hong aside. "I'm fine."

Liu Hong feels awkward, too, so he backs away and sits down a short distance from Lin Na. The staged argument and fight, which was hard to tell from the real thing, has exhausted much of their physical energy. In addition to not having rested for most of the day, they haven't had a drop to drink, so both their bodies are now on the brink of collapse. Liu Hong pants for a moment, before resorting to just lying down flat on the spot, but Lin Na is still minding her deportment, and makes do with leaning against the wall, and maintaining a half-reclining position.

After a while, when they have both somewhat settled, an unformed question bursts out of Liu Hong. "Do you really believe what you said?"

"Eh?" Lin Na doesn't understand the other's meaning.

"What you said just then, that the three generations of us... are all... losers..." Liu Hong just about brings himself to repeat this sentence.

Lin Na shakes her head. "That was just to provoke you."

Liu Hong shows his relief. After a moment more of silence, he asks, "Did you meet my son? He was very clever."

"I saw him occasionally, but... but not really any contact." Even talking seems to tire Lin Na further.

"He was really clever. More than the other children. If he'd grown up, he would be much better than me." Liu Hong stares at the ceiling in reverie. He is speaking with the unshakable pride of all fathers, and yet under these circumstances, that pride is inseparable from misery.

Lin Na is silent for a moment. There is a question that has been bothering her, which at last, she cannot resist asking: "Why... why did you leave the old man and your boy here?"

Closing his eyes, Liu Hong shakes his head, his expression full of agony. He hesitates, before answering, "How can I put it? I used to have a lot of money, but then I made some bad investments, and that turned into a lot of debt. My wife left with someone else, leaving me with the kid... I was working my arse off, and really had no time, nor energy..."

Before he finished, Liu Hong drew an even deeper breath, unable to continue. Lin Na remarks serenely, "We all have our burdens..." and says nothing more. The room once again falls into a quiet and lonely atmosphere.

IT IS ALREADY noon, and the sunlight is growing stronger, raising the temperature in the room. Even though the two people are sitting still and quiet, they feel sticky and parched. Due to dehydration, they are perspiring less and less, and can feel the heat building up within their bodies, leaving them uncomfortable and aching.

Being smaller, Lin Na is physically a little weaker, and is now struggling to cope. Shutting her eyes, she feels disorientated, unsure if she is falling asleep or passing out.

"Hold on, Lin Na!" In her daze, she hears Liu Hong's voice calling her. "We'll have another chance!"

A chance! The implications of that word act like a shot of adrenaline into Lin Na's bloodstream, and she struggles to open her eyes. "What chance?"

"I just remembered–" Liu Hong drags himself up to a standing position, his tone excited. "That safe, and the minifridge, are both chances!"

Lin Na stares at Liu Hong, lost, unable to understand him.

"These are all things that HE has left for us, so every single thing in here is a chance for escape. That bottle of water, the headphones, all of them! So we'll have more chances, at least two!" As he explains himself, Liu Hong walks over to the bed and picks up the minifridge, turning it over in his hand for a moment, asking himself, "But what use does this fridge have?"

Lin Na turns her gaze to the safe on the floor and says thoughtfully, "Perhaps we can think of a way to open this safe – there might be something important inside."

"Yes, yes, yes!" Liu Hong drops the fridge, and kneels down to investigate the safe, but is quickly disappointed.

"This is a six-digit combination, with a million possibilities. If we don't have the code, how can we open it?" He points to the dials on the safe as she moves closer to see.

After some thinking, Lin Na makes a deduction. "Since he has left us the safe, he must have also left us the code."

"Makes sense! Otherwise, why would he make a superfluous move?" Liu Hong looks at Lin Na admiringly, and then knots his brow again. "But where could the code be?"

"It must be hidden somewhere difficult to find. If it were easy, there'd be no point in locking the safe," Lin Na analyses, then suddenly, her eyes leap. "Or–"

Lin Na spins round, looking towards the phone on the bed. Liu Hong works out her meaning: or that person might give them clues to the code on the phone.

"He'll call again. We've been obeying his rules, his little game isn't over yet," Liu Hong mutters, as if consoling himself.

As if to prove Liu Hong's belief, the fuzzy electric rendition starts to play again.

"Ding ding dang, ding ding dang, ding dang rings the bell."

Lin Na leaps up, rushing over to pick up the phone, but does not say anything. Under the "rules" set by the master of the game, all she can do is comply without condition.

"You've failed again. Even though Lin Na made the right choice, the person you encountered does not want to help you."

The stretched-out voice on the phone continues, "I said very early on that for you to succeed in extricating yourselves, first Lin Na must make the right choice, but secondly there must be a truly kind-hearted person outside who will help you. Both of these conditions must be met. You have already failed twice, but there is another chance. And you are holding this chance in your very hand, Lin Na."

In my hand? Lin Na is astonished.

The man continues, providing the answer: "The mobile phone. One chance lies hidden within the phone you are using now. The keys have been disconnected, so there is no way you can dial – but I've installed a little app on this phone. If you press and hold the answer key, the phone will dial out to one of about five hundred random phone numbers I've put in the contact list. Not even I know who the owner of these numbers are, so you have no way of predicting what sort of person will be on the other end. I'll tell you, though, that while I can call you any time I wish, there's only about a minute's worth of outgoing credit. If, within this one minute, you can persuade the person on the other end to help you, then your prospects will be greatly improved. Good luck, Lin Na!"

As he had done on the several previous calls, the man hangs up as soon as he's finished his part. Lin Na places the mobile phone in front of her and fixes her gaze on it for a long time, excitement mingled with indecision on her face.

"One minute? How could we explain all this in one minute?" says Liu Hong slowly, incredulously, shaking his head. "Especially when the other party is a complete stranger to us... we'll be lucky if they don't just hang up on us."

"So we have to think about it carefully, how to make full use of the minute." Lin Na lets out a long breath, and then mutters, "How to communicate with the other party, what should be said?"

Liu Hong does not reply. Like Lin Na, he is frowning with concentration. Doubtless they have an incredibly thorny task ahead. What they are experiencing is so extraordinary that even Lin Na herself has yet to completely understand it. How could they make it clear to a total stranger in a mere minute?

After the longest pause, Liu Hong reaches a conclusion, waving his hand. "There's no need to communicate all this to the other party, because you can't explain any of it. You just need to ask them to call the police."

Lin Na cackles. "But why would anyone take us seriously? A completely random phone call..."

Liu Hong grins helplessly. "Let's pray to the heavens for protection."

After another long silence, Lin Na nods. "Well, that's all we can hope for." She grips the phone tightly in her right hand, her palms clammy.

"If we're done with thinking about it, let's just make the call." Liu Hong struggles to gather enough spit in his mouth to swallow, complaining, "I don't think I can cope much longer."

Lin Na puts the back of her left hand against her forehead, hesitating. She says, "Just a moment…" and slips back into a lengthy, nervous thinking process. There is nothing Liu Hong can do but sit quietly and wait anxiously.

At last, Lin Na builds up enough confidence and courage, lifts her head, lets out a heavy breath, and turns to Liu Hong. "OK, I'm dialling."

Nervously, Liu Hong holds his breath, fixing his eyes on Lin Na's hand. Hovering for a second, her thumb softly presses and holds the green key.

About five seconds later, a string of pitched beeps come from the phone. Lin Na and Liu Hong's hearts beat as swiftly as these tones. They can tell that the app has made its selection, and its random outcome may have the greatest impact on their fate. Where will the number be? What kind of person will pick up? Will they be kind-hearted? Or will they just be indifferent to the fate of others, like most people? The answer to all these questions will be revealed in just a few moments.

After the number has been dialled, there are five or six burrs of sound before the call is finally picked up.

"Hello?" It's a woman's voice.

"Please save us, we are in immediate danger!" Following her thoughts, Lin Na immediately blurts out how critical the situation is, as sincerely as she can.

"Who are you?" Although the voice is filled with suspicion and doubt, the speaker's voice is placid, and sounds like it belongs to a good mannered, middle-aged woman. This greatly raises Lin Na's hopes.

"You don't know me, but I desperately need your help. Just call the police for us, please!"

"You want me to help you call the police?" The woman is getting more puzzled. "Why don't you just dial 110 yourself?"

"Because I can't call from this phone. I can't explain right now. Please. Please take down this address and tell the police to come save us." Lin Na is speaking so fast, and finishes without taking a single breath – however, her words do not seem to have the intended impact.

"I'm sorry, I'm quite busy at the moment, and besides, I don't have a pen with me... please find someone else." The speaker is clearly about to hang up.

"No, please don't hang up, please don't...! I'm begging you!" Lin Na pleads with her wretchedly, her anxiety and fear seeping into her voice, choking it with tears. This seems to move her listener, who is now hesitant, and asks, "What's going on? Have you been kidnapped?"

Liu Hong is gesturing to Lin Na frantically, indicating that time is running out.

"I don't have time!" Lin Na's speech is almost indistinguishable from her crying. "Please remember, we are in flat 502, block 18, Gonglin New Village. Ask the police to come and save us!"

"Wait, Gonglin New Village, what was the number?" At last, the other party begins to listen to Lin Na's information, but at that very moment, they hear the dreaded sound of the line cutting and ending the conversation.

"Sorry, you have insufficient remaining credit, please top up," comes the automatic reminder, the scratchy recorded voice sounding cruel and merciless.

Lin Na feels a wave of numbness. She looks at the phone in her hand, her face the image of despair. Liu Hong bursts into a scream of rage: "FUUUUUCCCK!"

But then, the phone rings again.

With no time to think, Lin Na takes the call, quietly awaiting the mysterious voice's next instructions.

"Hello, are you there?" Beyond her expectations comes the voice of the woman.

"Yes, yes, yes!" Lin Na is both astonished and overjoyed. "You rang back?"

"I used call back," says the speaker. "I didn't hear that address clearly, can you repeat it?"

Putting her wits to work, Lin Na asks, "Can you see the number of this phone?"

The caller seems to be checking, and after a moment, replies, "No... that's a bit strange. My screen is only showing 'incoming call'."

"He's done something to disable the phone's ID," Liu Hong interjects hatefully.

Disappointed, Lin Na sighs softly. If they knew the number, they could get a friend or the police to call it. That would be an entirely different situation. All they can do now is pin all their hopes on this lady whose name they do not even know. Fortunately, the lady has at least shown that she is willing to help, and even called back, so they can talk more comfortably.

"We're in Flat 502, Block 18, Gonglin New Village. Please note it down and ask the police to come and rescue us urgently," Lin Na repeats.

"Mm..." The lady seems to be making some notes, and then she asks again, "What on earth is going on?"

Lin Na attempts to make a precis of the entire situation, but having heard it, the lady seems even more perplexed.

"This is too bizarre," she says on the other end of the phone. "I'm finding all this quite hard to believe."

"I'm finding it unbelievable, too, but it's happening. Please, you must believe me, I have no reason to lie to you."

Lin Na is talking with expressive anxiety. If the lady could see her, she would have fallen to her knees.

"Then I'll call the police for you first." The woman pauses, adding, "If this is a prank, it's not too late to stop it now."

"I would never do that. Please, call the police for us, thank you so much!" Lin Na says in a firm, resolute tone.

Amidst Lin Na's profuse gratitude, the caller hangs up. Lin Na looks at Liu Hong solemnly, unable to control her emotions, shedding tears of joy, and relief.

"It's alright, we're getting rescued! What are you crying for?" Liu Hong takes hold of Lin Na's shoulders, giving them a couple of strong squeezes.

Lin Na still looks like she's dreaming, as if not daring to believe that all this is real. Liu Hong flips over and stretches out on the bed. When he has calmed down, he asks, "So, let's think. What's the first thing you want to do when we get out of here?"

"I…" Lin Na lets her mind wander for a while, before replying, "I want to have a shower. I feel gross."

"Haha, women are women – even at this stage, that's still the first thing you think of." Liu Hong smiles. "Me? I think we should go out and eat and drink as much as we can. Gorge ourselves! How about it? There's a Fengming Lou just outside this block, isn't there? I'll treat you!"

Fengming Lou, "The Phoenix Call" is the most prestigious restaurant chain in the city, but when she hears the name, Lin Na blinks doubtfully. "Fengming Lou? Why would there be a branch here?"

"It's just outside, isn't it? You can see it from here." Liu Hong points at the window; perhaps due to over-exhaustion, he is loath to get up from the bed.

With a look of confusion, Lin Na walks to the window, looking out into the distance. As he had said, right next to the southern gate of the xiaoqu is a magnificent building, three massive hanzi characters in gold, glowing in the splendour of the afternoon sun: .

Lin Na's expression sets into grim mistrust. "Something... something isn't right!"

"What?" It isn't until Liu Hong hears the tone of Lin Na's voice that he sits up and questions her.

Lin Na ignores him, instead turning around to rush into the small bedroom. With each step, her face grows darker. Liu Hong realises that something is very wrong, and scrambles down from the bed to follow her.

Even though the window in the small bedroom has been neatly covered by the wooden planks, there are some unpreventable cracks between the uneven boards. Narrowing her eyes, Lin Na peeks out through them, and turns back, in despair. "We've been tricked. This isn't Gonglin New Village."

"What?" Liu Hong presses his eyes to the crack, straining to see as he asks, "Then where the fuck are we?"

"I don't know, I've never been here before! This isn't the room I lived in before. This furniture, this set up, they must all be replicas..." Lin Na stares incredulously at Liu Hong, wishing she could convey to him everything she has realised all at once.

Liu Hong seems to have understood at least some of this, and, astonished, he mutters to himself, "That's why he boarded this window up... because you'd remember the view on this side, he tricked us..."

"What do we do now? The police won't be able to find us!" Facing this sudden game change, Lin Na becomes panicked and flustered.

"Don't panic." Liu Hong steadies himself a little. "That woman will call again, so think quickly. How do we explain it to her?"

But Lin Na does not have the time to think about it, because at this very moment, the phone rings.

Lin Na looks at the incoming call on the display screen – it's the number of the lady who just called. She hastens to press the receive key, and does not even have a chance to speak before the indignant voice comes through: "I have just had a lecture from the police on 110 – do you find this funny?"

"I'm sorry, I had the wrong address," Lin Na interrupts in a panic.

"Fine, then tell me where you really are." The lady's tone is antagonistic and sounds as if she is trying to contain her resentment.

"I... I don't know." For a moment, Lin Na does not know how to reply, and stammers, "Oh yes, there's a branch of Fengming Lou just outside the main gates..."

"Right!" The caller cuts Lin Na short. "I'm very busy and have no time to listen to your nonsense. Goodbye."

The line flips to the dropped call tone, the caller obviously having hung up. Lin Na looks at Liu Hong, utterly destroyed. "She's hung up... will she call back?"

The answer is all over Liu Hong's face, now raw and set like iron. After the briefest effort to suppress it, the indignation in him finally explodes.

"Who does that bitch think she is?!" He flings his arms about, growling, "Too busy too busy too busy! All fucking excuses, she never believed us! One day, she's going to get a taste of the feeling of being abandoned by others!"

"It's all my fault, I didn't handle it..." Whether intimidated by Liu Hong's explosion or truly blaming herself, or just slipping once more into despondency, soft sobs start to escape Lin Na.

At this, Liu Hong's temper simmers down a little. Biting back his anger, he puts his hand gently on her shoulder, and reassures, "Don't cry, it's not your fault, you did all you could…"

Without warning, Lin Na throws her arms around Liu Hong, and her whimpers expand into painful heaving wails. He holds her gently. "Don't cry, we're still alive, aren't we? We'll get another chance, believe me, there will be another chance."

After a good while, Lin Na's wailing abates, and she leaves Liu Hong's arms. She wipes the sticky mess from the corners of her eyes, and trembling, tells him, "I'm so tired."

Liu Hong sighs softly. "If you're tired, then sleep."

Lin Na nods. Walking to her bed, she lies down, still gripping the mobile phone tightly in her hand. It is the last vestige of hope she can hold on to.

Liu Hong retreats to the main bedroom. He, too, is already over-exhausted, and not long after lying down on that big bed, quickly follows Lin Na into a deep, deep sleep.

THE TWO OF them sleep through until dark, when they wake from their drowsy state to the "Ding Dang Bells" ringtone of their lifeline. Lin Na opens her heavy eyes, finding herself in pitch darkness. Although she is awake, her faculties are slow and muddled.

Liu Hong dashes in from the opposite room, urging her, "Quick, check who's calling!"

Lin Na sits up and squints at the screen. "It's him – the

Man."

"Answer it, quick. Remember his rules, don't provoke him, and maybe he'll give us another chance, got it?"

Lin Na nods, puts the phone to her ear and presses the answer key.

"Lin Na, so far your behaviour has been excellent, and your choices have been correct." Although the voice on the phone is praising her, the tone remains cold. Then he switches the focus: "But you have still not escaped from the apartment. No matter how hard you try, the world outside refuses, in the end, to provide any real help. You must be very disappointed, and I am even more so. I am the one who has confined you to this apartment, but you should understand, it is not that heavy iron door that is cutting you off from the outside world.

"It's time to end this little game. This will be the last time I shall call you, and of course, you have gained one final chance of survival. Inside the pillow on your bed, you will find that I have left a letter for you, with instructions on what to do. But you alone are allowed to read it. Liu Hong must retreat to the other bedroom and close the door. As for whether or not you want to share the contents with him after you have read the letter, it is a choice I leave up to you. Goodbye, Lin Na."

The man hangs up. Lin Na's eyes instinctively shift to the pillow on the bed, and then to Liu Hong, pacing back and forth a short distance from her.

He knows what Lin Na is thinking, and nods to her. "Do as he says, I'll wait for you outside." Having said this, he takes the initiative to retreat from the room, pulling the door shut behind him with a solid click.

First, Lin Na puts the phone away, and then grabbing the pillow, places it on her lap. Gripping the pillow with both hands, she pulls the sides apart hard, and a split quickly forms. Lin Na pushes her right hand into the tear, tentatively exploring, and sure enough, finds a folded letter buried in the cotton wadding.

Holding the letter, she moves to the window, and under the moonlight seeping through the cracks between the boards, examines it. The letter consists of two pieces of paper, but the two pieces are not entirely separate. They are joined by a collection of points at the edge, and strictly speaking, should be called two parts of a perforated sheet.

The upper and lower parts of the letter each contain a paragraph of text. The upper sheet contains the words:

You must be very thirsty by now. Flip over your mattress, and you will find a bottle of water hidden in the bed board. This is my gift to you. Will you tell Liu Hong about this gift? Will he once again pour this bottle of water away? As long as you tear this part of the letter to pieces and hide it, then you will be able to enjoy the whole bottle by yourself.

The contents of the lower sheet are simple:

In the bathroom, between the cistern and the wall, I have left you a package. Your last chance of getting out of here alive is in that package.

Lin Na hurriedly reads these two paragraphs. She is too preoccupied to think about the details of the contents, and first gets up from the bed, flips up the mattress, and finds the bottle, as promised, embedded in the bed's base. Desperately thirsty, she takes it out, opens the stopper and takes a couple of hearty gulps. At once, a clear, cool and sweet feeling spreads from the tip of her tongue through her whole body.

"What's happening? Did you find the letter?" Liu Hong's voice comes from outside, edged with irritation.

Startled, Lin Na screws the lid on in a panic, and thrusts the bottle back into its hiding place, whilst her mind whirs at a flying speed: what to do now? Tell Liu Hong everything sincerely, or, as the letter suggests, hide the water and keep it for herself?

Lin Na is filled with the desire to enjoy this pure sweetness all by herself, but what they have been through together over the past day puts her selfish thoughts to shame. She feels locked by this contradiction, yet knows she has no time to think it over.

Lin Na searches hard within her to find any reason she can to support her next move, and quickly, her mind starts to lean one way.

Liu Hong might pour the water out again, which will do no good whatsoever! I cannot let him do that. But... whatever. I'll take a look at the last chance for escape first. We may have to hold out here for longer, so I should keep the water under my own control. Yes, before the situation is clear, hiding the water is the right choice. I can tear off the upper part, and show Liu Hong the lower, so it won't raise his suspicions.

As these justifications race through Lin Na's head, she has already made her decision. She rearranges the mattress, and tears the upper part of the letter off, hiding it in her clothing. After these tasks are done, she opens the door and walks out into the hallway.

"What happened? What took so long?" Liu Hong asks with suspicion.

"Well... the pillow was hard to rip open..." Lin Na

makes a placatory excuse, and at the same time, hands Liu Hong the lower section of the note. "Here's the letter, read it."

Liu Hong does not think about it any further, and taking the letter from her, glances over it, turns and strides straight for the bathroom, with Lin Na following close behind.

Behind the porcelain block, Liu Hong finds the "package" the letter is referring to – several items casually wrapped in a sheet of newspaper. Opening up the newspaper, there appears to be a new letter, and a sharp, polished knife.

Liu Hong grabs everything and takes it to the living room, and under the light, begins to read the contents of the letter, which says:

You must have noticed the safe, which contains the key to the security door in the front room. If you can open the safe, then you can simply leave the apartment. As for the six-digit code that unlocks the safe, I have already given it to you – it is hidden within the letter Lin Na has just found in the pillow.

There were two parts to the letter, a perforated double sheet joined together by a hundred points. I have carefully detached some of those points so that, if you count from the left, the number of the first broken point is the first digit in the code; continue to count from this broken point, and you'll find the next number, and so forth. Follow this method and you should be able to find the code very easily.

The crux of the matter lies in whether or not Lin Na

has already torn the sheet in two. If so, you will be very disappointed, and I'll be even more so. Despite undergoing so many hardships together, you are still incapable of caring for, and trusting each other. So, in the end, there is only one path you may walk: pick up the knife and read the contents of the newspaper. Only one of you shall survive.

Lin Na, this last decision, did you make the right choice?

Liu Hong holds up the lower half of the perforated letter that Lin Na has just handed him, looks at it in dread, and then turns to Lin Na, glaring, with eyes full of worry, suspicion and doubt.

Lin Na, who has also read the letter, feels as if an iron hammer has just smashed viciously into her chest, lying there so heavily it is unbearable. Seeing Liu Hong's burning gaze, she backs away in a panic, tears of guilt and regret coming to her eyes.

"You tore the upper section?" Liu Hong roars in despair. "Why?"

"I don't know... I didn't know there was a code..." Lin Na takes the upper section of the letter paper out of her pocket, her hand trembling, her mind blank.

With a quick dart, Liu Hong snatches the page away, and reads the contents. He seems to understand it all. His blood-shot eyes bulging, rage pours from his every pore, seasoned with hurt and dashed hopes. After an interminable pause, he breaks out into a wave of hair-raising, bone-chilling laughter.

"Well, well, well..." He fixes his stare on Lin Na, repeating, "Well, well, well..." again and again, but unable to say anything else. Lin Na huddles into the corner, not daring to meet his gaze, just keeping her head down, both her hands winding painfully into her long hair, whimpering constantly.

After who knows how long, Lin Na recovers her ability to think a little. She stops crying and looks up. "We'll have another chance... let's have another think. At least we have water now, we can survive for a few days..."

Liu Hong ignores her, his attention focused on something in his hand – the newspaper in which the knife and the letter were wrapped.

"What is it?" Lin Na remembers the last sentence of the letter: read the contents of the newspaper. She cannot resist moving closer, wanting to take a look.

Reading her intent, Liu Hong, face still dark, hands Lin Na the sheet. This is a paper from a year ago; its headline and prominent location direct her to a story she is more than familiar with.

"Seven days ago, old Mr Liu and his grandson were found dead in a rented property in this city's Gonglin New Village complex. They were found by their fellow tenant, who called the police. According to informed parties, Mr Liu, who was over sixty years old, lived in the rented main bedroom of a two-bedroom flat with his grandson. His son had left the city a few years ago for work commitments. On the 26th of June, their co-tenant from the room across from theirs detected a strong odour from their room. Because they have not seen the grandfather and child for numerous days, they called the police. When the police broke into the room, they found that old Mr Liu and his grandson had both, unfortunately, passed away. The forensic

examination has more or less determined that the cause of Mr Liu's death was a cerebral haemorrhage; and an autopsy of the three-year-old's corpse has revealed that the cause of death was starvation and dehydration.

According to the inferences of the official findings, the elderly gentleman died first, and due to the lack of survival ability and being trapped in the room, the grandson subsequently also perished. The approximate time of death of the pair is nine days ago, on the 17th and 19th of July. According to the co-tenant's account, a week ago they heard multiple instances of the child crying from within the room, which concurs with the coroner's informed speculation..."

"He's kept the newspaper, what... what does this mean?" As the "co-tenant" mentioned in the article, the news clipping strikes at the most painful part of Lin Na's memories.

"He's teaching us what to do – the last method of survival, only one of us makes it out." Liu Hong's tone and demeanour assume a sinister air, making Lin Na tremble.

Lin Na looks at her counterpart timorously. "No... I don't understand..."

"One person has to die... after their corpse begins to rot, people outside will notice the stink... Then they'll call the police, just like you did a year ago," Liu Hong says as he slowly draws nearer, closing in on her, pronouncing every single syllable in a slow and deliberate manner.

Lin Na finally notices the gleaming knife grasped tightly in the other's right hand. Horrified, she backs away into her small room, and asks, shaking, "What... what are you doing?"

"This is your own making, all your fault!" With monstrosity in his bloodshot eyes, Liu Hong lifts the blade to chest height, making his intent abundantly clear.

Lin Na screams, taking cover in the small room. She tries hard to shut the door, but Liu Hong does not give her the opportunity. Just as the door is about to be pushed shut, he rams into it ferociously. Lin Na's strength and weight are no match for him and the door slams open, the movement sending her unprepared body crashing onto the floor inside the room.

Brandishing the knife, Liu Hong lunges towards Lin Na, and in her boundless terror, sheer flight or fight instincts have her raise her foot and strike out hard against Liu Hong's ankle.

The joint, still swollen and livid from Liu Hong's tantrum against the front door, suffers under Lin Na's well-placed blow. He bites back a guttural groan, and his injured leg gives way. He tumbles down next to Lin Na, the knife dropping out of his hand.

Lin Na scrambles over and takes up the knife, at almost the exact same time that Liu Hong's large hand grips her neck from behind. Lin Na's pulse rises to a frenzy. Gripping the short blade's handle tightly, she thrusts it back blindly, again and again, not caring where it hits. And then her hand is jolted as it meets resistance. Evidently, she has landed a hit somewhere, and Liu Hong's hands, which were tightly clamped round her neck, gradually loosen their hold.

Lin Na frantically untangles herself from Liu Hong's grasp and, when she turns around, she is shocked by the scene. The blade has found its way right into his neck, and clearly wounded, he is now collapsed, defenceless, on the floor.

"Oh, god…" Losing her mind, Lin Na bursts into tears. She wants to come closer but is too scared to, and so stays on the spot sobbing and shaking. "I didn't mean to… I didn't mean to…"

Liu Hong is again calm amidst the frenzy. He puts his hand over his neck, panting heavily for a while, and then, cocking his head towards Lin Na, wheezes, "I… I don't blame you. You killed me… you… get to live…"

Lin Na sobs, her face red and swollen. "No, don't you die!"

"I have to. It'll take… about a week before people out there will smell the rot…

you'll need to eat. The little fridge, do… do you understand what it's… it's for now?" Liu Hong struggles to keep his eyes open, wanting to pass all the information onto Lin Na.

Having utterly lost her ability to think, she shakes her head. "No… there isn't any food here."

A final macabre smile lifts a corner of Liu Hong's mouth, and with the last of his remaining energy, he says, "It's me… I said I'd treat you to a meal."

The meaning of Liu Hong's words is too horrific, Lin Na is frozen. Yet, an even more horrific scene is about to shake her from her daze.

Liu Hong clasps his right hand around the handle protruding from his neck, and exerting a burst of energy, pulls the whole thing from the wound. The blade has already severed the artery, and as the blade is removed, hot red gore spurts out, like a small fountain. Liu Hong's body goes into violent spasms and with every buck, the blood geyser produces a fresh eruption.

Lin Na finds herself screaming hysterically, shrinking back as if her life depends on it, though the outer mist of the blood spray still floats over her.

This blood fountain continues for about ten seconds before subsiding, and Liu Hong no longer spasms. Lin Na's nerves are falling apart. She crawls over to Liu Hong, nudging his body. Petrified, she cries, "Liu Hong! Liu Hong!"

Liu Hong can no longer answer her call. But as she shifts his body, his tightly clenched left hand abruptly relaxes its grip, and something clatters to the floor.

Lin Na turns her gaze to it and is stunned to find a second mobile phone. She does not think about where it has come from, or why she is only seeing it now, but dives to pick it up and call for help, only to be met with disappointment: the keys of this mobile have also been rendered dead.

But there is another way to call, she has learned, and Lin Na presses and holds the green pick-up button, and about five seconds later, she hears the beeping of a number being dialled. Lin Na is seized by joy, for a split second, before every wisp of this gladness is shattered by that song. The song that should be joyous but now sounds like fear.

"Ding ding dang, ding ding dang, ding dang rings the bell…"

Lin Na becomes vaguely aware of a sensation, and plunges her free hand into her pocket, pulling out the original phone, buzzing, ringing, the display screen flashing with HIS call ID.

With an extremely complex set of emotions, Lin Na presses the receive key, and the heavy male voice begins to speak again, undistorted.

"Lin Na, I said that last time was the final call I would make, which is not incorrect, because this time, you rang yourself. The fact you are hearing this now proves that I am already dead.

"To me, death is not frightening, I died a year ago. When a man loses his wife, loses his father, loses his son, what need does he have to live on in this cruel world?

"But I was not ready to give up yet, and I did not believe that this world was entirely as cruel as I had experienced. I had imagined that there was a thread of hope, for someone like me to continue to stay alive.

"So, I set up this game, with you and I as the playing pieces. In the game, we would receive our punishment, in the game we would also seek our final chance to redeem ourselves. I told you from the very beginning, this chance is dependent on the concern for us from people on the outside and the choices we make.

"Yet the chance for redemption I had imagined never appeared in the end. Nobody cares about us, and at the most crucial point, your choice turned all my thoughts to ashes. This world is already beyond salvation, so all we can do is accept our final punishment.

"I have sentenced myself to death, but as for you? I have no right to do this. Yet, you will undergo torments, and endure the following days in darkness, loneliness and fear. You have nothing to complain about, because all of this my son had already endured, before he died."

"No, I won't!" Lin Na feels her mind exploding, and she shrieks in a multitude of agonies, but who is there to listen?

"Perhaps I am more fortunate than you, because at last, I have left this world, this hateful, despicable world. But why has the world become like this?"

The voice on the phone stops, leaving Lin Na's heart floating in expectation.

And then she hears the last words: *"When you tore off the top part of that letter, you already knew why."*

NOTES

SURVIVAL IS PERHAPS the most basic of human instincts, and survival horror is a genre that is universally relatable. There are plenty of successful books, films, and even videogames which revolve around their heroes, for whatever reason, finding themselves trapped inside a hostile space, sealed away from the outside, with their simple freedom robbed from them.

This horror novella by China's master of crime and suspense, Zhou Haohui, certainly offers that sense of tension, claustrophobia and threat, along with a damning indictment of a society in which people no longer have basic concern for their fellows, and the structures that have allowed this.

Like much of China's contemporary horror, the starting point for this story was a real-world incident. The author recalls hearing a social news report that became a hot topic some years ago, regarding an old man and a child. Their relatives had gone to work in other cities, leaving the two of them behind. The grandfather died suddenly, leaving his three-year-old grandson in the flat. With no one to care for him, the child eventually died of starvation and thirst. The neighbours had heard him crying but did not see it as their place to go and check on them.

In his story, Zhou had evidently recreated this real-life

scenario, but by putting his characters in a mortal game of survival, places the reader in a position to relive both the child's fear, and the emotional turmoil of those whose own inaction had allowed the tragic death.

I had to take my time with this piece, because it hit closer to home than I was comfortable with.

As an infant, I was left in the apartment whilst my mother went to work, and my father was out of the country. It was only when the neighbours heard me wailing through the walls that they somehow got the door open, and eventually arrangements were made for them to care for me in my mother's absence. This story had been so normalised in my upbringing, as a funny thing that had led to me having a second Cantonese family, that I quite casually told my circle of friends about it, only to be met with expressions of shock and incredulity. If Granny Chen had shown the same streak of reticence, I almost certainly would not be here today writing this.

Each of these pieces has been chosen to show the breadth of the genre, but I appreciated this piece at once for its complexity and familiarity. As a fan of English golden age crime fiction, its seal-off living quarters and the remote voice of moral judgement reminded me of Agatha Christie's And Then There Were None. Of course, contemporary China has its own set of social issues. A new generation is now feeling the heavy pressures to chase money and consume, which is feeding into a corporate culture of long work hours. Unregulated practices mean that whilst fortunes can be made from quick investment schemes, the risk of losing everything has led to mass bankruptcy. The widening gap between living standards, rising divorce rates and the necessity of migration for employment has increasingly led to a neglected portion of the population, left to fester in closed-off urban slums, or isolated in xiaoqu at the edges of China's most affluent cities and towns. These changes are happening quicker than the monolithic state can adapt to. The unfeeling and obtuse response from the charity that Lin Na's mother appeals to in the story feels like just the sort of unhelpful officiousness some organisations resort to, either overwhelmed by inquiries, or in the exploitation of the powerless.

Zhou weaves a deep sadness of social tragedies with a tale of remorse and survival that drains the emotions slowly and painfully, gradually tightening its suffocating grip, grinding down endurance and will, before raising hopes, only to smash them again. As the characters grasp desperately at last chances, we see them edge towards a brutal ending. At times, this story was draining, and even painful to translate, but I kept going, motivated by the belief that every sentence mattered. Every action, turn of phrase and flicker of emotion mattered. No matter how small or repetitive the detail, every element brought the reader deeper into the apartment with the two characters, and into their suffering mindsets. So, you should take pride in making it through to the very end of the story, and I know you will reflect on the little freedoms you have, how you treat others, and the last time you let yourself have a glass of water.

TI'NAANG

昔素

Su Min

1

PUSHING THROUGH THE thick green fog, I find myself on a
familiar little street. The pavement is wet and grey, while
the tedious sound of hawking at the 2-Yuan shop twines
about the low lampposts. The jumble of disordered shop
signs along the street is turned wretched white by the
lamps that have just come on.

What am I doing here? Oh, yes, I am going home; this
is the road back from school. Dad said I have to go home
straight after school.

The unbroken silhouette of the Xishan Mountains
imprints on the western horizon, together with the flow
of the river in the east. They press upon this tiny street,
making it long, narrow, and seemingly endless. I walk for
a long time, but never reach home. The 2-Yuan shop; the
clothes shop; the jewellers; the little fortune-telling stand
next to the jewellers, and the drowsy old granny on the
stand; and then the curtain shop; then the opticians...
these street scenes keep on repeating and repeating, as
if there is only this street left in the whole world. Little
by little, daylight disappears, the breeze from the river
becomes chilling, the dense, distant woods of Xishan

sway in the shadows. Everything that was familiar now feels strange, everything that was tender feels sinister. To avoid looking at the frightening black shadows, I lower my head to count the tiles on the pavement, concentrating on crossing over four bricks per step.

"Qianqian!"

Someone is calling my nickname, my mum's voice. I lift my head, look around, and see a lot of people standing with their backs facing me. As one, they all turn their heads towards me. Their faces are a blur, without expression. None of them... are real.

I WOKE UP in terror and stared at the ceiling in a cold sweat.

"Same nightmare?" Beside me, Liang Jiu held out a hand and stroked my chilled face. I took deep, practised breaths, waiting for this familiar terror to calm.

"Do we have to go?" I asked.

"We're getting married, I should at least meet your parents."

"I haven't been back for eight years."

"Just as well, then, it's time to go back and visit."

"What if you go, and you find that my family is even more terrible than you imagined? Would you leave me?"

Liang Jiu smiled. "Is there anything worse than being apart from you?"

We had been together for two years, and his smile had consoled me countless times, but this time, I was full of doubts and misgivings. I didn't want to disappoint him, so I returned his smile, just as I had done every other time.

2

As SOON AS we reached Jiangshan train station, that long-forgotten humid air clung to my face, and the local speech flooded my ears. Not one snatch of Mandarin could be heard.

"Your local dialect sounds fantastic. I can't understand it at all, it's just like being in another country."

Liang Jiu was delighted by everything strange or novel, and the language was gentle and warm to his ears. For me, it possessed an invasive intimacy, bluntness and crudity, and was reminiscent of reckless quarrelling and shouting.

"Of course, it's a southern language, so it's perfectly normal for you northerners not to understand it."

In fact, the topolects here, and those in the surrounding five brother towns, were all completely different, and mutually incomprehensible. Even the dialects of the villages in the surrounding hills had some variations from peak to peak. It was said that during the Civil War, after Dai Li had become the head of Military Intelligence, he had recruited a bunch of spies from the same village into the organisation, using their dialect as the secret communication method. Hearing that Dai Li was from our place, Liang Jiu had become very excited, blurting out that he just had to visit Dai Li's former residence.

Due to the narrowness of the town, we had hardly taken a few steps out of the station before we were on the riverfront. The riverbank had been repaired and made very tidy, no longer full of potholes. The people were the same as always, taking an after-dinner stroll along it in twos and threes. They walked at leisure, enjoying the shade of the green trees and the serene winding paths in the distance; all made an image perfectly befitting of all the tranquillity and placidity a small town should offer. But I knew, deep in my heart, that things here were never as simple as they seemed on the surface.

Directly ahead were three people: a man and a woman, who seemed to be a married couple, and another man following behind them, his hands full of carrier bags, as if returning from the supermarket. If you looked carefully, you would find that the placid, servile man looked exactly like the husband. The couple bumped into an acquaintance, and greeted them warmly, with typical chit-chat, whilst the servant-like man stood aside, not engaging in the conversation. None of the others even acknowledged his presence.

"Are they twins?" Liang Jiu asked, curiously.

"No."

This was just how this little town had always been; it was still the same after all this time, and I was beginning to regret bringing Liang Jiu back here.

"If you meet someone here, and then see them again, don't rush to talk to them. Wait till I greet them before you do," I urged him.

The dark green house in the small old district ahead of us was my family home. As soon as we entered the district, we almost immediately ran into Auntie Li, from opposite. She, too, was followed by a woman that looked exactly like her, except for being laden with shopping. As soon as she saw me, Auntie Li started to exclaim in a pantomime fashion: *"Well, goodness, isn't this the Zhang girl? It's been so many years, you're home at last! You've not changed one little bit. I recognised you straight away!"*

Politely I greeted her: "Hello, Auntie Li, I hope you've been well." I deliberately spoke in Mandarin, in order for Liang Jiu to understand, but he was baffled, just staring at the two identical people for a while, before following my lead and greeting the Auntie Li standing in the foreground.

She twigged his northern accent and looked him up and down. "Found a boyfriend from outside? What a handsome lad!" And then, without turning, added in the local language, *"Does your father know? Would he agree to you dating an outsider?"*

I really disliked the local habit of switching to the topolect in front of outsiders – it was rude. I replied vaguely with platitudes, and at last, got free of her.

Confusion was scrawled across Liang Jiu's face. "Is the identical twin gene particularly prevalent here?"

"Those are *ti'naang*," I replied.

"And what's a *ti'naang*?" Liang Jiu did not understand, because the word came from the Jiangshan topolect.

Should I explain to him? As I hesitated, a familiar dark red wooden door appeared in front of me.

"We're home," I said.

3

I HAD LOST my house keys a long time ago, so now I rang at the door like a guest.

The doorbell rang twice, but nobody answered. I could hear the sound of stir-frying in the kitchen. I pressed the bell again and heard hurried little scurrying steps. The door opened to reveal Mother. She wiped her grease-stained hands on her apron and took the gifts from Liang Jiu's hands with a face full of smiles, asking after our health. Father sat upright, in the middle of the sofa facing the door, inert, holding a half-smoked cigarette.

I had told my parents I was coming back today with my boyfriend, but they had not come to meet us at the station, or even asked the ti'naang to. I guessed this was intentional, just like he intentionally occupied the sofa, smoking rather than getting the door for us.

I tried hard to bite down my anger, and said, "Father, Mother, this is Liang Jiu, he's a journalist, he works for the news."

Before I'd even finished, his coarse voice unceremoniously tore through the apparent domestic peace: "So you still remember your way back, do you? What did you come back for?"

As always, my father, his face twisted by arrogance and egotism, knew exactly how to rouse my fury. I remembered the scene before I'd left home eight years earlier, when I had just graduated from the town's university, and wanted to try to find work in the wider province. In that authoritarian tone, Father had demanded that I stay and work for my hometown. I insisted I did not want to, and he said every berating, hurtful thing he could think of, describing me as absolute, worthless trash, telling me I could not survive outside of Jiangshan.

Later, I left Jiangshan, with an almost premeditated escape plan. I had spent six months accumulating as much money as I could, and in the middle of the night, I hopped onto a long-distance coach, running all the way to the north, as far away from this small southern town as I could. I did not contact my family for several years, and it was not until Father stopped bellowing abuse down the line in every call that I told them where I was living, and told him, in fact, I was managing very well in B******, with a respectable job, a decent salary, and that I had also met Liang Jiu. Yes, I was an adult who could make my own way in society, and no longer had to be scared of him, as I had been as a child.

So, I harnessed the dignity and decency of a grown-up, and announced, "I've come back to tell you I'm getting married."

"Like fuck you are! To an outsider?" he barked in local speech, and whilst Liang Jiu did not understand, he was clearly intimidated by Father's aggressive tone.

Mother rushed forwards to conciliate, taking my hand to pacify me, saying, "You must be tired from your journey. Why don't you two go to your room and take a rest?"

She had aged so much, almost becoming a dry and shrivelled old woman, totally devoid of personality. Father was still glaring at me with rage, the aggression burning in his eyes not at all dimmed by her intervention. I will just say it. Father's arrogant and domineering behaviour was the product of Mother's years of weakness and incompetence.

I threw down the luggage and dragged Liang Jiu back to my room.

This was the room I had lived in from primary school to university. The heavy curtains were firmly drawn, without a crack, blocking out all light, so that the room was in near darkness. I threw myself onto the bed, remembering countless nights from when I was little, when I had heard Father's aimless, drunken footsteps, and had dashed to switch off the light and dive under the covers, pretending to be asleep. I was not afraid of being found up late, but of my door being slammed open, the overpowering stench of alcohol, and his roaring curses that I had distanced myself from. Mother could do nothing, unable to protect either me, or herself.

"It's terrible, isn't it?" I said to Liang Jiu, who was standing very still in front of my desk, looking contemplative.

"Hmmm. You know, I've heard you talk about your father, but I never thought he'd be so harsh from the first meeting. But it doesn't matter." He was still smiling the smile that soothed me. "It's just the two of us, now."

He walked towards the window and threw the curtains open. The sun shone in so fiercely, I had to shield my eyes against the first assault, before I could make out the dust motes dancing in the bright air. My wooden bookshelves were coloured a vibrant orange by the sunlight, the dusty objects on them becoming more distinct. This room, which had been mine for fifteen years, suddenly felt alien to me, perhaps because in all that time, I had never opened the curtains. It was a habit I had maintained for years, until I'd met Liang Jiu, the person who opened the veil for me. Involuntarily, my eyes moistened.

"Liang Jiu, I'm sorry," I said. "I never told you the truth about my hometown."

I decided to tell Liang Jiu everything, about the monstrosity of this little town, its xenophobia, and the infinite pain and sorrow its deep-seated evil had caused me.

4

THERE WERE A lot of people that looked alike in Jiangshan – some of these were real people, others were the ti'naang of real people. The ti'naang were usually made responsible for a household's domestic chores, physical work, the running of errands, and anything their originals did not want to do, even replacing their originals in the workplace. When I was little, I could not tell the difference between real people and ti'naang, and would talk to the wrong person. As I grew up, I learned to be more adept at distinguishing between them, by observing other people's attitudes towards them. These ti'naang frequently appeared with members of households, but were never treated as family. They were looked upon like objects. The ti'naang themselves never showed any expression. They seemed totally lacking in what could be called a personality or a soul. I have no idea how long they have existed, but they became quite commonly used about fifty years ago, during the Civil War era. The town's oldest surviving ti'naang was that of Dai Li, which had been kept in the exhibition hall at Dai Li Museum, in his former residence.

I took Liang Jiu to see it. In the centre of the hall, on the ground floor of the museum and guarded by red velvet ropes, the ti'naang seemed to transcend the decades, quietly sitting in a traditional laoyeyi rocking armchair. He sometimes held his cheek in his hand in a pose of deep thought, and at other times, picked up an old-style lidded teacup to take a sip. His long face and straight nose were the exact replica of the Dai Li's in his portrait, his shining eyes brimming with loyalty and benevolence. His tightly drawn thick lips gave away his cruelty, though, conveying a suitable sense of mystery and inscrutability for a spy. I told Liang Jiu that ordinary tourists would just assume that this was an actor playing Dai Li – only the locals knew that they were seeing Dai Li's ti'naang, from all those years back.

Liang Jiu took a photograph of it. "You're staying it still

looks this way after fifty years? It won't age, or die?"

"They're copied from the original person's appearance at the time, and after that, their looks won't alter. They do age, but not in the same way as humans do. It's more like how things wear out over time."

"So what are they constructed from? Silicone? Or biological flesh like humans?"

"I'm not sure of the specifics. In our language, ti'naang means 'body substitute', or 'shadow'. I guess they are related to the puppets made by the ancients to ward off disasters."

"That's amazing!" Liang Jiu had become extremely excited. "Were they created by sorcery?"

"Nope, manufactured from The Workshop."

"Manufactured? So, what makes them go? Electricity? How come they can eat and drink?"

"They need to eat, drink and excrete like humans; after all, they were made to be used as spies in the first place."

It is said that during the Civil War times, Juntong Ju, led by Dai Li, carried out assassinations in enemy camps, and then created ti'naang that precisely resembled the dead person, before putting them in their place. These obedient ti'naang were, without doubt, their best spies. They were already sending ti'naang of themselves to execute dangerous missions, while the originals remained safe, plotting and manipulating the controls from the shadows.

After the Civil War, the ti'naang met the same fate as other spies, and became a permanently hidden secret. But in Jiangshan, that secret was an open one. In post-war times, the locals carried on producing and using ti'naang, not only for use in later wars, but for the convenience of their daily lives. Jiangshan had not been a very rich village, but with its farmland, manufacturing, and with the ti'naang to do the work, they were able to live very comfortably. They grew complacent with their plentiful little lives, and wary of outside disturbance. So "keeping the secret from outsiders" became the unspoken bond understood and agreed by all the principals of Jiangshan, and with this, came an ingrained culture of xenophobia.

My father also has a ti'naang. He was originally a Workshop technician, and when he was young, he was passionate enough about his job to go into work himself every day. Roughly after I turned ten, he lost interest in it, and got into the habit of sending the ti'naang in instead, while he stayed at home all day.

With nothing better to do, he started going out drinking with friends, and when he got drunk, he would bully Mother and me. He became bossy and arrogant, dictating orders on every little matter in the household, expecting to be obeyed with a glance. Inch by inch, he turned into a violent control freak.

Liang Jiu patted my shoulder soothingly. "Is that the root of why your relationship with him is so awful?"

"No. The root of the problem isn't my father," I said, "but my mother."

"Your mother? What has she done? She looks to me like a tender and caring mother, but… well, you don't seem to be close to her, either."

"I've just… always had the feeling that Mother is a ti'naang."

5

DUE TO THE xenophobia here, my mother, who was an outsider who'd married in, was always the subject of local criticism. They were full of their own superiority, thinking that anyone who discovered the town's secret would be insanely covetous of their comfortable and plentiful lives, and thought this was my mother's goal, with marriage at any cost. She suffered jibes and taunts from the relatives, the most outrageous of which was the time when Grandmother said there was not enough space around the New Year dinner table and sent Mother to sit with the ti'naang. Mother begged, in floods of tears, for Father to help her get her dignity back, but he could not bring himself to do it.

I watched them break into fierce arguments, after which, with no one to confide in, Mother could only cry alone or hold me, saying that she had only stayed because she had been pregnant with me. I lived in anxiety every day of my childhood, afraid that she would leave. Every time they fought, the next day when I got home from school, the first thing I would do was sneak into my parents' bedroom, open the wardrobe, and count Mother's clothes to make sure they were all there, checking if she had surreptitiously packed luggage. And only after checking that her slim dresses and her stiff, sombre looking coats were all still hanging neatly in the wardrobe, would I finally relax and go down to dinner. But one day, when I was ten, Mother did leave. When I came home from school, all the clothes were still there in her wardrobe, but she was gone.

I ran out to find her, from dusk until late into the night. Jiangshan was only so big, and there were just a few streets, but I could not find her anywhere. It did not occur to ten-year-old me that Mother might have already left by train, so I obstinately went through every inch of Jiangshan searching for her, not even letting the woods of Xishan go unsearched. I tried to tell myself that she had turned into some sort of little sprite, and was hiding in the crack of some tile, or behind a leaf, waiting for me to find her. In the dark night, the rustling of the forests, the mountains, and the dark shadows added to my feelings of horror. I pushed apart the thick bushes and shrubs, and used all my strength to climb up the mountain, following the uneven, well-trodden dirt path till I rolled on a loose stone, and fell.

I was knocked out. In my stupor-dreams, I was still looking for Mother. I dreamt that I had walked from the southernmost point of this narrow and long town, all the way to the northernmost, and in the end found her on a bench on the riverbank. Her body had been blown blue by the river wind, and she seemed in a lot of distress. I shouted, "Mother" as I ran over, reaching to hold her, but her arms became see-through, and the rest of her body began to slowly disappear, not a wisp to be seen. I was left clutching thin air, feeling devastated.

I woke up crying and opened my eyes to find a woman sitting by my bed, with a bowl of soup in her hands, which she was blowing cool for me.

Father, who was standing to one side, demanded harshly, "Why did you run off like a headless chicken? Didn't I tell you to come home straight after school? Do you know how long we've been looking for you? You really don't save us any worries, do you?"

I looked up and asked him, "Where's my mum?"

"What a stupid thing to say – your mother's sitting right here, isn't she?"

That woman looked up and smiled at me. Yes, she looked a lot like my mother, and was wearing one of her dresses, but her smile seemed very strange, and very remote.

She wasn't Mother.

I leapt off the bed and darted for the door.

Father grabbed me by the arm. "What do you think

you're doing?"

"I'm going to find Mother!"

"Did that fall give you brain damage? This is your mother!"

The woman who resembled my mother so much sat there quietly, looking at me, her expression full of imposition, and only after the longest moment did she call out my name: "Qianqian…"

"You're not my mother!" I screamed hysterically.

Father lost his patience, and, swinging his thick palm, sent the right side of my face into a rush of fiery pain. So, in the end, he used violence to force me to admit my apparently childish mistake, and to force me to call that woman Mother.

The longer I spent time with that woman, the more evidence I found that she was not my mother. For example, she cooked me tomatoes, which I hated more than anything. When she brushed my hair, she no longer tied it in the bows that I loved. The washing powder she bought was not the brand I knew Mother liked. From then on, she stopped fighting with Father, she no longer cried or kicked up a fuss, and completely lost her personality. When anyone else looked at her, it was in the same way they looked at the ti'naang.

"Do ti'naang have their original's memories?" asked Liang Jiu. He had already learned to pronounce the word "ti'naang" very well.

"No."

"Then how do they know how to do things?"

"There are experts who put the knowledge in them."

"Won't they develop a consciousness? I mean, do they have a sense of self?"

"No one here thinks so. They insist the ti'naang have no self-awareness, But I'm sure that's just to feel justified in ordering them about with a free conscience."

When he forced me to call that woman Mother, the animosity between me and my father began to breed. He started to force me to accept his arrangements in a lot of other things, such as going to extra classes, not having pets at home, and in countless other ways, instilling his will over me. That was how life worked, and this was the way of the world. But rebellious thoughts grew inside me day by day. I always resisted Father in secret, looking to seize the chance to prove that everything he had force-fed me was wrong. I did not understand why he had to make me accept a ti'naang mother. Was it so difficult to admit that my real mother had already run away and left us?

"So as long as he admits it, then your relationship can be mended?" Liang Jiu asked.

"He'll never admit it."

"But what if he did? Go and talk to him."

"No way. I know him, an egomaniac like him, would never admit his mistakes."

"Qianqian, you're avoiding communication."

This sentence struck me.

"Go and talk to him," Liang Jiu suggested again. "It's been so many years, you're a grown-up, so go and use the grown-up method, and talk to him. Even if it's just to get him to accept me."

"Mm." I nodded, solemnly.

6

EVERY AFTERNOON AT four, my father would invariably go out for a stroll, and Liang Jiu and I would take the opportunity to go shopping. Coming home, we became a whirlwind in the kitchen, planning to use a banquet of tasty dishes as a softener for the conversation with Father. I washed and cut the vegetables, while Liang Jiu gutted the fish. He was very skilled and nimble with the knife, and before long, the fish was not only gutted but also perfectly descaled. I watched his busily darting pale hands, and felt warmth in my heart, as if we had been married for decades. When the delicious-smelling dishes were all placed on the table, Father returned.

Seeing the table full of cooked food, a glint of surprise flashed across his eyes, but he quickly pulled his face rigid again.

I called him and Mother over to the table, motioning them to sit, and attentively poured him his favourite mijiu rice wine. "Father, this steamed jiyu broth was made by Liang Jiu – come and taste it while it's hot."

He refused to engage, and in his egotistical manner, announced, "I just went to talk to your future brother-in-law. His danwei has a job going: it's an office role, suits you. You start on Monday."

Running my life yet again.

"Dad, I already said, I'm going to marry Liang Jiu, and we're going to live in B*****. We'll come back every year to see you and Mother, but—"

"I won't allow it. You can't marry an outsider. You must stay in Jiangshan." He turned towards Liang Jiu and shouted, "You. Leave. I won't give my daughter to you."

I really could not take any more of this. "Dad. I've had enough…"

Seeing that I was reaching my limit, Liang Jiu said on my behalf, "Bofu, actually, today Qianqian wanted to have a frank conversation with you. There's a lot about you that she doesn't understand and finds confusing, so perhaps it would be better for the two of you to chat alone."

"What's there to talk about?" Dad said, coldly.

"For example, did you really replace the real bomu[35] with a ti'naang?" Liang Jiu cut straight to the chase with this question.

"You told an outsider about the ti'naang!" Father glared at me viciously. "You will regret this, I promise you."

"Outsider? This outsider is worth a hundred of you! You pushed my real mother away, and then replaced her with a ti'naang, you think I don't know?"

"How could your mother be a ti'naang?" He dragged Mother over, roughly pinching and pulling the flabby skin on her face, showing me just what a real, living person she was. "Take a good look, would a ti'naang get so old and flabby? Would it get so many wrinkles?"

It was true that a ti'naang cannot grow old, but my observations and judgements of many years could not be wrong either. There must be a way to make Mother's ti'naang appear to age with the years.

"I've worked it out!" I shouted loudly, as if solving a crime. "There isn't just one ti'naang of her, but every few years you have it replaced! You're the micro-design technician at The Workshop, so you must be able to sculpt the effect of ageing on every ti'naang, correct?"

Mother broke down, tears falling over her wrinkled face. "Qianqian, can you stop asking questions... we're doing this for your own good..."

"Stop asking questions? I'm right, aren't I? You could!"

---

35 Bofu and bomu, 伯父 and 伯母,terms for referring to an uncle who is one's father's older brother, and his wife, and by extension, also used for the parents of one's fiancée.

"We are doing what's best for you!" said Father.

"Nonsense," I said. "If you don't want to admit it, I'll find the proof myself!"

I turned and ran out of the home, with Liang Jiu chasing after me.

"Qianqian! Don't do anything stupid! Where are you going?"

"To The Workshop."

7

"THE WORKSHOP", TO the locals, was not a generic term. It had always referred to that one workshop, the one that produced the ti'naang. As early as the Civil War era, Jiangshan already possessed a highly developed production line for the ti'naang, to the extent of demarking the types of work minutely. There were people who specifically worked on making the moulds, those who made proof samples, those who trained in writing instructions for the freshly minted ti'naang. In the old days, almost the entire Jiangshan population had worked in The Workshop. Nowadays, even though there were far fewer skilled workers, the craft was by no means extinct. If anything, the technology has become more advanced. During the Civil War, moulds could only be made of people who had already been assassinated. Now, moulds could be made from the living. The fine detailing and accuracy had also improved, as has the complexity of what may be installed into them. My father was one of the micro-sculpture technicians, responsible for replicating the finest details of the body, such as the wuguan (eyes, ears, mouth and nostrils) and of course, the wrinkles.

The Workshop was located at the foot of Xishan, and whilst it had never claimed to be "hidden", my aversion to the ti'naang since my childhood has meant that I had never been here before.

It was after work hours, so its big, rusted metal doors were shut up under heavy locks, looking imposing and forbidding. When I was little, though, my classmates would boast that, whilst playing hide and seek, they sometimes climbed in through the window at the side of the building.

We moved round to the side, and sure enough, there was a little window. The wooden frame was now old and rotten, and Liang Jiu, using a tree branch as a pry bar, opened it with a single wrench. We were just about able to squeeze ourselves in through the square shadow.

With our phone screens, we groped our way forwards through the gloom, walking in turn past the mould-making room, the sample room, the calibration room, the recall room. These long-aged machines looked clumsy and blunt, but they were extremely precise and elaborate. Liang Jiu took photographs of every machine, gasping with shock between each shot.

The recall room was where the out-of-circulation ti'naang were stored. According to the rules, retired ti'naang must not be casually thrown out or destroyed, but stored here for spares, repurposing, or to be brought out again when the time demanded. If Mother had multiple ti'naang, then her former versions should be here.

"Stop with the photos, Liang Jiu, we need to get into the recall room," I said.

The recall room was immense, with four or five rows of stock shelves, each row comprising four layers of steel racks, on which piles of ti'naang had been placed, like sacks of rice. Some showed severe damage, some were filthy, and some were carefully sealed in a single layer of clear plastic. I searched around a few times, but could not find Mother's ti'naang. Instead, I found another familiar face. Mine.

I hauled out the ti'naang that had my face from the middle of a pile, and found that there was not just one of me. There were versions of me at different heights and sizes. Some were fresh-faced and infantile, some adolescent and ungainly, others almost adult... They were all wearing the clothes I used to own. A total of twelve. They seemed to range from ten-year-old me, to twenty-two-year-old me. Each one of them must have been Father's own handiwork.

Heaven and earth seemed to spin in opposite directions, as everything in my world crumbled. He was replacing the ti'naang, year by year, to disguise it as a real person, but it was me. I was the one that had been swapped out.

"Liang Jiu..." I call out to him automatically. "I am, I am..."

Liang Jiu was still taking photographs with zest. "I never thought you would turn out to be a ti'naang. I've hit the jackpot of this assignment."

His tone was full of the detached joyfulness of a bystander watching a drama unfold, a world apart from the tender and caring lover from before. Was it because he had found out that I was synthetic, that he was altering his attitude towards me so much? That he was now treating me like any other ti'naang?

"Thank you for bringing me to see such an invaluable site – this material is enough for me to do a huge cover story."

He packed away his camera, turned around, and was about to walk out. I threw my arms around him instinctively. "Don't you want me anymore? Is it because you've seen how terrible I am, and you want to leave me..."

"Please don't misunderstand – I never really intended

on marrying you in the first place, I only approached you because you're from Jiangshan."

He shrugged my arms off, pushing me to the floor. My leg got scratched by a hook in the steel rack, and fresh blood gushed out, splattering onto the floor.

Liang Jiu tutted. "Wow, that blood flows pretty much just like real blood." He pulled his phone out, bent down and snapped my wounded leg as his last piece of trophy material.

I watched him walk away, cold and indifferent. If the blood coming out of me was fake, then why was the pain I felt so real? Was I not a ti'naang? Should a ti'naang not feel heartache?

From the darkness, I heard a muffled thump, at which Liang Jiu, who was just passing the doorway, crumpled to the floor. The figure above him was Father, holding that branch in his hands. By his side stood Mother, still terrified out of her wits. Viciously, he brought the makeshift club down on Liang Jiu's camera, smashing it to pieces. Mother found the mobile in his pocket and smashed it to pieces. Looking at the floor, littered with my other ti'naang, the corner of Father's mouth twisted in pain.

"You've found out, after all…" he coughed out, stifled by emotion. "Qianqian, I'm sorry, your father couldn't protect you…"

Mother covered her face, breaking down in tears. "It's all your mother's fault. If I wasn't fighting with your father all those years back, you wouldn't have…"

Lost, I stood there, listening to them recount with remorse what had happened twelve years earlier.

THAT DAY, BACK when I was ten, I had come home from school while my parents were in the middle of a rage-filled argument. Hearing Mother say, "…and if it weren't for Qianqian, I would have finished with you long ago!" I ran out of the house. After their fight, when they found that I had still not come home, they went out to search for me all night. In the end, at the foot of the Xishan Mountains, they found my corpse, where it had fallen. Filled with remorse, guilt and the wish to undo the tragedy, their extreme sorrow led to their making a ti'naang of me. But they wanted a real daughter, and a standard "body double" full of input commands would have no sense of self, so could never be that. The concept of self required, as its foundational materials, the memories of a real person who had experienced development. So, in the end, my mother gave up ten years of her memories of me, but the price was that she lost those memories, and had her personality wrecked.

For the new me to hate tomatoes, it was because Mum remembered that I hated eating tomatoes; for me to like bows, it was because she remembered I liked to wear bows in my hair; my memories of the countless times I checked her wardrobe came from the countless times she had looked at her own wardrobe in sorrow, when she had wanted to leave; and my memories of madly combing every inch of Jiangshan looking for her were, in fact, Mother's memories of frenziedly looking for me.

Mother had never abandoned me – her love had been deeply implanted into my memories, becoming the foundation stone on which I built my new sense of self. And Father, from then on, swapped over a body for me once a year while I was asleep, sculpting my maturing face with his own hands. Every step he took he had to tread with extreme caution, staying on tenterhooks all day, worrying that I might get injured, worrying that others — or I— might discover that I was a ti'naang. That was why he watched my every step day and night, and like a bigot, demanded that I stay within his sight; it was his way of protecting me.

"But... who am I? What am I?" I was sobbing, holding my head.

Technically, I was definitely not Qianqian anymore. The real Qianqian had died long ago. I was only her ti'naang, her doppelganger. However, I did have a sense of self, and had done all these years. I had studied, grown up and lived like a real person.

Father and Mother held my uncontrollably trembling shoulders.

"You're ours."

8

I STAYED AT home for a few days, to recover from my wounds, before setting off with Liang Jiu to B****** City.

Before we left, Father insisted on swapping me into a new ti'naang that better resembled a thirty-year-old body. For some reason, the hostility between Father and me had lessened, and with that even came a strange sense of fealty.

Because few people ever left Jiangshan, Liang Jiu and I were the only passengers on the coach. Liang Jiu sat behind me, wordlessly. Once we returned to B******, he would actively apply for a transfer from the News Department to the Records Department, where he would, little by little, remove every record of, and clue to, the ti'naang. When all the related material was deleted, he was planning to resign, leave the news agency, leave B******, and finally return to the Recall Room in The Workshop. I would monitor his performance of these tasks, before resigning from my job in B****** City, bidding my friends farewell, and returning to

Mother and Father's side.

Before setting off, I reaffirmed my promises to listen to them, to look after myself when I was outside, to call them every week, and told them I would miss them, just like a good daughter should.

NOTES

THE FEMALE GOTHIC has been one of my favourite genres of horror, from the eerie attic in Jane Eyre and the swinging spectre of Villette, to the labyrinthine narratives of the Mysteries of Udolpho, and the murky Victorian secrecy in The Woman in White. I found much of this in the voice of Ti'naang. The lone woman, trapped in a hostile environment, having to make her way out under the watchful gaze of family and secrets which are always seen to be far more important than the individual.

The story that you have just read, and the one that was originally published, are not exactly the same. When I first read the story, I loved its concept and tone, but its ending seemed strangely disconnected. Liang Jiu slipped away, without evidence of the strange doubles, but otherwise unscathed and scot-free, and Qianqian's reunion with her parents was a soft, heart-melting affair, where she forgave their controlling behaviour and harsh treatment. It felt unreal.

Discussing the story with Su Min, she told me that Ti'naang had been written for 2019's Sci-Fi Gala, an annual event held during Spring Festival, where writers from around the world are given a theme to create from, and their short fiction is then published during the festive period for SF enthusiasts to enjoy. Having a downbeat ending to a Spring Festival story would be like having Scrooge dragged to hell at the end of A Christmas Carol, and so the story ended with the secret safe, and the daughter happily reunited with her family, despite the years of abuse, deception and control. I had already decided on the story, despite the oddness of the 'happy ending', when the author suggested a change. This is obviously not something I would ever ask, as an editor or translator, having immense respect for the creators and always preferring to truly represent the thought processes of the authors, but it felt here as though there was more to be told. After some discussion between us, Su Min wrote fresh final paragraphs, providing what she says is closer to her initial intentions. So I do hope you enjoyed the darker ending, which, whilst bleaker, at least lets us see the strength in Qianqian, and Liang Jiu getting his just desserts. Her reconciliation with her parents is not just a sign of accepting the systemic abuse.

The village of Jiangshan, with its idyllic exteriors, beneath which dark secrets are masked, their concealment the work of the whole village, seemed like familiar terrain for a Western audience, reminiscent of the village-based horrors of Hammer studios, or more recently, the films of Jordan Peele.

This story is set in Su Min's hometown. There really is a place called Jiangshan, which actually was the hometown of the republican spymaster Dai Li, who did use a regional language as a form of encryption. In Southern China, where there are a mind-boggling multitude of differing regional languages, topolects, and dialects, Su Min had noticed the habit of people reverting to their local languages when in larger cities, to keep their conversations from others. This, along with her hometown's local history, and the insular nature of those communities, all fed into a chilling tale of xenophobia and identity horror. The opening sequence, the dream of losing her mother and becoming lost in a supposedly familiar place, came from Su Min's own childhood dreams, which she says still occur in her adult life.

The Ti'naang themselves are also interesting. As the society of Jiangshan changes, the Ti'naang are no longer doppelgangers used for espionage, but have become the Ayi (literally meaning 'auntie'), the equivalent of 'the help'. In modern China, these are usually live-in migrant domestic helpers who take care of any duties from housework to childcare. Like the Ayi, the Ti'naang are essential to the running of the household but treated almost as automata, background things not even to be addressed, though Qianqian is seen as a special case. With the increasing social division in China, this is becoming less alien, as migrant workers head to first-tier cities to seek their share of the new wealth and find themselves in the same social isolation. We are never told of the inner workings of the Ti'naang, nor whether they are fully sentient and living this life without consideration, or modified to function on an emotionless level, either of which brings another level of horror to the story. The Hanyu term ti nang 替囊, means "body double", but as regional language plays such a key part in the story, I have decided to use a Romanisation of the local pronunciation, to emphasise the sense of the strange and alien surrounding these beings.

HUANGCUN

荒村

Cai Jun

1

A FEW WEEKS ago, I took a short trip along the Zhejiang coast, and had a most bizarre experience. Curious readers have pursued me with questions. Where did I go? I will tell you now – it was a place called Huangcun.

It all began with my latest book, "Youling Kezhan". This horror novel is set in a place whose name means "The Haunted Tavern", which was located in Huangcun – a small village in the mountains of Zhejiang, situated between a cemetery and the sea. Because it faces a stretch of deserted coastline, its name means "The Desolate Village". Actually, I had never been to Huangcun, because it was entirely my own fabrication – invented in order to provide the novel with a unique environment. Were it not for that book signing, Huangcun could have stayed existing only in my imagination.

This signing session for "Youling Kezhan" took place at a subterranean bookshop, and for some unknown reason, they had arranged it to start after seven pm. That evening, sitting at a table near the entrance of the shop, I signed for two hours straight. It was quite an effective sales strategy. At nine o'clock, when the bookshop started to pack up, and the traffic in the adjacent metro station gradually began to thin, I was sitting alone behind the table, head lowered, packing my things and getting ready to go home.

Suddenly I heard a soft rustling, and immediately raised my head. I saw a young girl standing before me – she was in a large, ill-fitting jumper, the bottom edge of which hung all the way down to the knees. She carried a cheap fake leather backpack, and her long black hair was tied back in a ponytail. She looked like a university student.

She clutched a copy of my novel in both hands, and with her eyes lowered, she placed it on the table without saying a word. I was a little distracted; the winters in Shanghai had a bite to them, and the heating in the bookshop had broken down, so I had been shivering with cold. She was the last reader to have made it in, and, despite having the author all to herself, she did not look pleased in the slightest. Without a word, she slid it towards me as if I was the cashier. I paused, lifting my head to observe her. It was a face with delicate features and was very likeable, even capable of generating a little tenderness in the viewer. I flicked the book open to its title page, and, looking into her eyes, asked, "May I have your name, please?"

She looked startled for a second, before lowering her eyes again, and answering in a tiny, thin voice, "Xiaozhi."

"Xiaozhi?" Oddly, it seemed like a better name for a flute to my mind. "Xiaoas in 'small', and zhi as in 'branch', yes?"

She did not speak, but affirmed it all with a nod.

I wrinkled my brow and wrote on the title page: "For Xiaozhi, with pleasure", before adding my signature. I returned the book into her hands, adding, "Thank you for coming so late in the evening, just to buy my book."

At last, she looked up at me, her eyes wide, as if she wanted to say something – her lips moved but no sound came out. I raised my eyebrows and widened my eyes at her, encouraging her. Finally, she took a deep breath, and said, "I come from Huangcun."

At first, I didn't understand, but she continued to focus her trance-like gaze on me, until I coloured a little – Huangcun? The place from my own novel? I stared at this strange girl named Xiaozhi, standing in front of me – had she leaped out of my book?

Under my piercing gaze, she buried her head again, mumbling a few barely distinguishable syllables that sounded like, "I'm sorry." She clasped the book, paid at the till, and dashed out of the bookshop.

Huangcun? My mind felt as if it had been gripped by something. I ran out of the bookshop, catching up with her just before the metro's ticket gate. She jumped as I touched her, spun round, and said awkwardly, "Sorry, can I help you?"

Actually, I felt even more awkward than she did. I wrung my hands nervously. "May I– Can I take you for a cup of tea?"

She hesitated for an instant. "OK, I can give you ten minutes."

Three minutes later, I'd led her to a teahouse just outside the station. Sitting across from me, she was still surprisingly taciturn, sipping the tea with a lowered head. I checked my watch: there was not much left of the time she had agreed to give me. I cleared my throat. "Sorry, you said – you come from Huangcun?"

Xiaozhi lifted her eyes at last, and fixed them on me, slightly dipping her chin in a nod.

"Where is Huangcun?"

"Just past Xileng, K**** City, Zhejiang province. Like it says in your novel: 'Huangcun was situated between the sea and the cemetery'."

Gazing into her black, jade-like eyes, I could tell she was not lying. "You're saying Huangcun really exists?"

"Of course it does. Huangcun has existed for centuries. I was born there, grew up there – I'm Huangcunese." She avoided my gaze, saying feebly, "I guess you've never been to Xileng Town, let alone Huangcun."

I suddenly felt fraudulent. "You're right. I have only seen Xileng Town on the map, and as for Huangcun? It was entirely my own creation. I thought the name suited the atmosphere the novel required. I had no idea there was a real Huangcun, and certainly didn't expect someone from the village to turn up at my signing. Thank you for telling me all this."

"Actually, I happened to be passing by this evening, taking the metro back to school, but then saw the advert outside the bookshop. I read your book a few days ago, and it left a deep impression on me, so I decided to come in, buy another copy and ask you to sign it."

"Ah, so it was a coincidence – I very coincidentally wrote a Huangcun that actually exists into my novel, and as someone from Huangcun, you also coincidentally saw me at a metro bookshop."

Xiaozhi nodded slightly.

I continued to ask, "You said you were taking the metro back to school? Are you attending university in Shanghai?"

"Yes, my second year."

I remembered the time and checked my watch. "The time you gave me is up."

"Sorry, I have an exam tomorrow and need to get back."

She stood up and hastened away, with her head still bent

low. It was then that I made another important decision – I ran after her and stopped her at the door. "Xiaozhi, when you finish your exams, you'll have the winter break, right?"

"That's right. When the holidays come, I'll be going home."

"Back to Huangcun?"

Xiaozhi seemed nervous. "Of course."

"I'd like to visit Huangcun, too."

"What?" She was clearly not prepared for this and shook her head blankly. "Impossible... that is not possible... please don't joke like that."

"I wasn't joking, I've already made up my mind. I want to go and see the place that appeared in my novel. It must be fascinating – you said that Huangcun was just like it is in my book, between the sea and the cemetery. Since there have been all these coincidences, then I must have a certain destiny leading me to Huangcun. Xiaozhi, all you need to do is show me the way."

She looked right into my eyes, and then, frowning, took a step back. I felt a current of mild horror emanating from her body. Her breathing had become shallow. "No, I don't know..."

Realising how awkward I had made this, I smiled. "Of course, we are only chance acquaintances, like leaves that fall into the same stream. You can say no to me. How about this? Take my card, and if you change your mind and decide that you would be happy to take me to Huangcun, give me a call?"

I thrust the card into the hand of Xiaozhi, who seemed at a loss, and like a small wild beast escaping from a hunt, she tore herself away and dashed out of the tearoom. Slowly I followed at a distance to see her off, as she disappeared into the streets on that cold Shanghai night.

She came from Huangcun.

2

TWO WEEKS WENT past, and Xiaozhi had not gotten in touch. I thought that perhaps she had already returned to Huangcun, or perhaps Huangcun had never existed, and she was just playing a prank. I had nearly forgotten about this matter, and the girl named Xiaozhi.

But early one morning, the phone rang. I picked it up, still drowsy from sleep, and heard the tiny thin voice of a girl... after a few seconds of stupor, my eyes widened with realisation – was it her?

It was. That morning, Xiaozhi had called me out of the blue, still with the same tone and halting speech: she agreed to my request to take me to Huangcun and would meet me at the intercity coach station the next morning.

I arrived punctually at the coach station. It was the peak of the Chunyun rush, and I only found Xiaozhi after squeezing through crowds for what seemed like hours. I waved at her, but she looked surprised, and could barely bring herself to nod back.

Half an hour later, Xiaozhi and I boarded a long-distance coach which terminated at K**** City, Zhejiang. She sat in a window seat, wearing a very thick coat and a scarf that covered her chin and cheeks. The coach drove out of the city, giving way to fields of yellow-grey farmland on either side of the Shanghai-Hangzhou motorway. The landscape became monotonous, and this dull and heavy journey was going to continue for seven hours. I felt more and more awkward. From the moment we got on the coach, Xiaozhi had not said a single word, and acted as if she was all but oblivious to me. As if there was an invisible railing around her, imprisoning her there, with a ten-thousand-foot abyss beyond it.

When the coach entered the Zhejiang leg of its journey, I could not hold back from asking, "Why aren't you saying anything?"

Xiaozhi at least turned her head a little to the side. "What do you want me to say?"

"Anything. It doesn't matter. Are you scared of taking me to Huangcun? Are you feeling last-minute regrets?" I looked directly into her eyes, and said in a low voice, "If you are, just say the word, and I will get off at the next stop and go back to Shanghai."

She pulled her scarf down a little, and said distantly, "No, I'm not regretting it, I just don't know what to say."

"Well, tell me about Huangcun."

"It's just an ordinary little village, with the sea on one side, and the cemetery on the other."

"And apart from that?" I tried to look into Xiaozhi's eyes, but she always avoided my gaze. I could sense something of horror concealed within her eyes, which she was giving her all to stop me from seeing. And it became my mission to dig out precisely what this something was, like a mysterious archaeological expedition. "I think you said that Huangcun has existed for centuries?"

"According to my dad, the ancestors of the Huangcunese came from the central plains. After the Jingkang Incident[36] during the Song Dynasty, they fled to Zhejiang with Zhou Gou, the Emperor Gaozong. Because they were refugees

---

36 Jingkang Incident – a major political turning point in the 12th century, when the Jurchen nomads seized control of the Song Dynasty capital in the Battle of Kaifeng and with it, the northern territories. Capturing Emperor Qinzong, they declared the Jin Dynasty that ruled northern Song territories until the advent of Genghis Khan.

from the remote lands, they could only settle in a deserted section of the coast.

"That would make it over eight hundred years old."

Xiaozhi turned her head back. The winter sun showered its rays on her face through the window, as if coating it with a layer of silver. Set off against the monotonous backdrop, her face began to look slightly more animated...

At three in the afternoon, Xileng came into view. The town was surrounded by continuous undulating mountain ranges. Like a lot of small towns along the Zhejiang coast, it was bustling with small businesses everywhere. Xiaozhi did not seem to like Xileng, pulling up her scarf till it covered nearly half of her face. We went through the station, and climbed up on a dilapidated bus, which would take us on to Huangcun village.

The bus headed along a country road, on either side of which were winter fields and sparse woods, all emanating an air of austerity. We went along a stretch of inclining mountain road, and the landscape grew bleaker and bleaker. Except for bare rocks, there were only a few low shrubs now and then, shivering in the cold wind. I stared at the scene beyond the window – this seemed a world away from the prosperity of Xileng.

With great difficulty, the bus cleared the steep hill, and I exclaimed in a whisper, "The sea!"

I could see the sea in the distance – a black sea. I'd seen the sea many times before, but in this desolate place, it felt distinctly different. It was hard to describe in words. Under the murky low clouds of dusk, the distant horizon was a blur, like a gloomy oil painting.

"Xiaozhi, have you ever read Jamaica Inn? It's strange, we only crossed a mountain, but it feels like we've gone from Zhejiang in China to the desolate south-western coast of Britain."

"I read it in high school. That's why I like your novels."

Hearing this, I was secretly pleased, and a little smug.

After about ten more minutes of jostling and bumping, the horizon opened up, and a giant stone gate appeared – we had reached Huangcun.

I helped Xiaozhi take her luggage down from the bus, and stood looking up at the intimidating, triple-arched, memorial stone paifang before me. It was over ten metres tall and covered with myriad complex stone carvings. In the centre were four large characters carved in kaiti calligraphy – 贞烈阴阳. Chastity Preserved Through Yin and Yang.

I did not know what was meant by these words, but seeing them on this huge stone arch sent a shudder down my back. It was getting dark, and the shadow that paifang cast over me filled me with deep and fearful awe.

Xiaozhi poked me. "What's the matter?"

"How strange, to see such a large stone memorial in such an inconsequential village!"

"This is a chastity paifang granted by the emperor. A few centuries ago, during the reign of Emperor Jiajing of the Ming Dynasty, a scholar from Huangcun became the jinshi Imperial Scholar and won high office at the imperial court. The emperor wanted to honour his mother, so he bestowed this memorial arch on the village." A cold wind blew in from the sea, and she brought her scarf up again over her mouth.

I considered the directions around the arches. To the east was a great outcrop of rocks and cliffs, beyond which the rolling waves of the black sea could be seen, thick with dark clouds looming on the horizon. On the other side was a chain of wild and overgrown mountain peaks. Beyond the chastity paifang was the Huangcun I'd sought in my dreams.

Through the tall arches, I could see ancient, tiled houses and new European-style buildings scattered through the plum and bamboo trees, the dark, cold light of the sea and sky reflecting off the tiles, tainting the whole village with its chill. I let out a soft sigh. "Now I understand why it's called 'Desolate Village'."

Xiaozhi led me down a narrow alleyway, lined with old houses on both sides. Despite being so crowded, I do not think I saw a single person. She walked with her head dropped, as if she had brought an unwelcome guest to the village. I began to feel anxious, asking softly, "Is there a hotel in Huangcun?"

She pulled at her scarf. "What do you think? Huangcun has been closed ever since ancient times. No one from the outside has visited for years."

I was shocked. "Then where am I going to stay?"

"Here," Xiaozhi said quietly, pointing to a large set of doors to one side.

This was an ancient mansion, with towering high walls all around it, and a pair of faded, mottled wooden doors tightly shut in front of it. There were large brass rings on each panel, and, borrowing the last dim rays of dusk, I could see three large characters on the tall and broad lintel: "進士第", Imperial Scholar's Residence.

Before I could react, Xiaozhi had already pushed open the peeling black doors. The threshold alone was almost a foot high, but she took a big step right across it. Turning to me, she beckoned. "Come on in."

Confronted with this great and imposing "Jin Shi Di", I stood shivering. "What is this place?"

"My home."

I stood, stunned for a moment, before carefully stepping across the threshold, asking in a reverent voice, "The jinshi was your ancestor? So the paifang at the gates of the village was granted by the emperor to your family?"

"Uh-huh," she answered disinterestedly.

I rubbed my eyes and looked up at the balcony of this "Imperial Scholar's Residence", and the unstable-looking side rooms. Facing the entrance was a hall with a Xieshan-style hipped roof. Against the tenebrous light of dusk that fell through the tall eaves, this ancient mansion looked even more spectral.

Xiaozhi did not go into the main hall, but headed through a small door to the side. I followed her closely, and we entered a second courtyard of the old house. This had an even smaller walkway and was surrounded by a two-storey xiaolou to the eastern, western and northern sides. All three wooden buildings were Xieshan-style, with carved windows, pillars and roof beams, reminding me of Feng Yansi's "Tingyuan shenshen shen jixu[37]", "how deep is the courtyard, it's impossible to know". I began to imagine the lonely sorrow of a young lady in ancient times, newly wedded and doomed to wander these vast inner yards day in, day out.

Without warning, a deep, thick voice sounded from behind me: "Who are you?"

The sound nearly frightened me to death, and, turning around unsteadily, I saw the outlines of a tall thin figure, silhouetted against an open wooden window.

Xiaozhi hastened to explain, "Dad, this is a teacher from our university. He's come to study the history and folk

---

37 蝶恋花:庭院深深深几许 – a famous ci poem by Feng Yansi, Southern Tang courtier and poet during the Five Dynasties period, composed to the Cipai tune pattern of the famous melody Die Lianhua, "Butterflies Love Blossoms".

customs of Huangcun."

So this was Xiaozhi's father. I exhaled. She was good at making things up, saying I was her university teacher, despite my being only a few years older than her.

"Welcome to Huangcun."

When Xiaozhi's father stepped out through another set of doors, I could finally see his face. He was a middle-aged man, with an emaciated, gaunt face, and deeply sunken eyes. But his complexion was nearly white, not how one would imagine the average rural villager's skin. He must have been very handsome in his youth. He came towards me with a smile. "Hello. I'm a teacher here in Huangcun, just primary school. Please, call me Mr Ouyang. If you don't mind, please feel free to stay at our home for a few nights. My daughter and I are the only inhabitants in this old house, and there are many empty rooms."

I turned and cast a glance at Xiaozhi, who I now knew was fully named Ouyang Xiaozhi.

The cold winter night gradually enshrouded Huangcun. Mr Ouyang led us to the front hall, and switched on lights which hung from the beams, illuminating the horizontal bian'e board, on which three characters were inscribed in Xingshu calligraphy: 仁愛堂, "The Hall of Benevolence and Love." Below the bian'e hung an ancient portrait on a scroll. Its subject wore a Ming Dynasty official's uniform, presumably the family's imperial scholar from the reign of Jiajing.

The hall stood empty, save for a circular wooden table at its centre, on which lay a sumptuous dinner. A paternal smile rose on Mr Ouyang's face, who said he'd known Xiaozhi was coming back today and so had especially prepared a table full of good dishes. As Huangcun was on the coast, it was, naturally, mostly seafood, which happened to suit my tastes. Mr Ouyang was not talkative and sat quietly, picking up neat mouthfuls of rice with his chopsticks. I saw that he had a small appetite, and hardly ate anything. Under the murky yellow light, his face looked completely bloodless. He was indeed the very model of the poor and dedicated village schoolteacher.

After dinner, Xiaozhi led me to the upper floor of the most northern, farthest back building. I followed with trepidation. We climbed steep wooden staircases and felt our way into a room on the first floor. Xiaozhi fumbled protractedly for the light switch, and when she flicked it, nothing happened. She stated, apologetically, "This room hasn't been used for a very long time, so the wiring has probably deteriorated. Wait here a moment."

Xiaozhi went back downstairs. I waved my hands around me, and felt a row of carved wooden windows, which were actually unglazed, with only a layer of window paper stuck to the frames. I stood alone in the dark. Through the paper of the window facing the courtyard, I could see a few stars peeking out where the covering was ragged in one corner. My heart began to beat more and more quickly, as I was seized by a compulsion to open the window. I reached towards it.

The window swung open, and beyond it, I saw a flicker of light in the darkness, bobbing and blinking like a will o' the wisp.

"It's okay! It's just me."

It was Xiaozhi's voice. She came in from the corridor along with the mysterious light, a kerosene lamp. I exhaled lengthily. "Don't scare me, please."

She chuckled. "Haven't you published dozens of horror novels? Why would you be scared?"

"Fear comes from the unknown." My eyes gradually

adjusted to the light of the lamp, its flickering red flames casting their strange glow over Xiaozhi's face. She was holding a thick roll of bedding, and placed the lamp on the wooden table, so I could see the room clearly. It was quite a large room, with a set of pingfeng screens in the middle, and a traditional shuita couch-bed behind that.

The weird thing was, the room was bereft of dust. It looked clean and tidy, rather than somewhere that had been uninhabited for a long time. Xiaozhi said, "My father likes cleanliness, so he regularly dusts these dozen or so empty rooms."

"Over a dozen empty rooms? Imperial Scholar's Residence indeed. But I need to ask, with only the two of you living in such a huge mansion, don't you feel scared?"

Xiaozhi quietly closed the wooden window. "We just don't have any other relatives left."

"Why did you say I was your university teacher?"

She knotted her brows and handed me the bedding. "You saw the chastity paifang at the village gates. The culture of Huangcun has been very conservative ever since those ancient times. If I told the truth, it would cause gossip. That's why I could only say that you are my teacher, who's come here to research history and folk customs. That way, my father would not misconstrue the relationship between us."

"Mm, then I'll be your teacher for a few days. But I'm not much older than you. Be careful of showing your toes through your shoes."

"Fine. My room is up on the west side. If you need anything, just call out, I'll hear you."

"Xiaozhi?" I looked into her eyes, procrastinating with my words. "It's nothing, I am just very grateful to you."

"I want to thank you, too, for carrying my luggage all

the way back for me."

I could not help but burst into laughter. "Your cases were so heavy! It nearly exhausted me. But you didn't agree to bring me to Huangcun just to get free porter service, did you?"

And then my eyes fell on the pingfeng screens that were lit by the obscure lamp light. I could just about make out some exquisite images. I hastened to bring the lamp closer.

It was a set of four vermilion screens, about two metres tall and four metres wide. The frame was made of wood in red lacquer which, although faded with time, still looked breath-taking under the lamplight. Each of the four individual screens of the pingfeng were painted with colourful images that looked as though they were composed before the mid-Qing era.

"Heavens, this is an antique!" I could not help but cry out.

I would have never expected such a fine piece to be in such a ramshackle place, and a stranger like me to be allowed to stay in the room where it was kept. How many treasures were hidden in this Jinshi Residence? Xiaozhi did not answer my question, though there was a strange expression in her eyes. I did not mind, my attention being fully taken up with the paintings on the pingfeng screens. The style resembled the illustrations in Qing editions of thread-bound books. Due to its age, the colours looked a little dull and washed out, but what astonished me most was the content of the paintings.

On the first screen from the left was a man and a woman; the beautiful woman was leaning against the door of a thatched cottage, whilst the man was carrying a travelling bag, as though about to go on a long journey. The two were gazing at each other with longing. The painting seemed to depict the parting of a husband and wife, or a pair of lovers, and faintly conjured up the sentiments in "the autumn maple leaves are crimson like drunken faces, so many of them in the woods, dyed scarlet by the tears from parting faces."[38]

The same woman was on the second screen, in tears of sorrow, and in front of her stood an odd-looking monk. The monk was holding a flute, handing it to the woman. I shook my head, unable to figure out the meaning of this painting.

The third screen featured an indoor scene, where the same woman sat alone on a bamboo mat, holding the flute to her lips, as if she were going to play. Suspended from the roof beam above her was a length of white damask – was she going to hang herself? The whole painting had an atmosphere of misery and death that made me shudder.

The fourth screen, still an indoor scene, showed a man in the middle of the room. Next to him was a large redwood coffin! What was more frightening was that the lid of the coffin was open. The man was also holding up a flute, his face inexplicably eerie. The hand I was holding the lamp up with began to tremble a little, and the light flickered, sending strange inky shadows swaying about on the screen, as if the man were ready to walk out of the painting. My hairs stood on end and my bones felt chilled, so I nearly dropped the lamp.

It took effort to speak again, but I managed. "Xiaozhi, this pingfeng is extraordinary, what do these four paintings mean?"

She frowned and paused for a long time, before saying serenely, "The paintings on these screens tell the story of

---

38 晓来谁染霜林醉? 总是离人泪, from Romance of the Western Chamber, a Yuan Dynasty zaju opera by Wang Shipu.

Yanzhi."

"Who is Yanzhi?"

The flickering lamplight cast a red glow over Xiaozhi's face. Softly, she began, "During the reign of Jiajing in the Ming Dynasty, there was a young couple in Huangcun. The wife's name was Yanzhi. Husband and wife lived a quiet and content life tending their farm, their only regret not having had any children. The peaceful days were soon disrupted by war, and the Zhejiang coast was often bedevilled with pirates from Japan. I think you know this period of history, don't you?"

"Of course, the Jiajing period was when those disturbances were at their worst, and Zhejiang was a major focus for pirate attacks."

"That year, officials came to Huangcun to recruit soldiers, and conscripted Yanzhi's husband into the army to fight the marauders. The couple were very much in love, but, facing the war, there was nothing they could do. Before he set off, Yanzhi's husband promised her that in three years' time during the Chongyang Festival, he would come home to her. If they did not meet face to face, then they would unite on that night, in death. In the days after he was gone, Yanzhi's heart never wavered. She endured the loneliness of the small mountain village, living alone, waiting patiently for his return. Time passed, and three years went by. Chongyang Festival was approaching, but there was still no news from Yanzhi's husband. Yanzhi waited by the village gate every day, but did not see her husband. On the day of Chongyang she ran into a mendicant monk. The monk could see straight away that something was bothering her, so he gifted her with a flute."

"A flute?" As she told this story, I could feel her eyes, half hidden in the darkness, shining with a strange light.

"Yes, the monk gave Yanzhi a flute, and bade her play it on that very night, to bring her husband home. That night, Yanzhi waited at home, having already prepared a metre of white damask, in case he did not return. She would hang herself from the roof beam and keep her promise to find him in the underworld. At midnight, there was still no sign of him, so she began to play the flute, just as the monk had told her to. She instilled in the melody all the longing and pain she had felt over the three years. On the night of Chongyang, this mournful and plaintive music drifted all night, spreading far and wide over the fields and mountains around Huangcun, and across the shore. When she had finished playing, Yanzhi had begun to tie the cloth around the roof beam, when she heard heavy knocking."

My heart felt like it had been seized. I gasped, "Yanzhi's husband came back?"

"Yes, under the pure and cold moonlight, Yanzhi saw that the man she had pined for day and night was indeed standing outside the door. He was still dusty from the journey and had not even taken off his armour or his helmet. Overjoyed, Yanzhi led him into their home, helping him out of his armour, bringing him cups of warmed tea. She was going to put all the tenderness she had accumulated over three years into the xichen[39] to welcome him home. Maybe it was due to the long journey, but his complexion was pallid, and his body was weak. He didn't even speak to her. Yanzhi could only gently lead him to bed and tenderly caress him to sleep. Over the next few days, the husband stayed indoors, as if afraid to go out. Perhaps he had deserted from the frontline. Yanzhi could not help

---

39 Xichen, 洗尘, literally "washing off the dust", a traditional Chinese social custom to present those that have taken a long journey home, or visitors from faraway lands, with a sumptuous meal to welcome them.

but see that something was strange with her husband, but nevertheless, they spent a few happy nights together."

"So, big reunion?" I found myself suddenly disappointed with this happy ending.

"No – one night, a few days after the husband's return, Yanzhi played the flute again. Maybe she played it for him, but as soon as he heard the music, he ran out of the door. Yanzhi ran after him, but could only see the pitch blackness of the desolate fields. Everything became enveloped in mist, including the withered woods into which her husband seemed to have disappeared. Yanzhi was full of remorse and searched outside the village for three days and three nights, without finding even a trace of her husband. He was like an illusion that had been devoured by the darkness and the sounds of the flute. More days passed, and several villagers who'd been conscripted at the same time as her husband came back. They told her that he had been killed in battle on the night of Chongyang. Yanzhi couldn't believe it, but so many people had seen him die, with their own eyes. Those who knew him well said that, on that night, on a battlefield thousands of miles away, her husband knew he would be unable to keep his promise to return home to his wife. So, in the heat of battle, he deliberately rushed to the front of his troops, and was killed by a volley of enemy arrows. He supposedly died a martyr's death in battle, but his friends knew he'd died for love, keeping his pact to his wife in death."

"So, on the night of Chongyang, who was the man that came home?"

"His ghost." Xiaozhi spoke these two words slowly. "It was the ghost of Yanzhi's husband, returning, as they agreed, on Chongyang Festival."

"I think I see. Yanzhi's husband died in battle on the

night of Chongyang, so that his hunpo could fly over the mountains and rivers, be borne on the wind, to be by the side of his beloved wife. When Yanzhi played the flute that the monk had given her, the mysterious sounds floated into the nocturnal sky, to guide the husband's lonely spirit home."

I was trembling in the frosty winter gloom as I spoke these words, but it dawned on me that the story was, at once, both romantic and horrifying in the extreme.

"What's wrong?" Xiaozhi inquired softly beside me.

I realised I had been lost in my own musings. "Excuse me, the story got to me a little. What happened to Yanzhi after that?"

Xiaozhi was just about to speak, when a most sinister sound came from outside – the sound of a flute! The ghostly music sliced through the dark nocturnal sky of Huangcun like a sharpened blade.

She paled, clasping her mouth with her hand, and flew to the window, but there was nothing to see in that obscuring darkness. The sound of the flute had scared me out of my skin and left my bones raw. I had learned the flute when I was little, and could still play a few tunes, but I had never heard such a dreadful melody.

Xiaozhi instinctively drew near me, and the action caused me to put my hands around her shoulders and squeeze. The flute music seemed to come from the mountains outside Huangcun, though we could not gauge the direction, and did not know how to react.

Xiaozhi lowered her voice. "No, I can't say anything more about it. You should get an early night."

I wanted to say something else, but seeing the fear on Xiaozhi's face, I could say nothing. Xiaozhi ran out of the room, and the ageing floorboards creaked. The sound, together with the flute, made my heart pound and my flesh creep.

After a few minutes, the flute playing suddenly ceased, and the ancient house recovered its all-encompassing silence. Now I was alone in this xiaolou, with a set of antique screens depicting a strange story – would its painted subjects step out of it in the middle of the night? I was no stranger to this kind of eerie tale.

I spread the quilts out on the shuìtà bed-couch and crawled inside swiftly. This was my first night in Huangcun, and both my body and my spirits were so drained, I fell asleep almost immediately.

During the latter half of the night, I woke to find myself shivering, sweat dripping from my forehead. A strange foreboding filled my mind, and my heart beat so fiercely I nearly suffocated. What was happening? I crawled up from the wooden bed-couch. The room was in complete darkness and deathly silence.

I pulled on some more clothes and stepped out of the room cautiously. Outside, there was a walkway with wooden railings. In the gloomy obscurity, I could barely make out the outline of this mansion – it was like an ancient grave.

My nostrils picked up an unusual odour. I turned my trembling head, shifting my vision to the room next door.

The glow of candlelight showed through the window!

My god, I nearly screamed. That was supposed to be an empty and closed-up room, so why would there be candlelight in the middle of the night? I finally got a grip on myself, and, wetting my finger with saliva, I quietly poked a small hole through the window paper.

I eased my face up to the window and glued my eye to the fresh peephole. The hole was just the right size, and

I could take in the whole room – a Ming or Qing style dressing table, and a lit candle, whose meagre, flickering light illuminated the back of a figure seated at the dressing table.

They were dressed in white and sat with their back directly towards me. Even though there was a mirror on the dressing table, it was blocked by their head so I could not see their face. From the outline of their body, though, I guessed she was a young woman.

She was holding a brown wooden comb, and slowly combing her hair. Her hair was long, sable and shining in the candlelight. She was sitting slightly to the side, her right hand holding the comb, and her left stroking her hair, which fell like a black waterfall down one side of her body. She sat at the dressing table, totally absorbed in the act of combing and combing.

On this bleak wintry night, in a dilapidated "Imperial Scholar's Residence", gazing through a peephole in a paper window, this scene made me feel as if I had travelled back in time.

I was so frightened that I worried I might let out a scream. I quietly took a step back, but realised my legs were buckling. I stumbled back to my room, and wiped the sweat from my forehead, but still dared not make a sound – because that woman was only a wall away from me.

I did not dare go back to sleep, so I just lay quietly, curled into a ball on the shuita. Though my eyes were tightly shut, the scene I had just witnessed kept playing across the screen of my mind.

Who was she?

3

EARLY THE NEXT morning, Xiaozhi was already in the front hall of the house, waiting to breakfast with me.

I said quietly, "Huangcun really is one of its kind. It fuels your curiosity, but also your dread."

"That's what I like about your novels."

"Xiaozhi, what exactly was the flute music last night? Why were you so frightened? Were you actually scared it might summon lonely spirits and wild ghosts?"

I was still too scared to tell Xiaozhi about the woman I had seen in the small hours, combing her hair.

"Shhh, keep it down!" Xiaozhi looked as though she wanted to block my mouth as she stared up at the portrait hanging in the middle of the main hall. The man in the Ming uniform gazed down at us harshly.

"Are you worried about him overhearing our conversation?"

Xiaozhi neither agreed nor denied it – she seemed greatly intimidated by the person in the portrait. "Of course, I don't believe in the ghosts and legends, but this is Huangcun, and it's not like other places."

"So there are ghosts and spirits in Huangcun?"

"That's not what I meant, but Huangcun has its own customs that you don't need to concern yourself with. Just hurry up and eat your breakfast."

I wanted to take a walk in the village, but she was desperate to stop me from doing so. She led me out of the village through a small path, and no one saw us. For the whole day, we strolled in the nearby mountains without a soul or house in sight.

After dinner, I heard Xiaozhi speaking with her father. They did not sound happy. When Mr. Ouyang came out of Xiaozhi's room, the way he walked resembled a jiāngshī in the night.

Quietly, I climbed the stairs of Xiaozhi's building, and pushed open her door.

"Excuse me, I heard a disturbance just then…" I felt a little awkward for a moment. Her room was very clean, with painted walls, a TV and computer – only the carved windows reminded one that this was an ancient mansion. "Has something happened? Does your dad think I'm disturbing your peaceful life?"

"No, it's not that." Xiaozhi seemed a little nervous, and automatically retreated to her desk. I noticed a framed picture on it. A monochrome photograph of Xiaozhi; she looked enchanting in it, only her eyes belied a hint of sorrow. However, there was some undefinable aura hanging about the photograph, and I could not help but ask, "Xiaozhi, when did you have this photo taken?"

She did not reply immediately, but after a long pause, stated distantly, "The person in that photograph has been dead for a long time."

"What? Are you trying to scare me?" I felt a little twitch in the middle of my palms.

"That's a photo of my mother."

There was a silence which hung in the room for a long time. I had never seen such a likeness between a mother and daughter.

"My mother passed away when I was very young. She died of an illness in that very building you're staying in, and Dad brought me up by himself. The only idea I have of what my mother looked like is from that picture," Xiaozhi said gently, but the melancholy in her eyes was exactly like that of the person in the photograph.

"I'm sorry." I looked at her with a twinge of guilt. Taking a deep breath, I said, "Your father must love you very much."

Xiaozhi did not reply, and the atmosphere in the room grew tenser still, so I hurried to leave.

I returned to my room, but dared not sleep. I kept the kerosene lamp lit, curled up on the bed-couch still fully dressed, and in the company of that lonely flame, I passed the time hazily until midnight.

The sound of the flute drifted into my ears. I leaped up, as if stabbed by a needle, and shook my head violently, hoping the music was just an illusion.

The flute played on, and, unable to resist my impulse, I tiptoed out of this "Imperial Scholar's Residence", my path illuminated by the kerosene lamp.

Midnight out in Huangcun was oppressively quiet, except for the unearthly flute-playing drifting down from the hillside. I walked out of the village gates, stood beneath the chastity paifang arches and gazed out over the surroundings. The continuous mountain range was like an imposing fortress in the night. I spotted the highest peak, and ran towards it, still carrying the lamp. Sure enough, the eerie flute music grew more and more distinct. I had found the right direction.

The moon shone bright, though its cold fingers barely pierced through the dark clouds to shine out over the expansive fields and mountains.

As I ran, I suddenly felt that the sound of the flute was now coming from behind me. I spun round and saw a mountain cave. Edged in faint moonlight, a black silhouette was standing at its mouth. The mournful music abruptly stopped.

Brandishing my oil lamp, I ran towards the figure. They did not move, standing there, rooted to the spot like a tree. I lifted the light so it fell on the figure's face. The lurid lamplight revealed a drawn and gaunt face.

"Mr Ouyang?" I cried out in astonishment. This shadowy

creature was none other than Xiaozhi's father! The bamboo flute was in his hand.

Mr Ouyang shielded his eyes, mumbling, "What're you doing up here?"

"What – what is going on?" In the deep of the night, on this lonely mountain peak, the moon and the lamp cast their dull light over Mr Ouyang's eyes, adding to his dismal air. I felt lost in the mystery of it all. "Were you playing the flute just then?"

"Yes. Village teachers get overworked, and I've not been in good health. For the last few nights, insomnia has kept me up." Mr Ouyang sighed, and his expression gradually recovered its equanimity. "I come to the mountains to play for a while, to soothe my nerves."

"I understand that, but your flute playing seems a little unusual."

"Because the flute itself is very unusual."

Mr Ouyang placed the flute into my free hand, and instantly, my fingertips felt a chill, and my hand began to tremor for no reason. With the light from the kerosene lamp, I took a good look at this flute – it was a traditional di, made of bamboo, about forty centimetres long. Its lacquered body had deepened to a brownish yellow. The finger holes were marked by plum-colour thread wound between them, and over the embouchure hole, stretched a membrane as delicate as a cicada's wing.

"You might not believe it, but this flute has centuries of history."

'How many centuries?"

"Xiaozhi already told you the legend of Yanzhi, didn't she?"

I nodded, guessing this was probably the source of the contention between Xiaozhi and her father.

"In Yanzhi's legend, a flute was given to her by a travelling monk." Mr Ouyang pointed to the flute in my hand. "And that is the one."

The right hand, with which I was holding the instrument, froze.

"You must still be unaware of how the legend ends." Mr Ouyang shook his head resignedly. "Yanzhi played the flute on Chongyang Night, and was reunited with her husband's spirit, or as the old folks called it, "The Ghost Husband". They spent a few nights together. When she found out the truth about her husband's death, she was heartbroken, and tried to take her own life a few times, but miraculously, she survived. After three months, she discovered she was pregnant."

"But her husband was a ghost! Does that mean it was a phantom pregnancy?"

Mr Ouyang solemnly shook his head again. "It was a miracle. The child she carried was indeed from the seed sown by the soul of her husband after he had died in battle. The heavens did not want him to be without an heir. As the child grew within Yanzhi, the villagers of Huangcun suspected her of straying into another's garden, like a red apricot tree that lets others pick its fruit. They insulted her with their vilest language, accusing her of all sorts of affairs, even of letting herself be taken by some vagrant. But Yanzhi always insisted she was innocent, and that she had kept her vow of chastity to her husband. In order to protect the unborn, she endured all the hardships inflicted on her, and after ten months, finally gave birth to her son."

"God, this story sounds a lot like The Scarlet Letter."

Hearing this tragic story on a cold winter night, I could not help but think of Hester, and the red "A" sewn on the front of her dress. She would rather have died than give up the man's name, seeing her daughter as a gift from the angel, willing to go through any sort of pain. This Yanzhi of Huangcun from centuries ago, was this the Chinese version of the Scarlet Letter? Or had she really been made pregnant by the ghost of her husband?

"Yanzhi and her son experienced all sorts of discrimination and humiliation. She raised the child singlehandedly, until she could send him away for tutelage. After decades of hardship, Yanzhi died from exhaustion, but her son managed to get top marks in the imperial keju examinations. He was promoted from county scholar, to jinshi, an imperial scholar with his name written in gold on the tablet signifying acceptance into the League of Heavenly Scholars. Later, the experiences of his mother became known to the emperor, who was touched by this story, and granted the village the chastity paifang, commending Yanzhi on her conduct."

I never imagined the story of Yanzhi would have had this sort of ending. Turning my head, I swept my eyes over the village below. "So, the chastity paifang at the gates was for Yanzhi? And the "Imperial Scholar's Residence" was built by her son? And you, Mr Ouyang, and Xiaozhi – are Yanzhi's descendants?"

"Correct. And this flute has been passed down by our ancestors."

I looked at the flute, and no longer wanting to be in contact with it, placed it quickly back into Mr Ouyang's hands. I probed, "So is the story of Yanzhi legend or history?"

"Nobody can say for sure, but over the centuries, the Huangcunese have believed it, and this flute, at least, is real."

Lost for words, I stared into Mr Ouyang's face. If Yanzhi's story was real, then this man standing before me, and Xiaozhi, were the descendants of the Ghost Husband? And the whole family living in the Imperial Scholar's Residence were a ghost clan? I could not help but back away a few steps, my mind flying to European castles full of vampires.

Gradually, the moon was swallowed up, and a gust of chilly, sea-scented breeze blew over the mountain slope, sending me shivering. When I raced down the slope, clutching the oil lamp, I passed under the chastity paifang, and my heart tremored inexplicably.

Returning to the "Jinshi Residence", I began to feel the mansion develop an air of gloom, increasingly growing to resemble Dracula's Castle in Transylvania...

In the sombre courtyard, a white figure flitted past. Its movement was inhuman and caused me to draw in a gasp of cold air. Thanks to my experience on the mountainside, I had grown bolder, and the more mysterious this old mansion seemed, the more terrifying, the more it piqued my curiosity. I dashed in the direction the white figure had headed, holding the lamp in front of me to light my path.

It appeared to be dressed in a white nightgown and had a head of long black hair – that young woman. The kerosene lamp faintly illuminated her body. Yes, it was she, the woman I had seen combing her hair the night before. She seemed frightened as she ran up the side stairs.

My heart pounded faster and faster. I pursued her closely, and at last caught up with her on the balcony of the first floor. I grabbed her arm, but my hand shot back as if I had touched a live cable, because she was so icily cold. I felt the aftershocks shiver up and down my spine, but still, she stopped. A sudden gust of frosty wind blew, sweeping her beautiful sable hair back with it.

"Who are you?" I asked, hoarsely. Slowly, she turned, her pale face exposed by the light of the lamp – Xiaozhi!

Heavens! I did not expect it would actually be Xiaozhi. Her complexion was wan, her lips purple from the cold. She must have been freezing in that biting northern wind, wearing only a thin robe. I took off my jacket and draped it over her. Gripping her shoulders tightly, I asked, "Are you OK? Coming out in just your night clothes in this weather, you'll catch your death."

She looked at me with glazed eyes and nodded blankly. I stroked her head of fine black hair, and felt my heart ache a little. "You're frozen through! Why did you come out like this?"

Xiaozhi still said nothing, her expression a mixture of strangeness and nerves. Then without warning, she touched my cheeks, and my nose. My heart tightened under her glacial fingers.

I shook her by the shoulders. "What's going on? I don't want to see you get hurt."

With this, Xiaozhi panicked. She struggled out of my embrace, and bolted like a small wild animal, down the stairs. I ran after her, but missed a step, tripped, and rolled down the stairs.

When I wrenched myself back up, there was no trace of Xiaozhi, only my coat, discarded on the floor. I looked up at her room, but the lights were already out.

Returning to my room, I put my coat back on, and once again wrapped myself in the quilts. I lay there, gazing at the pingfeng opposite me, with my eyes halfway between open and closed, thinking about Xiaozhi's strange behaviour. So the young woman combing her hair in the next room was also her? But why did she come out and do this in the middle of the night?

Xiaozhi's glazed eyes appeared in my mind – she had not seemed fully conscious just then, but muddled, as if half asleep. All of a sudden, I remembered a plotline from my own novel...

Yes, this was a definite possibility. Xiaozhi looked lost. Even though her eyes were open, her mind still seemed asleep – these were all the symptoms of a sleepwalker.

She herself would not be aware of this – to her it would just be a dream, she would not know that her body got up and acted her dreams out.

I took a deep breath and let it out. I never thought Xiaozhi would have a sleepwalking condition; maybe she was not even aware of it herself. Huangcun was truly a maddening place. Tiredness began to overwhelm me, and slowly, I closed my eyes...

4

AT SEVEN IN the morning, I opened my eyes. The light shone through the paper windows onto the pingfeng screens, giving some life to this ancient house.

I could not take it anymore. I had thought Huangcun would be a romantic and interesting place, but now it was infinitely terrifying. So I decided to leave. Immediately.

Xiaozhi was in the front hall. Her complexion looked remarkably normal, not at all as it had been while she was sleepwalking the night before. I felt it better not to point it out. I lifted my head to look at the portrait under the bian-é plaque of 'Hall of Benevolence and Love'. The man in the portrait seemed to look back at me. That would be Yanzhi's son, with a ghost for a father. I did not dare let myself think about it further, and quickly finished breakfast.

"You're leaving?" Xiaozhi could already tell from my attire.

"I'm sorry, I shouldn't have come to Huangcun, and I certainly shouldn't have interrupted the peaceful life of your household."

"I knew you wouldn't last long." Xiaozhi bit her lips. "Will you ever come back to Huangcun?"

"I don't know." I looked into her innocent eyes, but I was thinking of the moonlit scene on the mountain slope the night before. "What about you? Once you graduate from Shanghai University, will you still come back?"

Her eyes had a troubled look to them. Lowering her voice, she answered, "I will definitely come back. Even if I die far away, I shall come back."

I shuddered, her words causing a strange sensation. At that moment, I smelled the distinct scent of rotting orchids, emanating from Xiaozhi's person. It rushed into my nostrils and lungs, making me bitter and sad from the bottom of my heart.

Slowly, I walked to the door of the "Imperial Scholar's Residence". Standing by the high threshold, I turned and fixed my eyes on Xiaozhi. "We may not ever see each other again. Take care."

There was that melancholy again, in Xiaozhi's eyes. She seemed to want to say something, but I had already stepped over the threshold of the ancient mansion and dared not turn back. With my head thrust down, I walked forwards, wanting to eliminate all the gloom in my heart. When I came to the bottom of the paifang, I looked up at those words above the central arch – "Chastity in Eternity". Suddenly it seemed a little ridiculous and pathetic.

I hitched on a pick-up back to Xileng, but the coach to Shanghai had already left, and the next one was not till four in the afternoon. That meant a few free hours. So I went to the cultural museum of Xileng, and rashly asked for the curator. I stuck to the headspace of the identity Xiaozhi had fabricated for me, presenting myself as a researcher of history and folk customs. The curator was evidently taken in and let me barrage him with questions about the paifang and Huangcun, and helped me understand a few things.

The curator was a man in his early fifties, and, on hearing my line of enquiry, fell into deep thought for a while before disappearing into the archives. He came back with a facsimile. I skimmed through the dense text, which had been made from an ancient monument, so lacked any punctuation, and was extremely hard to decipher. I concentrated intently, holding my breath and examining it word by word. After an entire afternoon, I finally understood the content of this document.

Now, I will give you a brief, modern language outline of the facsimile's contents.

In the reign of Emperor Jiajing, when the South-Eastern Wokou troubles were severe, Ouyang An of Huangcun was conscripted into the army. Before he set off for battle, he made a pact with his newlywed wife that they would unite three years later on Chongyang Festival. If they did not see each other, they would each take their own lives to honour their word.

Yet, when the agreed time was reached, three years later on Changyang, Ouyang An was still thousands of miles away in Guangdong, fighting for his country. He knew he would not be able to honour the agreement, and so decided to die for love on the battlefield. On the night of Chongyang, the officers and the Wokou were engaged in fierce battle. Ouyang An ran to the front of his regiment, and as a result was shot by a volley of arrows and fell immediately. But Ouyang An did not die in battle, only passing out from his heavy injuries. He was found, barely alive, by local fishermen. When Ouyang An had recovered from his wounds and was about to go home, battle had once again erupted between the officers and the Wokou. One of the Wokou leaders escaped, and ran into Ouyang An. Ouyang An cut off the head of this chief, unexpectedly accomplishing a great feat, and was granted office by the imperial court.

Not long after that, the Wokou were put down, and Ouyang An returned home in finery. But when he arrived home to Huangcun, he learned that his wife had, according to their pact, hanged herself and taken her own life on Chóngyáng night. Grief-stricken, as if his liver and guts had been shattered, he felt he could no longer remain in the mortal world alone. Before he took his own life, he wished to see his wife one last time. So, secretly, he dug open her grave. When he opened the coffin, he was astonished to find that her body had remained intact, and that there was a strange flute placed next to it. Ouyang An had a great mansion built, and his wife's coffin carried into it.

Over the next few years, Ouyang An seldom left the house, keeping himself confined to its depths, where he had hidden his wife in her coffin. Every year, on Chongyang Festival and during Spring Festival, he would take the flute from his wife's coffin and play it in the middle of the night. This continued for many years, until on a snow-swept Xiaonian night, when Ouyang An was playing the flute again, a miracle took place. Strange noises came from his wife's coffin, and he opened it to find his wife slowly waking up. Beside himself with joy, he carried her to the bed, and fed her light congee every day, until at last her health was restored.

The wife that had come back to life was still young and beautiful. Again, they were able to live a quiet and peaceful life. They even had a son, who later won the Imperial Scholar position, and the emperor, touched to hear this story, granted Huangcun a chastity paifang, on which the words "Chastity Through Yin and Yang" were composed by his majesty and written by his very own hands. Not long after the paifang arches were erected, Ouyang An and his wife passed away, almost at the same time.

After reading the facsimile, I was profoundly shaken. Those blurry words on the monument were still swimming around in my eyes as I rubbed them. "Where did this facsimile come from?"

"It's an epitaph."

"An epitaph?" Immediately, I connected this to the large cemetery near Huangcun. "Is it Ouyang An's?"

The curator nodded. "Twenty years ago, a Ming Dynasty tomb near Huangcun was raided by looters. A primary school teacher from Huangcun, Mr Ouyang, called the police, and an archaeology team was quickly dispatched to salvage the raided artefacts. As the descendant of the owner of the tomb and the reporter of the crime, he was allowed to accompany the excavation, along with the archaeologists. I was there, too. The excavations found that, buried inside the tomb, were the skeletons of a man and a woman, and this relatively well-preserved epitaph.

The stone tablet on which it was carved was taken to the city museum to be added to its collection, and it was then that I made this facsimile of the inscription to keep in the town museum, which is why you've been able to read it."

The bones of a man and a woman? That must be Ouyang An and Yanzhi? So, they really had existed, even their bones had been found... and then I remembered something that made me nervous. "Was anything else found in the tomb?"

"Most of the grave goods were taken by the robbers. But there was a flute found at the site, lying next to the bones of the subjects, in very good condition." The curator sighed. "It's a shame. At the time, the site was in great chaos, and we didn't have much control over the situation. Not long after its discovery, that flute mysteriously disappeared. This was the biggest regret of the whole operation."

A flute from a few centuries ago? My hair prickled. "Curator, has Mr Ouyang read this epitaph?"

"Of course he has. He is the descendant of the tomb's occupants, and he took part in the salvage and excavation process, and actually helped in the production of this facsimile. I remember that he seemed exceptionally shocked, because the details recorded on the epitaph had not been in the Huangcun legends about the chastity paifang."

"The legend of Yanzhi?"

"Yes, her story has been propagated in Huangcun and many other nearby areas. There are over a dozen versions of the legend, most of which have been tinted with mystery and esotericism. People believe that Yanzhi's spirit is still there. But when this epitaph of Ouyang An emerged, it rendered all the other legends drab and dull. Perhaps the truth can only be found inside the grave."

"Do you believe the account in this epitaph was the truth?"

"We do not know for sure. From the angle of historical research, the reliability of the epitaph as a source is much higher than that of secondary texts, and certainly supersedes all these various folk legends. Because – the dead and their stones have no reason to lie."

The dead and their stones have no reason to lie? It was true – in this world, only the living would lie. Suddenly, I felt I had fallen into a mystery in the style of Akira Kurosawa's Rashomon.

It was not until I pulled myself out of my contemplation that I realised it was already half past five, and that I had missed the last coach back to Shanghai.

As I hurried out of the museum, night had already fallen on Xileng. A gust of arctic wind blew past, bringing with it the scent of burning. Around me, every household was burning paper money and silver foil in front of their doors. I could even glimpse some of their ancestral tablets.

Oh, heavens! I'd lost track of the days in Huangcun. Today was Xiaonian eve, the twenty-ninth of the twelfth lunar month, and tomorrow would be Chuxi, New Year's Eve. Custom had it that Xiaonian was a time for making offerings to one's ancestors. Every household would burn paper money to send it to the next world, and bow before their ancestral altars to pay their respects.

My thoughts turned again to the story in the epitaph – Ouyang An had played the mysterious flute on Xiaonian Eve and caused Yanzhi to come back to life. Today was Xiaonian Eve, and that mysterious flute was in the hands of Xiaozhi's father, whose wife had died at a young age. As the descendant of Ouyang An and Yanzhi, would he try to re-enact the ancestral miracle, and summon his wife's ghost?

In that instant, I made a decision – I must get back to Huangcun immediately. I must uncover this secret.

The Xileng bus had stopped for the day, so I had no choice but to take out my torch and follow the country road that led to Huangcun, walking across the desolate mountains and fields.

Two hours later, just as I was about to reach Huangcun, I suddenly heard the sound of spectral flute music, like the ebb and flow of nocturnal tides, slowly flowing into my ears. Amidst the fearful melodies, I ran and ran, until I was out of breath, and I began to see the vague shadow of the giant, three-arched stone paifang, towering in the dark like a fortress – I was at Huangcun.

At that moment, the flute music on the mountain faded again. Not stopping to catch my breath, I dashed straight to the "Imperial Scholar's Residence".

To my surprise, the large doors stood open, and I raced straight through them. Pointing my torch into the gloom of this ancient house, which seemed wrapped in a layer of strange mist, my heartbeat hastened. There seemed to be no one in the cavernous hall, so I turned to the courtyard at the back. The entire Jinshi Mansion had become silent as a tomb.

I rushed into Xiaozhi's room. The light would not turn on, so I swept the room with my torch, but there was not even the shadow of a ghost there. Stepping out of the room, I saw in the building where I had been staying a weak streak of light.

I hastened to the source of the light in that xiaolou, and gently pushed open the door to the room where I had stayed – that kerosene lamp was lit again, its flickering flame lighting up the inky room, and through the set of pingfeng screens, I saw the outline of a young woman.

"Xiaozhi!"

I dashed round the screen. It was indeed her, wearing her nightdress, her black hair hanging loose, looking at the pingfeng, trance-like. I clutched her icy shoulders, and she slowly turned to me. Her tragically beautiful face looked forlorn, but her eyes were completely dull and empty when they looked at me – she was clearly sleepwalking again.

I shook her shoulders. "Wake up."

Xiaozhi did not answer, she only blinked, her eyes shining like obsidian gems in the ghostly light.

Gazing at the last painting in the pingfeng screens, I said, "Yanzhi's story. Perhaps your father didn't tell you that there is another version that was dug out of the tomb."

She paused, turning her head, and called out, "Lost soul, will you return?"

I froze. It felt like these words had not left her mouth, but had been channelled directly into my mind, and that voice… it didn't sound like Xiaozhi's! Even the eyes looked different from hers.

The gloomy lamplight shone over her eyes and hair; in her white sleeping dress, she resembled the ancient figure from the screens.

She was not Xiaozhi!

Her shoulders were so devoid of warmth, her eyes so strange, I felt fear in my bones, and took a big step back. "Who the hell are you?"

"That's Xiaozhi's mother."

The heavy and oppressive voice behind me made my hairs stand on end. In the lugubrious light of the kerosene lamp, Mr Ouyang's thin and cadaverous face appeared, as if out of thin air.

He glided to the side of the woman, still holding that mysterious flute in his hand, and said chillingly, "You have seen what you should not have."

Trembling, I shook my head. "What is going on? Isn't Xiaozhi's mum long dead?"

Mr Ouyang replied in a voice devoid of warmth, "She died twenty years ago, not long after Xiaozhi was born. I'd been away on a long business trip, and when I returned, her mother had already passed away from illness. But I was unwilling to accept her death – I couldn't be without her. Devastated, I no longer wanted to live in this world. Soon after that, our ancestral tomb was raided, and I went in with the archaeology team. We dug out this mysterious flute, which I took in secret, and the epitaph, which I studied. The story of my ancestor gave me incredible inspiration. I believed that as long as I used the same method as recorded in the inscription, I would be able to bring my wife back to my side."

"That's why you often went up the mountain in the middle of the night, to play this flute?"

"Yes. Do you know the power it possesses? It could bring your loved one back to you – yes, she is back." The expression in his eyes, as well as his breathing, became more and more desperate. He gently stroked his wife's hair. "Whenever I play this flute at night, she would come to Jinshi Di without a sound. Even though I have grown old, she is forever young and beautiful. The music guides her home, she combs her hair in her room, and takes a stroll in the courtyard."

I remembered what I had seen in Xiaozhi's room. The picture of her mother from when she was alive was the spitting image of Xiaozhi. No wonder I had mistaken her for Xiaozhi. I gazed at the ghostly couple before me. The young and beautiful wife looked up, meeting the eyes of her aged and haggard husband, and their gaze broke my heart – he loved her deeply, no matter if she were dead or alive. Even though mortals and ghosts were separated by the worlds of Yang and Yin, he longed for his lover to come home.

Mr Ouyang chanted, slowly, "Once one has seen the sea, no other waters can compare. Once one has seen the rain and clouds of Wushan, no other scenery can compare."[40]

I felt an aching pain in my heart. This was Yuan Zhen's Lí Sī, for the commemoration of his dead wife. Then I remembered Xiaozhi. "What about Xiaozhi? Where is she?"

Mr Ouyang did not answer. Suddenly his eyes grew very wide; he held up his hand and pointed behind me.

As I turned to look, I felt a spell of giddiness – in the ghostly lamplight, the pingfeng screen was glowing faintly. The Ming Dynasty woman in the painting now held the flute to her lips, and was playing...

The floating, lilting music washed over me like waves, and engulfed me like a dark tide, and I lost all consciousness...

5

WHEN I CAME to, it was early morning. I ached all over, my head thrummed, and I felt disoriented. I remember what had happened the night before and shot up from the floor of the ancient room.

"Xiaozhi! Xiaozhi!" I ran down the stairs, shouting, but there was not even a shadow left in the whole of the

---

40 曾经沧海难为水, 除却巫山不是云 - From Five Poems of Yearning for the Departed, by Tang Dynasty official and scholar Yuan Zhen. See note on p29 in Immortal Beauty.

"Imperial Scholar's Residence". I looked through all the rooms, and found nothing except for thick layers of dust, as if no one had stepped foot in there for years. Xiaozhi's room was completely empty, except for that photograph of her mother.

What happened? Where did they go? Where was Xiaozhi and her father? I was still shouting for her, but the old house was as silent as an ancient grave. Xiaozhi's long-dead mother, Mr Ouyang's invocation of her with the flute – was this a nightmare, or a terrible hallucination?

No, I dared not think any more about it.

I ran out of the towering double doors of the "Imperial Scholar's Residence", and at last, found some signs of life in Huangcun. People were putting up Spring Festival banners on their doors. Yes, today was Chuxi, New Year's Eve, and it was time to go home for the nianfan meal.

I went straight to the village committee and found the head of the village. No longer holding back, I questioned them about Xiaozhi and Mr Ouyang.

What came from the village head caused my nerves to shatter and my legs buckle under me. Mr Ouyang had been dead for some time. He had passed away three years earlier from cancer, dying in that very house. The village head had helped to prepare Mr Ouyang's body for burial himself since his wife had died from some illness at home twenty years before that, when he was away for work.

As for Xiaozhi, the village head sighed. "The girl was so smart and got into Shanghai University. It was such a shame that, a year ago, she was caught up in an accident on the city's metro, and was gone, like a wilted young flower, like a piece of fallen jade."

My heart was already numb. I put my hand over my mouth to hold in my scream, scared they would think I had gone mad. The family of three from the "Jinshi Di", were already dead – how could this be possible? Who, then, were the Xiaozhi and Mr Ouyang that I had seen and spoken to?

But I could not say any more, fearing that the villagers would think I had gone mad, and have me thrown in an asylum. I could not stay in Huangcun for another moment. Perhaps this place belonged solely to a bygone era, to those strange tales told in thread-bound books.

Xiaozhi – my mind and heart called out to her, even as my body carried itself out of Huangcun. The imperial gift of the chastity paifang stood there, upright and immovable, like a giant tombstone.

Farewell forever, Huangcun.

EPILOGUE

RETURNING TO SHANGHAI, I went to speak to a friend who worked in the metro company. He told me that a year before my signing, at the station next to that bookstore, there was a major accident; one of the trains had pulled into the platform, and a twenty-year-old university student had tripped and fallen onto the tracks, being crushed to death by the train instantly. The student's name was Ouyang Xiaozhi.

My friend did not notice the tears that quietly rolled down my face. It was only then that I realised that I had irrevocably fallen for Xiaozhi, a girl who had died a year before I'd met her.

This was a tragic yet beautiful story, so I decided to turn it into a novelette. If Xiaozhi had not come to me on the evening of my book signing, if she had not taken me to Huangcun, I would never have known this story. In the vast sea of people that is the city, she and I had encountered each other. This was her gift to me – she said she liked my novels, so she gifted me with inspiration and an exquisite story.

Will I ever see her again?

A few days later, on the way home, I walked past a street peddler, and felt as if my heart had been pierced. Out of the corner of my eye, I saw a flute – immediately, I squatted down to study it. It was about forty centimetres long, the body lacquered a brownish yellow, with plum-colour threads wound between the finger holes, with a sheet of membrane over the embouchure as delicate as cicada wings.

Unimaginable.

The cold dusk wind ruffled my hair as I held the flute, trembling. I stroked it softly, as if caressing the soft skin of a woman. The body of the flute was freezing. I felt tendrils of cold energy seep through my fingers and into my blood, blurring my vision. And then, emerging from the blur, was a face I had dreamed of and yearned for with my soul.

I took some money out and paid for the flute, carefully wrapping my coat around it, as if it were a living being. Night was slowly falling, and I hastened home. I did not go into my apartment, but walked straight up to the rooftop terrace.

The terrace at night was positively arctic, the biting wind slipping through my clothes and piercing my bones, and I was already standing unsteadily. Up there on the rooftop, gazing around into the distance, Shanghai at night lay beneath me with all its allure, splendid lights from countless skyscrapers, like a dream world.

Xiaozhi, where are you?

I took out the flute from my embrace and looked up at the vast heavens. All I could see was the mysterious night, on which the new crescent moon hung like a hook. With pure moonlight pouring into my eyes, I could not help but lift up the flute, and put it to my lips. I took a deep breath, letting the freezing air pour down my nose, my throat, fill my chest, and burst open those dust-locked doors at the bottom of my heart.

Holding the air for a moment, I exhaled that breath as if I had regained a new life. Gradually, warm air flowed into the flute, swirling round and round its slim pipe body, crashing against the walls, whimpering, generating a sad resonance, which then merged into lilting waves that flew from the other end of the instrument, and floated far into the mysterious night sky.

Immersed in the mellifluous music of this ancient flute, my consciousness began to blur – and then again came that unusual scent of orchids, and a feeling, as if a long and slender finger had gently come to rest on my shoulder.

NOTES

THE GOTHIC HAS always been important to me, but I grew up in a culture which does not drip with the tropes of occidental gothic aesthetics. There are few ruinous stone castles or ice-carved mountains, but that leads to an interesting question. Is there a Chinese Gothic?

Chinese art and fiction are often filled with deserted temples at night, deep winding recesses of old mansions, mysterious melancholic melodies emanating from traditional instruments, exhumated camphor coffins, single lit paper lanterns blown about in the desolate wilderness, where the night wind howls like ghosts, and ethereal female figures with long black hair and flowing snow-white hanfu... Yes, there IS a Chinese Gothic tradition, and it is just as filled with awe, mystery, dark and picturesque imagery. Cai Jun's traditional ghost story expresses this Chinese Gothic in all its mesmerising charm.

This novella is also an exploration of how national, regional and local histories can haunt a place and its people, and how traditional 'virtues' such as chastity became a heavy millstone on women's shoulders, rather than a celebration of their righteousness. Aside from the fear and fright, Cai Jun's remarkable imagination and unique descriptions of sensations brings us closer to what it might feel like physically to be haunted, to come into contact with the supernatural. As a horror writer with post-humanist concerns, much of Cai's appeal lies in his writing of marginalised human characters, zombies and ghosts alike, with empathy, compassion and love.

As one of the most popular horror writers in a society with monumental reverence for education and learning, Cai Jun stands out like a black sheep in a snowy flock. He confesses that he has never received any formal education past high school, and at the age of nineteen, arrived in Shanghai to work in the post office. After a few years, having a job became a habit, but he discovered that he could make a much better living from writing. When he was at primary school, he dreamed of becoming an archaeologist; when he was in secondary school, he dreamed of becoming an artist, and even considered entering an art academy. In reality, he fell into writing almost by accident, and even today, says he feels like blushing whenever he hears himself being referred to as an 'author'. Nevertheless, there is little doubt that this author has become one of the major names in China's contemporary horror community and was one of the first authors I wanted to 'collect' for Sinophagia.

The idea of an author summoning a fictional place they have created in their imagination into real life must have appealed to Cai Jun, because after this story, he returned to this locale to write two full-length novels set in this strange sleepy town, 'The Huangcun Apartment' and 'The Return of Huangcun'. He has always intended that in Huangcun, Love would be ultimate eternal theme, traversing history, time, and reality.

THE DEATH OF NALA

娜娜之死

Gu Shi

1

MY SON HELD Nala's corpse up to me.

The kitten's head had fallen backwards, her fur no longer silky or smooth, her body limp with death. I could not help but think back to when I had brought Nala to him, two months ago.

That day I held Nala and presented her to him. "Do you like her, my treasure?" I asked him, making sure my tone was as soft as it could be. "Do you like the little kitty?"

He hesitated for a long time, before putting aside his toy bear Duomi, and placing his hand on the kitty's head, who let out a soft mew.

"Careful!" I was a little nervous. My son liked to break his toys, so I hoped the same thing wouldn't happen to Nala.

My son looked startled, instantly jerking his hand away and shoving it behind his back.

"My treasure," I asked again gently, "do you like her? Isn't she adorable?"

My son glanced up at me and silently shook his head.

I had known this might happen – it was a rare

occurrence that my son took to anything. There was a time when, even as his biological mother, I could not help but think of him as a natural born monster, but my husband remained adamant that his coldness was just the nature of boys. "They're not like girls," was how he'd put it to me.

The psychologist's advice had sounded a lot more effective than my husband's unfounded opinion. My doctor thought that the child was more likely to identify with things that had names, creating an illusion of anthropomorphism – like that bear he had named Duomi, and which he had indeed come to cherish.

So I asked my son, "Shall we give the kitty a name?"

He stayed silent, fixing his gaze on the kitten in my arms. She was treating my arm like a mother cat's belly, holding out her two front paws and kneading it left and right, attempting to squeeze out the milk.

"What is it doing?" my son asked.

"She's hungry," I replied. "She wants milk."

The kitten kept on kneading until she actually fell asleep on me, her mouth latched on to a decorative bobble on my sweater, looking incredibly cute. My son took in the whole scene, and suddenly, bursting into tears, he howled, "I hate it!", tearing his voice hoarse. "I hate it!"

"Shh, my treasure." I rushed to calm him, holding out my hand to point at the TV, attempting to divert his attention to the Disney film. "Look, doesn't the little lioness look like our kitty? Shall we call her Nala?"

He continued to cry.

"Shall we, my treasure?" I asked again.

His only answer was a continued stream of incessant sobbing and screaming.

2

NALA'S CORPSE LAY across my son's hands.

As a mother, of course I knew that I ought to react to the situation at hand immediately, but for a minute or so, I felt nailed to the floor, my body refusing to move. Nala was such an adorable little creature. She often gazed at me with those dark brown eyes, as if giving me all her trust and love, yet now she was dead.

It felt like an age before I heard my own voice. "How could this happen? How is Nala dead?"

"She kept on crying, but I wanted to sleep... so I tied a plastic bag over her head, so I wouldn't hear her." My son looked at me timidly. "But, but, when I woke up, she was like this... Mummy..."

His voice felt like poison shot straight into my heart, and I sensed my body turn cold, icy, as if the one who had died was me, not Nala.

He approached me, sobbing softly. "I didn't know it would be like this..."

But I knew he had done it on purpose. Every time he destroyed one of his toys, he would cry like this. Each time, he would cry meekly and timidly, his eyes blurred with tears, but in those moments between outpourings, he would clearly be observing me, like a devil dressed as an angel.

The child was only five, and his face told the whole truth.

I raised my hand, but instead of flinching back, as I had expected, he stood there looking at me expectantly. This made me hesitate, knowing that if I punished him, it would mean his actions were forgiven, and I would immediately become the one at fault. He waited,

and, seeing the rejection in my eyes, slammed Nala's

body to the floor. I fell to my knees and rushed to pick her up. The corpse was stiff and ice cold, its fuzziness feeling downright nauseating. How strange this was, that when she was alive this feeling had inspired so much affection, and now so much repulsion. I ran into the bathroom, retching, and threw up violently, tears and spit mingling with my tumbling vomit as I emptied my guts. I heard my son's crying again, knowing he had done something wrong and wanting to placate everything with his tears.

No.

I cleaned up, and went out to face the culprit, the sinner. He cried out dramatically through his tears, "Mummy, I was wrong." He reached out, attempting to grab the corner of my gown, but I flung him aside.

He turned deathly pale, and stared at me as if stunned, the tears immediately drying up. Suddenly, he turned, and grabbing hold of Nala's body by one leg and wrenching open the balcony door, hurled her straight out from the 13th floor.

He turned back to look at me, and there was a gut-wrenching scream, but I had no way of telling if it came out of his mouth, or mine.

3

NOT LONG AFTER that, my husband left his job to work locally, and our family of three were reunited. For a while, I thought the incident with Nala would eventually pass, but it seemed to have left a vague shadow across my heart, a wound that left me utterly incapable of bestowing any tenderness on my son. More time passed, and he began to attend primary school. One day, he came home with a stray cat to feed.

"Mum, do you like her?"

A cat.

It felt as if something was struggling with all its might to surface in my memory, and I did not answer his question. My son stroked their head affectionately, bathed them, and insisted we take them to the vet to be vaccinated. He even spent his own pocket money, buying tins of food.

I tacitly consented to all this, but I knew that it wasn't the cat he wanted to please. Whenever he carried out these chores, he always kept his attention closely trained on me from beginning to end.

It was precisely because of this that I could never forgive him. He never felt any real remorse, he did not know what he had done wrong – his only control was in evading punishment, to protect himself. I, however, had never been able to read anyone as clearly as him, my son.

Everything I saw made me tremble with fear.

"Mum, look how adorable it is." At last, one day, losing patience in this continuing performance, he asked me, "Shall we call her Nala?"

His eyes were crystal clear, the eyes of a child, but they displayed the purest provocation and malice without a hint of concealment. I looked at him, shocked, cold filling my body.

"Shall we?" he repeated, smiling as his chubby little hand stroked the kitten's neck.

I stood there, rooted and dumbstruck, until my husband ragged the boy into his room and locked the door. The kitten was dropped, and with a mournful cry they struggled to edge towards my feet, rubbing against them ingratiatingly.

My husband picked them up and put them in the carrier

on the balcony. "I'll take it to the shelter tomorrow," he said with resolve when he came back in.

Perhaps my years of coldness had at last infuriated Son – I tried to convince myself, and this was his revenge. So, I forgave him, and the incident should have ended there. We were still a happy family. But heaven knows, from that night, Nala would appear in my dreams.

Dream after dream, night after night, they all revolved around Nala. Sometimes the colour of her fur would change, sometimes she was not a kitten, but a puppy, or a bunny, but no matter what form she took, I always knew she was Nala. The dreams would begin happily, a furry little creature with a large pair of eyes, curled up next to me asleep, as if I was her shelter against all the storms in the world. And then for one reason or another, I would have to leave her side for a while. I would never want to leave, I would turn back to look at her, and she would be there asleep, her little paws nuzzled against her face.

"Nala," I would call, and then she would lift her head to look at me.

We would both know this was the last time we would see each other.

The dreams do not have endings. As I walk away, my fear grows deeper and deeper, until at last, I struggle into wakefulness, my whole body dripping with sweat.

Eventually, my husband noticed, and asked if I was having nightmares. I told him I dreamt of Nala, I kept dreaming of her.

He decided to get me counselling.

This seemed like making a mountain out of a molehill, but he was adamant. As I waited for him in the hospital corridor, I overheard faint moments of his conversations with the doctor.

"I thought she had already gotten through it."

"For women, it can be too much to get over," said the doctor. "Has anything unusual happened recently at home? Perhaps something that has triggered her memories of what happened then?"

"Oh yes, it's my son, he adopted this cat..."

Their voices grew softer, and then it was my turn to speak with the doctor, alone.

He asked about Nala. He wanted me to tell him about her appearance, and what she was doing in the dreams. At first, I was able to talk clearly, but then, it was as if there was a grate in my throat that the important words could not get through, and then a wall that nothing could pass through.

The doctor's decision was for me to "face the facts."

That sounded ridiculous. Families facing the death of pets was an everyday thing. I'd just had a more agitated reaction, probably because I'm a loving person, or perhaps because my son's entirely malicious performance had left me so extremely disappointed.

A natural born monster.

"Shall we call it Nala?"

I could almost hear his voice – the murderer! He had not suffered the consequences of his actions, and I, his mother, had no way of punishing him.

"You need to face this," the doctor said. "Face reality."

He said I needed to stay for treatment. I refused. This was not a counselling clinic, it was a psychiatric institute.

"I'm not crazy!" I said to my husband. "It's just nightmares, you're overreacting!"

He cast an imploring glance at the doctor, who silently shook his head.

4

I WAS LOCKED in a room, a comfortable little room with no TV, no phone, no computer, and apart from the doctor, no contact with anyone. After a month, I gave up protesting, so at least he would consider that I had "calmed down" enough. On this fresh, sunny morning, the doctor played me a recording of a telephone conversation.

The recording had been made three years earlier, of a phone call I had made to my husband, who was stationed abroad at the time.

"She was just like a kitten when she was born." My words, in a soft and gentle tone. "Even her cries were practically mews."

I had wanted my husband to hear her, as if she were right in front of him, so I had recorded her voice, her soft, thin and rhythmic crying.

"Mew," she cried.

"Listen, listen," I said.

"How about we call her Cindy? That's my favourite name," he suggested.

"Sure," I said. "But yesterday I told Tom her name was Nala. It's from a cartoon he's been obsessed with lately."

"Haha, then Nala can be Tom's pet name for her."

The doctor switched off the recording.

"Do you remember now?" the doctor asked. "Cindy was your daughter, who died three years ago. You and Tom called her Nala."

No, Nala was a cat, a cat with big brown eyes.

So, he starts playing another recording, where my voice sounds very anxious. "Tom doesn't like her, I'm so exhausted. When are you coming back? I really can't manage two small children on my own."

"Darling, I really can't get away right now. Why don't you get someone in to help?" His voice at the other end of the line dripped with apology and guilt, while at this end of the line came Tom's voice, out of control: "Mummy Mummy MUMMY MUMMY!"

"OK, OK, I'll find a nanny, I'll arrange some interviews tomorrow." That had been my reply.

So, in order to attend the face-to-face interviews at the recruitment company, I'd had to be away for two hours. Before I went, I took one more look at Cindy sleeping in her cot; she was rubbing her face with her tiny hands. "Nala." Seeing that my son was close by, I called her by this name instead, and then she woke up, opened her beautiful big eyes, and looked back at me.

My little angel, Cindy – Nala – my precious daughter.

Nala was not a cat.

She was my daughter.

I covered my ears, and screwed my eyes shut, but still, I was unable to stop that horrifying moment flooding back into my memory...

When I returned home from the recruitment firm... my son held Cindy's corpse up to me.

The baby's head had fallen backwards, her skin no longer rosy or warm, her body limp with death.

NOTES

GU SHI IS primarily known for her science fiction, so the fact that this, her only attempt at horror writing, is bereft of any supernatural or technological McGuffin, speaks to the strength of her skills in capturing characters and situations beyond the tropes of genre. During the initial reading for this story, the translation and in every re-read, I have felt the same deep sense of shock and gut-wrenching discomfort.

Like everyone else in her generation in China, Gu Shi was an only child, her mother often telling her she wished she could have had another child. This short story was written in the build-up to the relaxation of the Single Child Policy in 2013, which allowed couples to have a second child, if either of them had been an only child. The Single Child Policy has been in place for decades, and needless to say, domestic media stirred with news reports and public debates on the subject. Gu Shi's idea for the story arose from the concerns that some single children would not want a sibling, assuming that a brother or a sister would take away the love of their parents, and also, that those who had grown up without siblings would not be prepared to deal with situations that multiple children might create.

Apart from these imagined fears, it is also worth looking at how this is a story about gender. The mother has to balance the roles of managing the house and the children, whilst the husband is away. She placates the son, whose coldness his father dismisses as accepted male behaviour, and in the end, it is again the male psychologist who waves away the psychological damage our protagonist suffers as hysterics and weakness. As a victim of neglect and pressure, she is punished with incarceration. The most horrific violence in this story, perhaps in this whole collection, is visited on an infant girl, whose tragic fate is minimised, forgiven and erased. This story would never be "The Death of Simba".

Mental health has been a notoriously neglected and

stigmatised topic in traditional Chinese culture. With their characteristic stoic natures and Confucian reverence for reserve, it is still considered unseemly to display strong emotions in public, let alone any signs of mental unease. Unsurprisingly, this has disproportionately impacted on women. The unfair pressures placed on them in domestic matters, including child-rearing, is amply highlighted in this fictional tragedy.

Even with my 'Westernised' parents and education in the West, I was still brought up with an aversion to discussing mental health. Mental illness was something that happened to other people, and would lead to them being taken away. Only recently have there been some conversations within China about stress, mental wellbeing and neurodivergence.

As the purpose of horror literature is to induce fear for either entertainment, reflection, or both, I felt as though this story would make the most fitting impact to end this anthology, as it was what one of my readers described as, "the story that most made me want to hurl the book away". So thank you for holding on to it for the final few pages.

I do hope that you have enjoyed this little collection of short stories, novelettes and novellas, and that when your skin has stopped creeping, you may feel brave enough to delve deeper into the world of China's horror literature.

ACKNOWLEDGEMENTS

I WANT TO thank my partner and editor, Joseph Brant, for their insights in horror fiction and their unwavering support for my work on China and its cultures, even during very difficult times in their own life. I want to thank Michael J. Rowley for initially commissioning this anthology with Solaris, for his commitment to broadening the horizons of Anglophone SFF, and his trust in my expertise and skills as a curator and translator. I want to thank PR and Marketing Manager Jess for throwing her genuine passion for horror and SFF behind her fun, thoughtful and well-prepped campaigns, not only for Sinophagia but in the continued promotion of the award-winning Sinopticon. And a thank you to new Commissioning Editor Amanda who has had to adopt Sinophagia halfway through its gestation, for recognising that it requires a unique and culturally appropriate approach for a first in its field.

As this very rare but very frail fledgling finally takes to the wing, I am grateful to many people who went out of their way to help me or gave me the benefit of the doubt. Ra Page, CEO and founder of Comma Press, who helped to put me in touch with one of the major voices I wanted to seek out. Leary Li who handles English markets at the FAA for his efficient help in facilitating collaboration with his company, his proactive approach to finding solutions and the continued exchanges on the SFF industry. Tao Cui of Tianjin Wenxuan Media, a small group of like-minded and experienced publishing professionals dedicated to China's genre literature, who has been instrumental in helping me track down the voices I wanted to find and amplify. I am grateful to Senior Literary Consultant He Chaoqun, who took the time to explain the current horror taboos in China, for listening to my plans and goals, taking a chance, and helping to bring the authors I sought on board with the project.

I want to thank every one of the contributors for agreeing to be part of Sinophagia, despite the current attitudes towards horror literature in China, especially Yimei Tangguo and Zhou Dedong for replying to some mad woman sending them private messages out of the blue. I am so delighted to be able to feature their insightful social horror works in this collection.

And lastly, I want to thank all my readers for being adventurous, stepping out of your comfort zones and investigating an alien take on an already discomforting genre. I hope you will find your reward in these stories, not only in the thrills and shivers, but perhaps some insight into another culture and its society.

ABOUT THE TRANSLATOR
AND EDITOR

XUETING C. NI was born in Guangzhou, during China's re-opening to the West. Having lived in cities across China, she emigrated with her family to Britain at the age of eleven, where she continued to be immersed in Chinese culture, alongside her British education, realising ultimately that this gave her a unique a cultural perspective, and bridging her Eastern and Western experiences.

After graduating in English Literature from the University of London, she began a career in the publishing industry, whilst also translating original works of Chinese fiction. She returned to China in 2008 to continue her research at Central University of Nationalities, Beijing. Since 2010, Xueting has written extensively on Chinese culture and China's place in Western pop media, working with companies, institutions and festivals, to help improve understanding of China's heritage, culture and innovation, and introduce its wonders to new audiences.

Xueting has contributed to the BBC, Tordotcom and the Confucius Institute. She has created non-fiction works, including *From Kuanyin to Chairman Mao: An Essential Guide to Chinese Deities* (Weiser Books), *Chinese Myths* (Amber Books) and curated fiction in translation, including *Sinopticon: A Celebration of Chinese Science Fiction* (Solaris).

Xueting is currently working on a range of projects, including a book on the culture of wuxia storytelling. She lives just outside London with her partner and their cats, all of whom are learning Mandarin.

ABOUT THE CONTRIBUTORS

The Girl in the Rain by Hong Niangzi
Published in Chinese in a collection by Yellow Mountain Press, 2011.
HONG NIANGZI, known as The Red Lady, is a woman of Miao ethnicity from Pushi, Hunan, who currently resides in Shenzhen, Sagittarius. She has published sixteen novels, and seven collections of prose and short stories. This includes her **Seven Colour Horrors** novel series, considered a must-read for Chinese horror fans. Her **Green Silk** was among 2018's Top Ten Thrillers. CCTV (like China's BBC) have broadcast adaptations of **Red Brocade, Emerald Door** and **Green Silk** on separate occasions in their after-midnight programme. The Red Lady's strange and unique literary flair, brilliance in story construction, dynamic style and solid training, astonish and delight in equal measure. With her visible achievements within the genre, she has been given the title "The Empress of Horror". Her work has been selling well in Italy, Korea, Taiwan and Vietnam. She has been published by major magazines across the country, and has a readership that reaches far and wide.

The Waking Dream by Fan Zhou
*Published on **Non-Exist SF**, 2022*
FAN ZHOU is a new writer who has just begun her writing career, alongside a very ordinary day job. She spends her spare time creating stories of conspiracy and crime, totally unrelated to her day job. She wishes that all the conspiracies and crimes in the world were just stories.

Immortal Beauty by Chu Xidao
Published in Chinese on rongshuxia.com, 2002
CHU XIDAO holds a Master's degree in literature, is a member of the Shanghai Writer's Association and has been creative director to an advertising company. Now an independent writer, she works mainly on novel and screen writing. Her novel-length works include the **Demon Born** qihuan fantasy series, the **Heavenly Light and Cloud Shadows** series, part of the Jiuzhou Universe, and the novel prequel to Huayi Brothers film "Detective Dee: The Rise of the Sea Dragon". She was also head script writer for Hunan TV's "Warrior of Destiny".

Those Who Walk at Night, Walk With Ghosts by She Cong Ge
Published in Chinese on Tianya.com, 2010
SHE CONG GE is the pen name of Xu Yufeng, born 1977 in Yichang, Hubei. In 2010, while working as a construction worker in Pakistan, he began writing and publishing his supernatural horror "Ghost Stories of Yichang" on Tianya.com. In six months, the work had gathered forty million views on the site and propelled the writer to fame online. These stories were published in print in 2011, as part of **Records of Strange Tales**, and again as part of **Ghost Stories of the Yangtze** outside China. In 2013, he left his job at the National Chemical Engineering Group, to join Beijing's Cyzone Film and Media Ltd, where he has headed the literature division ever since. Filming rights for his xuanhuan (Eastern fantasy) novel series The Master were bought by IQiyi in 2016. Many of his other thriller and horror novels such as **Snake City** and **The Secret Tunnel** are being adapted into TV and film. He has even starred in the internet drama **Once Upon a Time in Forbidden City,** for which he wrote the script.

The Yin Yang Pot by Chuan Ge
Published in Chinese on zhihu.com, 2018

CHUAN GE, self-professed "story grave-digger", is a writer of suspense whose strength lies in short to medium-length suspense fiction. His signature work for short fiction is **The Yin-Yang Pot**, and for medium length fiction, **The Dark Peach Blossom Spring**.

Shanxiao by Goodnight, Xiaoqing
Published in Chinese in Fantasy World magazine, 2007
GOODNIGHT, XIAOQING, also known as Xiao Qing, was born in the '80s, and is a superstar writer with good looks, one of the "hot authors" jointly endorsed by rongshuxia.com, jjwxc.com, sina.com and many more major online publishing platforms. Her avid fans proudly refer to themselves as the Qing Clan. Her long series of Qing's Classical Treasury, which includes **The Lament of the Water Dragon, Ghostly Fragrance** and **Distant Shadows** has earned her millions of followers online. Some of her devoted fans have even adapted her works into four-panel comics. Her printed works include "The Imprisoned Fox", "The Journey of the Sword" and "The Avenger's Song".

Have You Heard of Ancient Glory? by Zhou Dedong
Published in Chinese on zhihu.com, 2020
ZHOU DEDONG, renowned author, is considered China's "godfather of suspense fiction". He has been editor-in-chief of the youth magazines Youth and Motto, and the women's magazine Friends. He has published over ten books in print, and been translated into many languages. His signature works include "Door", "The Ghost Wedding" and "The Curse of Lop Nur". His latest work is "The Respected Mr Qin Ling".

Records of Xiangxi by Nanpai Sanshu
Published in Chinese in The Nine Gates Sect: The Xiangxi Days, 2021
NANPAI SANSHU, or "Third Uncle of the Southern Sect", is

the pseudonym of Xu Lei, writer, scriptwriter, and a member of the China Writer's Association. He is also the chief executive of Quantum Multimedia Entertainment, and a leading figure in China's thriller and adventure fiction. Ever since his signature work **The Graverobber Chronicles** were published in 2007, the series has sold over 20 million copies. Following this success, Third Uncle has expanded the Chronicles universe, into subsequent series such as **The Zanghai Flower, The Sand Sea** and **Records of the South**. The story of the Iron Trio continues in novels such as **The Lost Tomb: Reboot**. From its original literary origins, Graverobber has developed into an enormous product chain, a multi-media industry that includes manhua (comics), donghua (animation), film, TV and other derivative products, with a net worth estimated at over 20 billion RMB. Since 2016, Third Uncle has chaired various official creative associations in Hangzhou and undertaken a lot of charity work. In 2019, he won the Mao Dun Award for Best New Writer, and the Internet Literature Award for Best New Writer.

The Ghost Wedding by Yimei Tangguo
*Published in Chinese in **The World of Suspense** magazine, 2006*
YIMEI TANGGUO is the pseudonym of Zhou Qin. One of the most renowned female suspense writers, she likes to write love stories under the cloak of horror. Her readers have likened her to a poisoned sweet, because her words are addictive, like a drug. As soon as she began publishing on Tianya.com (major global Chinese social media platform), she bloomed like a strange flower, attracting millions of dedicated fans. Her sharp writing style, and alluring plotlines, have quickly made her a star. Her astounding creativity and talent have brought her many chart-topping novels, including **The Rat Skin Jade Figure, The Crazed Claw,** and **Ghostly Intentions,** as well as three novels published across Asia, cementing her place as the unshakable queen of horror.

Night Climb by Chi Hui

CHI HUI is a writer, editor and former deputy chief editor of Science Fiction World. She has published over ten sci-fi and fantasy novels, including **Terminal Town 2030** and **Synthetics 2075**. She is the winner of famous awards such as the Galaxy, Nebula and Coordinate. She has published works in English on Clarkesworld, was a contributor to The Reincarnated Giant collection, and her **Algorithm of Simhuman** was nominated for the Locus Awards.

Forbidden Rooms by Zhou Haohui
Published in Chinese in **Legends of Past and Present** *magazine,* *2007*

ZHOU HAOHUI, renowned writer of suspense, screenwriter and cutting-edge director, author of the **Death Notice** series, is considered China's Keigo Higashino, and is one of the best writers in the genre. Seasons one and two of the web adaptation of Death Notice made 2.5 billion RMB, becoming the hottest suspense drama in China. Season three received over a hundred million views in four days within its release, generating 130 million views of related topics on Weibo.

Ti'naang by Su Min
Published in Chinese on 2019's **Chinese SF Gala**

SU MIN is a science fiction writer and playwright. Her representative short works include **The Earth's Reflection,** **Ti'naang** and **The Post-Consciousness Era**. **The Post-Consciousness Era** has won the Gravity Award (voted for by the readers) for Best Short Story. Her sci-fi short film script **The Reconciliation** won the China Science Association's Star of Youth. Her numerous works have been translated into English, Japanese and Italian. She has contributed to the writing of **The Three Body World Guide** and has published her own collection of shorter SF works **The Post-Consciousness Era**.

Huangcun by Cai Jun
Published in Chinese in Mengya magazine, 2004
CAI JUN is an author and screenwriter, and a member of the China Writer's Association National Committee. He has published about thirty novels, including **Spring Night, Guardian of the Cemetery** and **The Longest Night**; and sold a total of fourteen million copies. He has been published by major literary journals such as "Harvest", "People's Literature" and "Contemporary Bimonthly". He has won multiple awards including the Mao Dun Award for Best New Writer, Liang Yusheng Award for Outstanding Contribution and the Hundred Flowers Literature Award. He has been translated into over ten languages including French, German and Japanese. Many of his works have been adapted for TV, film and stage.

The Death of Nala by Gu Shi
Published in Chinese in World of Suspense, 2014
GU SHI is a speculative fiction writer and a senior urban planner. Her short fiction works have won two Galaxy Awards for Chinese Science Fiction and four Chinese Nebula (Xingyun) Awards. She published her first story collection, **Möbius Continuum**, in 2020. Her stories have appeared in English translation in the collections **Book of Beijing** (2023), **The Way Spring Arrives** (2022), **Sinopticon: A Celebration of Chinese Science Fiction** (2021), **Broken Stars** (2019), **Clarkesworld** magazine, and **Current Futures, XPRIZE's science fiction ocean anthology** (2019). Her stories have also been translated into Italian, Japanese, German, Romanian, and other languages. Her novelette **Introduction to 2181 Overture**, Second Edition is a finalist for the 2024 Hugo Awards.

CONTRIBUTORS' COPYRIGHT NOTICES

FIND US ONLINE!

www.rebellionpublishing.com

/solarisbooks   /solarisbks   /solarisbooks

SIGN UP TO OUR NEWSLETTER!

rebellionpublishing.com/newsletter

YOUR REVIEWS MATTER!

Enjoy this book? Got something to say?

Leave a review on Amazon, GoodReads or with your
favourite bookseller and let the world know!